MAP

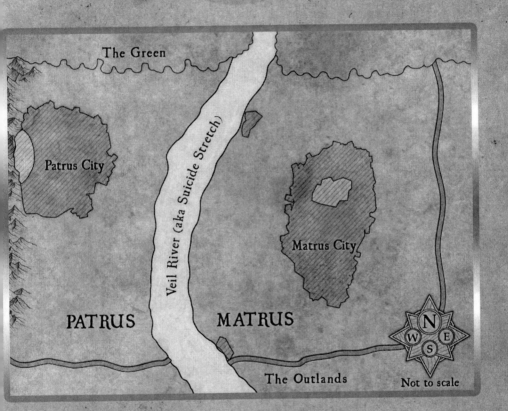

The Green

Patrus City

Veil River (aka Suicide Stretch)

Matrus City

PATRUS

MATRUS

The Outlands

N
W E
S

Not to scale

NIGHTLIGHT PRESS

Copyright © 2016 by Bella Forrest

ISBN-10: 1535197722
ISBN-13: 978-1535197724

First Edition

THE
GENDER
GAME

BELLA FORREST

DEDICATION

*To my readers, for every kind comment, email and review.
I would not have come this far without you.*

PROLOGUE

My sweating palms slipped against the handles of my bike as I cycled at a pace I hoped would not look suspicious. I tried to fix my eyes ahead on the perfectly even road and not keep glancing over my shoulder at the makeshift wooden trailer I was pulling behind me.

As the uniform townhouses on either side of me grew sparse, so did the light. By the time I arrived at the edge of town, the sun had set.

I had been lucky so far. I hadn't passed anybody I knew, and nobody had halted me to ask where I was going.

I slowed to a stop once I reached the end of the last concrete road on this side of the city. Catching my breath, I wiped my palms against my blouse. My lower back felt sticky with sweat. And I had run out of water.

But I was almost there now.

I repositioned my throbbing palms on the handlebars and my feet on the pedals of the bike when a voice called behind me.

"Violet? Is that you?"

I froze.

I knew that voice. It was one I'd grown accustomed to hearing every Monday, Wednesday, and Friday. Ms. Dale, my defense trainer.

What was she doing in this part of town at nightfall?

I forced a casual expression to my face and twisted around.

The fluorescent street lamps illuminated the tall, lithe brunette standing on the sidewalk outside Georgette's Laundry. She was clutching a bundle of white sheets.

"Good evening, Ms. Dale," I called back.

"What are you doing out here, Violet?" she asked.

My jaw twitched as she left the sidewalk and approached me.

"Trashing Ms. Connelly's old china," I explained, a response I had thought up long before leaving my room this morning.

"Oh, I see," she said, her eyes moving from my three-wheeled trailer and returning to my face. "Wish I had someone to run *my* errands." She grimaced at her laundry.

I managed a half-smile.

She lingered a few seconds longer before glancing back at the launderette. "Right, well… you'd better be on your way. You know the junkyard gets creepier the later it gets."

"Yeah," I murmured.

"See you Monday."

She turned on her heel and I let out a slow breath. Gritting my teeth, I faced forward again, my eyes focusing on the narrow cobblestone path that branched off from the end of the road. I cycled for another fifteen minutes down the winding route, past the suburban cottages and misted greenhouses until I reached a pair of corrugated iron gates— the junkyard's entrance. Pulling the gates open just wide enough for my bike to fit through, I rolled it inside. I gazed around the sea of color-coded trash containers, wide-eyed. Nobody was around. *So far, so good.*

The overpowering smell of artificial mint filled my nostrils as I wound around the containers toward the back of the enclosure. The chemical the hygiene department sprayed in here helped to mask the odor of trash, but had the tendency to cause a dull headache.

Arriving at the last row of trash containers lining the back wall, I stopped. I grabbed the handles of the container directly in front of me and slowly eased it forward to reveal the brickwork behind it. I hurried to the wall and sank to my knees on the ground. My fingers fumbled along the bricks, feeling for the tell-tale gap. Finding it, I gained a firmer grip and coaxed it out of place. Then I worked on the previously weakened bricks behind it and above it until I had created a hole just large enough for my frame to squeeze through.

I had to be quick now. Quicker than ever. If someone spotted me here like this, all my days of preparation, all my sleepless nights, would be in vain.

I darted for the wooden trailer hooked to the back of my bike and, clutching the clasp that was holding the lid securely shut, I unfastened it. My heart was hammering against my chest as I opened it.

Curled up in the cramped wooden crate, knees drawn to his chest, eyes tightly closed, was my eight-year-old brother, Timothy.

My eyes moved over the mark etched into his right hand. The mark of a black crescent.

The mark that had changed our lives forever.

It took a few seconds for him to unglue his eyelids and realize that it was finally time to climb out. His black hair clung to his moist forehead as he raised his head to look at me. His gray eyes shone with fear.

I leaned over and wrapped my arms around his midriff, helping him step out. He winced and groaned against me. It killed me to think of how much time he'd been holed up in that box.

But it wouldn't be long now.

It wouldn't be long.

"Come on, buddy," I breathed. "Cad will already be waiting for us."

I pointed to the dark gap in the wall. He glanced at me uncertainly before lowering to his hands and knees. He scurried through. I followed immediately behind him. A chill stole through me as we emerged on the other side.

I swallowed hard as I gazed around at the seldom-frequented surroundings. At least, what I could see of them. We were standing amid a slushy marshland, pale and glistening beneath the strip lights that lined the exterior of the wall. Fifteen feet away flowed Veil River, above which hung a dense gray mist. The river was wide, so wide that the opposite bank was a blur even in the daytime when the mist was thinner.

We crept as quietly as we could through the sludge, toward the edge of the vaporous water. I continued to reassure Tim in whispers that Cad would be waiting in his rowboat, just like he'd promised. Only a little further up… but as we reached the river's border, neither Cad nor his boat were anywhere to be seen.

"Where is he?" Tim gasped.

"He… He's got to be along here somewhere. Let's move up the bank a bit more."

I led Tim further up the river through the marsh, knowing how much danger we were in now. My whole plan had revolved around Cad being here, waiting for us, so that Tim could immediately board his boat. We shouldn't be roaming in the open like this. Wardens could spot us at any second and the consequences would be catastrophic.

"Oh!" Tim hissed, making me jump. "There's a boat!" He jabbed a finger toward the river as Cad's competitive rowboat came into view.

Warm relief washed over me. *Thank God.*

Cad closed the distance between us, an apologetic look on his unshaven face.

"I'm so sorry," he whispered, as he bumped the boat against the bank. "I had some, uh, unexpected complications. You know, with Margot. She started asking me where I was going and… Let's just get this done."

I turned to my brother and bent down. Wrapping my arms around his thin waist, I lifted him up. But before I could pass him to Cad, he struggled against my grip, forcing me to replace him on the ground.

"Wait, Vi!" he breathed. Tears moistened his eyes. "When am I going to see you again?"

My voice caught in my throat. How could I answer a question like that? What could I tell him? I didn't want to lie and say that I would see him next week, next month, or even next year. Because once he reached the other side of the river, I didn't know if I would ever see him again.

I cupped his face in my hands and planted a firm kiss against his forehead, his nose, then his cheeks.

"We'll see," was all I could think to whisper.

My chest ached as I thought of returning home to the orphanage tonight to sleep alone in my room. And tomorrow, waking up without him. How I would have to maintain complete ignorance as to his whereabouts to everyone in the city.

I pushed the thoughts aside.

"I love you, Tim," I said, hugging him tightly as I buried my face in his hair. "Don't forget it."

"I love you too, Ma," he whispered.

Ma. How I despised it when he called me that. *And now of all times...*

Gripping him firmly, I pried his arms away from my neck and rose to my feet.

"You need to go," I choked.

Tears streamed down his dirty cheeks as he finally let me pass him to Cad, who hauled him onto the boat.

Even as Tim left my grasp, every part of me remained holding on. As Cad sat Tim down and, with a grim nod of his head, began to row away, I couldn't let go.

My eyes stung as I gazed through the mist at their retreating shadows.

I had already imagined this moment in my head long before tonight. I'd pictured myself standing on the muddy bank, staring out over the water and waiting until the mist engulfed the boat. Until I lost sight of them completely.

But now that it was happening, I couldn't handle it. It only made Tim's departure seem all the more final. All the more conclusive.

I turned and began wading back across the marshland, but after barely five steps, I stalled.

Three hunched shadows loomed near the wall. Three large, black dogs. Sniffers. And behind them, two tall, broad-shouldered women in deep green uniform. Wardens patrolling on their nightly rounds of the wall's perimeter.

I dropped down, flattening myself against the wet ground, the panic in my chest almost suffocating me.

It was too late.

They had seen and sensed me. Growls ripped from the dogs' throats as they closed the distance. But it wasn't the end of the world if I was caught out here. As long as—

"Watch out, Violet!"

Tim's scream.

My blood ran cold.

Stupid boy. Stupid, stupid boy!

The dogs' and wardens' attention instantly shot to the water, where the outline of Cad's boat was still visible.

Losing all interest in me, the five of them dashed to the water's edge. One of the women pulled out a whistle from her pocket and blew it before barking a command to the dogs.

"No!" I cried, stumbling after them.

In spite of its toxicity, the dogs leapt into the water, their powerful legs navigating the current twice as fast as Cad's oars as he attempted to speed up and escape.

Two of the animals reached the boat and leapt onto it, causing Cad to topple into the river. One of the dogs closed its jaws around Tim's shirt and tugged hard, pulling him over the edge and into the water.

My vision became tunnel-like. All I could see was Tim being pulled through the water, back to the bank. I attempted to swoop in and grab him as the dog arrived at the shore, but one of the women leapt at me. Tripping up my already shaking legs, she tackled me to the ground.

"Violet!" Tim screamed again. I gazed helplessly as the second warden locked his inflamed arms behind his back and began dragging him away.

Back toward the wall.

As the woman straddling my hips drove a tranquilizer dart into my shoulder, that scream would become the last memory I ever had of my brother: A marked boy.

CHAPTER 1

Eight years later...

"**M**errymount Mill," read the sign hanging above the entrance of the graystone windmill. "*Facility for Convicted Juveniles.*"

I wrinkled my nose, flexing my fingers around the handle of my tattered suitcase.

I had no idea why it was called Merrymount. There were no "mounts" around here, or anywhere in the flat land of Matrus—mountains were a luxury enjoyed only by our neighbors in Patrus. And nothing about this towering brick building, or the shriveled brown fields that surrounded it, could be described as *merry*.

But I ought to start getting used to it. This was to be my residence for the next two years, assuming I behaved myself.

This would be my third home—if a detention facility could be called that—in five years. A textiles factory deep in the countryside, about twenty miles from here, had been my first, and a sewage plant on the other side of the city, by Veil River, had been my second. A flour mill certainly beat the latter.

If I managed to keep myself in line here for the next two years and successfully complete my seven-year incarceration period, I would be on track for reintegration into the city a few days after my twenty-first birthday… whatever life the Court expected a girl with no family to live after having spent her adolescence locked away from society.

And I had better not slip up. I'd already rebelled against the Court at the age of eleven by committing obstruction of justice, and after being convicted of womanslaughter (albeit involuntary) via the use of a weapon (even if it was a dinner fork) a few years later, there would be only one fate left in store for me if I didn't get through these next two years without first-degree infractions. It would be straight to the city labs, where I would be put painlessly to sleep without further trial or consideration.

There would be nobody to miss me, I supposed. I no longer had my younger brother. He'd been flagged as "excessively domineering" in the matriarchy's screening lab when he was eight and consequently deemed an unfit member of Matrus' peaceful society. A score of five out of five for both aggressive tendencies and insubordination was essentially the kiss of death for any Matrus-born boy. Tim was a slave in the coal mines in the Deep North now. Or so I'd been told. I hadn't seen him since the day I'd failed to smuggle him to Patrus.

After I'd been caught and sedated by the riverside, I'd been forced to spend the next two weeks in isolation—my first taste of imprisonment. The more I begged to be sent to the mines with my brother, the more I was ignored. I even tried to locate the aircraft that transported the boys to the North once I got out, but I was caught near the hangar and thrust back into isolation with the stern warning that if I stepped out of line again, I would be locked up long-term.

Over the years, I'd eventually managed to see the futility in pursuing Tim, but the day I gave up looking for him was the beginning of a steeper downhill slide. A slide that I still struggled to find reason to fight against. And my anger simply fueled my rebellion.

But I had to fight it now, and keep my head down, unless I truly did have a death wish.

My aunt, uncle, and cousin Cad might miss me if I was gone, though I almost never saw them as they lived on the other side of the river in the patriarchy of Patrus.

Then there was the owner of my old orphanage, Ms. Connelly. She had always been kind to me, though she'd probably be senile by now, assuming she hadn't died already. The few childhood friends I'd had would have moved on with their lives. None of those friendships had been deep.

"Keep moving, Ms. Bates," my escort said to me, nudging me in the shoulder. She was a green-uniformed warden armed with a crossbow; a stocky woman nameless to me and about half a foot short of my height.

The warden ushered me through the doorway and we emerged in a small reception room whose walls were lined with lockers and hanging white aprons. An oval desk stood opposite the doorway, behind which sat a plump middle-aged woman with cropped brown hair and horn-rimmed glasses.

"Violet Bates," she said, glancing up. Her lips, lined with plum-colored lipstick, pursed. She rose to her feet with a black registry book and wound around the table to approach us. She paused a few feet away, eyeing me shrewdly. "Nineteen years old."

I nodded curtly.

"Almost a clean record for the past four years," she went on. "Two minor incidents of violence against fellow inmates, involving punching."

I nodded again, swallowing. Those punches had been well-deserved.

She furrowed her brows before concluding, "Right, I know where we have space for you. Follow me. My name's Ms. Maddox."

Ms. Maddox led me through a back door and we arrived in what I could only assume was the main place of work in this mill, a vast circular room filled with aisle upon aisle of grinding and sifting machinery. I sneezed. Everything in here was dusted with white particles.

She led me across the room to a staircase. By the time we'd reached the top, my calves were burning and Ms.

Maddox was positively wheezing. I'd counted eight floors in total.

"You're right at the top," Ms. Maddox explained, panting as we turned into a dim, worn gray-carpeted corridor lined with wooden doors. She stopped at the sixth door to my right and turned the handle. She pushed, but the door didn't budge. She huffed in frustration. "Josefine!"

There was a span of silence before a vague voice replied, "Yeah?"

"You have locked your door again! Were you not reprimanded just last week for this?"

A bed creaked. Light footsteps sounded. A chair scraped and the door slowly drew open.

A waifish girl who looked no older than nine stood barefoot in the doorway, wearing a checkered brown dress. Her face, splashed with freckles, was round and framed by a ginger mop of short, yet wildly curly hair. The apples of her cheeks were high and plump, her small lips pursed and heart-shaped. She had a look of righteous indignation in her large—almost bulbous—green eyes.

Her fingers flicked to the chair at her side. "It wasn't *locked*," she muttered, scowling.

"Obstruction of entry to dormitories is forbidden," Ms. Maddox countered. "I do not want to have to remind you of that again."

The girl rolled her eyes exaggeratedly and retreated into the room. Ms. Maddox led me inside. The windowless room was square-shaped and held very little, save for a bunk bed which Josefine had just climbed onto, the chair, a rickety table, and a chest of drawers.

"Well, this is Josefine Rankin," Ms. Maddox explained.

Josefine scrutinized me through the jungle of her low-cut bangs as she perched on the top bunk.

"Hello," I said, offering her a small smile that she didn't return.

"The bathrooms are situated to your right when you walk out the door, at the end of the hallway," Ms. Maddox explained. "Meals are served at eight, two, and seven-thirty. Work finishes at seven p.m. each day. Lights out at nine-thirty p.m., no exceptions. You should be asleep by ten p.m. Wake-up call is four a.m. You have thirty minutes to get up, get washed, and be downstairs in the work room."

I grimaced. Wake-up call here was one hour earlier than even the sewage plant.

"I trust that Josefine will answer any questions you may have," Ms. Maddox ploughed on. "At four-thirty a.m. tomorrow, you'll be given a briefing of your tasks. It's ten to eight now, so you'll have to wait until tomorrow morning for food."

My stomach was rumbling after the long journey to get here, but I was used to skipping meals.

"You'll find that most of the same rules apply here as they did at Divedun Sewage as well as at the textiles factory," Ms. Maddox continued. "Wardens roaming the building night and day, routine searches when entering and leaving the dining room, etcetera, etcetera."

"Right," I muttered. I'd been searched before embarking on the journey to Merrymount, too. Nothing sharp was allowed in my suitcase, not even nail clippers. That was why there were never mirrors in the dormitories of these facilities, only in the bathrooms, which were monitored by wardens.

"I'll see you tomorrow morning," Ms. Maddox concluded. She backed out of the room and clicked the door shut behind her.

I turned slowly to the bunk, resuming my focus on Josefine. I cleared my throat. "You, uh, sleep up there, I assume."

Josefine nodded.

"Okay…" I heaved a sigh before dumping my suitcase on the lower bunk. I sat down, spreading my palms over the mattress and gauging its softness. A little softer than my previous bed. Not that this was saying much.

I removed my boots and rolled off my socks, stretching out my legs and toes. I sat there for a few minutes in silence, staring at the blank wall opposite me. Then I glanced at Josefine, who was still sitting in the same position, knees drawn up against her chest, arms around her shins.

"Going to the restroom," I murmured, before leaving the room and taking a right turn down the corridor.

The bathrooms were clearly marked at the end and I moved inside to find a showering area and a row of sinks and cubicles. I stopped in front of one of the sinks to splash my face and caught my gray eyes in the mirror. I hadn't slept much last night and it showed. I looked like crap. My skin, lightly tanned by the sun, appeared dry and lackluster, and my black shoulder-length hair, normally dead straight, was crimped and escaping in all directions from my pony tail. I shook it out, running my fingers through it, before heading to a stall to relieve myself.

When I returned to the sinks, another girl had entered—a girl I recognized instantly. Her features were ratty, with thin lips, a protruding upper jaw and lanky brown hair that clung to her scalp like a helmet.

Vera Sykes. A girl who had almost caused me to gain a third infraction over the past five years due to a run-in I'd had with her back in the textiles factory. I had not seen her since.

She looked just as surprised to see me, her eyes widening a fraction as she stared. But then she turned away abruptly, deciding to ignore me. She washed and dried her hands before sweeping toward the door. Though, as she brushed past me, she moved a little too close—managing to nudge me in the back. Then she sped up, hastening through the exit.

Idiot.

I couldn't stand girls like Vera. Girls with neither brain nor backbone. Her way of surviving the facilities was by becoming the full-time ass-licker of whoever she deemed the toughest person in the block… or the toughest person who could stand to be around her. She'd been friendly with me for a couple of days before I'd started avoiding her. After that, she'd gone behind my back and revealed her second face.

Though in fairness, I wasn't good at getting along with people my age in general. I struggled to connect and was often labeled a loner. Not that I minded. Making friends in facilities like this wasn't encouraged. It wasn't supposed to be a social club and that was one of the reasons girls were uprooted and made to rotate the facilities.

I returned to my room to find Josefine lying on her back, staring up at the ceiling. She didn't look at me as I entered, though she addressed me for the first time. "What's your name?"

"Violet."

"And… how did you wind up here?"

I sat down before turning my mind heavily back to that fateful day at school. It had been a sticky Monday afternoon. I'd been fourteen years old when a girl two years my senior, whom I'd had a history of discord with, had picked a fight with me in the dining hall because I'd objected—in no timid words—to her jumping the line. We'd started with bare hands, and would have continued that way if she hadn't scooped up a fork. I'd reciprocated to ward her off, not to plunge the fork into her throat. But she had launched at me at exactly the wrong moment, and at exactly the wrong angle. She'd died in the hospital a few hours later.

After that, my life became one of slavery to my country. Waking up at the same time every day, being carted from one chore to the other. And trying to stay out of trouble. I'd gotten into a few fights—only two of them recorded—but I had been careful to avoid the use of actual weapons. Weapon usage by anyone other than an authorized warden was strictly prohibited throughout Matrus; it was one of the most basic commandments of our monarch, Queen Rina.

I didn't feel like spilling all this history to Josefine now. So I just replied, "I got into a fight with a bully... What about you? And how old are you, by the way?"

I took a seat in the chair so that I could see her as we talked. She'd positioned her head closer to the edge of the bunk and was looking at me now.

"I'm eight and a half... I'm only supposed to be here for another two weeks," she replied. "Mom was taken to the Drewsbury Center while I got stuck here. We got caught."

I frowned. "Caught?"

"Caught without permission, trying to return from Patrus. We wanted badly to move back here—it's our home. I was born here and so was Mom. But the Court was telling us we'd have to wait two weeks for approval. We couldn't wait that long. Mom was going mad, and she was going to get into a lot of trouble if we didn't leave Patrus right away. So she traveled back with me in my uncle's rowboat… We left Dad."

It was disturbing that Josefine should be put in a facility like this one, which was filled with girls convicted of far worse crimes than premature migration. Her crime had not even been hers, but her mother's. But this was common of the Court's decisions. They were known to make statements, however harsh, to discourage the public from even considering infractions. Matrus' government frowned upon residents who decided to move to the patriarchy in the first place, so making it difficult for them to return ensured that they thought long and hard about their choice.

"How come you went to Patrus to begin with?" I asked, although I hardly needed to. There weren't a lot of reasons that women who were born and bred in Matrus would migrate to Patrus.

"Because of my dad," Josefine responded grimly. "He was born there. He moved to Matrus because my mom asked him to. They married here and he took her name. But he couldn't survive here. He begged Mom to let him take us back with him."

"… And your mom couldn't bear it in Patrus," I finished. Just as marriages only usually lasted in Matrus if Matrus was all the man had ever known, the same was true of marriages in Patrus; women born there were conditioned to the ways of life in the patriarchy. They didn't suffer from culture shock as Matrus-born women did.

A woman in Patrus had about as many rights as a pet animal. She couldn't legally reside there without being owned by a man, and even with a husband she was limited. She couldn't go out by herself, she couldn't work, drive, or own money or property. I'd even heard that their physical appearance and clothes were dictated by the man, if he so chose, and arguing was completely taboo. Women were dependent to a humiliating degree.

I'd spent the last five years of my life as a Matrian prisoner, but even so, I was sure that I still held more dignity than I would in the patriarchy. I had never crossed the river to Patrus, as I suspected no self-respecting Patrian man would want to cross to Matrus, either (unless it was on business).

Things weren't a lot easier for men here. Any Patrian male wishing to migrate to Matrus had to first undergo a full background check to shed light on any potential disruptive tendencies. Only if the man was deemed to be a low to moderate risk (it was rare for any Patrian male to be considered a "low" risk) would he be allowed to be coupled with a Matrian woman and adopt her last name. Retaining his ego was out of the question. No matter what qualifications he might have arrived with, he would be relegated to an occupation of repetitive manual labor—only sons of the Court were allowed to pursue the sciences or other intellectual professions. They weren't allowed to own property or assets, although they were allowed to drive and roam by themselves. This extra leniency shown toward them was made up for by the harshness of Matrus' legal system — there was little male-committed crime in Matrus for a reason.

Such differing upbringings between Patrian-Matrian couples were all but impossible to reconcile in the long term. Veil River was known colloquially as Suicide Stretch, and there had been more than a few incidents of couple suicides over the years.

Hook-ups between the nations usually only happened if one of them had an occupation that required them to spend time on the other side of the river, like trade officials, or negotiations ambassadors. The majority of women in Matrus either chose a Matrian partner, or opted to be without a partner completely and conceive in an insemination center. My mother had chosen the latter to have my brother and me. And if I ever decided I wanted a child, I would do the same.

I didn't need a man in my life—not even a Matrian male—and from all that I'd been told by my mother before she died, I was better off without one anyway. *Better to remain always self-reliant. Self-reliance means you're in control. Don't ever think you need a man for happiness.*

Besides, even Matrian husbands were a headache with all the accompanying paperwork and responsibility they came with. These days I had a hard enough time being responsible for myself.

Josefine shuddered, horror swimming in her irises. "You don't know how bad it is in Patrus for us girls, Violet..."

From the few papers I'd managed to get a glimpse of in the communal areas of my last facility, the situation wasn't about to get any better. The newly ascended King Maxen was proving himself to be a more ruthless monarch than his recently deceased father. He was rumored to be pouring a staggering amount of resources into the development of a new pharmaceutical drug that anesthetized emotions while sharpening logic and intellect—hardly the makings of an empathetic people. Reporters feared this would make Matrus' dealings with the nation only more strained in the years to come. Patrus' emphasis on drug development worried them especially, as Matrus' thus-far unrivaled expertise in the fields of biology and medicine was the one thing Matrus truly had to offer Patrus in exchange for water and fresh crops from the verdant mountainous region. Matrus could survive without Patrus' trade, but it would make life more austere for all of us.

Things hadn't always been this way.

According to our history books, centuries ago, Matrus and Patrus didn't even exist. They were one group of people, one band of survivors of the Last War that toxified vast swathes of the great land once known as America. The troop discovered a small haven amidst the wasteland of Appalachia—a haven that was the stretch of mountainous land now occupied by Patrus. All the survivors used to live on that side of the river, men and women. It was only after they began the work of building a new civilization that political divide struck. It started with a party of women protesting against the colony's quickly forming male-dominated leadership. The party believed that if men were allowed to prevail again, they were simply creating a replica of the former testosterone-driven regime that had led everything to ruin. They argued that if they were to learn anything from the past and stand a chance of building a better future, women must finally take the reins.

But the men in power refused. No satisfactory headway was made after countless meetings and protests. Thus, the female party had a choice: stay and essentially bite their tongues, or leave and put their beliefs into practice elsewhere. They opted for the latter after discovering that the land on the other side of the river, while not as conducive for living as their current side, was still habitable compared to everywhere else they had searched. And so began the split. It wasn't only women who chose to follow the female party in founding Matrus— a percentage of men agreed with their manifesto and followed them too. Similarly, a portion of women chose to remain under male rule. The most outspoken of the female party was put forward to lead Matrus as queen—Queen Daphne the First—and soon after, the first king was appointed in Patrus (whose name slipped my mind).

To say that both nations had come a long way since their founding must be an understatement. We had so many structures and amenities and rules and restrictions in place now (not to mention the increase in population) that I found it hard to imagine what it must have been like in those pioneering days, hundreds of years ago. Certainly there hadn't been as many rules so early on—though, if I remembered my history correctly, the screening of "violent" boys was instituted by Matrus' politicians pretty quickly, as well as the building of aircraft that were used to discover the mines in the Deep North…

Josefine was quiet. Her expression had turned somber, distant.

I left the chair and sank into bed where I began rifling in my suitcase for my nightclothes.

"Do you have any brothers or sisters?" she asked. An innocent change of subject.

My throat tightened. "No." I lied.

"Me neither," Josefine murmured.

I was glad that she didn't say anything more after that.

After changing into my pajamas, I rummaged in the side pocket of my suitcase until my fingers ran over a thin smooth square and my mini-flashlight. I dimmed the ceiling light before crawling beneath my blanket.

I switched on the flashlight, illuminating the most precious item I possessed: a faded photograph of a boy with eyes and hair like mine. My brother, at five years old, three years before he'd failed the screening. It was a picture of him on a swing, a broad grin splitting his chubby, mud-smeared face. A snapshot from a time when our life was happier.

The photo had a bit of tape still attached to the back from where I had fixed it against my bedpost in my previous room. I stuck it against the wall now, level with my pillow, and stared at it long into the night. Far past ten o'clock. I replayed the months, weeks and days before his capture over in my mind and wondered if there was anything I could have done differently.

I didn't think so. My brother was what he was. A fault in Matrus' system.

Surrounded by Josefine's snores, I switched off the flashlight.

CHAPTER 2

I felt like death when a blaring alarm sounded the next morning at exactly four a.m. I'd have to face the consequences of falling asleep so late for the rest of the day.

Josefine leapt out of bed and I clambered groggily after her. Gathering up our clothing, we moved to the showers which, thankfully, were separated into stalls.

After washing and dressing, Josefine and I followed the crowd milling down the hallway, heading for the staircase. I spotted Vera up front, standing next to the largest girl among us. The girl's hair was so short and her build so wide, one could have easily mistaken her for a man from behind.

I kept my eyes down, avoiding people's gazes, as we piled down the long staircase. On reaching the ground floor, we entered the work room and lined up in front of the machinery. At four-thirty a.m. on the dot, Ms. Maddox entered the room, holding her black registry book. One by one, she called out and ticked off our names.

Facility registers were usually in chronological order, rather than alphabetical, which meant that the girl who had been called out before me—the troll of a girl I'd spotted earlier, Dina Bradbury—must've arrived just shortly before me.

"All right," Ms. Maddox said, snapping her book shut. "Work begins."

Everyone began moving to the machinery, while Ms. Maddox approached me and explained my responsibilities. I understood and quickly got the hang of the grinding machine she was asking me to monitor. It wasn't a difficult task.

The hours blurred into one another, as I was used to them doing, and I stopped looking up at the clock.

Finally, it was time for breakfast; we exited the mill and trudged along a pebble path toward a bleak brick building a quarter of a mile away which served as the dining hall. A buffet was already laid out. I'd lost sight of Josefine in the crowd, so I lined up with the rest of them and piled my plate with hot food. We were only allowed one plate per meal, so everyone filled it to spilling point.

I was still looking for Josefine as I turned to search for somewhere quiet to sit. Then I caught a glimpse of her fiery red hair on the opposite side of the room. She stood with her back against the wall, while Dina loomed in front of her.

I couldn't spot any wardens around; perhaps they were outside the door, waiting until the crowd in here settled down.

Forgetting all about finding a quiet spot, I dumped my plate and cutlery down on the nearest table to me and weaved through the crowd toward them. My eyes trained on Josefine as she picked up one of her bread rolls and handed it to Dina. Before she could do the same with her second roll, I stepped between the girls and gripped Josefine's arm, guiding the roll back to its rightful place on her plate. My gaze was steely as I glared at Dina. Although we were actually almost the same height and roughly the same age, physically, she was much larger than me. This was the first time I'd seen her face up close; her eyes were small and spread too far apart to be attractive, their color dark brown, almost black. Her forehead hung low, and metal braces glinted against her teeth.

"Who are you?" she asked, her eyes narrowing.

"I'd like to ask the same," I replied calmly.

My eyes fell to the roll on her plate that belonged to Josefine. Before she could react, I snatched it up and returned it. Clutching the young girl's shoulder, I pulled her out of the corner Dina had bullied her into and stood in her place.

"I suggest you keep to what's yours," I whispered.

Dina's broad cheeks flushed and a muscle in her jaw twitched. Anger glinted in her eyes. Her disposable plate creaked in the tightening grip of her meaty hands. But then she backed down, as I'd known she would, and turned on her heel and steamed away. I knew a coward when I saw one.

Dozens of eyes were on me as I escorted Josefine to the table where I'd left my plate and cutlery. Nobody had touched it.

I pulled up a chair for Josefine next to me and we both sat down.

"You make sure you stay away from that girl, okay?" I told Josefine as I dug into my porridge.

The girl looked shaken as she picked up a piece of apple. She glanced nervously at Dina, who, having taken a seat across the room from us next to her new crony Vera, was glaring daggers our way.

"And don't look at her," I said. "Giving her attention makes her think she has power over you. Ignore her."

Josefine resumed her focus on her plate. She took a bite of everything but the two rolls, which were the most substantial food she'd collected. So I gave her my untouched sandwich. "Eat this. It hasn't been contaminated by Piggy Hands."

That brought a smile to Josefine's face. "Thanks," she mumbled. She accepted and began munching.

We spent the next fifteen minutes in mostly silence as we finished eating, and then a bell warned us that breakfast was drawing to a close. We had to get a move on.

Josefine and I picked up our plates and left the table to get in the line leading up to the trash cans. After I dumped my plate in the waste, someone brushed into my right side. I turned to see that it was Vera. She had a comically solemn look on her face as she leaned back against the wall and crossed her arms over her chest.

"Mind where you're going," I muttered, before taking Josefine's hand and leading her away.

"You really shouldn't mess with Dina, you know," Vera called after me. I didn't give Vera the satisfaction of turning around and asking why, but she offered it herself. "I'm serious, Violet Bates. I share a room with her... You don't know where she's come from."

Oh, please.

I sped up with Josefine and exited the dining hall, Vera's irritating voice fading out in the crowd.

I asked Ms. Maddox if Josefine and I could share a work station after lunch and she agreed. She allowed us to choose one in the far end of the room, as far from the other girls as we could be. After an hour or so, Josefine seemed to put thoughts of the incident with Dina behind her and became chatty. She asked me more questions about myself; particularly, she was interested in my parents. I told her that I didn't know who my father was and that my mother had chosen to conceive my brother and me in the city's insemination center. She had died from complications during my brother's birth.

"So you do have a brother?" Josefine asked.

"Not anymore."

"What happened to him?"

I hesitated before replying, "He failed the test."

"Oh, I'm sorry," Josefine said, subdued.

She understood that there was only one kind of test that a boy could fail in Matrus, and it had nothing to do with education. Other than the basic ability to read and add up numbers, boys weren't given an education like girls were, just an apprenticeship in manual labor.

The same was true of the girls in Patrus who weren't allowed to attend school like the boys. The only semblance of training they received was domestic.

I was grateful when Josefine redirected the conversation. Talking about Tim was painful. She asked what my favorite subject at school was and I immediately thought of my defense training. My lessons with Ms. Dale had been the highlights of my week. Ever since I could remember, my dream had been to become a warden when I grew up. There was something about their toughness, their strength, that I had always admired. I had never pictured myself pursuing any other occupation.

That had lasted up until the age of eleven when Tim had been captured.

A lot of things had changed in me after that. I'd found myself getting into fights easily and had visited the doctor for medication to ease my bouts of anger. Once Tim had gone, all of the attraction becoming a warden had previously held for me evaporated. After my brief spell of imprisonment for trying to smuggle a marked boy to Patrus, I'd still continued my defense training because, well… it was the only thing I really knew how to do well. And Ms. Dale had encouraged me to continue. She'd told me I had a natural instinct for fighting and that it would be a shame to let it go to waste. Maybe when I got older, I'd change my mind. I didn't think so, but I followed her advice.

Although it had been a long time now since I'd had any formal training, my instinct had never really left me. And over the years of incessant manual labor, my body had kept fit and strong. Plus, I'd grown in height.

"I wish I could be brave and tough like you," Josefine sighed wistfully as she dipped her hands into a trough of flour.

"You can be," I told her. "It's about your mindset. Refuse to be browbeaten. Like this morning. You didn't have to hand over your bread rolls. You could have refused, pushed past her, and gone outside to look for a warden."

Josefine nodded. "I suppose I could've," she mumbled.

I took my turn in asking her questions—her own favorite subjects, her dreams and aspirations. She told me she wanted to be an environmentalist like her mother. She wanted to help improve the soil in Matrus so that we could produce more natural foods and import less from Patrus. A noble career. I wished I had such a strong vision for my future once I got out of here. I still had two years ahead of me, but Josefine's focus made me feel I ought to start thinking more seriously about what I was going to do with the rest of my life.

By the time it was time to stop work, I had developed a thorough liking for the young redhead. Perhaps it was just her age, but she reminded me of my brother—not the timid and shy side of her, but the fiery, feisty side that bubbled to the surface on occasion. I hoped she wouldn't lose that as she got older. If she received the right training and diet, she'd make a good fighter. Unlike my brother, she wouldn't be penalized for her boldness. Unless she started doing stupid things like brandishing dinner forks in a fight.

We hung up our aprons in the reception room and headed back to our room, where I picked up my nightclothes before heading out again to take a shower. My hair badly needed a wash and I was feeling dusty in the most unexpected of places from having spent the day in the mill.

I stood for a while in the shower, relishing the warm water gushing down my back. Showers, like rain, always had a way of calming me. The pitter-patter beat, the incessant contact. Nothing made me feel sleepy faster. But my shower turned lukewarm too soon—an unpleasant quirk of detention facility bathrooms. Wardens didn't want girls dawdling— they never wanted girls dawdling. I hurried to finish washing my hair before it could go ice cold. Then I dried, dressed, and left the bathrooms.

My eyes were beginning to droop as I returned to our door and I wanted nothing more now than to climb into bed and lose myself in sleep, even if it did mean skipping dinner. But my pleasant daze was disturbed as I arrived to find our door ajar. That was unlike Josefine, and I was sure that I'd left it closed.

When I pushed the door open, I saw Josefine trembling on the floor, her right eye bruised and puffy. Surrounding her were the contents of my suitcase, scattered all over the room. My gaze shot to my most prized possession. Tim's photograph had disappeared from my wall. And on my pillow... lay a pile of shreds. The only relic I had left of my lost brother, destroyed.

"Dina?" was all I managed to breathe.

Josefine whimpered a "Yes."

That photograph had survived with me through a lot of shifts and upheavals. The thought that it should be ripped from me like this, by that... that animal...

I wanted to both scream and cry at once. But instead, I surrendered to an emotion I had gotten to know all too well, and felt all too often, over the past eight years.

Anger. My fury consumed me and every fiber of my being felt like it was burning up.

I couldn't even bring myself to care if what I was about to do would prolong my sentence by months. Feeling my fists connecting with that monster's face would make it all worthwhile.

My chest heaving as I attempted to regain some semblance of control, I thundered out of the room.

That girl is going to regret ever crossing paths with me.

CHAPTER 3

I stopped the first girl I came across in the hallway—a rotund fifteen or sixteen-year-old—and gripped her shoulders. "Which room is Dina Bradbury's?" I demanded of her in a menacing whisper.

"I-I don't know," she stammered, trying to shrug away.

Cursing beneath my breath, I let her go before moving on to the next girl, and then the next. The fourth girl I stopped knew which room Dina resided in, and the moment the answer left her lips, I hurtled there.

Arriving outside the door I burst in, my fists balled so tight my short nails dented my flesh.

Dina was standing on the opposite side of the room with her back toward me. I couldn't see what she was doing exactly, but as she twisted around, her eyes bulged. I had found her alone, with nobody to obstruct my path to her.

I lunged forward and grabbed hold of her shirt. Swinging a leg behind her knees, I sent her crashing to the floor.

I leapt on top of her, pinning her down. Then I began pummeling blow after heavy blow against her face.

She groaned, her large form struggling beneath me as I straddled her hips. Her head shifted from side to side, trying to avoid my beating. Then she raised a hand and managed to catch the next punch before it could connect. Her grip closed around my fist and I fought to maintain my dominance as she twisted forcefully beneath me. She managed to dislodge me with a speed I hadn't been expecting, getting me on my side. She thrust her knee upward to collide with my groin, but I shielded myself with my shins. We broke apart, scrambling to our feet. Her nose was already bleeding. Next, I would squash it flat.

I was about to close in on her again when, to my confusion, she reached into her mouth. When she withdrew her hand, she was holding the top and bottom layers of her braces.

Removable braces.

She'd managed to keep them from the wardens.

My pulse raced as I realized what she was doing. She quickly broke off the smooth rubber seal at the end of each of the wires, leaving them bare and pointed. Then she held a brace in each hand, positioning the wiry ends between her fingers so they stuck out like claws.

As she lashed out with her right arm, I swiped it with mine, knocking it away from me.

She has weapons. I can't get caught up in this. I need to get out of here, my brain was telling me, and yet my mind and emotions were dictating a different thing entirely.

I hadn't hurt her enough yet. I wanted to break her nose. Give her a black eye. Split her cheekbone. I wanted to give her some kind of permanent scar so that she would always have something to remind her of what she had done to me.

She swung out at me again, this time with both hands. I ducked, but not fast enough. She managed to catch my right shoulder, splitting the fabric of my shirt and etching a stinging cut into my skin.

And then she launched all her weight toward me at once, crushing me against the floor as I had done to her. She raised both hands and attempted to bring them down against me, wires pointed downward. I gripped her wrists, stopping them a few inches away from my body, using every muscle in my arms and shoulders to keep the wires from plunging into me. Catching the glint of malice in her eyes came as a wake-up call. I realized in this moment, she was as crazy as I was.

Neither of us are thinking straight.

Even though my rage was still running wild, this was just stupid. Really stupid.

So she ripped up Tim's picture. I can try to piece it back together again. But I can't get involved in this.

What the hell am I doing?

As I strained beneath her weight, I struggled to slip out of the lock she had me in.

I had made my bed, and now I was forced to lie in it.

If I'd had longer nails, I could've dug them into her flesh in an attempt to loosen her grip. Instead, I had only my bony fingertips to use to press down hard against her pressure points. I managed to make her left hand release its hold on the brace, but with this hand now free, she used it to clamp around my neck, crushing my windpipe.

As I gazed into her dark eyes and fought to breathe, I wondered if she would actually go so far as to kill me. Maybe Vera had been right in her warning. Maybe Dina was insane.

My vision started going hazy, and I couldn't even yell out for help. I scooped up the brace she dropped, but every part of me was screaming to not go down that road. Not to even cut her arm in an attempt to free myself. That slope was far too slippery. I was already on my last warning.

I wriggled wildly, forcing her to reposition her body in order to maintain her dominance. And as she did, I was finally able to put my legs to use. I slid both knees upward in one forceful thrust, causing her to jerk forward. Her hold on my neck loosened.

I gasped, heaving oxygen back into my lungs. My instinct was to immediately brace myself for another attack... but it didn't come.

Then I realized that my right hand—the hand that had been clutching her second brace—felt moist. In fact, my upper chest and right shoulder felt moist, too. A trail of moisture.

My eyes refocusing, I scrambled to sit upright, heaving her weight off of me.

Harrowing déjà vu washed over me as I stared at Dina, lying on the floor while choking and clutching her throat, blood spilling from her neck and pooling around her.

The door shot open behind me.

A scream erupted. Vera Sykes's scream.

"OH, MY GOD! VIOLET'S KILLED DINA!"

I haven't killed her! I thought to myself in a panic. *She's still alive! She just... She just needs to get to the hospital, dammit!*

But the amount of blood that was spilling from her throat... As Vera raced away, shrieking for the wardens, I already knew what would happen next.

CHAPTER 4

Footsteps pounded outside. Five wardens spilled into the room—Vera and several other girls looming behind them.

I was in a daze, still not believing what had happened. My sodden hands were trembling as two wardens flipped me over and pinned me against the floor. The other three picked up Dina and rushed her out, before dragging me to my feet and pulling me into the hallway after her.

My blood pulsing in my ears, everything around me was a blur. As we approached Josefine's and my room, I managed to catch a glimpse of her terrified face, but they pulled me right past her. They wouldn't bother to stop to collect my things. What use would they be to me now?

We arrived at the stairwell and my feet dragged and tripped as we wound our way down the steps. Reaching the ground floor, we moved through the work room and the reception where Ms. Maddox was sitting. I didn't even get a chance to witness the expression on her face. I was forced forward as the wardens escorted me out of the mill.

We came upon four more wardens here. Two of them raced off around the side of the building, returning in two trucks. Dina was loaded into the back of one, myself into the other. As they slammed the doors shut behind me, I was plunged into darkness — the nightmare replaying over and over in my mind. Those few seconds before Dina's end. My knees thrusting upward. The moistness of her blood. Her choking.

The vehicles trundled down the long track that led to the city, but it sounded like they parted ways as they reached the end — mine split to the right, Dina's to the left. Both headed to different destinations. Very different destinations. I clutched the base of my seat as beads of sweat formed on my upper lip.

The road was bumpy. My elbows and the back of my head banged against the walls, but I could hardly make an effort to hold myself still. It was as though the life had been sucked out of me already. Everything seemed pointless.

I'd imagined this moment a number of times since claiming my first life. I'd imagined this journey, across the bumpy outskirts of Matrus, blending into the smooth roads of the city, where the labs were situated. A small part of me had always known that my anger would get the better of me again.

Closing my eyes, I lost track of time.

Finally, the doors opened, letting in a stream of street-light. Hands grabbed me and pulled me out and I found myself standing on a sidewalk, my surroundings not what I had expected them to be. I was not outside the labs, but the gates of Frenton, another detention center—the most central to the city. Then I reminded myself that this should not be surprising. It was nighttime and lab technicians didn't work at night. Of course, I would spend the night in a cell and be taken to the labs tomorrow morning.

The wardens led me to the main rectangular gray build-ing and into a reception area where they picked up a set of keys from the woman behind the desk. Then we walked along a hallway before moving down a stairwell, down, down, down, until we reached what had to be the lower-most floor. We arrived at the end of a hallway lined with cells, all empty. They stopped outside the third one on our left and thrust me inside.

After locking it, they strode away, leaving me to the deathly silence.

I wasn't sure what to feel. Somewhere within me still blazed my perpetual flame of anger, indignation, and resentment. But deeper than that, there was more. There was abandonment. There was betrayal. There was a hollow sense of grief. For years, I'd been grasping at straws in an attempt to find meaning to my life, purpose to my days. As much as my country had been the cause of my darkest depths of depression, it had also picked me up from them. It had forced me to keep going in *some* direction, even if it wasn't what I would have chosen for myself. In many ways, being imprisoned had been the best thing that could have happened to me. It had taught me to stop feeling and to simply concentrate on *doing*. We were worked hard and weren't given time for much else. Days were comfortably numb.

But now, as I sat here alone and taskless in the gloom, I didn't know how to still my mind. Almost decade-old feelings resurfaced, clawing at my chest and heart, threatening to overwhelm me.

Through it all, questions broke above the surface, surging like bellows in the wilderness.

What am I?

Why am I here?

Where did I go wrong?

When and how did I become a person unworthy of living?

Do I truly deserve to die?

So lost was I in my mind's tempest that I didn't notice when the prison doors finally opened and the wardens stopped right in front of my cell.

I gazed up at them, my vision focusing. These women were different wardens from the ones who had dropped me off here. They escorted me out of the holding cells, up the staircase, and back to the ground level. I gazed through the windows. It was still dark outside.

Where are they taking me?

The air had a certain feel to it—a crispness—and the crows had started cawing, indicating the imminent daybreak.

Perhaps they wanted me to be first in line.

We crossed the courtyard and approached a different truck than the one I'd arrived in. They locked me inside before piling into the front and starting the engine. We drove away from the compound, the quiet, neat streets lined with pastel-colored townhouses bleeding away on either side of me. I hadn't visited this part of the city for years and we passed places I hadn't seen since I was a child: the Racelle Art Gallery with its luminous mural-clad exterior, the multi-columned, whitestone Krisler Theater, the pebble-dashed City Library. I'd forgotten how pretty Matrus City was.

The sky was clear as I looked up. The stars glistened down on me, as if taunting me. It was a beautiful morning to be my last.

My heart palpitating, I tried to focus on the road. We met a crossroads, and I expected the driver to turn left down Wester Road, which was the most direct route to the labs. But she didn't. Instead, she carried on straight ahead, deeper into the center of the city.

"Where are you taking me?" I couldn't help but ask. My voice sounded scratchy. It'd been hours since I had last spoken.

Neither of the wardens bothered to answer.

The situation only became stranger when I realized we were nearing the royal quarters… The palace.

I wondered if there had been new labs set up recently that I wasn't aware of. But as we continued to make a beeline toward the royal quarters, it became clear that we were heading to none other than the palace compound itself.

What is happening?

We glided down the final road that led to the high wall surrounding the majestic tower which served as the queen's and her courtiers' residence. Constructed from white stone and dotted with tall windows, it loomed over thirteen floors. The queen was reputed to live at the very top, occupying the highest two floors with her daughters.

Upon our arrival at the cast-iron gates, we were searched before they allowed us inside.

I had never been on this side of the gates before, I had only seen the occasional photograph in the papers, and my eyes struggled to take in the incredible sight. Surrounding the tower were geometrical gardens whose lawns were almost too green, flowers almost too large and vibrant. Ornamental fountains spiked with stone fish gushed out water. Quaint stone paths wound through the grass and flora, leading up to the main entrance of the tower: double shiny steel doors.

"Why am I here?" I asked again.

"Just follow," the warden holding my right arm replied.

Arriving at the steel doors, the wardens knocked. The doors whined open seconds later. A chambermaid wearing a starched white dress appeared on the other side as though she'd been expecting us. She led us across a luxurious lobby to a rug-clad sitting room before taking her leave. The wardens sat me down on a silky padded chair, then assumed positions on either side of the door.

As we waited—for what, I could still only muse—the only sound to distract me was the ticking of an old oak grandfather clock in one corner of the room.

Then I heard more footsteps. The doorknob twisted and clicked and a man stepped inside the room, a man I recognized. His hair was light—almost white—blond, and his face sported a thin goatee. His eyes were powder blue, his skin sallow. His features were altogether so fair and pale, he looked washed out. I had seen his face in the papers before; he was the only male consultant to Queen Rina's Court—a scientist whose name was Alastair Jenks, if I remembered right. Born and bred in Matrus, he was the son of a member of the Court, and a distant relative of scientist Ianto F. Jenks, who had pioneered the methods of screening boys—the same methods that were still used today in the matriarchy.

I felt a biting pang of resentment. If it weren't for Alastair and his family, Tim might have never been taken and I might not be here now. We might still be living in the orphanage, or maybe I would have taken a job and started earning enough to become his official guardian, and for us to move into our own home. Tim might have begun an apprenticeship.

Why has this man come to see me?

He had entered armed with a crossbow and a shoulder bag. I eyed the bow's loaded tip. Perhaps I had been right about the wardens not wanting to wait until the main labs opened. Perhaps he was going to finish me off sooner: now. I had no idea why a man of such high status would do it personally though, and he didn't move any closer. He strode to a chair near the clock and sat down, his weapon resting casually on his knee. Then he let out a subdued cough, clearing his throat.

"I have some news for you, Ms. Bates," he said, his voice nasally and off-puttingly high-pitched. "Ms. Bradbury passed away in the hospital about an hour ago."

My heart stilled.

"I also have a proposal for you," he went on. "A proposal that I suspect you will not refuse." He paused for a moment, scrutinizing me. "A situation has led Her Majesty and the Court to find use for a person with... your type of background. We have been watching the detention facilities, waiting for the right young woman to whom we may offer this opportunity."

"Opportunity?" I managed.

"You took defense lessons with Ms. Dale up until the age of fourteen, did you not?" he asked, as though I hadn't spoken.

I nodded.

"The opportunity involves embarking on a mission which, if successfully completed, would suspend your sentence. It would allow you another chance to redeem yourself and reintegrate into society. Your previous crimes would be erased from your record. Forgotten about. You would essentially be starting from a blank slate..." He raised his almost nonexistent brows. "How does that sound?"

My anger had given way to bewilderment and I couldn't stop frowning at him. What mission could be so important to the Court that it would cause them to erase two counts of womanslaughter from my record? I felt shocked that they would even consider compromising their principles in such a gross manner.

"What mission?" I asked.

"Before I explain," Alastair replied, "I will warn you that after receiving this information, you will need to make an immediate decision. Take up the challenge, or not. And if for some reason you decide the latter, you will receive your due injection without delay… This room will be the one that you die in." His voice lowered. "Think carefully, Ms. Bates."

In spite of my bias against the scientist, I wasn't sure that there was anything to think about. This mission would offer me the chance of a new life and freedom from detention facilities. Maybe the rules in Matrus would even change someday and allow the boys in the North to see their families. Maybe I would discover happiness.

Besides, however dangerous this mysterious mission could turn out to be, anything was better than death… *Wasn't it?*

CHAPTER 5

"I understand the choices you have laid out," I told the scientist stiffly. My voice had dropped several tones deeper than normal. "I accept the offer. Tell me the details."

Alastair's mouth twitched. I guessed that was the closest he would get to a smile. "Very well," he said, putting down his crossbow for the first time. He began to pace the room slowly. "Recently we had a break-in at the Court's labs—*my* lab, specifically. Some valuable items were taken. Specimens. After a thorough investigation, we discovered who the thief was. Unfortunately, we had a snitch in our midst. A double agent, bribed by Patrus. She has been caught and reprimanded"—*put to death, without a doubt*—"but the damage has already been done. There is, however, one specimen that we believe is still salvageable. The most vital of all of them. It is the result of thousands of hours of experimentation and research." Alastair paused to drag a small table in front of me. Then he placed a hand into his bag and pulled out a tightly rolled-up piece of paper. He dropped it onto the table and unfurled it, revealing a map of Patrus.

He moved a forefinger over the paper, resting it atop the city to the far west, where the mountains were located.

"Fortunately, we, too, have somebody on the inside," Alastair went on. "An agent of our own who has infiltrated Patrus' high society. He resides several miles away from King Maxen's palace and their newly renovated laboratory, which he has discovered is where the specimen is being kept… Now, this is where you come in. He wants assistance to recover it."

My stomach clenching, I leaned over the map. "What is this 'specimen'?" *And what makes you so desperate to get it back?*

"What the specimen is," Alastair replied, "is of no consequence to you. The only thing you need to know is what it looks like." He moved again to his bag, drew out three photographs and planted them on the table next to the map. The pictures depicted a strange silver object in the shape of an egg. It was perched on a stark white table, supported by a transparent glass tripod.

"This silver egg," Alastair said, "is what you need to retrieve. It's hard to tell its size exactly from these pictures, but it's not too large to carry. Its length is about that of my briefcase, its width a bit narrower." He raised his bag up for me.

"What would I have to do, exactly, to recover it?"

"That will be made clear soon enough," he replied. "Once you reach the other side of the river."

My chest constricted. *The other side of the river. They're going to cart me off to Patrus.* Out of one prison and into another. For there was no way a self-respecting Matrian woman could describe Patrus as anything other than a prison.

Alastair still hadn't made it clear why they had been waiting for 'someone like me' to come along and assist with this task—a convict who had no experience in matters of robbery or espionage. I could only assume that this mission wasn't something a lot of people would volunteer for. People with lives, family, and choices.

"You said that other items were stolen," I said through a dry throat. "Other specimens that are pointless to reclaim. Why then is it not too late for this one?"

"The silver egg's shell is a protective casing," Alastair replied. "It's designed to self-destruct if forced entry is attempted. But, regrettably, that is a matter that's up for contention. Although I am in possession of its only key, the casing technology is still in the early stages of development. The inventor cannot guarantee that Patrus will not find a loophole if they work long and hard enough... hence, time is of the essence. We must retrieve the egg soon."

I glanced again at the map. "But how can I go to Patrus on such short notice? Wouldn't I need to go through immigration procedures? Or apply at their General Hall for residence? I would need to wait for—"

"Our contact can speed up the entire process to three days," Alastair replied, cutting me short. "He's able to pull a few strings... Getting there expediently will not be an issue. The issue for you will be *staying* there—and safely. Staying there in a way that you can execute the mission without hindrance. Which brings me to my next point: you must marry our contact."

"What?" I thought I had misheard Alastair.

"You must marry him, Violet," he repeated, with unmistakable enunciation.

"M-Marry?"

"Yes," he replied bluntly. "Marriage is the only way a Matrian woman—or any woman for that matter— can have an existence that's even semi-worth living in Patrus. Our insider will sort out your papers, and when you arrive, he will marry you and take you under his wing. Then he will provide you with the details you require to execute the mission."

My voice was still trapped in my throat, but my mind raced with questions.

Who is this man? What is his occupation? What does he look like? How old is he?

"Do you have a picture of him?" I asked.

"Yes," Alastair replied. "You'll need to recognize him once you arrive at the dock."

He retrieved a photograph from the side pocket of his bag and handed it to me.

I found myself staring down at a clean-shaven man with a smart, trimmed crop of black hair, thin lips and a narrow, triangular jaw. His exact eye color was hard to make out from the photo. Somewhere between gray and blue. He looked perhaps in his mid-twenties. I found him neither attractive nor repulsive, though I wasn't used to judging men in either respect. Heck, I wasn't used to judging men at all. Other than Tim, I hadn't had significant close contact with males and didn't think I'd ever need to. I sure as hell never thought I'd end up coupled with one.

"His name?" I rasped.

"That isn't required yet," Alastair replied.

I swallowed, my eyes boring into the man in the photograph, as the word swirled around and around in my head like a nightmare:

Marry.

CHAPTER 6

After showing me the photograph of my soon-to-be husband, Alastair was done answering questions. He took the photograph back from me, telling me that he would give it to me again when it came time for me to leave. Then, after replacing the map and photograph in his bag and gathering up the crossbow, he led me out of the room. Two wardens were still waiting outside the door.

He turned to one of them and said, "Take her to a guest room." Then he addressed me. "While preparations are underway, you should be using your time productively. I will solidify your schedule for the next three days and have you notified after eight a.m."

I barely even had a chance to nod before Alastair strode away.

The wardens flanked my sides and escorted me down a winding hallway till we stopped outside a door that revealed a small suite containing a single bed, a bathroom and a kitchen area.

The wardens remained outside, closing the door behind me. I moved to the bed and slumped down on the mattress. My limbs were exhausted. I should try to sleep, but I couldn't conceive of attempting it. I was still struggling to wrap my head around my meeting with Alastair.

Less than an hour ago, I'd been preparing myself for certain death and now here I was, on the verge of entering a marriage.

Being thrust into the land of Patrus.

I recalled the fear in Josefine's eyes as she had spoken of the state of the patriarchy these days.

Will it really be worse than my current life? I couldn't see how it wouldn't be. Even though I was a Matrian prisoner, I was still respected as a person in my own right. As an independent entity. As a woman. In Patrus, I would be deemed incapable of being anything but some man's shadow. An accessory. A pet. No rights. No voice.

I couldn't imagine anything more daunting.

Even though I wore sweaty, soiled clothing, I curled up beneath the blanket and nestled my head deep into the pillow. Doubt and fear still swirled in my mind as dawn arrived sooner than I was comfortable with. I remained in bed until someone rapped against my door at eight-thirty a.m.

I stumbled toward the door but it opened before I could reach it.

It was Ms. Dale.

Her appearance in the palace was both surprising and comforting. It felt like an age since I had last seen her, though it had only been five years. Her face displayed more creases than I remembered it having, and her hair was visibly graying. Her physique, however, looked as tight as ever. She was shouldering a large backpack.

She cracked a small smile at me, which I couldn't help but return.

"Violet," she said, moving inside. "How are you?"

I shrugged. What did she expect?

"Mr. Jenks sent me. He informed me that you are to embark on a confidential mission to Patrus and over the next few days, he wants me to help you brush up on some skills."

"Oh."

Defense skills.

What exactly does he have planned for me in Patrus?

"We're to start now, so I guess you should get ready."

"Okay." I turned away from her and moved to the bathroom.

"Also," Ms. Dale added, "I brought these for you." She slid the backpack off her shoulders and withdrew an outfit that filled me with a sense of nostalgia. Sturdy shoes, long pants and a top made of durable, stretchy black fabric that was almost impossible to tear. I remembered her lending me a couple of uniforms just like this during my early teenage years.

I flung the clothes over my shoulder. "Thanks."

"And… I should also mention that Mr. Jenks's preference is for us to go to The Green to train."

"*What?*"

"Yep," she replied.

The Green was the dense forested region that ran across the entire northern border of both Matrus and Patrus. The river that separated the nations also ran through it, and that was one reason why its water was so toxic.

The Green's biosphere was not deemed safe to take up residence nearby; the trees and vegetation were noxious. But it was also avoided for another reason: the wildlife that lived there.

"Why does he want us to train there?" I asked. "What's wrong with your training rooms? Don't you still have them?"

"I do," Ms. Dale replied, almost apologetic. "But Mr. Jenks said that training in The Green will make it more of a… high-stress scenario. Apparently, that's something you're going to have to get used to."

My jaw tensed.

"The Green won't kill us," Ms. Dale went on. "We'll only be there for a few days during the daylight hours."

I felt nervous that this mission might turn out to be more dangerous than I'd thought. Though, given the stakes and the weight of the prize I had been promised should I succeed, it would be naïve of me to think it would be easy or of moderate risk.

It was with a tighter throat that I entered the bathroom. I hurried to brush my teeth and take a shower. After drying myself off, I bound my hair into a tight knot atop my head before slipping into my new clothes.

Ms. Dale was waiting patiently for me on the edge of the bed. Her brown eyes rose to meet mine.

"Your breakfast was delivered." She pointed to the bedside table, where a tray of sandwiches had been placed along with a jug of water. I picked at and drank as much I could stomach before returning my focus to Ms. Dale.

"You ready?" she asked, cocking her head.

"Yeah," I muttered, even though I felt anything but.

Two wardens followed us as Ms. Dale led me out of the palace, across the gardens, and toward the main gates of the compound. Reaching them, she turned to me and said, "Wait here with the wardens. I'll fetch my truck."

She returned about a minute later driving the same old truck she'd owned five years ago. The wardens escorted me through the gates and piled into the backseat, sandwiching me between them before giving Ms. Dale the go-ahead to leave.

I had been hoping that I could be alone with Ms. Dale for the next three days; that she would be deemed enough security. But apparently the wardens still considered me too much of a threat—to what, exactly, I wasn't sure.

The streets were all but empty as we rode through them, which meant our journey to The Green passed faster.

Soon the outline of the forest and its halo of greenish mist began to creep into view. A wiry fence was all that separated the mass of trees from the countryside, because there was nobody to keep out. Nobody ventured here, just like nobody ventured into The Outlands either—the desolate wilderness beyond Matrus' eastern and southern borders.

Well, almost nobody. There had been cases of rebels venturing north particularly; usually mothers of marked boys who were mad enough with grief to think they could find their son if they just walked far enough. They paid no heed to the impossible size of The Green.

As much as Matrus' leadership made efforts to emphasize that every law and restriction instituted was for the sake of our nation's — and womankind's — long term peace and well being, and that it was only because of a long history of misbehavior by men that we were in this position to begin with, their assurance wasn't enough for a minority of women whose lives had been touched by the screening. Whenever I thought of my brother, it still wasn't enough for me. But I hadn't lost my mind. At least, not yet. I had learned enough about the world outside from Ms. Connelly and almost every teacher I'd had in school—nobody who tried to escape came back.

Their words still haunted me now as we closed the final distance. The truck stopped in a meadow, a quarter of a mile before The Green started. Ms. Dale slipped out and trudged around the vehicle, opening up the trunk. She pulled out two breathing masks and handed one to me while placing the other on herself.

She addressed the wardens. "I'm sorry. I thought I had a couple more masks back there."

They frowned as Ms. Dale took my arm and guided me out of the truck. Without a backward glance, she began traipsing across the field of brittle grass toward The Green, pulling me along behind her.

I sensed that she didn't want the wardens shadowing us, either.

In any case, the two women had no choice but to wait in the vehicle unless they wanted to risk getting sick.

"Stay within earshot," one of the wardens called after us.

"We'll do our best," Ms. Dale replied. "But I must go wherever is most conducive for training…"

I could feel the atmosphere intensifying the closer we drew to The Green. The temperature also seemed to spike, though perhaps that was just me working up a sweat. I found myself wishing that my clothes weren't so tight, that my shoes were made of a thinner material.

As the mist pervading the trees began to touch us, Ms. Dale stopped and reached into her bag again. She pulled out a gun from the back compartment and two pairs of gloves from a mesh side pocket. She handed one pair to me and we both pulled them on before continuing.

We reached a narrow door in the fence. Ms. Dale drew out a key, unlocked the door, and pushed it open. My breathing sounded labored as we stepped through it and entered the first line of trees. From the outside, I never would have guessed the mist was this thick. I could hardly see more than ten feet in front of me. We wouldn't have much warning if an animal came charging for us.

We had entered a world of low-hanging trees bursting with green sap. Moss-covered boulders, purple mush-rooms, and dead wood littered the deep, moist under-growth. Slimy vines that resembled snakes hung down from the canopy of leaves—a canopy so thick, it was rare to catch a trickle of sunlight. The lighting was gloomy and altogether surreal in its greenness.

Ms. Dale strode a step in front of me, her gun at the ready. Sweat trickled down my forehead behind my mask as we ventured deeper.

After thirty minutes had passed, I was sure we'd traveled well out of the wardens' earshot. Ms. Dale was obviously not afraid of me. Not only did she have the skills to easily overpower me, I doubted she truly believed I'd become the criminal the wardens made me out to be.

She stopped abruptly. I followed her gaze straight ahead through the trees.

"Do you hear that?" she whispered.

"What?" It was a struggle to hear much other than my own harried breathing beneath this heavy mask.

"Listen closely," she said.

As I strained to hear, I realized what she had noticed—a low buzzing, coming from somewhere in front of us, in the distance. A buzzing that was growing louder.

My heart skipped a beat. "Red flies?" I whispered.

"Sounds like it, doesn't it?" she murmured grimly.

Ms. Dale began scanning the ground around us. She darted with me through the trees until she located a hollow trunk. She pulled out another object from her backpack, an aerosol container, and sprayed the hollow. Shiny black centipedes the length of my hair squirmed out, worming themselves into the brushwood. Then Ms. Dale pushed me inside. I cramped my body up as small as I could to make room for her to crawl in next to me. There was enough room for us to sit side by side while still having a view of the outside.

The buzzing was hard to miss now. It thrummed in my ears.

Ms. Dale sprayed the aerosol again, through the opening of the trunk and into the forest's atmosphere. She acted just in time. A few seconds later, a blur of brown zoomed through the undergrowth with a dense red cloud moving at an alarming speed close behind. It was a wild boar, running for its life from a swarm of huge blood-colored flies. It darted out of sight, the flies maintaining their close pursuit.

I could only be grateful that it was the animal they were chasing, rather than us.

Ms. Dale and I waited stiffly until the buzzing faded, then climbed out of the hollow and straightened.

"So, Violet," Ms. Dale muttered, brushing off her pants. "Now you've seen it for yourself. The flies do exist."

"Yeah," I said, my throat hoarse. Those flies were supposed to be vampiric. They attacked in swarms and if there were enough of them, they could drain an animal or even a person to the point of death. But I was already facing certain death by execution if I failed this mission, and I trusted that Ms. Dale was trained to deal with this environment.

"Let's continue," she said curtly. She handed me the aerosol can. "You carry this for now."

During the next stretch of our journey, the occasional squawk of a bird made me jump, and I was introduced to yet more insects—jumper bugs and rope leeches—as well as a silver python that looked large enough to swallow me whole. But Ms. Dale deftly guided me onward.

She stopped again as we arrived at the first clearing we had come across since entering The Green. Taking the aerosol container from me, she roamed its perimeter and sprayed generously. It was some kind of pest repellent, evidently, but it also had a side effect of clearing the mist, making our vision a little clearer.

Then she moved over to a fallen tree whose carcass was thriving with new life. She scraped away the weeds and moss from its surface, then placed her gun atop it, along with her backpack, opening the bag's zipper.

"Come here, Violet," she said.

I approached and stood next to her as she began to empty the bag's compartment of… more weapons. Guns— large and small. By the time she'd finished, her backpack had shrunk to a fraction of its previous size.

My eyes met hers. "You're going to train me to use… weapons?" I whispered.

"Yes," she replied. "At the request of Mr. Jenks."

My eyes trailed over the assortment of guns. Only wardens, authorized warden trainees, or professionals like Ms. Dale were allowed to handle weaponry. All of my defense training to date had consisted solely of physical contact.

Now I couldn't help but suspect that putting me into a "high-stress" situation wasn't the scientist's main motivation for wanting me to train in The Green. He probably wanted to keep all this undercover as much as possible, and the primary appeal of this location was its isolation.

"So I have just three days to perfect my skills?" I asked.

"I don't expect you to be perfect," Ms. Dale replied. "But I do expect you to become proficient. Once you're in Patrus, as a woman, it's highly unlikely you'll find an opportunity to train or practice… You'll be lucky to get hold of a gun at all."

"Then what's the point of training?"

"Because it will push your comfort zone—something you need to get used to for your time in Patrus. Moreover, it's what Mr. Jenks wants, so let's start."

She set up a target—a rotting log—before picking up the nearest weapon to her, a handgun. She began demonstrating how to stand, aim and fire. She hit the target dead in the center, several times over, before passing the gun to me. It felt cold and heavy in my gloved hand. And so very foreign.

I spread my feet apart as she instructed, assuming a firm stance before taking my aim. I missed wildly.

She made me try again and again, until I got closer to the target. It took me all of two hours to hit the exact center.

"Good," Ms. Dale said. "Let's move on to something larger."

Great. Larger and probably noisier.

I had been on edge the whole time, constantly glancing around the clearing, afraid that our noise would draw unwanted attention from the creatures of The Green.

Ms. Dale picked up the gun with the longest barrel and handed it to me after a brief explanation of the differing mechanisms between this and the previous firearm. Then she allowed me to fire. It didn't take me nearly as long to succeed in hitting the target with this. I was warming up, I supposed.

She made me try out a third gun, and then a fourth. By the time three p.m. struck, I was famished.

"We'll continue practice after lunch," she said, taking my gun from me and resting it on the dead trunk along with the others. "Let's head back. There's food in the trunk."

As she placed the backpack on her shoulders without the guns, I frowned.

"You're just going to leave those here?" I asked.

"Yes," she said. "They'll be here when we return. It's not like there are thieves roaming around in this place."

We traipsed back the way we'd come and returned to the truck. The wardens looked thoroughly bored. Judging from the bag of dirty napkins on the floor in front of the passenger's seat, they'd found something to eat already.

It was a quick lunch and we rested for another fifteen minutes before returning to the clearing for our afternoon session.

We resumed where we had left off, and by the time darkness began to close in—which was as early as six-thirty due to the denseness of The Green—I had worked with every single weapon Ms. Dale had brought with us. I'd definitely had my comfort zone pushed, but once I'd gotten the hang of the technique, it wasn't nearly as difficult as I'd envisioned. Wielding a gun had started to come naturally to me. That didn't make me any less afraid of the weapons, though—not so much of being shot at as afraid of the damage I could inflict with them myself. I had a hard enough time controlling my fists.

We packed everything up, headed to the truck, and journeyed back to the palace. It was late by the time I arrived in my room. We'd hit rush hour on the way back and been delayed. Ms. Dale told me she would greet me at nine the next morning.

Except for a chambermaid to bring me some dinner, nobody came to see me that night. I'd thought that Alastair might, but perhaps he wouldn't bother until the papers were ready—supposedly in two days.

With my arm muscles sore and body aching, I slept far more easily that night, though my slumber was punctuated with a nightmare involving echoing gunshots, red flies, and silver snakes.

The next two days passed in much the same manner as the first, except that Ms. Dale varied the weapons she taught me to use. On the second day, we focused on crossbows and knives, and on the third, she brought along a sack full of more common objects. Every day items that could be turned into weapons, like pens, rope, and hair pins.

We met with a few more scares from the wildlife—like a pack of wolves Ms. Dale warded off with an explosion of gunshots, and a horde of venomous spiders raining from the trees. But otherwise, thanks to her experience in this environment, things went as smoothly as I could have expected them to go.

I could have sworn, though, at one point, that I actually saw the shadow of a person darting through the trees—or some other kind of creature that stood tall and upright. But it vanished quickly, before I could even point it out to Ms. Dale, leading me to conclude it was the mist playing tricks on my eyes.

At the end of the third day, we finished half an hour early and sat together on the log, steeling ourselves for the journey back.

I sensed melancholy in my trainer. Melancholy that I shared. Neither of us knew when, or if, we would ever see each other again.

She gazed down at her gloved hands, her feet grazing the soil.

"I saw that you were a disturbed girl," she said quietly. "But I never thought it would come to this."

I stared at my own hands. "Neither did I."

"I wish I could have done something to help keep you out of trouble. I know you cared about my opinion."

"I doubt there's much you could have done," I muttered. *I was on a collision course.*

I was beyond wanting to explain the details of the murders I'd committed to Ms. Dale, because the details didn't matter. All Matrus saw was that I had claimed two lives.

"Maybe encouraging you to pursue the occupation of a warden was a mistake on my part," she said, as though she hadn't heard me. "Maybe you should have been channeled into something tamer, though it would've been a waste. You were my best student."

I dug my nails into the log. She was speaking as though this second lease on life I'd been granted by Alastair was hardly much better than being put down.

"Ms. Dale… Did Mr. Jenks really not tell you any details about the task ahead of me? Nothing at all?"

My trainer hesitated for a moment, then shook her head. "He didn't give me specifics, because he said they were not required… I will say one thing, however." Shifting on the log, she twisted to face me. Her expression was serious, her brown irises glimmering in the pale evening light. "Once you reach the other side of the river, trust no one, Violet. Do you understand me?"

Swallowing, I nodded.

CHAPTER 7

After Ms. Dale returned me to my room, I was left to wait alone. I didn't know when Alastair would come for me. The papers were supposed to be ready, but it was possible they could be delayed.

There was nothing I could distract myself with; no books or newspapers. I ended up taking a long shower to wash my hair free of all the gunk that had accumulated in it from The Green. When I emerged in the bedroom in my bathrobe, I was surprised to find a chambermaid waiting for me. I hadn't heard her enter through the noise of the shower.

"Mr. Jenks wishes to know if you are ready for a reception," she said, her voice a tad monotone.

"Uh, yeah. I will be in a minute."

She nodded and exited the room.

Grabbing some fresh clothes that had been placed in the closet for me during the day, I quickly dressed and draped my hair in a towel.

I moved to sit down, but my nerves would not allow it. This was it. My last night in Matrus. Wringing my hands, I paced up and down the far end of the bedroom until footsteps sounded outside the door. There came a polite yet sharp knock.

"Come in," I called.

The door glided open. In stepped Alastair sporting a deep blue suit and carrying his crossbow again, followed by... I could not believe my eyes.

Queen Rina.

The queen of Matrus herself.

I hardly knew how to react. I stared, rooted to my spot and gaping at her as she glided into the room after Alastair, who closed the door behind them.

She wore a long, brown, padded-shoulder dress that clung to her tall, slender frame. Her appearance was striking, but not beautiful. Her features were too severe for that. Her face was long, the apples of her cheeks sharp. Framed by thin, slanted brows, her eyes were narrow, their color almost black—like her short bob of hair.

"Your Majesty," I murmured. I should've fallen to my knees before her immediately and kissed the back of her right hand. But I couldn't physically bring myself to do it. The same stinging resentment I'd felt toward Alastair surged up in me and I remained standing, holding her gaze.

I had all but forgotten about Alastair until he dropped a gray folder onto the bed in front of me.

"Everything is lined up," he said. "Your papers have been filed with the immigration department. After Her Majesty and I leave you, go through this folder carefully. You will need to memorize all details contained within it. Not only memorize; you must live them and breathe them. The photograph of our contact is also in the folder— keep it safe. You should be ready to step out of this door at midnight tonight. I will come to collect you and drive you to the port, where you will take a late ferry to Patrus."

"O-Okay," I said, my eyes returning to the queen. As if mirroring me, consciously or subconsciously, she, too, had remained standing, even though there was a seat only a couple of feet behind her. Her gaze was still on me, and I suspected that it had never left. It was hard to read her expression though—what she might be thinking. How she might be judging me. Her face was stoic, quite devoid of clues. If she disapproved of my reception of her—or rather, lack of it—she wasn't showing it. Neither was Alastair. He appeared too busy with the matter at hand to think of much else.

"I must also impress upon you one more thing, Ms. Bates," Alastair plowed on. "Something that, really, should be obvious to you by now, since you seem to be a sharp girl.

But it's important for me to emphasize all the same." He stepped back from the bed and stood level with the queen. "Matrus cannot risk a war. Our nation is founded on peace. The type of mission you are about to undertake is, admittedly, not orthodox. But sometimes drastic actions are necessary, especially since we are simply reclaiming what is ours. Even despite this fact, if King Maxen got wind that you were sent on our bidding, if you somehow caused yourself or our contact there to be outed, the consequences could be crippling not just for you and him, but for your entire country. Patrus would see it as an affront—at a time when relations are already strained. Hence, you cannot be too careful. Pay close attention to everything our man tells you."

I stared at the scientist as he finished. Even if I was successful in retrieving this mysterious egg, how would Patrus not suspect that Matrus was behind it? I didn't understand what would be stopping them from finding out, and then probably tracing everything back to me—the newly arrived Matrus girl with magic papers.

The Court must have thought this through though. They weren't stupid. I supposed things would become clearer once I reached Patrus, but this truly did seem to be a tricky situation.

Both Alastair and the queen exuded an air of tension as they studied me. I found myself considering again how curious it was that they should select me for this task out of all their citizens. Couldn't they have waited for a more suitable—and experienced—person? I would have thought that a man would be better suited. He could in theory blend in better and move about freely. *They must be desperate to get the job done.* The thought came with a feeling of empowerment—something I hadn't experienced in a while. *If they're as desperate as me... then they need me, just as much as I need them.*

The queen stepped forward, closer to me, and rested her hands against the bedpost. Then she spoke for the first time.

"Ms. Bates," she said, her tone deep and commanding. "You may not understand the full implications of this mission now. I do not expect you to. You are young. But if you keep your courage, if you pull through this with strength and determination, you will go down as a hero to your people. In spite of your past, you are still a child of Matrus. And now you must fight for her. You must bear this responsibility with tenacity. With enthusiasm and passion. You have a nation behind you, Ms. Bates. During whatever trials you may face, always remember that."

She let her words hang in the air before pursing her lips and giving me a firm nod. I supposed that she expected me to feel roused now. Raring to go. Honored at the opportunity to put my life on the line. It was my home that I was fighting for, after all.

But I didn't feel anything like this. Instead, my mind was ticking.

"Your Majesty," I said, bowing my head just a touch. "I understand the weight of this responsibility, and what is at stake should I fail. For this reason, I believe it would be wise on your part to give me an extra incentive... an extra personal incentive. This would ensure that, on both a conscious and subconscious level, I will be making my best effort at all times."

As her brows rose, I could practically hear the question pass through her mind: *What could be more personal than serving your homeland?* But she didn't shoot me down.

"My proposal is simple," I dared continue. "If I succeed, allow me to visit my brother, Timothy Bates, who was transported to the coal mines eight years ago."

Her nostrils flared slightly as she breathed in, her eyes moving fleetingly to Alastair's. She hadn't been expecting me to attempt to get something out of this deal above having my own life spared.

She gave it a minute of thought before a smile cracked her porcelain face. "All right," she said. "If you succeed, and return with the egg without creating trouble for Matrus, then you shall visit your brother the very next week."

It was as though a light switched on inside me. My heart swelled with joy and an anticipation I could hardly contain. When I'd taken a shot at setting my own terms, I hadn't dared to hold much hope that the queen would bite. But my suspicion had been correct: both she and her Court were as desperate as me.

Tim. He would be sixteen now. How would he have grown? How would he have changed? I felt jittery at the thought of seeing him again. It would be unreal. A dream. It still hadn't quite sunk in what I had just negotiated for myself.

I bowed before the queen this time, and in spite of all the obstacles I knew were up ahead of me, I smiled more fully than I had in years.

"I will succeed, Your Majesty."

CHAPTER 8

I didn't have long till midnight. After the queen and the scientist took their leave, I sat cross-legged on the bed and opened the gray folder. Along with the photograph, it contained a three-page letter of recommendation signed by a Mr. Lee Bertrand. As I continued to read through the letter, I soon realized that Lee Bertrand was the man I was to meet on the other side of the river. The man I was to marry.

He was recounting in small, neat handwriting how he and I had first met, three years ago during one of his visits to Matrus to inspect lab equipment. How, in spite of our distance, we had maintained a relationship all these years, him visiting my home whenever he frequented Matrus. He explained that I was an orphan who had received little education and had worked in a bakery for all of my adolescent life. I was "one hundred percent clean, with no history of disease or promiscuity". And, as one could note from the picture they'd received of me—*what picture?*—I was "more than pleasant to the eye". He would marry me posthaste and take full responsibility for me the moment I set foot on their side of the river. He ended with the assurance that I would make "an innocuous addition to the society of Patrus".

My mouth had dried out by the time I had finished. I sat there, staring at the pages.

I wasn't sure whether to feel insulted, intimidated, or relieved that Lee had thought all these details through for me, leaving me only to memorize them. I brewed in a mixture of all three for the next half-hour as I read the letter over several times to ensure I didn't miss anything. I wasn't used to this—having things done for me. Least of all by a man. I had never relied on a man before in my life, for anything. But if I wanted to stand a chance of seeing my brother again, it looked like I was going to have to get used to it.

Time passed quickly. I managed to force myself to sleep for an hour and a half, and then it was time for me to get ready.

Alastair arrived at midnight precisely, carrying a small, yet completely empty suitcase. I frowned at him as he handed it to me.

"You will be provided with everything you need once you reach Patrus. But it will look odd if you arrive carrying nothing at all."

I slipped the folder inside the case to give it some use, and then the two of us departed from the palace. Alastair hadn't bothered to bring any weapon with him this time, at least not that I could see. He seemed to have gained confidence that I wasn't going to try anything. Of course I wasn't now. He'd be an idiot to think I might.

He led me outside the royal compound's main gates, where a long white car with tinted windows was waiting for us. He opened the door to the backseat and held it for me as I slid inside, before slamming it shut and seating himself next to the driver. The car moved forward.

I gazed through the tinted panels at the quiet city as we sped away toward the dock. I lost track of time, and soon, direction. My eyes glazed over as I attempted to mentally steel myself for what was to come. A risk-filled mission whose details were still a mystery to me, and marriage to a man I'd never even met. I'd never felt more unprepared.

My stomach grew tighter as I lowered my window to let in the air. It was becoming colder, sharper, and moister. My eyes refocused on the streets of modest townhouses. We were almost at the water.

Soon, we were driving through the steel gates that led directly to the road that lined the misty dockland. There was only one ferry operating at this time, its round lamps gleamed through the fog of the river.

I climbed out of the car and Alastair led me to the narrow rope bridge connecting the jetty to the ferry. We stood stoic for a moment, holding each other's gaze.

"How are you feeling?" he asked. He looked tired and anxious.

I didn't want to admit that I was afraid. My feelings were none of his business. I just nodded stiffly.

"All right," he said, dropping his voice to a whisper. "Remember everything we've told you. We are depending on you, Ms. Bates. Don't forget that."

I doubted I would.

He gave me a twitch of a smile before walking away.

I found it a bit disconcerting that there had not been any talk at all about how I would return to Matrus after the mission. That was a bridge they apparently weren't willing to cross until we came to it.

As Alastair returned to the white vehicle and the driver pulled away, back toward the safety of the city, I crossed the rope bridge and boarded the boat.

Other than the captain, who sat in the control cabin with her head buried in a newspaper, there was only one other person on board—an elderly woman wrapped in a woolen shawl near the back. I sat a few rows in front of her and gazed out of the window, my eyes scanning the dark, vaporous waters.

If only my brother could have boarded one of these, I couldn't help but think. *If only he could have made it to Patrus and been accepted there...* It would have been relatively easy to arrange clandestine visits with him if he'd resided just across the river—compared to not knowing his whereabouts at all.

I pulled my thoughts back to the present. Reality. *Focus.*

"What's bringing you to Patrus?" The old lady behind me spoke up.

I twisted reluctantly to face her. "I'm, uh, moving there."

Her eyes bulged. "Are you really?"

"Yup." *Really.*

"Who's the man?" she asked.

"A scientist."

"What kind of scientist?" she asked, rising from her seat and moving to a row closer to me.

I wished that she would have stayed where she was. I wanted to sit in silence, mentally prepare for my arrival, not be hit with a barrage of questions. But I supposed that this would be good practice for me. A test run, to see how well I had memorized, and how naturally I could spout off, all the lies.

"I can't say, to be honest," I replied. "His work is high-level. He's not even allowed to tell me the details."

"I see," she murmured.

Then she fell quiet. Though I could practically hear her thoughts. Because the same thoughts ran through every Matrian's head whenever they came across a woman making the move to the other side.

Poor thing.

What a waste.

She'll never last.

She offered me a weak smile. "You must really love him."

Yeah...

I fixed my attention firmly out of the window to make it clear that I was done talking. When the ferry left the dock five minutes later, we were still the only two passengers. I watched the bank grow further and further away, until the mist became too dense for me to see it anymore. I stood up and walked to the opposite end of the boat. Being a warm night—or morning— it was unpleasantly stuffy inside. None of the windows could be opened, to prevent spray entering the boat. I had never touched the river water directly, but I had seen its effect on other people, and if you ingested too much, it could be fatal. I hoped my brother hadn't swallowed much when he fell into the river that night he'd been ripped from me.

The ferry sped up, forging its way through the mist. Due to its thickness, when Patrus' bank finally manifested, it came with little warning. I witnessed Patrus' dockland in clarity for the first time. Warm orange lights glittered along the lengthy wooden jetties, illuminating a myriad of boats that looked quite different from those you'd find in Matrus. Most of them appeared to have been constructed primarily with leisure in mind rather than mere functionality, with shiny, attractive exteriors, spanning several floors and complete with open rooftops protected by transparent shields. There was also a bay reserved exclusively for competitive rowboats—like my cousin Cad's.

Our ferry slotted into an empty bay and stopped. I let the elderly woman walk ahead of me, though she stopped to chat with the captain, leaving me to step out alone onto the empty jetty.

I breathed in, scenting the atmosphere as a gust of wind caught my hair. It was breezier on this side of the river.

I cast my eyes around, trying to find my bearings… and my host. Lee Bertrand. He was supposed to be waiting for me.

Clutching my suitcase, I moved away from the vessel. There was a road beyond the docks, and behind that was a towering wall, just like we had in Matrus. No overwhelming difference between the lands so far.

Lee had to be around here somewhere. I caught sight of shadows moving near the cargo ships, further along the shore. But I was apparently alone…

Then I spotted movement to my right and a man wearing a dark brown coat appeared from behind a lamp post. He sported a tartan cap that shaded his face.

I was hardly breathing as he closed the distance between us. The breeze carried his fragrance, sharp and citrusy, and stopping a couple of feet in front of me, he removed his cap, allowing the dock lights to illuminate his clean-shaven face.

"Ms. Bates." His voice was deep and low.

"Mr. Bertrand," I whispered, my grip tightening around the handle of my suitcase.

His narrow lips formed a smile that reached his eyes—eyes that were more blue than gray.

He looked younger in person and there was a slight boyishness to his features, which I found kind of comforting.

I reached out to shake his hand, but he instead closed his fingers around mine and held it gently.

"Let's go," he said beneath his breath. "We'll talk later."

He remained holding my hand as he reached across me to remove my suitcase from my grasp and carry it. He pulled me away from the river, toward the road. We reached the sidewalk and stopped in front of a black motorcycle that leaned against a lamp post.

He attached my suitcase to a holder at the back of it before lifting up the seat to reveal a hidden compartment which stored two helmets. He handed me one, which I proceeded to strap to my head while he did the same.

He pushed the seat back down. "After you," he said, patting it.

I straddled it, moving as far back along the seat as possible. Clutching the handles, he positioned himself in front of me. I felt embarrassed and uncomfortable to place my hands on his shoulders, but as he coaxed the engine to life, I had no choice. We rolled off the sidewalk, slipping onto the deserted road where we picked up speed. The chill of the morning amplified, my skin tingled with goosebumps.

We drove close to the gray brick wall for about two miles before Lee eased our pace. An opening emerged: a pair of wide, gold-plated gates. As we passed through them and reached the world on the other side, my jaw slackened.

Sprawled on either side of us were vast artificial lakes, exploding with fountains made to glimmer in the darkness by brilliant underwater lights. The tall spurts of water shot up to varying heights, swaying in the wind as if in a dance. Droplets sprayed the road and touched us.

I had seen pictures of these lakes before, but the photographs did them little justice. The expanse of clear, shimmering water felt almost like a taunt to their neighbors—Matrus couldn't even conceive of such waste.

But Patrus could afford it, just like they could afford other extravagances, thanks to their fertile mountain region. I glanced there now, toward Patrus' peaks. Their majestic outline loomed closer, and I felt an unexpected rush of anticipation to see them up close.

As soon as the lakes and fountains ended, towering apartment blocks began. They spanned ten floors, and each block was separated by lush lawns and illuminated gardens. The buildings were beautiful to look at. Their smooth steel exteriors gelled with dark wooden panels that lined the balconies. Each block boasted a terrace garden, vines spilling over the rooftops like hair. Being situated on this prestigious entry road to Patrus, of course, only the affluent could afford to live here.

The broad road led us past miles of this development until the blocks gave way to a different kind of architecture and we arrived in an expansive community of large two-story houses. These were clearly family homes— many of the front yards contained swings and other play-ground equipment, and they had garages large enough to fit three vehicles.

As Lee sped up, I held him tighter. This was the first time I'd been on a motorcycle. He could probably tell from the pressure of my fingertips against his shoulders.

We joined a highway and to the left of us, more suburbs slipped away. To our right was apparently the beginnings of Patrus City— a halo of orange light overhung a sea of densely-packed buildings. Buildings, tall and short, wide and narrow; shops, arenas, eateries, offices, houses.

Then Patrus' famed Crescent River came into view. It acted like a moat for the king's residence, a magnificent five-turreted stone palace built against the cliffside of a mountain. The river set the king's home aside from the rest of the city, on its own little island.

Lee forged onward and began a route that led us into the foothills of the mountains. We wound upward, higher and higher, and began to pass more residences, albeit at longer intervals. These houses were all very different and more extravagant than any I'd seen so far. Spanning four levels, they were stark white and triangular-shaped, their walls more glass than brick. Racing cars and powerful motorcycles filled the driveways.

Higher and higher we climbed, until we had gained a bird's eye view of the ground: the glittering city to the north, the eastern and southern suburbs… and Veil River, so far away now in the distance.

Finally, Lee pulled into the empty driveway of a triangular villa identical to all the others that lined this mountainside. The only distinguishing factor about his was a neatly trimmed row of flower bushes lining the ground floor.

As Lee stalled the motorcycle, he slid off and I stepped off after him, steadying my knees as the gravel crunched beneath my feet.

His crop of black hair was mussed from his helmet and draping down near his eyes. He slanted a glance at me, then gestured to the front door. "Shall we?"

We approached the entrance and barking erupted from behind the door, making me jump. As we stepped into a dark hallway, a large shaggy brown dog leapt up at me, front paws against my waist. I patted the dog's head awkwardly. I didn't have much experience with animals. The canine's tongue wagged, swiping at my wrists.

"Come on, Samuel," Lee muttered, slipping a hand through the dog's collar and pulling him into an open doorway before shutting him inside. "Sorry," he said with a roll of his eyes. "He doesn't get visitors very often."

He switched on a light, and led me through to a spacious open plan kitchen-dining room. The floors and ceiling were wooden, as was the kitchen table. A beam hung over it, dangling half a dozen pans. A granite counter stretched the length of one wall, immaculately clean and tidy. White blinds were drawn against the wide windows.

Lee removed his jacket and hung it over a high-backed chair, revealing his true physique. It was slimmer than his bulky coat had made him out to be, but I guessed fairly attractive.

I wasn't wearing a coat. Just a plain, long-sleeved top and black pants. I sure hoped that he *did* have clothes sorted for me. I didn't even have a change of underwear.

"Can I get you something to eat or drink?" he asked, drawing up a chair for me.

"Uh, a drink, please. Just water."

He filled up a tall glass from a crystal canister and handed it to me. His lips curved again in another fleeting smile. The thought that he might be as nervous as me about this whole situation brought me a thread of comfort.

I had to remind myself that he was not like the other men in Patrus, even if he pretended to be to the outside world. He belonged on the other side of the river, my side. He was a Matrian male. He should understand what I was going through in coming over here.

"So," he said, breathing out. "Welcome, I guess."

"Thanks," I said, letting out my own stifled breath.

With both of us sitting opposite one another beneath the bright kitchen spotlights, perhaps he felt as bare as I did. As awkward and exposed.

"How was the journey?" he asked, pouring a glass of water for himself.

"It was fine…" I struggled to embellish my answer.

"Do you have my picture with you?" he asked. "And my letter of recommendation?"

"Yes."

"Okay. You may as well hand those back to me. You only needed to carry them in the unlikely event that you were stopped by someone before I met up with you on the dock."

Lee had placed my suitcase on the floor near my feet. I stooped down and retrieved the gray folder, handing it to him.

"Thanks." He glanced briefly inside it before stowing it away in one of the kitchen drawers. He resumed his seat and placed his hands on the table, twisting his silver watch. "So, I'm sure you want to know more about me."

"Um, yes."

"My full name is Lee Desmond Bertrand. Named Lee by my father, Desmond by my mother. I am twenty-five. On paper, I'm native to neither Matrus nor Patrus. In fact, I was born in the middle of Veil River. Literally. My mother was fleeing from Patrus to Matrus to give birth to me, but timing was not on her side."

He paused to sip from his water.

"Why was she fleeing?"

"Her relationship with my father was a tumultuous one. She had wanted to move back to Matrus even before she fell pregnant with me, but my father forbade it. He wanted me to be born in Patrus. Being a migrant and a woman, there was nothing she could do at the time except go along with her husband's wishes, obviously. But she plotted an escape the night she went into labor, a plot that went horribly wrong… I was lucky to have survived."

"Did she survive it?" I wondered.

"Yes. She died a few years back."

"Oh, I see. So… you have no true nationality?" I posed.

"I have allied myself officially with Patrus, though my loyalty has always been with Matrus, like my mother's was. My mother was spotted on the river by a Matrian the night she gave birth, and she and I were taken to the city hospital. I managed to spend the first ten years of my life in Matrus—and they were my happiest years—before my father reclaimed me. But in the strict sense of the term, yes, you are correct…I have no true allegiance to any nationality."

"And how did you become… this?" I asked.

"Let's just say I was still young when I came here, and my father's position was of great benefit to me… Honestly, the less you know about this particular subject, the safer you and I will both be."

I pursed my lips. "I see."

He glanced around the kitchen. "I've been in this residence for the last three years. I live alone with Samuel, with no siblings or family in general to bother us. My father died a year ago… My duties are down in the lab, near the palace. It takes about half an hour to commute by motorcycle, depending on the time of day. I will be out a lot during the week, sometimes also at the weekend."

"What sort of work does a scientist in Patrus do, exactly?" I asked. "I read about a pharmaceutical King Maxen has commissioned development on…"

"Yes. Patrus is trying to become as proficient as Matrus in the fields of biology and medicine. King Maxen wants to catch up, become as competent in them as Patrus is in architecture and engineering… But the new king has no intention of playing fair, of building from scratch based on their own research and merits. He wants a head start. Upon his ascendance to the throne, infiltrating Matrus' lab was a logical first step. He wants to reverse-engineer what was taken in the raid and work out how to recreate it… Of course, he knows that there's not much Matrus can do to fight back; he uses Queen Rina's reluctance— and practical inability—to start a war to his advantage."

I lowered my brows. "In all the years you've been under-cover, what sort of missions have you been on for Matrus?" I couldn't help but ask, even though I suspected that he would be reluctant to answer.

"Never a mission, per se," Lee replied. "So far, the neces-sity hasn't arisen. I have been Matrus' eyes and ears, report-ing back what I see and hear from the higher levels of the patriarchy, so they can plan and take action according-ly on their side. That's why you're here to assist with the task ahead, because I cannot do everything on my own.

And I can't be caught. My presence here and the trust the authorities have in me are extremely important to Matrus."

He lapsed into silence, his blue gaze still on me. I wondered whether he wanted me to talk about myself a bit, though I was sure that he'd already been told everything about my history.

"I-I understand… Will there be some sort of test by the authorities for how well you know me?" I asked. "Or how well we know each other? Before we're allowed to, uh…"

"Marry?"

I was glad that he spared me the word. "Yes," I managed, heat creeping to my cheeks.

He shook his head. "Sometimes it is required. But it won't be in my case." He swallowed the last of his water, surprisingly cool about the subject. I ought to be like that, too. This wasn't a real marriage. It was just an arrangement. An arrangement that would allow me to stay safely in Patrus, and that would be annulled as soon as our job together was done.

"I noticed you didn't shake my hand, back on the dock," I said, changing the subject. "Is that something you don't do here?"

"It's not something that's done between the sexes." He heaved a sigh, pushing his glass aside. "There is a lot that you're going to need to pick up on while you're here… This is going to be a long discussion. Are you sure you don't want something to eat?"

I was feeling less nervous now than when I'd first come in. I realized that I was hungry. I definitely could stomach something. "I'll eat," I acquiesced.

He rose to his feet with a smirk. "And that brings us to another 'don't': Don't ever tell anyone that I've cooked for you."

CHAPTER 9

Lee's dinner was delicious — no doubt the freshness of the produce contributed a lot to the flavor. The food was simple, with basic herbs and spices, and the core ingredients were enough to make it take off.

I ate more than I had intended to and after I finished, I found myself leaning back in my chair, holding my stomach.

He eyed me with amusement, setting down his own fork. "Had enough?"

"Yeah. Thanks."

He hadn't wanted to talk much over dinner. Maybe because he hadn't wanted to ruin my digestion, but now his mood became more serious.

"There are a lot of rules you're going to have to absorb. A lot to bombard you with at once. But I plan to keep you under my wing as much as possible. You'll learn the ropes as we go about our activities. You'll never go out alone, and when I'm gone, you'll stay in the house with Samuel and not answer the door to anybody."

It sounded like what I was used to: a prison life. I wondered how different my days would end up being on this side of the river, after all.

"Tomorrow we will have a tight schedule," Lee went on. "In the morning, I'll need to take you shopping. In the afternoon, we have an appointment in the marriage hall. We will sign the papers and be wed. Then, in the evening, I'm going to take you into the lab to meet my associates and, most importantly, show you around."

My head spun. A tight schedule was an understatement. "Your associates... you've told them about me already, I assume?"

"In brief," he replied. "I told them the same day I found out you were coming over here. It wasn't really a surprise to anyone that I should keep it a secret; I'm not exactly known to be a talkative person when it comes to my personal life... Anyway, don't worry about them. They won't be very interested in talking to you. Men don't talk much to women here — they'll ask a few polite questions, and that will be that."

"Won't they be suspicious that you're bringing a Matrian girl into the lab?"

"We won't stay long enough to cause suspicion," he replied. "We'll do a quick walkabout and then head off. But it'll be enough to give you a bearing on the place."

After another pause, he stood up. "Wait here," he said.

He headed out of the room while Samuel padded inside. The dog wagged his tail and nuzzled his head against my knees before slipping it onto my lap. He sat down in front of me, and I stroked his ears until Lee returned.

Lee was carrying a red folder, which he laid on the table. One by one, he pulled out what appeared to be profiles of a dozen men, each sheet containing a headshot along with personal data.

"These men will be obstacles in retrieving the egg from the lab." He tapped a finger on the photograph in the center of the table in front of us, a photograph of a young man who looked more beast than man compared to the others who, although tough-looking, were fairly well-groomed. His dark brown hair draped down to his shoulders in waves. His forehead was low and wide, his face rough and unkempt. But he struck me as handsome in spite of his roughness. I was instantly attracted to his physical appearance—something I couldn't say in the case of the other men scattered over the table, or Lee for that matter. His deep-set eyes radiated a fierce green even in the photograph. "Viggo Croft" was his name.

"These are the wardens in charge of security surrounding the labs and the palace," Lee said. "They have received the highest level of training Patrus has to offer. They are the best of the best when it comes to protection around here. You'll often spot them roaming the border of the Crescent. Especially Viggo. He's the chief coordinator and very little gets past him… He resigned from the force about a year back, due to 'irreconcilable differences' with the man who was chief at that time—he clearly has a strong independent streak—but got himself into a spot of trouble with the law while he was on leave. At the time, King Patrick struck a deal with him that if he returned to the force to work for the next four years without pay, the infraction would be expunged."

"What was the infraction?" I asked, feeling a spike of curiosity.

"Obstruction of justice," Lee replied.

That had been my first infraction.

"Anyway," Lee continued, "the point is, he's not managing the security by choice at the moment. It's a service that he's forced to perform in order to avoid jail."

He paused, eyeing the papers. I wasn't sure how Lee's "point" was actually relevant to the task at hand.

"So… guards are always around? Day and night?" I asked.

"More or less."

"Then how exactly do you plan to retrieve the egg if they're constantly stalking the place?"

Lee sat back in his chair. "With difficulty… But we'll take this one step at a time. Tomorrow in the lab, I'll show you the location of the egg, and then we'll discuss the next step."

His response didn't sit right with me. I didn't like being fed information in dribs and drabs. "I'm not a Patrian woman," I reminded Lee while keeping my tone polite. "I'd like to know the full extent of my role in this mission."

Lee breathed out. "I understand that, Violet. But I'm saying this for your own sake. I don't want to overburden you with so much information now. You've just arrived."

Hm. Maybe he was right that I ought to give myself a bit of landing time. I needed to know more about the mission, more about the risks and the dangers that I was about to be thrust into, but if he told me everything that was on his mind now, I doubted I'd get a wink of sleep, and I needed to be fresh for the day ahead.

Deciding not to press, I glanced back down at the profiles. "Are you on speaking terms with these men?"

"Yes," Lee said. "Though I try to stay under their radar as much as possible, in case you haven't gleaned that yourself by now."

"Have you ever met King Maxen?"

He nodded darkly. "Yes, a few times. I've been summoned to visit him before along with other members of the board."

"What's he like?"

Lee grimaced. "He's everything that you've read about in the papers. Ruthless and fiercely intelligent, with a demeanor personable enough to influence people and get things done. A deadly combination."

We lapsed into another stretch of silence as I gazed through an open window and down at the mountain.

Samuel let out a snore. He had fallen asleep with his head still on my lap.

"Maybe that's our cue." Lee chuckled.

I slipped myself out from beneath the dog, lowering his head to the carpeted floor against his paws before heading out of the sitting room with Lee.

So far, Lee had given me no reason to feel uncomfortable around him or think that our relationship would be anything but businesslike and perfunctory, the same as if he'd been a woman. In fact, his personality struck me as rather flat and bland (something that was not uncommon among Matrian males).

But even in spite of the ease I'd come to feel around him, my heart couldn't help but quicken as we climbed the staircase to the next floor.

He's going to give me my own bedroom, right?

Thankfully, as we arrived on a landing, he took a right turn and led me to what was clearly a guest bedroom, containing a single bed. The view from here was prettier than downstairs. I even spied a stream flowing near the road that I hadn't noticed before.

"There's a single outfit for you to wear tomorrow in the cupboard, along with a night dress and underwear," Lee told me, pointing to a mahogany chest of drawers in one corner of the room. "Hopefully they'll fit. Tomorrow, we'll equip you properly."

"All right."

"Well, I'm heading to bed," Lee said, backing out of the room. "See you in a few hours."

After we bade each other good night, he closed the door behind him. I moved to it instinctively, searching the back of it for a lock. There wasn't one.

Although I felt almost guilty for it, I found myself dragging a chair to the door and barricading it… taking a page out of Josefine's book.

CHAPTER 10

I woke up to the sound of drilling drifting up from somewhere beneath me. I was in a daze as my eyes shot open and I took in my strange surroundings. Then I remembered. *I'm in Patrus.*

My head ached dully as I headed to the bathroom. I'd eaten too much last night and I felt dehydrated. I drank from the cold water tap before washing and looking at my outfit, which turned out to be a modest blue dress that stopped just below my knees, and a light gray woolen cardigan. I rarely wore dresses even before I was incarcerated, but this one wasn't too bad. The bra was too large, however. I strapped it on anyway before pulling on the dress and buttoning up the cardigan. Lee had also helpfully provided me with a watch, made of silver like his.

I padded out of the room and into the corridor, which was almost blindingly bright. Sun streamed in through a skylight in the ceiling, warming my skin.

Amidst the drilling, I heard the clinking of cutlery and I headed down to the kitchen to find Lee already dressed. He sat at the table looking clean-shaven and bright-faced, in front of a bowl of what looked like oatmeal. He wore a smart gray suit, his black hair combed neatly back.

"Hi, how did you sleep?" he asked.

"Pretty well, thanks."

"Good. I was going to come and wake you up in ten minutes. You should eat some breakfast." He gestured to the stove, where a pot of warm oatmeal sat. On the counter next to it were a bowl of deep pink berries and a jar of honey. I helped myself and took a seat opposite Lee at the table. The berries were the sweetest, most succulent I had ever tasted, and the milk was creamy and rich. Much better than my usual breakfast.

Lee was watching me as I finished, his expression thoughtful. "I suppose I've been in Patrus too long to appreciate the food like you do. I've forgotten how good it tastes compared to Matrus."

Although much of Matrus' fresh produce was imported from Patrus, they gave us the worst of their harvest, always keeping the best for themselves. Not that I could blame them. Matrus would do the same if they were in Patrus' position.

"Where's that noise coming from?" I asked as the drilling continued.

"I have someone down in the garage fixing my third motorcycle," he said. "Hope it didn't disturb you."

"Not really."

I found it funny that he had three motorcycles when there was only one of him. It wasn't like I'd be able to ride it; Samuel would sooner be granted permission than me.

I finished my breakfast and noting that I was done, Lee straightened before speaking. "Right," he said, glancing at his watch. "It's time for us to head off. Are you ready?"

"Yes."

"Okay, wait here. I'll be down in a minute."

I roamed the kitchen as he left and stopped at a window that was slightly open. Even though I was feeling nervous about the day ahead, the beauty of the landscape lifted my spirits a little. The luscious greenery. The fresh air, fragrant with morning dew and the scent of pinewood. The swallows, chirping and soaring over the treetops.

I supposed I could better understand the lure of Patrus for even a Matrian woman now that I was here. If you could ignore everything else that went on in this place—the lack of rights, and the fact that you were basically a prisoner of your husband—the land was beautiful. Vibrant, verdant, closer to nature than Matrus was, and maybe ever would be. There was little to no feeling of shortage on this side of Veil River. The population being smaller than that of Matrus probably helped. There was more wealth and resources to go around in general. The quality of life in a purely material sense was superior even for a woman. I had yet to witness real Patrian society for myself, but so far, I wasn't feeling as daunted as I'd expected.

"Okay," Lee said as he descended the stairs and entered the kitchen. I turned to see him holding a brown wallet, which he slipped into the side pocket of his pants.

"Let's go."

Samuel followed us to the door before Lee shut and locked it. His motorcycle was where we had left it, in the center of the driveway and the gravel crunched beneath our feet as we approached it. Lee handed me a helmet and then the engine roared. We headed out of the driveway, slipping onto the winding road that led down to the city.

It was quite surreal how different everything looked in the daytime. Seeing everything in color, I gained a whole different perspective of the mountain road and the triangular villas that lined it.

We soon began to pass vehicles rolling up the mountain, and as the slope lessened and we arrived on flatter ground, we joined a highway that hummed with many more—at least half of them motorcycles.

I found myself peering into the windows, curious to glimpse the passengers. I spotted some families—wife and husband in the front, kids in the back—but mostly, the vehicles were occupied by lone men. On the way to work, I guessed.

The sky was almost cloudless overhead as we neared the city. Lee branched off the main highway onto a narrower street filled with restaurants before we arrived in a communal parking area.

I got off, steadying myself as I gazed around. The parking lot was practically empty.

"Now is the best time to go shopping," Lee said. "While most men are at work. Early morning and evening are when it gets most crowded."

"So how come you're not at work?" I asked as we drew away from his motorcycle.

"My hours are more flexible than most," he said with a half-smile. "Besides, I have a day off today — I'm getting married, remember."

His hand closed around mine as he led me out of the parking lot and onto the street of restaurants. His leading me like I was a child felt weird, but I understood that Lee had to behave differently while we were out. All of the restaurants were closed at this time, except for a couple of cafeterias.

The streets were immaculately clean, and I had to say that this aspect of Patrus reminded me very much of Matrus—their attention to hygiene. Even the exteriors of the buildings were well-maintained, many of them appeared recently repainted.

He led me down a narrow alley and we emerged onto another road that was populated with shops that catered specifically to women. Clothes boutiques, hairdressers, and salons surrounded us.

Lee's brows furrowed as he glanced over my hair and nails. "We'll pay a visit to Ciantro's first." He pointed to a storefront that appeared to be a beauty and hair salon combined.

My hair was the same as it had always been: long, dry, and unstyled. And my nails… well, they were what they were. Given the environment that I had been living in for the past several years of my life, there had hardly been any point in putting effort into them.

We crossed the road and entered Ciantro's, catching the attention of a tall, skinny man with a perfect coif of blond hair.

He smiled as he looked from me to Lee.

"Morning," he said jovially, moving to the reception desk. "And what can I do for you today?"

Although he was inspecting me, he was clearly asking the question of Lee.

"Just a wash and style for the hair," Lee said. "And"— he gestured to my hands—"a… whatever you call a hand treatment."

"Manicure," the man replied with a grin.

"Yeah," Lee said. I glanced around the pristine white salon. We were the only ones here.

Lee offered me an encouraging smile before nodding toward the man, indicating that I follow him.

The man led me to a chair in front of a sink and after telling me his name—Tyler—began washing my hair. He didn't talk as he worked—just the odd question about my usual "hair routine", which warranted a very short answer. After cleansing my hair, he dried and styled it.

Staring at the finished result in the mirror, I was glad that Lee hadn't told him to do anything drastic. I still looked like myself… just shinier.

Then he took me to the opposite end of the salon where he worked on my nails for the next forty-five minutes—a process that I found tedious. I was relieved when he finally was done, and allowed me to return to Lee, whose head had been buried in a newspaper most of the time.

Lee smiled warmly, his eyes lighting up as he looked over the finished result. He pulled out a platinum card from his wallet and swiped it against the machine on the counter. Then we said thanks and goodbye, and left the salon.

Next, we headed to a clothes store a few doors along. When Lee asked me what sort of thing I liked, I admitted I wasn't really sure. I'd grown up on mostly hand-me-down pants and shirts in the orphanage, and detention facilities didn't exactly provide the opportunity to develop a sense of style. The attendant—another perfectly groomed and extremely knowledgeable man—ended up helping us out. After trying on dozens of outfits, we ended up with two bags full of clothes —mostly dresses, but a fair amount of pants and shirts too (which pleased me). Lee said that dresses were advisable for me to fit in with the general dress code of women in Patrus, though I could wear fitted pants and shirts occasionally (and obviously I would wear whatever I wanted when I was in the house).

I knew a lot of women adored shopping—in Matrus, too—but I wasn't one of them. The first hour was a novelty, but after that it became rather dull to me, like watching someone poking at my nails had.

I hadn't been paying attention to the prices, since Lee hadn't, but I suspected it would've cost him *a lot* of gold. The materials were all organic and high quality, unlike what I was used to wearing.

Since we weren't having a proper ceremony, Lee told me that a traditional wedding dress was not required, but that I still needed something elegant. We ended up choosing a well-tailored long indigo-blue dress that, according to the attendant, made my eyes "pop". Whether they did or not, I couldn't deny that it looked nice. Not me, but nice.

By the time we left the shops, it was nearing one o'clock. We headed back to Lee's motorcycle, where we offloaded the bags. Then he turned to me. "So, we don't have time to return home before the appointment. You can change into the dress and shoes we picked out for the marriage now."

We dug into the bags and retrieved the items before he led me to a building of public restrooms nearby. As I moved into one of the shiny, steel-gray stalls to change, my throat went dry and I started perspiring more than I should have on a day of such a moderate temperature. I had to remind myself that there was no need to feel nervous. *This marriage is fake. It won't mean anything.*

After pulling on the dress and slipping into the shoes, I stepped out of the cubicle and stared at myself in the mirror. My hair hanging down my shoulders in soft waves, the blue dress hugging my frame at the most flattering of places, I didn't remember the last time I'd felt so feminine. Perhaps when I'd tried on my mother's makeup as a kid.

Drawing in a deep breath, I tore my eyes away from the mirror and rejoined Lee outside.

I kept my gaze on the ground as he offered his arm to me, though I could feel his eyes pass over me in polite admiration.

"You look perfect," he said quietly.

An odd feeling swirled inside me. That was the first time I'd been complimented by a man. I wasn't sure whether I liked the attention or not.

Lee cleared his throat. "Right, so, uh... we're not far away. About five to ten minutes' walk. It'll be easier to go by foot from here."

I held his arm a little harder than I had intended as I focused on keeping my walk steady in my new shoes. We first returned to the motorcycle to drop off the clothes I'd changed out of, and then, leaving the street of women's boutiques, we wandered down another narrow alleyway. We passed several more streets after that—streets with barber shops, men's clothing stores, as well as other shops retailing furniture and food. We didn't exchange a word as we walked for the next ten minutes, until we finally arrived outside a tall, red-brick building with a sharp, protruding spire.

"Central Matrimony Registration Office."

We stopped outside the entrance. Finally, Lee and I met each other's eyes as he straightened his jacket.

"Okay." His Adam's apple bobbed. "In we go."

He pushed open the door and held it for me as we stepped into a sterile reception room. The lighting was white and bleak, the carpets a dull shade of green. A wide desk lined the wall opposite us, behind which sat three men in black suits. The man in the middle—a middle-aged bald guy with a heavy goatee—stood as we approached. A perfunctory smile spread across his lips.

"Good afternoon, Mr. Banks," Lee said, holding out a hand for him to shake.

"Afternoon, Mr., and soon-to-be Mrs., Bertrand," he replied.

My hand instinctively moved to shake his, but I caught myself and instead gave him a brief nod, which he returned.

"Do follow me."

Mr. Banks led us through a door to our left and guided us into an office. Here, he circled around a black wooden table and sat down, while he gestured for us to do the same in the two seats positioned in front of us, opposite him at the table.

He ducked down and opened a drawer, reemerging with a pile of papers, which he placed in front of Lee, and handed him a pen. Then Lee began to sift through the pages, signing and dating multiple sheets. Once he was done, he handed the papers back to Mr. Banks.

Then Mr. Banks withdrew a single sheet of paper and passed it to me. "Read it and sign, please," he requested of me.

My eyes trailed down the page. What I was reading was a declaration of oath to give up every freedom a woman took for granted in the land of Matrus, for the sake of my "husband". The language of the document didn't bother to soften the blow as it concluded:

"I hereby declare my full dependence on and submissiveness to Lee Desmond Bertrand, who will take responsibility for my speech and actions, as well as ownership of any possessions previously deemed my own."

It was like a deliberate affront to Matrus-born women. The document was designed to intimidate. As if a Matrian's transition to Patrus wasn't already difficult enough. Even coming from being a prisoner to my homeland, I found it an affront to my identity. Gritting my teeth, I scribbled my name and the date in the same manner one would strip a bandage from a wound. I would have been hurting a lot more if I'd been a regular upstanding Matrian citizen.

Mr. Banks slid the paper back to his side of the table and glanced over it briefly before nodding. "Good," he said. "Now…" He dipped behind his desk again, opening another drawer, before appearing this time with a small black velvet pouch.

He handed it to Lee, who opened it and drew out a single golden ring, then Lee twisted in his chair to face me.

"Do you, Violet Bates," Mr. Banks spoke up, "accept Lee Desmond Bertrand as your lawfully wedded husband?"

My voice caught in my throat as I stared at the ring. I realized that it was engraved with a name. *"L. D. Bertrand."*

It became clear to me in that moment that Mr. Banks would pull out no second ring. There would be no exchange of vows, either. Just a single vow. A single ring.

A single leash.

This ring means nothing, I reminded myself again firmly. *I'm not actually getting married. Lee won't be my husband. We are business partners and this is all just an act.*

I gulped before answering: "I do."

CHAPTER 11

After Lee placed the ring on my finger, our business in the marriage office was done. On exiting the building, we both took a moment. As I stood on the sidewalk, the fresh air against my skin was soothing. I couldn't wait to get out of this dress. Out of these shoes. Out of Patrus.

I had to keep my mind on the prize at the end of the tunnel: my brother—seeing him again would be all the reward I needed.

Lee gestured to my ring and said in a low voice, "Whenever we're out of the house, you should wear it. It's important that you have it on you at all times in case something happens—in case you get separated from me. You will be safe with that ring."

I narrowed my eyes on him. "What do you mean by 'safe'?"

He began to walk me away from the building, back to the alleyway at the other side of the street. "Let's just say there are some less-than-gentlemanly men here in Patrus."

Okay…

"I don't mean to worry you," Lee went on. "Most men here are decent, albeit different from what you're used to. Just keep the ring on your finger, eyes to the ground, and you'll be fine… Now," he said, looking straight ahead at the street we were about to emerge on—the street filled with women's shops. "I suggest we head home for lunch. By the time we eat, we won't have long before we have to return to the city for our lab visit this evening."

I'd hardly spent any time in Lee's house so far, but it was already feeling like a haven compared to the rest of this disconcerting place.

Lee and I changed into more comfortable clothing when we got home. He had cooked a lot the morning before and frozen the leftovers, so we ended up finishing them off for lunch.

As we sat at the table, I couldn't stop thinking about the marriage office, keenly aware of the new weight on my finger.

"Patrian marriages," I said, chewing slowly, "do they all take place in an office like that? Are there no proper ceremonies, like we have in Matrus?" *Are they all so perfunctory?* was what I was curious to know.

"No," Lee said, dabbing the sides of his mouth with a napkin. "There are traditional ceremonies here, too. Some men opt for lavish arrangements, while others prefer to keep it low-key. It just depends on the man... and how much he takes into consideration the preferences of his bride."

"I see," I muttered. Whatever weddings took place in Matrus were almost always accompanied by ceremonies. Even if they weren't grand or lavish, efforts were made to hold a small gathering at least.

"Well," Lee said, finishing his meal and standing, "I'm going to take Samuel out for a walk and then we can head off. In the meantime, feel free to do whatever you want around the house. Make yourself at home and maybe freshen up for this evening. I suspect we'll end up going to a restaurant for dinner, so we could be out fairly late."

My eyes followed him as he moved across the room to drop his plate in the sink and then headed out of the kitchen. He called for Samuel and led him to the door.

Finishing my food, I rose from the table and moved to the window, peering through the blinds as they left.

I glanced furtively at my ring again before walking to the sink to wash up the few dirty dishes.

Make myself at home. That was something I'd had to try to do a lot over the last decade, though I hadn't had a true home since my mother died.

I headed to the bathroom and after splashing cool water on my face, I decided to wander around the house a bit. I found myself roaming the stories of the triangular building, gaining a better understanding of Lee in the process. He really didn't like clutter, we were alike in that sense, and there were hardly any ornaments or decorations, except for the odd abstract painting on the wall. His own bedroom—bigger than mine but hardly containing more—also held a single bed.

There was an exercise room on the second floor, containing dumbbells and several large pieces of equipment, and next to it I discovered a library. Its walls were lined with tall glass bookcases, and I noticed he had an awful lot of books on guns, explosives and other weaponry, a lot more than he had about biology, which was supposed to be his primary occupation—this kind of unnerved me. Then there was a whole shelf dedicated to psychology.

I picked a book up—one about the history of arms development in Patrus, which listed every single gun invented by Patrian natives—and sat down with it in an armchair. A few of them were familiar to me from my training with Ms. Dale. Although I was sure the weapons I'd trained with had been produced in Matrus (it would be rather hypocritical for Matrus to import goods as destructive as guns from Patrus) the design was practically identical.

I paged through the dusty pages until Lee and Samuel returned, both panting as they moved inside. Apparently their walk had turned into a jog.

Lee headed to his room to take a shower and get ready for the evening—something for which he only needed fifteen minutes. Then he was downstairs again, looking crisp and fresh as ever, wearing a new suit—deep burgundy in color.

Leaving the house, we rode back down the mountain to the city, while the sky darkened overhead. On arrival at the lab—a seven-story building whose walls consisted entirely of shiny, dark-tinted glass—Lee punched a code into a number pad and the gates drew open, allowing us inside. After parking and removing our helmets, Lee took my right hand and planted it firmly around his arm before leading me through the revolving doors.

My heels clacked against the sleek floors of the reception area. There was nobody behind the long white desk, even though a phone was ringing. Lee moved to it and, leaning over the counter, picked up the phone.

"Hello?" he answered, frowning. "Oh, Viggo. Yes, Lee here. Nobody's behind the desk. Why were you calling? Maybe I can help. Huh. Okay, yes." Lee moved behind the desk and examined a computer. Then he read out a string of numbers. "Did that work? Okay."

Lee hung up and looked at me. "That was Viggo Croft," he murmured, moving to my side. "The code to the back gate was changed, he was calling in for it. He'll be heading here—"

A door creaked from some distant part of the building. Then footsteps grew louder. A door opened to our left and in stepped a tall, handsome man with a mane of dark brown hair. Wearing a trench coat and heavy boots, he looked less unkempt than in his photo, with just a little stubble darkening his thickset jaw, though he had a scar across his right cheek which I hadn't noticed in the photograph. His olive-green eyes swept over the room and landed on us. They paused on me for but a second before he gave Lee a brief nod and headed across the room to another door.

"Viggo." Lee spoke up before he could reach it. He took my hand and led me toward the warden. "This is my new wife, Violet." My attention was drawn momentarily to Viggo's hands as we neared; his knuckles were red and raw, like he'd punched someone or something one too many times without adequate protection.

Viggo's eyes returned to me, his right brow raising a fraction. He nodded, his expression remaining stoic. I nodded back just as curtly.

Then his focus resumed on Lee. "Good evening, Mr. Bertrand." He turned and left the reception.

The room went quiet, still, in his absence. As though his presence had brought with it an aura of tension.

"Well," Lee whispered, blowing out softly. "That was quick..."

"Yeah," I said dryly. "He didn't seem to approve of me."

Lee chuckled. "There aren't many people he does approve of, apparently. He's a loner. Lives in a cabin by himself up in the mountains."

Lee fell silent, his eyes narrowing like he was straining to listen to something. Then he said, "Do you hear that?"

I strained to listen and nodded. I could just about make out voices murmuring somewhere in our vicinity.

"My colleagues, a few rooms away. The work day is over, but they often hang around in the evenings… Anyway, let's take a look around."

We moved to an elevator and Lee punched the button for the seventh floor.

"There are seven levels in total, as you can see," Lee said, trailing a finger over a map of the facility that hung against the elevator door. "The lab is huge with hundreds of rooms. It's recently been renovated and expanded," he explained. "It was less than half the size only last year."

That would explain why everything looked so new and shiny.

Arriving on the seventh floor, I realized why Matrus ought to be afraid. I wasn't a scientist, but the apparatus contained within these labs looked sleek and sophisticated. The building itself seemed to be almost as large as the city lab in Matrus. That was saying a lot, considering that Matrus' lab was also used for routine euthanasia of criminals. In Patrus, from what I knew, they didn't bother with all that hassle. If somebody committed a serious crime like murder, they were publicly hanged.

"Are you aware of everything they're developing here?" I asked Lee in a whisper as we moved along the wide hallway and peered through open doorways of the labs.

"Not everything," he said. "But a fair amount. A lot of time and resources are going toward developing the 'smart drug'. Its official name is Benuxupane," he added. "The drug has already been formulated and deemed fit for consumption. Several scientists in this lab are going to take it within the week."

"Will you?"

He shook his head. "No."

"Do you know the real reason they're developing it? What exactly do they plan to do with it?"

"Matrus' news channels have basically got it right," Lee muttered beneath his breath. "Emotions are a hindrance to King Maxen's plans."

Before I could ask anything more, we turned a corner and arrived outside a closed white door, next to which was a screen. Lee swiped his thumb, and the door opened.

We emerged in another lab, the largest I had seen so far, with row after row of tables lined with microscopes, Bunsen burners, and specimen racks filling the room from wall to wall. Around the edges were glass cabinets, some containing books, others piles of folded lab coats… but as we roamed the lab, one in particular caught my eye. Lee noticed where my attention had flown, and it appeared that this was where he was leading me.

"You've spotted it, haven't you?"

It was hard not to spot. One of the glass cabinets was unique from the others. It didn't have shelves, and the glass looked much thicker, even reinforced. Perched in a tall, black metal tripod was a silver egg. *The* silver egg. I moved up to the cabinet and stared at it. I couldn't believe it was just here... visible to anyone entering this lab. Just a few feet away from me.

I turned to Lee in confusion. "So this is definitely it?" I asked.

He nodded. "This is the egg."

"Can't you open this case?" There was a number pad next to it.

He grimaced. "No. I'm not high up enough to access the code."

I dared reach out and touch the glass. "But it's just... glass. Couldn't it be broken easily?"

Lee reached for my hand and pulled me back. He began leading me to the other side of the lab. He didn't answer until we'd exited and returned to the corridor.

"We ought not linger in that room," he whispered as we made our way to the elevators. "As for the glass, yes, it could be broken if enough force was applied. You're talking about explosives, though. That glass is tough as hell. It wouldn't be so simple as smash and run... and then"—we moved into the elevator and he hit the button for the ground floor—"of course, you'd have to escape Patrus… Trust me, if it was simple, I would have done it already. Remember also that we cannot get caught—neither you nor I. If one of us was, they would quickly place the blame on Matrus."

I was mired in confusion. We had to retrieve the egg from the glass cabinet, but at the same time, nobody could suspect that it was us? What about when we suddenly went missing? Even if Lee didn't come with me, but stayed behind, what about me? I'd had these doubts before, and Lee still had not clarified them.

"You'd better start giving me details," I said irritably, no longer able to hide my frustration. I was fed up of being led blindly along.

"I will," he said. "Tonight, when we get home."

The elevator reached the ground floor and we stepped out. "For now," he said, his tone raising and brightening, "I ought to take you to briefly meet my colleagues." He glanced down at me, an artificial smile on his lips, clearly indicating that I assume the same. "We got married today, remember?"

Right.

He led me across the reception area toward a pair of double doors. Before pushing open the door, Lee whispered, "The head scientist of this lab is in here. My boss, Richard. He's the overweight one."

He replaced my arm through his and walked me inside.

A group of ten men were gathered around a billiards table, all of them older than Lee—I suspected in their mid-forties—except for one, who looked about the same age, perhaps in his late twenties.

My eyes lingered on the short, rotund man with blond hair and a thick mustache. Richard.

"Lee!" the youngest man cheered.

"This is your girl?" another man spoke up. "Violet, did you say her name was?"

"Yup. My wife," Lee said through his plastic smile. He displayed my ring finger to them.

"Good man," the younger guy said, patting Lee on the back.

"Thanks, Simon," Lee said.

Richard and the others weren't nearly as informal as Simon. They nodded politely and murmured, "Congratulations."

Lee took a seat with me on a couch, accompanied by Simon and three others who abandoned the game. Richard also strolled over.

"How many more days of leave will you be taking?" Richard asked Lee, his voice rich and throaty.

"Oh, I'm not entirely sure, Richard," Lee replied. "As you can imagine, Violet and I have a lot to catch up on and a number of things to adjust around the house."

"I understand. Let me know once you have a date."

"Of course."

Lee fell into five minutes of small talk, throughout which nobody bothered to address me. If I wasn't a guilty spy on a hazardous mission for Matrus, I would have been annoyed by that. As it was, I was relieved that the attention was kept off me and Lee tackled all the questions.

Lee stood up. "Well, we're off to have dinner," he concluded. "I'll catch you around."

"Where are you going to eat?" Simon asked.

"Uh…" Lee said, slipping a hand into his pocket. He bobbed thoughtfully on his feet.

Before he could reply, Simon suggested, "How about The Red Boar? We were planning to go there ourselves tonight. I'm pretty starved now, in fact. You could join us."

Lee hesitated, but apparently struggling to find a polite way to turn Simon down, replied, "Okay. Sounds like a plan."

Other than Simon, four others accompanied us: Luke, Frederick, James and Rocco. The others remained in the billiards room, except for Richard, who headed home.

Lee pulled back with me as the men exited. "The restaurant's not too far from here," he said beneath his breath, "about twenty minutes by car. Though it's in an area I'd hoped to avoid. Not the end of the world though, as long as you stick with me."

On exiting the lab, we headed to the parking lot where Simon offered to drive us in his vehicle. I sat in the back, while Lee sat in the passenger's seat next to Simon. We drove out of the lab compound and passed road after road that was teeming with life. Men with their wives and children populated the sidewalks, milling in and out of shops and restaurants. These were the same streets that had been almost empty earlier in the day.

I sensed us approaching the river that encircled the palace by the subtle change of atmosphere, the breeze seeping through the car windows becoming crisper. We reached a parking lot at the end of a long promenade, beyond which were the river's gushing currents and the tall, well-lit walls of the palace. On our side was a long line of bars and eateries. I immediately noted the lack of women and children in this area.

"There's the place." Lee pointed it out to me. A bright red sign depicting a muscly boar hung above a large, dimly lit restaurant, outside of which was an open-air enclosure of tables. Our group managed to secure a table from a group who'd just finished eating as we arrived.

I didn't have an appetite as we sat down and eyed the menus. I always felt tense around strangers, and particularly these men who were potential obstacles in accomplishing my mission. I told Lee to order me whatever he was having before leaning back in my seat, half in and half out of the conversation sparking up among the men around me. I'd hoped that, as uncomfortable as the meal might be, it would at least prove to be interesting; that they'd talk about their work, and the types of experiments they ran all day in that monstrous lab, but apparently work talk was reserved for work hours. Their primary topic of conversation became a major event that was due to take place soon, a cage fight between two of Patrus' most skilled professional fighters.

I found it endlessly strange to listen to them talk about fighting as a sport, something that people watched for entertainment, when in Matrus any sort of physical combat was discouraged to the point that even a punch could have somebody reprimanded.

Violence was taboo in my world, as much as women getting jobs was in theirs.

"What are your hobbies?" Simon turned to me and asked as the food arrived.

Oh, someone's deigned to ask me a question.

Hm. Hobbies? What hobbies would be deemed acceptable here in Patrus for a woman? Cooking was the first that sprang to mind. Ironically, I actually couldn't cook to save my life. Lee was a better cook than I could ever hope to be.

It felt like the only thing I knew how to do well was fight.

I was glad when Lee helped me out. "Other than being a bread artisan, Violet is a painter. An *excellent* painter."

I scoffed internally.

"Wonderful," Simon replied, sipping from his glass. "Next time I come to visit Lee, I'll have to take a look."

Yeah... Good luck getting yourself out of that one, Lee. He'd have to go hunting for some unsigned paintings to brighten up his walls, though it shouldn't come to that. I was still holding out hope that this mission would only take a matter of days (then I could see my brother again as early as next week!)—though I'd been given no reason to hope this. Nobody had mentioned a timeframe yet, neither Alastair nor Lee.

"What are *your* hobbies?" I returned the question to Simon, hoping to divert the attention away from myself.

But as Simon began to answer, I hardly heard him. Something—someone—caught my eye across the tables.

It was my cousin, Cad. Cad, whom I had not seen in years.

He was with two other young men I guessed were friends. The three of them were moving toward our eatery, already scanning for a seat among the outside tables. He hadn't spotted me yet, but that wouldn't last long if I didn't get the hell out of here. Being surrounded by Lee's colleagues, I didn't have the time or ability to explain anything to Lee, of course. I immediately turned my back on Cad while lowering my hand beneath the table to grip Lee's knee. I held it firmly, hoping to instill in him my urgency.

"I-I'm sorry, Simon, you'll have to excuse me... Lee, where are the restrooms?"

Lee looked confused, but nodded toward the entrance of the restaurant. "At the back, near the bar. I'll come with you."

"It's all right," I murmured, biting down on my lower lip. "Stay here. " I feared the two of us standing at once would attract more attention our way. Cad might even think that we were a couple freeing up a table.

There was a moment of hesitation in Lee, when I feared that he would insist on coming with me all the same. But it was just the back of the restaurant. That could hardly be considered leaving him—could it?

I tore away from him, trying to make my retreat as undramatic as possible, even as I was forced to walk sideways so that my face remained obscured from Cad, who was nearing closer and closer with his friends.

The restaurant was huge. It had four main entrances, and I could hardly see through to the back of it as I stepped inside because of all the men moving around. I spotted the sign for the ladies' restrooms at the back, but to my dismay, they were closed for maintenance. *Closed. How could they close the restrooms?* The men's were open on the other side of the bar. *Dammit.* I was still the only woman in this place that I could see, so I supposed they'd hardly had any complaints.

I backed into the shadows as best as I could while trying to keep a tab on Cad's movements, which was hard with all the bobbing heads. I caught a glimpse of him entering the building with his friends—obviously having failed at finding a table outside. They were making a beeline for the bar, which meant I needed to move again and fast, but I had effectively backed myself into a corner. There was only one path I could take from here to the main aisles that led to the doors, and that would mean crossing straight in front of Cad.

If he saw me now, it could be a disaster. He would cause a scene and demand not only that I explain myself, but also that I go to see his parents. I wouldn't be able to shake him off and he wouldn't believe the lies that I'd fallen into a romance with Lee. Cad would know that it was impossible. And if any of those scientists heard him talking or discovered we were related… it would be far too much of a footprint for me to leave in Patrus.

My palms were sweating as I kept my gaze trained on the out of service sign on the restroom door and their conversation floated in my ears above the rest of the noise in the pub. They were talking about rowing, Cad was, apparently, as keen a boater as ever.

It was strange to hear my cousin's voice again. Strange, yet comforting. I felt a bittersweet twinge in my chest, wishing I could greet him. But I couldn't stand where I was much longer without looking seriously odd. I sensed that a waiter would be the first to ask me if I was all right.

I twisted ever so slightly, just enough to glimpse the nearest exit. If I moved tactfully, I could slip around the back of Cad and his friends' chairs while they weren't looking. Then I could get lost in the crowd and make my way back outside. I could rejoin the dinner and tell Lee that I was feeling sick and that we needed to leave.

But before I could even begin my attempt to move around them, Lee spoke up behind me.

"Violet?"

He'd come to see if I was all right. And he either had not been informed about my cousin or simply hadn't seen or recognized him.

I was already picturing Cad turning to Lee, and then following Lee's gaze toward me. I didn't have time to think. My gut instinct took over and I found myself darting forward, past the out-of-order sign and into the ladies' bathroom.

My heart raced as I gazed around the stalls. I spotted a window above the line of sinks and, kicking off my shoes and hanging them over one wrist by their straps, I climbed onto the sink and pushed it open. Gripping its frame, I hauled myself up to find myself above a trash yard around the back of the building.

Swinging my legs over, I leapt and landed on the roof of a trashcan. I slid off, tearing the hem of my dress in the process, and landed on the puddle-strewn ground. I quickly slipped my shoes back on before hurrying toward the gates that marked the exit of the yard. Thankfully, they weren't locked. I rushed through them while trying to tidy my hair and straighten my dress. Taking a deep breath, I leaned back against the yard's wall.

Lee would probably go barging into the ladies' room after me and suspect that I had climbed through the window. I guessed he would climb through, too. I would wait here for him to emerge, and then the two of us could roam back to the tables before taking our leave.

I couldn't help but wonder what was going through his head right now, though. He might be doubting me, thinking that I'd decided I wanted to get out of all of this and tried to escape while I thought I could. If I hadn't had a reunion with my brother dangling ahead of me as a carrot, the notion of running away would probably be tempting, but even that would require a level of insanity I didn't possess. I'd be caught, and probably thrust into jail… And jails in Patrus were rumored to be a woman's worst nightmare. I would be better off in a Matrian detention center any day.

As for Cad, I'd gotten out of the building before he had been able to see me properly. The most he would've seen of me was my back. Although Violet was not a very common name, I had to hope that he'd write it off as a coincidence and not think any more of it.

I clasped my hands together, waiting tensely. The street was dark, except for a single strip light a few hundred yards away. It cast eerie dancing shadows on the brick work surrounding me.

Where was Lee? Why was I still waiting for him? It occurred to me that maybe, rather than climb through the window, he might've gone around the front and would be making his way to the back alley now.

I started moving toward the crowded street that ran perpendicular to the alley. I'd feel easier waiting where there were bright lights and people, but as I had almost reached the busy sidewalk, a group of men turned the corner. Big, heavy-set men with identical tattoos—a solid black square beneath the left ear. They had the rough appearance of farmers or manual laborers: sun-tanned skin, windswept hair, baggy clothes, and clunky boots.

Almost colliding with me, they stopped abruptly, their eyes raking over me curiously. Balling my hands into fists, I kept my eyes firmly on the ground while attempting to dodge and slip past them. But one of them—a man with a pockmarked face and a jungle for eyebrows—apparently wasn't done looking at me. He moved directly in front of me, blocking my path.

"What are you doing alone?" he asked.

"What business is that of yours?" I said through gritted teeth. He clearly wasn't a warden.

I moved to push past him but again he obstructed my way, taking a step closer to me this time.

"She's too well dressed to be a stray," one of his companions muttered.

I glared into the eyes of the man looming over me, refusing to be intimidated. I could have flashed my ring to show him that I had a guardian, but I wasn't a Patrian girl. And I wanted him to know it. He couldn't just push me around.

I could tell that my stand aggravated him. His arm shot out to grab my wrist, but I had already predicted his movement and with a sharp chop of my right hand, I knocked his arm aside and jerked backward.

His eyes lowered to where I had struck him, which would soon show bruising, and then raised to me again in disbelief.

I hadn't been sure why Lee had been hesitant to come to this part of town, but perhaps men like these were the reason. The man surfaced from his surprise and lurched forward, giving me no choice but to remove my stupid heels again and hurry back. I was feeling angry and frustrated enough to get into a physical fight with him, but I wasn't quite that stupid. Even if I outsmarted him, which, judging by the slowness of his reflexes, wouldn't be all that difficult, now more than ever I had to control my temper. Plus, he wasn't alone.

As I ran, the voices of schoolchildren chimed in my ears. *Violent Violet, Violent Violet.* My nickname at school. I'd become notorious early on in my life for finding trouble. But if I didn't stop now, I would only be digging a deeper grave for myself.

The man, and now his companions, pounded down the street after me. I wasn't sure what he intended to do if he caught up with me. Beat me for my insolence? They were apparently on the lookout for "strays", a term I hadn't heard before, but I could take a good guess as to what it meant. Women who, for whatever reason, found themselves living in Patrus with no male to act as a guardian. No guardian in this country equated to less than zero rights. Unsupervised women became like lost children, wandering the streets at risk. According to my knowledge, this was one of the reasons why polygamy was allowed in Patrus—to give Patrus-born women plenty of options, and ensure they never had to be without a man.

But even though I was aware of all this, my pride wouldn't let me flash my ring at my pursuers and my hands remained tightly balled. The guy would only take my show of a ring as fear, weakness on my part. And there was nothing I hated more than giving a bully what he or she wanted.

Reaching the end of the alleyway, I glanced behind me. There was still a fair distance between us. Though my speed had been hindered by running in bare feet over the coarse concrete, I had gotten a head start.

I looked left and right, sparing a couple of seconds to figure out which would be the most direct route, before hurtling to my right. I'd been in such a rush, I hadn't noticed a man crossing my path at exactly the same moment and I found myself slamming into a hard chest. I staggered back, gazing up at a familiar face. Not Lee's. But Viggo's.

Based on the surprise on his face, he hadn't been sent to find me by Lee. He was obviously just doing his regular evening rounds. Next to him was another man, a warden I recognized from the profiles Lee had shown me the night before.

My pursuers' footsteps behind me stopped short, and I twisted to see them do an almost comical abrupt about-turn and head off in the opposite direction.

"What are you doing without your husband?" Viggo asked me in a low, disapproving tone.

"I'm on my way to him now," I replied tersely. I considered turning the guys who had been chasing me into Viggo and his companion, because I was sure that harassing a woman the way that guy had was against the law. Even though females were supposed to never be unsupervised, it couldn't be *legal* for men to prey on "strays".

Viggo gripped my arm firmly. His palm felt rough and warm. He pulled me out of the darkness of the alleyway and into the bustling street.

"Where is your husband?" he repeated.

"I last saw him in The Red Boar," I muttered.

"You are not supposed to be alone," he said tersely, glancing at my ring, which was visible now that I'd unclenched my fists. "Surely your husband has told you that?"

"I'm not alone," I said, probably too snappily considering I was talking to a warden now. "He's just around the corner. We accidentally got separated in the crowds."

Viggo retained his grip on me as we headed down the street, but I shrugged him off when we turned a corner. *I'm not a damn child.* I had already put up with Lee holding me earlier, I didn't see a reason why I had to put up with Viggo when he wasn't even my "husband". I didn't bother to check Viggo or his partner's reaction to my assertion of independence. But although he stayed close, he didn't try to resume his hold on me.

We walked in steely silence until we reached the restaurant. Lee was bouncing on his feet near our table, looking bedraggled with worry while speaking into a phone. His eyes gleamed with relief as he noticed us approach. Relief, but also doubt and disturbance. A dozen questions must have been roaming his mind, but he would have to wait until later for an explanation.

"Violet," he gasped, taking my hands and pulling me to his chest.

Viggo cleared his throat. "With due respect, Mr. Bertrand, I would keep a better eye on this one… She has a rather adventurous mind for a bakery girl."

Viggo's green gaze rested on my face once more. Then he turned on his heels, his long trench coat billowing in the breeze as he and his companion stalked away.

CHAPTER 12

Lee was understandably shaken. The others looked confused, too and I was forced to address all of them, even as I looked around for Cad, praying that he hadn't come back out here.

"I'm sorry," I said. "I, uh, I needed to use the restroom but it was out of service. I found a back door and went through it. I hoped to find another restroom nearby, but I got lost." Here I turned to Lee, and tried to look apologetic. "I'm sorry, it was stupid of me. I guess I'm still getting used to the rules."

Lee slid an arm around my waist before facing his colleagues. "I need to get my girl home, gentlemen. I apologize. Enjoy the rest of your evening."

To my relief, he led me away from the restaurant, and firmly out of Cad's potential view. We returned to the teeming sidewalks, where Lee stopped to hail a cab—one of the dozens of blood-red cars roaming the roads at this hour. It was of course too risky to discuss anything mean-ingful in the back of a cab. We waited until we arrived back at the lab, where we had left Lee's motorcycle. Only as Lee started the engine and we rode off did he speak.

"What just happened?" he asked. I could feel how tense his chest was as I gripped it.

"I'm sorry," I breathed. "I spotted my cousin, Cad Thorne, and there was no way I could think to warn you. I had to get out of his sight."

Lee let out a deep sigh—of relief, I could only assume. "Well, I'm glad that was the reason," he muttered. "I hon-estly thought you might've tried to do a runner."

"No," I reassured him.

"You'd be a fool to attempt it," he said.

"I know." *For more reasons than you might be aware of.*

I told Lee about the men I'd encountered in the alley-way, looking for "strays".

He tensed up again. "God, Violet. Alleyways are the absolute *worst* place for you to stand at night. Especially in that part of the city. Guys like the ones you ran into are known to snatch even married women. They take females away from the city and surrounding suburbs, deep into the mountain region. There are a number of scattered towns in those harder-to-reach areas which are inhabited pri-marily by peasants, though frequented by city men more than the state would like to admit… Let's just say they're not places you'd enjoy visiting."

I took the hint. Men seemed to be able to get away with using women for their own dark deeds here in Patrus, unlike in my homeland. Any untoward approach by a man toward a woman in Matrus would be the last thing he ever did. It virtually never happened.

"Did you show them your ring?" Lee asked, rounding a corner and joining the main highway that led to the foothills.

"Yes," I lied. It was easier to lie than attempt to justify why I had not.

As he lapsed into silence, I recalled the last unsettling words Viggo had spoken. He had already guessed something wasn't right about me.

"What did you make of what Viggo said?" I dared ask.

"Well, obviously, getting into trouble the day after your arrival wasn't the smartest idea. *Especially* not with Viggo." Lee sounded pissed off.

I blew out a breath. "Look, I'm sorry, okay? If Cad hadn't arrived, I wouldn't have left you. How does Viggo even know about me being a bakery girl?"

"I told the guys in the lab," Lee said through his teeth. "I guess he overheard the conversation or was privy to office gossip."

We spent the rest of the journey in silence; a silence that was broken only by Samuel as we entered the house.

Lee headed straight to the staircase after locking the door, without a backward glance at me.

"So what now?" I asked, hands on my hips as I stared at his retreating back. "You said you would finally tell me the actual plan."

Lee paused in his ascent, but didn't turn around. "I know," he muttered. He hung his head, reaching to rub his temples. "But as I said, it's unfortunate it was Viggo who found you… Just give me a bit of time to clear my head and consider if anything needs to change. I'll still tell you the plan this evening. I promise."

I watched in annoyance as he disappeared up the stairs, while I was left with a slobbering Samuel.

I moved to the kitchen, and, since I hadn't actually eaten anything for dinner—I suspected Lee hadn't either—I rummaged in the fridge. We had already finished all the leftovers, and there were no other precooked items here that I could see. I ended up grabbing a slab of butter and some bread from the cupboard over the sink. Pulling up a chair at the table, I buttered a slice and chewed glumly.

Whatever was ahead of me, this sure hadn't been the best start.

When Lee came back downstairs, I was still sitting at the table, paging through an old newspaper I'd spotted on one of the seats. It was actually extremely interesting to see the way Patrus presented the news. Their excited tone when reporting their advances was so at odds with that of

Matrus when covering the same news. And the types of advertisements that appeared in between the pages were also... interesting. I struggled to find a single one that didn't feature a scantily clad girl. *Modeling is apparently one profession that is excusable for women here...*

I set the paper down as Lee took a seat opposite me.

I raised my brows expectantly.

"I've thought about it," he said, leaning back in his chair and rocking slightly. His demeanor was calmer now. "Tonight could have been worse." His expression softened as our eyes met. "I'm sorry if I was harsh earlier. You just have no idea how stressful it was not knowing where you went. When you ran, I honestly did believe you'd lost your senses and were trying to escape... So..." Pressing his hands together, he sat forward. "Now you've seen the egg. You know where it's located, and hopefully could find it in that lab in the dark if you had to... In a few weeks, the city lab's ten-year anniversary will take place. A banquet will be held to commemorate the occasion. It is not a widely-publicized event; it's reserved specifically for the scientists who work in the lab, and members of the king's council have also been known to attend. The night of this banquet will be the perfect time for us to strike."

Weeks. My stomach plummeted—I had hoped this would be over in days. The thought of staying in Patrus for so long terrified me. If tonight's mini-fiasco was anything to go by, I was sure to mess up again. My nature wasn't designed to handle this environment.

I stared at him, frowning. "I don't understand. On a night when so many important people are together in a room, wouldn't security be higher than usual?"

"Yes," Lee replied. "But that shouldn't hamper anything, if all goes to plan… Give me a minute."

He retreated from the room and returned a minute later carrying the same folder he'd brought in yesterday, along with a second green-colored folder. He opened the latter and pulled out a map. Unfolding it, he spread it out on the low table in front of us. It was a plan of the lab, each floor and all its rooms clearly marked.

He pointed to the lowest level, a few doors along from the reception area. "This is the events hall, where the banquet will take place. What's required is a big distraction that will keep everyone's attention on the ground floor, leaving the highest floor"—his finger traveled up the map and rested on the large laboratory that held the egg—"unwatched," he concluded. "We won't need long to do the deed anyway. Just a few minutes."

"What kind of distraction do you have in mind?" I asked.

"Explosives," Lee replied. "In the weeks to come, my plan is to install them inside the building near the hall so that when triggered, the blast will be so destructive, security's immediate occupation will simply be attempting to get everybody out alive."

I realized that I had stopped breathing. "So, you're saying it's probable that some of the diners will lose their lives in this?"

Lee nodded and I swallowed the lump in my throat. Having committed womanslaughter twice, claiming lives shouldn't be anything to make me flinch. But of course, those incidents had been accidents. These would be cold, premeditated murders. I wasn't a murderer. I was a girl with a difficult temper. "And the egg?" I asked. "I don't understand how—"

"I'll figure out the distraction, while you will take care of the most important business: the egg."

"I'd need explosives to blow the glass."

"Yup," he said. "We'll have to work on equipping you with some. Then you will seize the egg—setting off a hot-wired alarm in the process, which will be ignored for a good while due to the commotion downstairs—and make your way up to the roof." He traced my route on the map. "There is a stairwell near the egg's lab, which leads up to the rooftop."

"The roof? Assuming I actually manage to get that far, what happens once I get up there? And won't the building itself be shaken to its core from the explosions at its base? Won't it be alight and crumbling?"

"I'll be careful in my choice of explosives," Lee replied. "The building will be burning, of course, but you'll be quick. Your focus will be extricating the egg and getting to the rooftop... I will meet you up there, and we'll have pre-arranged transport for the two of us."

I glanced back down at the map. *Transport for the two of us.* I could only think that meant that Matrus would be sending an aircraft to carry us both back over the river to safety...

"I still don't understand how we wouldn't be instantly blamed though," I said. "Especially if we were absent from the dinner and—"

"First," Lee said, "we won't be absent from the dinner—we'll need to discuss the specifics of this nearer the time. Second, I also won't stay away from Patrus for long in the aftermath. Once we've returned the egg to Queen Rina's palace, I'll come back discreetly, and reintegrate myself into the scene. As for your absence..." He grimaced. "Trust me when I say it's not difficult for husbands to hide their wives in Patrus. Most wives hardly go out anyway. There was a murder case last summer where it took five years for the man to be convicted, simply because nobody noticed his wife's absence."

My jaw dropped.

"It can be that bad," he assured me. "Especially if the woman is from Matrus. She typically has no family over here. Another option could be to say that you died in the blast. That might be a better way to play things... Then as for the issue of *who* will take the blame if not us..." He looked me in the eye. "Who do you think could be used as a scapegoat?"

Used. I didn't like that word. Still, I racked my brain. "Um… Well, it would need to be someone with regular access to the building. Someone who knew it well, and… if the bombing was to make any sense, it would have to be done by somebody who had a reason to hold a grudge against Patrus. Someone who was discontented with their life here." My voice trailed off as Lee nodded. "Who are you thinking?" I asked him.

Slipping out the red folder, he spilled the wardens' profiles out on the table before his forefinger settled on a single one.

Glaring up at me was the rugged face of Viggo Croft.

CHAPTER 13

"Viggo?" I clarified as I stared down at his picture.

"Yes," Lee said. "He fits the bill excellently for a potential anarchist. Let me explain to you a bit more about his background and it should be clear why… I told you that he got into trouble with the law for obstruction of justice."

I nodded. *Just like I did.*

"Well, the circumstances surrounding that are rather interesting. Viggo used to be married—to none other than a Matrian woman. She was an emissary at the time they met. She tried to move over here but, you guessed it, found the adjustment to Patrus' culture extremely difficult. As the official story goes, her and Viggo's relationship had been tense for months. One night they got into an argument, after which she stormed out, alone. Although Viggo went out after her, she managed to shake him off and lose him. She wandered the whole night as an act of protest and, as the early morning hours drew in, she came upon a couple of drunks who had less than noble intentions.

"Fortunately for her—or unfortunately, depending on how you look at it—she had been trained in self-defense by Viggo. She stopped their assault and escaped, but she ended up killing one of the men in the process. Given that there were no neutral witnesses—only she, the victim and his accomplice were present at the scene—she had no way to prove that she had been acting in self-defense. Viggo found her in the morning, stumbling back toward their home. After she told him what had happened, he tried to cover up her crime… obviously knowing what would ensue for her. He made an attempt to ship her back to Matrus, but failed. She was taken before the judge, and—given that she was already guilty of having left her husband and roaming the streets unsupervised at night—there was little sympathy for her in the trial. Long story short, she ended up being sentenced to hanging."

Hung for acting in self-defense. The sheer injustice caused the blood to drain from my face.

"Viggo was to serve four years in jail for his act of dishonesty. But, given his skill and the value he added to the city's security force, jail time was deemed a waste for him. He was made a special offer: resume his position as a palace warden and serve without pay for four years… He's in his second year now. His wife's death has obviously scarred him. He moved away from the city and set up in a cabin in the mountains a few weeks after the hanging.

He's never been the most approachable of guys, but since he lost her, he's notorious for being tightly strung—as you may have noticed."

Lee rose to his feet and paced in front of the window.

"So, in sum, we have a man with a clear grudge against the state, who has lost his wife, and is now leading a life that's been forced upon him… Men have snapped beneath lesser burdens." He caught my eye. "But just as important as all of this," he went on, "is that he was made chief coordinator. He has access to the lab… It would honestly be hard to think of a more suitable person to lay the blame on."

My stomach tensed. *An innocent person.* We would be framing an innocent man, who had obviously already been through hell and back. This didn't sit right with me. At all.

"There must be some other way we can pull this off," I breathed. "I can't believe that laying the blame on someone else is the only way. What if it we didn't set this up as a terrorist attack but instead… I don't know, some other kind of explosion in the building? It's a laboratory, Lee. Surely there are other exploitable options?" *Options that don't involve a beating heart.*

Lee shook his head. "I've thought this through, Violet. I've thought this through for days. I understand your hesitation to frame an innocent person—of course I understand. I feel as uneasy as you about it. But this is the only way we can convincingly pull it off without laying the blame squarely on Matrus. Remember, Patrus stole the egg from Matrus in the first place. We are only retrieving what is ours."

'What is ours'. You mean what is the queen's and her army of scientists'. An object whose contents I still had no damn idea about.

I pursed my lips, my stomach continuing to churn.

"So," Lee continued, his voice becoming more subdued. "The next question is, how exactly would we go about setting the man up as an anarchist? How would we make it convincing? How do we make sure that he's at the right place at the right time?"

I didn't feel like offering any more suggestions. Lee had apparently already thought all this through, anyway.

"The first issue," he said, "is that we need to be able to track his movements, and understand his day. We need to be aware of when he's doing his rounds by the Crescent, when he's at home, and when he's at the gym or in the cage."

"Cage?" I interrupted.

"He's a professional cage fighter. That's what he does for money these days. Takes as many fights as he can while off work."

"Oh. I see." I recalled the conversation Simon and Lee's other colleagues had regarding the sport's popularity here in Patrus. "How would we track him?"

"Come with me," Lee said, gesturing to the door. I rose and followed him to his bedroom where he sat down at his desk in front of a computer monitor before pulling open a drawer and lifting out a ball of metal foil. Within it was a semi-transparent gel-filled capsule that I almost didn't notice because of its minuscule size. In the center of it was a black dot. I leaned closer. Some kind of… square object? My eyes weren't sharp enough. I would need a microscope to be able to describe it better.

"What is it?" I asked.

"An ingestible tracking device."

My eyes shot up to meet Lee's.

"Are you *serious*?"

"Yup," Lee said. "Swallow it down with some water, and it will embed itself in the gut—staying there for up to three weeks."

Ugh. "Where did you get this thing?"

"It was developed in Matrus, actually," he said. "I picked it up from Alastair during my last visit to the queen's palace. It's so tiny, you wouldn't even notice it gliding down your throat when swallowed with a gulp of liquid. He'll never know it's inside him, and it'll pass through naturally on its expiry."

"H-How would you actually make him swallow this?"

Lee refolded the foil around the capsule and placed it in my hand. "The question is, how will *you*?"

CHAPTER 14

"Slipping Viggo this tracker will be your first task," Lee explained. "And it needs to be done as soon as possible. He has a fight tomorrow night on the outskirts of town. I'll drop you off there, and you'll need to figure out how to do it."

Lee opened up his cupboard and pulled out a stiff shirt and an even stiffer gray suit. The shirt and jacket were padded around the shoulders. A man's outfit.

My lips parted.

"Try this on," he said.

As I pulled the costume on over my clothes, it was surprisingly lightweight and comfortable. I looked in the mirror. My chest, which didn't bulge much anyway, could easily pass as a man's. The shirt was amply bulky.

"This is a temporary measure," Lee said, eyeing me over. "I have a body suit for you, too." He rummaged in his closet and pulled out an actual skin-colored male body suit, complete with bulges in all the right places. "But I figured that'd really be throwing you in at the deep end. This gray suit will be enough for tomorrow."

He replaced the body suit in the cupboard, and then drew out a wig of curly black locks and strips of facial hair.

"This is insane!" I said.

Lee looked half amused as he applied my wig and then the facial hair with a thin, transparent adhesive. By the time he was done, I was a black-haired man with a mustache and a generous beard. The facial hair helped to cover the softness of my jaw. I would have laughed in disbelief at how realistic it looked had I not been so tense.

"However you figure out the logistics, this task shouldn't be too difficult," Lee said. "Remember, it'll be nighttime. I'll give you this, too." He brandished a cap and planted it on top of my head. "Oh, and lenses, to be doubly sure…" He left for the bathroom and returned with a rectangular silver packet, as well as a narrow white and blue box. He split the packet open and told me to tilt my head back while he applied the lenses. I hadn't expected the application to be so uncomfortable, but he managed it. When I looked back in the mirror I had dull brown eyes. My eyeballs had gone reddish with irritation, my tear ducts working overtime.

"Your eyes will get used to them," Lee assured me.

"And shoes," I murmured. "I guess I can wear the ones I arrived here with. They're unisex. But then there's the matter of my voice. What if I need to speak?"

"You should try to avoid speaking at all costs," Lee said. "But in case you can't..." He held out the small box so that I could see the front of it. Bold, jagged black letters stamped across the packaging announced the product as "*Deepvox*." He opened the box to reveal it was stuffed with tablets.

"You're kidding me."

"Nope." Lee laughed. "This is actually a thing here. Swallow one of these and it'll deepen your voice for up to twelve hours. Designed for men who aren't happy with their natural tone."

"*Go deeper. Last longer*," was the brand's slogan.

"What are the side effects?" I asked, dubious. I squinted at the tiny, almost illegible print on the side of the box.

"Your throat might get sore," Lee said. "But that's nothing that can't be solved with some warm honey and ginger tea. You should get used to it after a while, anyway."

How many times was I going to have to swallow these things? How many excursions would I have to make before leaving Patrus?

For the sake of my sanity, I figured that it was best to only look one step in front of me at a time.

"I should test the product now to see how well it works on me," I said. "And how quickly it will work."

We headed to the kitchen where I helped myself to a glass of water.

I swallowed one of the small round pills gingerly and waited with bated breath. Nothing happened at first, other than my heart pounding. Then I began to feel a constricting, tingling feeling at the back of my mouth. It wasn't strong enough to hurt, just enough to be unpleasant.

"Say something," Lee said.

"Hello." A noticeably deeper voice blurted from my lips. Not quite deep enough to pass me off as a man, though. I consulted the product's description; it said it could take up to an hour for the pill's effect to fully come into play.

"I suggest you take three tomorrow evening to be safe," Lee said. "Otherwise, I guess you're ready."

Lee had to go out early the next morning, which left me alone in the house with Samuel. As I washed up after breakfast, I already knew the wait for this evening's excursion was going to be tedious. Tedious and nerve-wracking.

I ended up gathering a pile of books from the library and sitting out in the garden; the mild temperature and mountain breeze helped to calm me. I took a seat in a deck chair and tried to forget about the time for as long as I could, until I could no longer ignore Samuel's whining. I finally acquiesced to his requests to play ball and remained busy with him until lunchtime. I brought food outside for both of us so we could sit in the sun and eat, and then spent the rest of the afternoon indoors. I had roamed every room in the house by now, but I still had not set foot in the basement. On heading down there, however, I discovered the door was locked.

I huffed and returned upstairs.

I had deliberately eaten until I felt stuffed again, hoping to make myself feel drowsy so I might be able to get some solid sleep before Lee's return. I had been awake most of the night before, tossing and turning and worrying. The food was beginning to take its toll and I slipped into my bed and managed to pass the rest of my alone time in slumber.

I woke up to the sound of the front door unlatching, and Samuel's barks as he scurried to the door.

Yawning, I staggered out of bed, splashed my face with cold water, and headed downstairs.

A black canvas bag was waiting by the doorway, filled with some kind of heavy, rectangular weight. The door was open, and I caught sight of Lee crossing the drive and returning with an identical second bag.

He quickly closed the door and turned to me, rather out of breath.

He planted down the second bag next to the first and reached into his pocket. He rummaged and pulled out a square piece of card: a ticket to the event at Brunswick Arena. There were to be four fights that evening; Viggo and his opponent, "Seamus Vanguard", were up first.

"Keep this ticket somewhere safe," Lee told me. "And don't forget to bring it with you."

I stowed it in my pocket, my focus returning to the bags. "What are they?" I asked.

"Explosives," he replied over his shoulder as he descended to the basement. Then he changed the subject. "By the way, we should leave in less than an hour."

I sensed his unease. As a Matrian male, Lee wasn't a naturally aggressive person. Less aggressive than me, I was sure. I doubted any of this came instinctively to him.

"Okay, I'll start getting ready." I dragged my feet up the stairs to Lee's room. Opening the cupboard, I pulled out all the parts of my costume and quickly slipped out of my clothes and pulled on the shirt and suit. I decided to leave the whole facial hair thing to Lee, but did make an attempt to apply my wig.

Lee arrived a few minutes later, carrying the lenses and the pills. Once he finished my cosmetic appearance—leaving my eyes feeling sore and watery again—I took the pills. After ten minutes, my voice had deepened enough to be passable as a man's, even if a slightly effeminate one. But by the time we arrived at the Arena, it should have deepened further.

I stuffed my ticket into the jacket pocket while Lee equipped me with a pager and, of course, the all-important ball of foil. I was also sure to remove my wedding ring.

As we were about to step out of the house, Lee's phone rang.

"Hello?" Lee answered. His expression went serious. "Yes. Yes. It's going according to plan. Yes."

After a few more *yeses*, Lee handed the phone to me. "It's Alastair," he whispered.

Alastair? I took the phone and pressed it to my ear. "Mr. Jenks?"

"Ms. Bates?" he replied. It was strange to hear his voice again. He felt like another universe away.

"Uh, yeah. It's me. I just took some Deepvox pills."

"I see. How's everything going?"

"Okay, I think." I replied, frowning.

"How are you finding Patrus?" he asked.

How does he expect me to answer that? "Uh, not exactly pleasant." *Not that Matrus' detention centers were pleasant, either.* But at least there my sense of worth wasn't constantly being affronted, and I wasn't under so much stress.

"Okay, well, I won't keep you," he said. "I'll check in with both of you again soon."

With that, he hung up. My eyes turned to Lee in confusion. "What was that about?" I asked.

"Wanted to verify for himself we're both still on the job," Lee replied. "Make sure I hadn't lost you." He opened the front door and we strode out into the night. "Anyway, I think you should start focusing now," Lee said as we donned our helmets and climbed onto his motorcycle. "Visualize what you need to accomplish tonight in your head."

Lee drove me through the tail end of rush-hour traffic to the outskirts of town—suburbs to the south that were noticeably rougher than the city or any other areas I'd passed so far. The streets were not as well cleaned, the buildings shabbier, and the men roaming around looked generally more unkempt. I was still unable to spot a single woman amidst them.

Lee parked the motorcycle in a bay on the sidewalk opposite a tall, round building, the first two floors of which were occupied by a noisy, smoky eatery. He led me across the road and around the side of the building where we stopped outside a set of open, peeling, red double doors. I poked my head through to find a stairwell leading downward.

"The arena is through there," Lee whispered. He backed up against the wall of the building and glanced nervously to the left and right. "As you can see from the ticket, we're a bit early. Not a problem, though. Just go through those doors and show your ticket."

"What time will you come to pick me up?" I asked.

"Viggo's up first and his fights rarely go past one round. Let's say… giving time for any possible delays… eleven."

"That late?"

"Well, you shouldn't just leave straight after Viggo's fight. It's considered discourteous and you might draw unwanted attention to yourself."

"Okay," I said. "Where exactly will I meet you?"

"Where I've left my motorcycle now," he replied. "I'll be hovering somewhere in that area and watching for you."

I nodded again, my palms and forehead breaking out in a sweat.

"What happens if I get caught?" I asked.

"You've just got to make sure you don't."

Great.

Lee lingered for a minute longer, readjusting my fake hair, which had gotten disheveled after the motorcycle ride. My eyes still felt irritated, but since he didn't remark on them, I assumed they didn't look too odd. I doubted teary eyes was a great look for a Patrian man.

Drawing in a deep breath, Lee took half a step back and gave my left shoulder a reassuring squeeze, then turned and headed back to the main road. I didn't wait to watch him disappear from view. I hurried through the double doors and down the staircase. I had work to do.

The door awaiting me at the bottom was open and unguarded. Stepping inside, I found myself surrounded by an arena that was smaller than I had expected. It could probably fit about three hundred people, which wasn't exactly tiny, but not grand like I had imagined the venue of a national sport would be. Not much pride had been taken in the aesthetics either. The seats were made of garish red plastic, and the walls and ceilings were rough and unpainted, the brickwork clearly visible. But maybe this was all intentional; I supposed that it added to the atmosphere.

I turned my mind back to the conversation I had overheard with Lee's colleagues, when they had been excitedly talking about a fight that was to take place in a few days' time. I couldn't remember the name of the arena where it would take place, but it hadn't been Brunswick. I was sure of that. Maybe Viggo's career hadn't taken him to the big leagues.

In the center of the room was a cage in the shape of an octagon. It had two entrances and the mesh walls were constructed from thin malleable metal, and the edges of the cage's floor itself looked painfully sharp. Their ridges were pointed; if someone slipped against them with the right amount of force, they could easily cause serious damage. Probably even hospitalize someone. I guessed this was deliberate though—making their environment as rough and treacherous as possible to up the stakes and keep the men on their feet at all costs.

I roamed around the arena, mulling over my task, until voices came from the door near one of the back rows of seats. Two men strode into the arena carrying lighting equipment and two small foldable tables.

I moved back into the shadows and took a seat, trying to remain as inconspicuous as possible while they set up the lights. They unfolded the tables in front of each of the entrances. Then more men came in with more paraphernalia. Some carried chairs and boxes of food, while others carried towels and first-aid equipment. Finally, I spotted something interesting—a man carrying in two containers of water. He set one down on the tables at either entrance, where two flasks had already been placed.

More banging and commotion ensued while they rigged up all the final lights, and then everyone retreated through the back door. I wondered if anyone had noticed me at all yet, or whether they'd just chosen to ignore me.

Either worked for me. The main thing was that the room had become empty again. This was my window of opportunity—a window I had to grab with both hands now that the fight was drawing so close.

I left my seat and made a beeline for the nearest cage entrance. The flask on this side was helpfully labeled with the name of Viggo's opponent. I sped around the cage to Viggo's side. Glancing over my shoulder, I hurriedly opened the flask. It was already filled to the brim. I retrieved the foil ball and unfurled it, dropping the transparent gel capsule into the water. It blended in so well that I had to make an effort to search for it. It floated on the surface, too, which meant he'd likely swallow it in his first or second gulp.

Footsteps sounded in the stairwell. Replacing the lid, I jerked back from the table and resumed my seat.

I exhaled slowly, wiping my palms against my pants. *Okay. It's done. The worst is over.* Now, hopefully, all I had to do was wait.

Twenty minutes before the fight seemed to be the magic time of arrival—the arena began filling quickly and within a matter of fifteen minutes, every single seat had been taken, leaving many forced to stand. With five minutes to go, the main doors were closed.

The excitement in the room was palpable, and I was surprised to see many women accompanying their husbands.

Dressed to the nines, in front of me sat three of them in a row, sandwiched by their husbands.

In between flicking their perfectly coiffed hair, they were gushing about the fight that everybody else seemed to be so breathless about: Croft versus Vanguard.

In spite of my nerves, I couldn't deny that I was excited, too. Attending this event was unique—an adventure. Something I'd never imagined myself doing in my whole life. I suspected this would be the high point of my stay here in Patrus, so I probably ought to make the most of it.

The lights dimmed, leaving a single spotlight to blast down in the far right corner of the room. Boos erupted as a tall, sculpted man stepped out, bare from the waist upward. He was bald, and every visible inch of his bulging physique was etched with green-ink tattoos. His face reminded me of a shark's—angular, with a broad, flat nose and a cruel, crooked mouth.

Wearing yellow shorts trimmed with gold, 'Seamus "Sharp" Vanguard' made his way to his entrance and climbed into the cage. He skipped around the enclosure— bowing in four directions while gnashing his teeth and beating his chest—before retreating into his corner.

Then the spotlight sped to the far left corner of the arena. Cheers erupted before Viggo even came into view. When he did emerge beneath the glaring beam, the crowd went wild.

"There he is!" gasped one of the women in front of me through the deafening applause.

He wasn't introduced with a nickname like Seamus. Just Viggo Croft.

Viggo looked quite different in his role as a fighter. His hair was tied back, revealing the full breadth of his jawline. His physique was muscled, but in a more understated—and, in my opinion, very attractive—way compared to his opponent. Although their weight must be even, Viggo was taller, leaner, and I suspected more agile. His knuckles were tightly bound in bandages, and his shorts were plain black.

I found my butt sliding to the edge of my seat as he prowled down his aisle and swept into the cage. He didn't offer the audience any introductory performance like Seamus had; he simply planted himself immediately in his corner.

A man sporting a blue shirt and white gloves moved to the center of the cage and beckoned both fighters forward. After he informed them that they were to obey his commands without exception, a bell rang. The commencement of the fight was announced by the booming voice of a man whom I was sure must have popped a Deepvox pill or two. *Nobody's voice is that deep.*

The two men circled for a few seconds before Viggo drew in. He aimed a front kick at Seamus's chest, causing him to stagger toward the edge of the cage. Seamus, trying to regain a central position, threw a flurry of punches, but Viggo blocked them deftly before counteracting with a powerful right hook that knocked Seamus to the floor.

The crowd erupted.

"He's got the takedown!" one of the women in front of me squealed.

Viggo pounced on the man before he could rise, pinning him down and raining punches. Seamus held up his elbow, attempting to block them, but Viggo was too overpowering. He came in with blows not only to the side of Seamus's face and ears, but also against his kidneys. Seamus, daring to come out of pure defense mode, shot up a punch toward Viggo's face, but that only opened himself up. Viggo hammered down a punch so hard I found myself wincing, and the next thing I knew, Seamus had gone still and the referee was calling a stop to the fight.

My eardrums ached from the cheers.

Viggo rose to his feet. Although he had won, there wasn't the slightest trace of victory in his expression. He barely even made eye contact with the crowd. He looked uncomfortable, forced into the situation. I knew that feeling.

Everybody stood and clapped. Whistles ricocheted around the arena.

I watched with bated breath as he was handed his flask by a man in a black shirt. He swallowed a few mouthfuls before handing it back. That should have been enough for the capsule to glide down. I guessed Lee would know soon enough.

Viggo didn't hang around to soak up the adoration. As soon as the referee announced him as the official winner, he swept out of the cage as swiftly as he had arrived, strode down his aisle, and exited the basement.

As everybody settled back down to wait for the next fight, I tuned into the conversation the women in front of me were having.

"When is that guy going to move on to bigger things?" a blonde was saying. "He doesn't belong in this dump. Such a waste of talent!"

"He's been approached by the big league a bunch of times already, Vanessa," a man, presumably her husband, replied. "He turns down their offers again and again. He doesn't want a bigger spotlight."

"He's twice the man most big-league fighters are," a brunette chimed in. "Cruz. Rosen. Croft would knock them out. He'd be top of his division!" She shook her head sadly. "He'll fade away if he doesn't move up in this game."

"Maybe that's what he wants," a second man retorted. "Whatever he's doing this for, it's clearly not legacy."

The conversation died down as the next fight was announced. The lights dimmed, and once again the spotlight shone on the far right corner of the arena. This was to be a "middleweight" fight. Terrence "Trump" Wilson versus Bernard "The Beast" Hill.

As the two opponents made their way to the ring one after the other, I was shocked to see a huge chunk of the audience get up and leave the arena. They really had just come to see Viggo, only they weren't adhering to the etiquette Lee had advised me to follow.

I understood why so many left. Professional fighting was still a complete novelty for me, but even I found the second fight slow and plodding. Neither had the skill or agility of Viggo to make it an interesting match. It went on for five rounds, and by the time the winner was announced, three quarters of the arena had left.

I felt bad for the fighters as they bowed, and clapped harder in a feeble attempt to make up for the lack of noise.

But those women were right. Viggo didn't belong here.

I checked my watch. Lee was due to collect me in ten minutes. I made my way to the exit before the next pair of fighters could enter the room and climbed up the stairs, out into the open air. I headed to the main road and crossed to wait by the bay to make it easy for Lee to spot me when he arrived.

After a couple of minutes, a familiar figure exited the bustling eatery. Draped in a long trench coat, hood pulled up over his head to shadow his eyes, Viggo was carrying a bottle of water and a bulging paper bag. I realized he was heading right for me. Or, rather, the motorcycle bay, and I moved discreetly backward, trying not to stare as he approached a beetle-black motorcycle.

He seemed too intent on leaving the arena to even notice me standing nearby.

A part of me was tempted to congratulate him for the fight just for the hell of it, but I bit my tongue. Of course, that would be a stupidly unnecessary thing to do.

He stowed his items beneath the seat, swung himself onto it and roared away down the road, in the direction of the mountains.

When Lee arrived at eleven on the dot and asked if I'd placed the capsule, there was a lump in my throat as I replied, "I did."

CHAPTER 15

After I gave Lee details of how I'd planted the tracker, he asked, "So how was the fight?"

I couldn't deny that I had enjoyed it. "It was good."

But I didn't feel good about what we were doing, in spite of Lee's assurance that we were doing nothing wrong— that we were simply retrieving a stolen object. But Viggo hadn't stolen it, he was just a foot soldier. Someone just trying to survive, like me.

I wished that the banquet was sooner, not only so I could see my brother sooner, but so that I would not have to carry around my guilt for so long.

I realized that the only way I could get through this would be to stop thinking about what I was doing. Adopt tunnel vision. Do everything required to ensure things ran smoothly so that I could get out of here, see my brother and then, assuming I couldn't wrangle a way to stick with him permanently, reintegrate myself into some form of existence back in Matrus… and try to move on with my life. I'd probably look to move somewhere far away from everybody—like Viggo had done—to reduce the odds of getting into trouble again.

Numbing myself shouldn't be too much of a challenge. My years spent in detention facilities had made me good at that. Blinders on, head down, same routine day in and day out. Just get through the day. I had to see this mission involving Viggo Croft like everything else: threading needles, sifting flour, or shoveling crap.

This was all simply another detention, where I had no choice but to do as I was told.

Once I adopted this mindset and stopped considering consequences, I felt lighter and I was better able to engage in Lee's conversation.

"Viggo knocked out the other guy in the first round," I told him.

"Yup." Lee smirked. "No surprise there."

I wished that professional fighting was a thing in Matrus. If it had been, I might not have ended up in so much trouble with the law. I'd have had other ways to let off steam.

"If I was a man," I muttered, "that's what I would be doing." This was probably the first time I'd ever truly considered what it would be like to be a man.

"Fighting? It's not all it's cracked up to be," Lee said. "It's a hard, hard life."

Yeah, well, life is hard whatever you do.

Reaching the foothills, we let the quieter atmosphere halt our conversation: the gentle mountain winds, the fragrance of the soil at the end of a warm day.

Samuel was asleep when we returned to the house. We headed immediately to Lee's bedroom and drew up chairs at his desk. He switched on the monitor and pulled up a detailed map of Patrus. Roaming it, I spotted four flashing red dots. They were all stationed near the city center.

"You're tracking other people, too?" I asked.

"Yes," he replied. "There are a few whose help I've needed, and I've had to keep an eye on them. There's Viggo," Lee said excitedly. He pointed to a red dot that I hadn't even noticed yet. It was up in the mountains, some distance away from Lee's home. While we were situated on the southwest side of the palace, he was northwest.

It seemed that he had already reached his home by now, as his dot appeared stationary.

"So," Lee said, leaning back in his chair, looking relieved. I reached up to peel off my mustache. "Step one is completed," he said. "You successfully tagged him and we can now monitor his movements in real time."

"Next, I suppose we need to figure out his schedule," I muttered, pulling off my wig and removing the rest of my scratchy facial hair.

"I agree. We need to know what, if anything, he plans to do on the night of the banquet. This should be easier than what you did tonight. Viggo has little time to vary his schedule. When he is not working as a warden, he's typically either fighting or preparing for a fight. He trains at a gym in the city, and behind the reception desk is a schedule of all the booked sessions, as well as each of its members' upcoming fights. You'll likely need to hang around for a bit and wait until the receptionist goes for lunch, but the arrangement would be similar to tonight. I'll drop you there and give you about half an hour—I'm sure within this time you'll find an opportunity. There's usually only one receptionist behind the desk and since we'll be arriving just before lunch, he'll have to take at least a short break to fetch his meal… We'll do it tomorrow—leave here at eleven-thirty in the morning, okay?"

Okay… Another risk for me. But I understood why; Lee was more valuable than me in Matrus' eyes.

I sat with Lee a little longer, staring at the map and watching the red dot that was Viggo.

Then I left his room and headed to my own. Entering my bathroom, I removed the suit, took a quick shower, and changed into my nightclothes before climbing into bed.

As I drifted off to sleep, I returned to the Brunswick Arena. The electrifying atmosphere flooded my mind: the bright lights, the roaring of the crowd… The mass celebration of physical prowess.

That night, it was me in the cage instead of Viggo, and opposite me, a stocky blonde female inked with green tattoos, whose face uncannily resembled a shark.

CHAPTER 16

I decided to wear the full-body suit for this lunchtime's excursion to Viggo's gym. Since I would be roaming in the daytime, rather than lurking anonymously at the back of a shady arena, I figured that I would feel less nervous with it on.

Lee donated three outfits to me: jackets, shirts, and pants, and I spent the morning tailoring them so that they would fit me properly. I pulled the pants' ends up by a few inches before adjusting the jacket and shirts. My time working in the textiles factory had been useful after all.

As for my shoes, I decided to wear my own again, the same as last night. They were kind of scrappy, but they'd do.

I also took four Deepvox tablets two hours before we were due to leave.

By eleven-thirty, I was ready to leave. My voice had sunk deeper than the night before, not fight-announcer deep, but deep enough to pass as a real man.

I couldn't stomach a lot of brunch, and it seemed neither could Lee. He was just as nervous as me.

Lee headed upstairs briefly to check on Viggo's location, and returned to report that Viggo was near the palace, as expected. He also placed a small red rectangular object in my hand, and a miniature notepad and pen in my pocket. I stared at the red object, turning it over in my palm. On one side was a blank screen.

"It's an advanced pager. Smaller and less conspicuous than a phone, it will vibrate when I trigger it"—he drew out an identical red object from his right pocket—"and a message will pop up on that screen. You can also send a message to me if you need to. As for the notepad, use it to note down the dates... So, are you ready?"

I nodded.

"Then let's go."

The gym was fancier than I'd expected it to be. It was a stylish steel structure spanning four floors, perched right on the bank of Crescent River.

Lee dropped me off one street away. "I'll be back in about forty-five minutes, but I'll send you a message when I arrive."

"Okay."

I strolled casually across the road, keeping my eyes firmly focused on the ground. Reaching the building, the glass doors opened automatically and I stepped into a cool reception room with slate-tiled walls and black marble floors. A minty hue hung in the air.

I dared to raise my eyes and gaze around the room. To my pleasant surprise, it was empty. Perhaps it was lunch break already. This meant I had to be fast; I had no idea when the receptionist would return.

Withdrawing the notepad, I planted it down on the table while leaning over and scanning the desk for the big ledger Lee had spoken of. It was one of the first things I spotted—just to the left of me. I reached down a hand and lifted it up before paging through it. Indeed, Viggo's schedule had been marked there, and it was a busy one. His heart might not be in the fighting, but nobody could fault him for his dedication to the sport.

I kept a keen ear out for sounds of the receptionist returning, but I had time to flip through the schedule a second time to be doubly sure that I had not missed any pertinent dates or times. He wasn't booked in for any-thing on the night of the banquet. That was the day we were most concerned about.

I replaced the ledger on the table, careful to reposition it exactly how it was, and ambled away from the desk.

Glancing up at a clock that hung above the main entrance, I still had loads of time. Only five minutes had passed. Not wanting to hang around in the reception area, where I would likely have to engage with the receptionist when he returned, I took off down the corridor to my left, deciding to explore the gym a bit. There were no signs indicating special permission was required, and the doors at the end of the corridor leading deeper into the gym were wide open, so I assumed that nobody would object.

The corridor's walls were made of glass, allowing me to peer into hall after hall of cages as I walked. Each hall contained two or three cages, and the walls were lined with lockers and benches.

I stopped at the fifth hall, where two fighters were going at each other in a cage. I watched as they grappled on the floor, each trying to wrestle the other into a choke hold. The loser eventually tapped the floor, and his opponent released him.

I continued exploring, passing more halls, until I reached the end of the building. I stopped and turned around, but wasn't willing to retrace my steps to the reception so soon. I didn't want to return there until I had to leave the building.

I entered an empty hall. I was better off sitting in here and waiting, rather than roaming around where I was more likely to run into trouble.

I moved to one of the benches closest to the back wall and sat down. My eyes traveled all around the room, taking in every detail with interest. There was a line of punching bags hanging from a thick metal rack on the opposite end of the room.

Another ten minutes passed as I waited for Lee's message.

Retrieving the pager from my pocket, I punched in a message and sent it to him. Just two words: *I'm done.* It took him about a minute to reply, *"OK. Stay where you are. I had to head to another part of town. I'll be there ASAP."*

I sat back on the bench, blowing out a breath. I was not great at waiting.

My eyes returned to the punching bags. Slowly, I stood up and made my way over to them. Balling my fists, I landed my first punch against one. It was heavy, barely budging. The outer fabric was also rough, as though specifically designed to cause calluses and harden skin.

Glancing around the room again to check that nobody had entered without my noticing, I landed a harder punch in the center of the bag, causing it to sway away from me before swinging back. I punched again, and then again. My knuckles weren't used to this abrasion, and they were already feeling sore, but it was in a therapeutic way. I continued punching, though when I sensed my skin was about to break, I switched to kicking. Luckily, the clothes I was wearing were not too tight. I removed the jacket, since it was making me hot and stuffy, and began attacking the bag with kicks. Back kicks, front kicks, side kicks. I practiced everything I remembered from Ms. Dale's training sessions.

It felt good, really good, to awaken muscles I'd forgotten about, feel the stretch, the burn in my thighs as I pushed myself harder. Although I did keep an ear out for the sound of the pager vibrating in my jacket pocket, I got carried away and stopped checking the entrance to the hall as often as I should have.

When I glanced up a few minutes later, it was to see a couple of fighters had entered and were heading my way. I stopped kicking, turning to face them, suddenly extremely conscious of the fact that I had discarded my jacket. I felt grateful I had worn the body suit.

The fighters, I soon realized, weren't heading for me, anyway. They merely glanced my way briefly before climbing inside a cage much like I'd seen at the Brunswick arena. Strapping fingerless gloves around their fists, they began to fight.

They didn't seem to mind my presence, so I refocused my attention on the punching bag and continued.

When the pager finally went off another ten minutes later, I was expecting it to be a message from Lee, telling me to hurry outside and meet him on the street. But instead, he'd sent a message informing me that, "There's been a delay. Will be at least another thirty minutes. Sorry. Keep yourself out of trouble."

I wondered what had happened and hoped nothing had gone wrong. I returned to my kicking, albeit with less focus than before.

I got distracted by the fight going on to my left and kept glancing their way. I found myself predicting who would win, even though they had barely started. I figured it would be the shorter one, the man with a mop of ginger hair, who was showing more initiative and daring than the other. As the sparring went on, I became more and more sure of my prediction. And then the ginger managed to trip the other up and pinned his arms behind his back, holding him until he grunted in defeat.

I tried to keep myself looking busy—I didn't want them to think that my attention was on them, and the last thing I wanted was them watching me. I was dressed very differently to them, but at least the clothes I was wearing today were casual - the shirt was loose, as were the pants.

After five more minutes of sparring, there was an audible yelp. I could have sworn that I heard the crack of bone. The ginger had injured his friend during a particularly frenzied takedown. The friend's right ankle looked bent out of shape—probably broken.

The ginger apologized before helping his friend out of the cage and taking him down the hall, no doubt to get medical assistance.

Once again by myself, I was feeling a bit tired of nonstop kicking by now. I took a pause and approached the cage the guys had been fighting in. I moved closer to it, standing on my tiptoes and peering through the mesh. The ridges of this cage were not as nasty as the one I'd seen the night before in the Brunswick Arena, but they still weren't padded. Not something you'd want to fall on.

My breathing quickening a touch, I felt the urge to climb inside it, to see what it was really like on the inside. I climbed into the cage, my feet slipping slightly over beads of sweat.

I moved around its circumference, running my fingers over the mesh. I imagined what a thrill it must be to enter a cage like this on the night of a fight. To be surrounded by crowds chanting your name. What a rush would come with looking your opponent in the eye and having full freedom to make them submit to you.

The pager in the pocket of my jacket, which I had brought in the cage with me over one arm, buzzed again.

"Still delayed. Will keep you posted."

Resuming my focus on the room around me, I heard footsteps outside, moving along the corridor. I hurried out of the cage and made my way back to the punching bags as someone entered the room. The same man returned without his injured friend and headed to the same cage they had sparred in.

He began throwing air punches, flexing his limbs on his own.

He caught me staring at him this time and stopped punching to address me.

"Haven't seen you around here before," he remarked. "You had a good kick going on there…"

I felt my cheeks heat. Now was the moment of truth, the moment to put Deepvox's claims to the test… "Thanks." My voice boomed across the hall, a little louder than I had intended.

"Just joined?" he asked.

"No, actually," I replied. "But I'm considering it."

He tightened his gloves. "How's your punch?"

I shrugged.

"Want to spar?" he asked. "I've got a fight coming up next week and could really do with a partner."

I glanced down at my watch. There was still time, but seriously? Was I about to say yes? I supposed I could exchange some calculated punches with him, but there was no way I could get hit in the face, or start grappling or wrestling with him on the ground. My disguise wouldn't hold up under that sort of strain.

"I'm recovering from an injury myself," I told him. "Lower back. Can't move so fast and can't afford to be knocked down … I'll throw a few punches, as long as it's not near the face."

I didn't sense danger in doing that with this guy. He didn't strike me as the talkative type; the only reason he'd struck up a conversation with me to begin with was because he'd lost his sparring partner… He might not even bother to ask me my name.

"Okay, cheers," he replied, holding the door to the cage open for me.

I double-checked the pager one last time to verify no message had arrived from Lee without my noticing, and since it was still blank, I left it with my jacket at the foot of the cage steps. Then, flexing my wrists, I stepped into the cage.

A spare pair of fingerless gloves like this guy's were hanging from a hook. He offered them to me, and I quickly bound them around my knuckles, which were already red and sore from my assaulting the punching bag earlier.

Then, knocking my gloves together, I faced him.

"Not gonna take off your shirt?" he asked.

I shook my head. I wasn't planning to roll up my sleeves, either.

"All right... let's box."

We met in the middle, and I realized that he was more or less the same height as me, our arms about the same length. He swung the first blow. I dodged and returned one. We danced around the cage, neither of us connecting much, until I seized a small opening and knocked him—perhaps a little too hard—in the gut. He staggered back, taking a few seconds to recover before we went at it again.

"How did you learn to fight?" he asked, eyeing my fists with more wariness than a minute ago.

"Self-taught."

I upped my pace, keeping him distracted so he'd stop asking me questions. He caught my shoulder with a right hook, though I was careful to keep my face protected. As our sparring progressed, a realization dawned on me. This fighter and I might just be two people in an empty hall, but the fact that we were man and woman made this moment feel suddenly epic, sweeping, groundbreaking. Nobody in the world might know it—not even my male accomplice—but we were making history. I doubted any man and woman had ever stood on such equal ground before since time began in Patrus and in Matrus. The male in front of me was looking me in the eye without prejudice, without bias or discernment—as I was looking at him. The thought filled me with such euphoria that I found myself quite breathless, in a daze; so much so that I almost missed blocking a punch.

If only more people could experience this, was all I could think to myself.

I didn't want this sparring match to end. I wanted Lee to leave me alone for at least another half-hour so that I could continue immersing myself in this feeling... but then the pager buzzed.

I dropped my fists, my heart dropping along with them like a heavy weight.

"I'm sorry," I managed, stooping to my jacket and retrieving the device.

"I'm outside", said the message.

I turned back to the fighter, whose name I still hadn't asked, and shook hands with him. "I've got to go," I said before hurrying out of the room, although a piece of me remained in that ring with him.

As I moved along the hallway back toward the reception, my fingers reached up to check that my facial hair was all still in place. Now that hard reality had returned to me, I was afraid that I'd gotten too carried away and all that dancing around might have loosened it. Maybe the mustache was slightly less firm than before, but altogether the hair felt okay. Nothing was going to drop off during the time it took me to return to Lee across the road.

As soon as I stepped through the door, I kept my eyes on the ground and hurried forward, not even glancing to the reception desk, though I sensed someone there.

I let out an internal sigh of relief as I reached the main exit. Out of view of the receptionist, I threw caution to the wind and raced up the twisting stairs. But as I turned the corner to climb up the final flight, I almost collided with someone. I staggered back too quickly, and before I could find my footing, I tripped down several steps until my back hit the stairwell wall.

It was Viggo.

Standing in his trench coat and looking more imposing than ever from his elevated position five steps above me, he had stopped in his tracks and was gazing down at me.

What was he doing here? He couldn't have been here for training—his schedule had made no mention of it.

I straightened and averted my eyes to the stairs, attempting to recover and act as though nothing had happened.

Indeed, I expected Viggo to also continue descending right past me, but to my horror, he stayed exactly where he was. And when I reached his level, he reached out a hand and gripped my upper arm. I found myself being scrutinized by his hard stare, his face inches away from mine.

Crap.

I stopped breathing as his right hand moved to my face. The next thing I knew, I felt a tug on the skin above my upper lip, and then his hand was drawing away again, clasping my fake mustache between his fingers.

I swore in my head. What were the odds of me getting caught as I left the building? And by Viggo of all people?

Viggo seemed to have a penchant for turning corners at the most unexpected of moments.

His frown deepened. "Would you like to explain this?" he asked, his voice dangerously low.

Viggo was one man who definitely had no use for Deepvox.

My mind went into a panic. *What do I tell him?*

My angst was hardly helped by my pager going off again. Lee must be wondering where I was. *Dammit.* I was so close to Lee. And yet I was stuck.

As Viggo's eyes lowered to my beard, I realized there was no point in concealing my identity any longer. He seemed to have already detected that my beard was fake, too, and once that came off, there would be nothing to hide the softness of my jawline. He might even recognize my bare lower face. He'd seen me twice already.

As my mind raced for what explanation I could possibly give him, I realized that it ought to just be as close to the truth as possible. That was the best way to lie.

"I'm sorry," I whispered.

"Sorry for what?" His face contorted.

"I-I'm not a man." The words sounded weird coming from my deep throat.

Glancing nervously up and down the stairwell, I gripped one corner of my beard and stripped it off like a piece of wax. Next, I reached for my wig and unclasped it, letting my long hair fall down my shoulders.

All that remained now were my lenses. But Viggo didn't need me to remove those.

"Mrs. Bertrand."

"I'm sorry," I repeated, my voice constricted. "I've been having a tough time getting used to the ways of Patrus. It's hard never being able to roam by myself. I just wanted a little freedom. To roam the city without my husband holding my hand... My husband approved of this. He thought it would help with the transition."

Viggo's eyes widened. "He approved of you masquerading as a male and roaming the city by yourself?"

"How else do you think I got hold of this costume?" I replied. "He gave it to me. But I am *not* by myself," I added quickly. "My husband has been following me around from a distance, to make sure I don't get myself into trouble.

He's just on the other street. I can take you to him now if you don't believe me."

"I will have to take you up on that offer," he replied darkly.

Stuffing the facial hair into my right pocket along with my notepad, pager and pen, I moved past Viggo and hurried up the staircase. My pager buzzed again. Lee was getting nervous.

"That's my husband," I explained to Viggo as we surfaced on the road. I pulled out the pager and glimpsed the latest message.

"*?????*"

I showed it to Viggo, who grunted.

"What were you doing in the gym?" he asked me.

"Well, I wondered what was in that pretty glass building. I watched some fighters training, roamed around… Fighting isn't a sport, you see, in Matrus. I've worked in a bakery all my life, but I always wished I could've become a warden."

Viggo's expression soured. I could practically read his thoughts. *You're not missing much*, I imagined him thinking. He made no attempt to hide how much he hated his job.

We reached the other side of the road. I led Viggo round a corner until we arrived at the end of the second road along, where I caught sight of Lee waiting. He was standing next to his motorcycle, glancing up and down the street and clutching his pager in his hand.

"There he is," I murmured, pointing to him. "He lost track of me after I went into the building," I explained. "I should have told him I was going inside."

Lee soon noticed us, and instantly froze. I imagined him cursing in his head as he hurried forward, closing the gap between us.

"Violet?" he asked, his voice strained with confusion. "What's going on?" His eyes flitted to Viggo.

"Lee, I'm sorry," I said, moving to him and clutching his arm. "You told me not to wander into any buildings, but I did. The gym on the river bank."

There were undercurrents of confusion in his eyes, but he was quick to play along. Admirably quick.

Viggo didn't need to say anything. He just stood there, glancing from me to Lee in cold disdain.

"Dammit, Vi." Lee exhaled sharply. "I take risks and go to all this trouble to give you a sense of freedom, and this is how you repay me? Doing the first thing I forbade you to do?" Lee's grip around me tightened. "This'll be the last time I trust you." He turned to Viggo. "I understand of course if you need to report us, Viggo. Mark it as an infraction on my name. Even though I was following her, we were stretching the rules, no doubt about it. But I do promise you this will not happen again... We've just been having a difficult time with her adjustment. I hoped keeping her on a longer leash would help us make things work."

I prayed that would get to Viggo. If it didn't, I didn't know what would. He had experienced firsthand the difficulties of a Patrus-Matrus marriage, with his own wife struggling with the constraints Patrus' laws put upon its female residents. I hoped there was a place of compassion within his heart that he would draw on to not judge us so harshly.

Viggo's gaze remained sharp as it continued to roam my face. But then his jaw clenched, resoluteness setting in. "I'll let you off this time, since you were nearby. But if I do witness it again, I'm sure you understand I can't be so lenient…" He cleared his throat and averted his eyes, settling them on some distant point at the end of the road. "As you know, here in Patrus, rules are rules."

CHAPTER 17

After Viggo strode away, both Lee and I let out a long, slow sigh.

"God," he muttered, turning his back on the warden and rubbing his face in his hands. "That was not something I *ever* want to repeat." He glanced at me. "What on earth happened?"

My relief gave way to mild irritation. "What happened to *you*? What took you so long?"

"I had to go pick something up." He gave me a meaningful look. I guessed that meant more explosives or some kind of other equipment necessary for our mission. "But things got delayed. How did you wind up with Viggo?"

"I was hanging around the gym," I began. I decided to omit the little sparring match I'd had. I didn't see the point in mentioning it. It would only make him more nervous. "I tried to keep myself away from the reception area, to avoid awkward questions. I ended up roaming around the training halls. When I finally got your text and was making my way back up to the street, I bumped into Viggo. Like, literally bumped into him. My mustache got knocked off and he noticed. I figured it was best to just come clean after that—as clean as I could."

Lee nodded as he raised the seat of the motorcycle and pulled out our helmets. "You did the right thing. It's likely he's seen this trick played before. I'm certain we're not the first couple to think of it."

I found the idea quite revolutionary as we mounted the motorcycle and Lee kicked us off down the street. That this could be an old trick played by women who found themselves in Patrus but wanted more freedom hadn't occurred to me. Where had Lee actually gotten such a realistic costume? Had he really made it all himself, or had he purchased it? I guessed there must be some kind of underground market for them and I wondered how many women I'd mistaken for men since arriving here in Patrus. Especially at night, when streets were packed and it was far easier to go unnoticed.

Maybe some Patrian females aren't all that different from Matrian ones after all.

Maybe others, too, have experienced the rush I did back in that gym.

As we traveled back through the city toward the mountains, I found myself eyeing everyone on the sidewalks, examining the faces of the men and trying to spot any slight hint of femininity. But then Lee started traveling too quickly and I could no longer continue with that game.

"Anyway, none of this is the end of the world," Lee said as we entered the house. "In fact, we could twist this to our advantage."

"What are you thinking?" I asked, removing my shoes at the doorway.

We entered the kitchen and sat down around the table.

"Where's your notebook?" he asked.

"Here," I said, digging a hand into my jacket pocket and handing it to him.

Lee stroked his jaw as he paged through it, leaning back in his chair. "Hm. Okay. Interesting... And good. So far, he has nothing booked the night of the banquet. As you know, we can't have him having an alibi that evening..."

"How do we turn my collision with Viggo today into an advantage?" I asked again.

"Well, I was actually surprised that Viggo was so lenient with me. He isn't the type to dish out leniencies." Lee paused, glancing up from the notebook. "As hardened as he seems on the outside, he obviously does have weaknesses... I think he has a thing for Matrian girls."

"Well… he married one, so I guess he'd have to…"

Lee sat forward. "I think our strategy from now on—at least in regards to you—has become a lot simpler."

"What do you mean?"

"This further development of… rapport… between the two of you, shall we say, could be used to bridge the gap between him and us more."

"Bridge the gap? Why would we—?"

"We'll need to find a way for you to keep him isolated on the night of the banquet. To keep him away from anyone else's eye. In order to do that, you're going to have to make him go somewhere… Don't ask me where yet—that's something we'll have to figure out. But for any of this to happen, he's going to need to trust you. Gain his trust, and we have more control over him when the night arrives."

I lowered my brows at Lee. I would hardly describe what had happened today as "further development of rapport".

"Of course, another thing that works to our advantage in all this," Lee went on, "is that he needs money. That's the reason he fights in the first place; it pays well compared to other jobs…"

I crossed my arms over my chest, waiting for him to tie all his threads together.

He stood up and moved to the kitchen counter. Planting his palms down on the surface, he turned his back on me. He fell quiet for about a minute before drawing in a thoughtful breath and turning round again. His blue eyes rested on mine with a gleam of optimism—enthusiasm, almost—before he said, "Let's meet Viggo again tonight. I have a proposal to discuss with him…"

CHAPTER 18

After Lee revealed his plan to me, we spent the rest of the day at home, monitoring Viggo's movements. According to the gym schedule, he wasn't due to visit the gym tonight, nor did he have any fights going on. Which meant he would in all likelihood head straight home after work. As evening came around, we watched his red flashing dot make its way toward the mountains, straight from the city center. Once he'd entered the foothills, Lee was confident enough about his direction for us to leave ourselves.

I didn't need to wear a suit this time. We rode out of the driveway on Lee's motorcycle, but instead of taking the usual route down to the city, we headed further upward, higher into the peaks.

It got chillier as we ascended, and I found myself grateful Lee had suggested I wear a jacket. It was silent up here too and soon we came to the end of the residential area and entered a long, deserted stretch of winding road that led us northward toward Viggo's territory.

It was a pity that the sun had gone down, as the verdant landscape sped away on either side of us. I imagined this place would have looked stunning during the day, with brooks bubbling beneath bridges, lots of trees. We reached an open plateau, allowing us an unrivaled view of Patrus beneath us. It was a fairly clear night, and beyond the glittering sprawl of Patrus City, I could make out the deep black stretch that was the river and then, beyond, the hazy glow of Matrus' borders. I couldn't say that the sight made me feel homesick. Anxious to get back, because of the prize that awaited me, but not homesick.

Lee thundered the motorbike forward at a speed that made me nervous. "How much longer?" I asked him. My deep voice hadn't worn off yet.

"Maybe ten minutes."

Ten minutes proved to be about accurate. A bungalow—which was really not much more than a glorified log cabin—came into view at the end of a dirt track. A familiar beetle-black motorcycle was parked outside its porch, next to a three-wheeled trailer that I guessed he used to transport larger objects. The building looked like only a one-bedroom, with perhaps enough space for a small living room, a kitchen and a bathroom. The large square windows were closed off by shutters, though a spill of warm light glowed through their cracks.

As Lee killed the engine and we got off the motor-bike, we stood in silence for a few seconds, taking in the peaceful atmosphere. It was like another world up here. The middle of nowhere. The closest houses were settled nearer to the foothills, miles beneath us by road.

Lee reached for my hand, giving me a reassuring squeeze before the two of us approached the front door.

Lee knocked three times and my stomach clenched as I caught the sound of a door clicking, then heavy footsteps moving toward us.

A bolt was drawn, and then the front door creaked open. My lips unconsciously parted as Viggo towered before us in the doorway, bare-chested. He wore a pair of loose black pants, and clutched in one hand was a roll of cotton wool, in the other some kind of medicated oint-ment. His bare knuckles were red and glistening.

"Mr. Bertrand?" Viggo said, his eyes widening as they swept from him to me.

"Viggo," Lee replied calmly. "I do apologize for intrud-ing like this. I won't take up much of your time, but I would like to speak to you about something."

Viggo paused, still frowning, before allowing us inside.

We stepped into a narrow hallway lit by a hanging gas lamp, its walls and ceilings made of logs. A rough wicker carpet lined the floor, and the hallway opened up to four different rooms.

Viggo led us through the first door to our left, into a sitting room. A fire crackled in the hearth and before it sat one sturdy armchair. That was the only piece of furniture in the room, save for a low table upon which sat a metal jug and a damp cloth. Viggo set down his bandages and ointment on the table. He grabbed a shirt which hung at the back of his armchair and pulled it on before turning back round to face us.

"It's about Violet," Lee said, his arm moving to my waist. "We're trying to figure out how to make things work in the long term. As you noted, she has an adventurous mind. Even though her work was domestic, she still of course has the spirit of any Matrian woman... My days will become much busier soon. I will have to return to work, and I will not have time to accompany her places... But our meeting earlier got me thinking, and I have come to you with a proposal."

Viggo's gaze froze on Lee, his right brow lifting.

"You spend the most part of every day in the city," Lee said. "I would like to appoint you as Violet's second guardian and have her accompany you for at least a few hours every day, when it's convenient. It will get her out of the house on a regular basis, and I would pay you, naturally, for the service."

Whatever Viggo might have been expecting Lee to say, it sure wasn't that.

"What do you mean, *accompany me?*"

"I mean just that," Lee replied. "Let her walk with you. Be your shadow. It will allow her to explore the city, as she's itching to do, and gain a greater understanding of our culture and residents."

In other words, it'll be like walking a dog. As my husband, Lee had full right to appoint guardianship of me to any other man, with or without my consent.

Viggo's green eyes rested on me, his expression serious. At least he appeared to be considering the proposal.

"I'm not sure this would be approved by head office," he said.

"I doubt you'll have trouble," Lee said. "It's not breaking any laws to bring a girl with you to work."

"Hm… How many hours exactly?" Viggo asked, resuming his focus on Lee.

Lee shrugged. "It can vary. I'm sure we could come to an understanding. Though it would make sense if she came into the city with me in the morning, for work; I could bring her to you, and then either you could drop her back home during lunch break, or you could bring her back to the lab and I could drive her home with me at the end of the day… Whatever works; I'm flexible. As for payment," Lee went on, "I'll pay you the same hourly rate you ought to be receiving as an inner-city warden. Just keep a tally of the hours and let me know."

That ought to be an attractive proposition for Viggo.

He leaned against his chair, glancing down at his knuckles, falling into thought. Lee and I waited patiently.

Finally he looked up. "All right," he said. "I'll accept the offer, but understand that I will back out at any time if things get… complicated."

"Naturally," Lee said, a relieved smile spreading across his face. "Assuming things do go smoothly though, I would say this arrangement could go on for at least a few months, depending on how long Violet takes to adjust to our culture… And could we start tomorrow?"

Viggo rose to his feet, slanting me a glance. "I suppose."

"Great," Lee said. "I'm planning to go back to work in the morning, so I'll drop her off with you on my way to the lab if that suits you. Where do you plan to be at, say, eight-forty?"

"Head office," Viggo replied.

"Perfect," Lee said, rubbing his hands together. "Now, we won't eat up your evening any longer. Thanks again for your time. I hope this can be an arrangement that benefits us both equally."

Viggo merely nodded before shaking Lee's hand. I instinctively reached mine out too—forgetting that this wasn't something done in Patrus. But before I could withdraw it, to my surprise, Viggo accepted my hand and shook it firmly. *Beneath his layers, maybe he's a rebel like me.*

Our gazes locked for three tense seconds.

Then Lee took my arm and led me to the exit.

CHAPTER 19

The next morning, I washed and changed into pants and a shirt and opted to wear my flat shoes again, since I'd likely be doing a lot of walking.

I couldn't deny that the idea of spending hours with Viggo was daunting. I didn't know what we'd talk about. I imagined us spending time in awkward silence. But that wasn't how it was supposed to go. I needed to try to make him warm to me. To even become his friend, if that was possible. Viggo seemed to guard himself against everyone, a friend only to himself. But there had been that handshake. That little crack in his exterior I might just be able to widen.

Lee and I made our way through rush hour and into the city. We passed the lab and he drove me to a tall gray building with a pointed roof near Crescent River. This was the wardens' head office, apparently. I didn't get to see much of it though, before Viggo appeared, waiting for us.

"Thanks again," Lee said, reaching for the small of my back and pushing me closer to Viggo. "You have my number, right? Just let me know if you decide to drop Violet back at lunchtime, or if she'll stay with you until the end of the day. See how it goes."

Viggo nodded.

"See you, then," Lee said before returning to his motorbike and riding away.

Viggo and I stared at each other.

"So, uh…" He nodded up the road, to our right. "My transport's that way."

My mouth dry, I followed him up the busy road to where he'd left his motorcycle. He had me sit on the seat first, and I was relieved to feel my fingers curve around a metal bar at the base of the seat, meaning I didn't have to clutch Viggo for dear life as we roared into the road.

We wound our way deeper into the center of town—not far away from the alleyway where I'd bumped into him the other night—and he parked on a street lined with shops.

"This way," he muttered, jerking his head further up the road.

He stalked forward, and I hurried to match his pace. After allowing the two of us a couple of minutes of silence, I asked, "So what does your day actually consist of as a warden?" I was genuinely curious. I wondered what the similarities were between the jobs of wardens here and in Matrus.

Viggo's eyes remained straight ahead of us. "Various things," he said vaguely. "During the daytime, there aren't usually a lot of incidents. It's on night shifts when things tend to get more… disordered."

"Disordered in what way?" I asked him.

"This city is at a junction with the mountains. There's a whole mix of guys who pass through, many of them of the opinion that they are above rules. We watch mostly for thieves, illegal substance dealers, traffickers, and of course… potential strays." Here, he glanced my way.

"What do you do with 'strays' if you find them?" I asked.

"It's our job to keep them off the streets," he said, turning a corner. "Those we find are taken to Gerter House—a shelter on the other side of town—before reintegration is attempted. Having them roaming the city merely makes it a target for the exact kind of men we work to keep out."

"Which are…?"

"The dregs from Porteque, basically." He seemed to sense my questioning stare as he added, "A spread of towns in the mountains, further west."

"Oh." *Gerter House.* I hadn't known they had an official shelter for women. I guessed they had to put them somewhere though, especially if Matrus didn't accept them— the Patrus-born females. "What causes women to become strays in the first place?"

"They're mostly runaways."

"And how are they reintegrated?" I ventured. I was aware that we were skirting a sensitive topic.

He paused as we approached a road. He looked left and right before herding me across it to the other side. "The first step is to find out where they came from, who their guardian is. Once that's discovered, a team identifies the reason for their wandering. If they ran away like most, they're returned with a cautionary warning. If the issue is more complex, like abandonment, then… well, some women grow old in Gerter House," he finished with a grim clench of his jaw.

That was depressing.

We lapsed into silence as we continued Viggo's route through the city. His eyes were sharp as a hawk's as he glanced around. I noticed the way others responded to his gaze, quickly averting their attention and continuing about their business. Though many of them lingered on me a little longer. Maybe they thought I was a stray who'd been caught.

With Viggo's popularity in fights at night, and his constant appearance around the city during the day, I imagined he was kind of a celebrity here in Patrus. As childish as it was, it made me feel kind of special to be walking with him.

"What made you want to be a warden?" I asked.

"It matched my skillset," he replied shortly.

He was probably wishing I didn't talk this much.

"Like I told you, I fancied myself as a warden back in Matrus," I went on regardless. "Even sneaked to a few defense lessons when I was younger, and when I had the time. Just never got the opportunity to follow through on the dream."

"I've never set foot in Matrus," he replied, "but in Patrus, the novelty soon wears off."

"Why's that?" I asked, recalling Lee's story that Viggo had retired from the force even before his wife had been sentenced.

"It's called life," he replied dryly. "Things lose their shine when you get too close to them."

I sensed there was a deeper resentment over his work as a warden than he was letting on. But I let it go.

"So… you've never visited Matrus, not even once?" I asked.

"The furthest I've ever gotten is its dock."

"And you've never been curious to visit?"

"No."

I blew out. "So… you're working a job you don't like. You apparently live by yourself in the mountains… What's your game plan?" I asked.

"Game plan?"

"What are you working for? What gets you out of bed in the morning?"

"I have obligations," he replied curtly.

"Do you have any family?"

He shook his head. "None to speak of."

"I guess I wonder what motivates you to take on extra work," I dared say. "My husband told me you're also a fighter."

He grimaced. "If you must know, I'm not getting paid for my time as a warden, nor will I for the next two and a half years. I earn my money through fights. As for my 'game plan', once the years are up I plan to buy a larger patch of land, further away from the city."

He was obviously expecting me to ask next why he was acting as a warden without pay. I avoided the subject, since that was too close to his wife for comfort, and I already knew the answer.

"Why do you want to live so far away from everyone?" I asked.

"I just do."

His answers were becoming increasingly short, so I figured I'd give him a break from questions. I didn't want to annoy him too much.

I realized we were nearing the street where I had come to get my hair and nails done, and gone shopping with Lee—the street consisting entirely of women's shops.

As we passed the hairdresser, Viggo asked me a question of his own. "Do you regret coming to Patrus?"

I was surprised not only that he'd asked a question, but also by the directness of it.

"No," I lied. "I mean, it's been difficult leaving behind my old life and entering one so very new, but I don't regret it. It was the only way I could be with Lee."

He went quiet for a few moments before remarking, "You don't strike me as a girl who'd be happy here long-term. It's pretty easy to spot the ones who'll last and those who won't... For women, curiosity isn't a quality that's rewarded here."

"Yes, I know..."

"Hey, Viggo!" a voice chimed from across the road.

Two men were standing there, wardens in long coats and heavy boots. I found it interesting that, although all wardens in Patrus wore a similar style of clothing, there appeared to be no official uniform. Perhaps they used that to their advantage; they could sneak up on unsuspecting suspects more easily.

The men crossed the street and approached us, their eyes glued to me.

"Who's this?" the blond man asked.

"Mr. Bertrand's new wife," Viggo replied. "I've been appointed as her temporary guardian."

They looked rather confused as to how that could have come about, but they didn't ask further questions. One of them retrieved a piece of paper from his pocket and handed it to Viggo.

"Back gate of the lab's code has changed again. Here it is."

Viggo nodded in appreciation.

Then the men parted ways with us, continuing down the road in the opposite direction.

"So do you roam the streets all day?" I asked. "Don't you get tired?"

"No to both questions," he muttered.

"Then?" I cocked my head to one side.

"In about ten minutes, I have an appointment with the owner of an arms store, one of the largest in the city. There was an attempted break-in yesterday—while the store was closed. Nothing was stolen, but I need to examine the site, as well as discuss precautionary methods to put in place to keep it from happening again."

Attempted break-in at an arms store, earlier yesterday.

I wondered, could that have been Lee? The reason for his delay in picking me up from the gym? He'd seemed pretty tense.

"Is there a lot of theft around here?" I asked.

"No," Viggo replied. "The state's punishments are severe. We're talking about dismembered limbs, or in some cases, hanging."

In Matrus, criminals were treated differently—at least, the women were. If a female committed a serious crime, even so far as murdering someone, she was given a second chance. A thorough period in detention facilities, to see if she was capable of and willing to redeem herself. Matrus' men, on the other hand, were not treated with such leniency. If they murdered or plundered, it was immediate euthanasia. Indeed, from a male's very birth they were subject to close scrutiny. They were regularly monitored in their early years for traits that went against Matrus' culture—a domineering temperament, with a strong inclination toward violence and aggression—and between the ages of eight and ten, they were put through the ultimate test to decide whether they were fit to reside in Matrus. The screening employed a combination of genetics and psychology to determine which boys would be forced to leave Matrus and flown off to the mines in the north.

I didn't know what went on during the tests or how exactly they worked. They were usually conducted in the lab near the queen's palace and the details weren't public knowledge.

All I knew was that my brother had come out shaking, and bearing the mark of a black crescent on his right hand. His virtues had been deemed too close to those of Patrus. And of course, the queen and her council didn't want boys like him piling into Patrus. It wasn't in Matrus' interest to help increase their neighbor's population of strong-willed men.

"There isn't much theft in Matrus, either," I told Viggo. "More serious crimes are also rare… Do you know about its justice system?"

Viggo scowled. "'Justice' hardly seems the right word."

I bit my lip. I couldn't exactly argue with that.

"But yes, I'm aware of the ins and outs," he added. "Euthanasia versus hanging, corrective detention for females, jail for males, pseudoscientific screenings, murdering pre-pubescent boys, etcetera, etcetera."

I stalled, my hand shooting to Viggo's arm. "*Murdering?*" I breathed, gripping him hard. "Where did you hear that?"

Viggo rolled his eyes. "Come on, what do you think they do with all those boys? You really believe they're carted off to mines? Do you have any idea how large and organized they'd have to be to contain the increasing number of males, year after year?"

He shrugged me off and continued walking. It felt like a steel ball had materialized in the pit of my stomach.

I dragged my feet forward to keep up with him.

"Do you have any evidence?" I choked. "Any evidence at all? Or is it only a suspicion?"

Viggo was eyeing me curiously now, apparently not prepared for or expecting such a strong reaction from me. "It's a suspicion," he admitted. "Of course, I have never traveled to the Deep North to verify whether the boys are actually there. I don't have access to an illegal aircraft, nor would I have reason or permission to fly there in a legal one."

I let out a breath. I'd truly feared for a moment that Viggo might have evidence. But that would make no sense. Queen Rina had promised me a reunion with my brother. Would she really have lied about that? I didn't want to consider that question. I couldn't start thinking that my brother might be dead. Not after my hopes had been raised sky-high about seeing him again in a matter of weeks. He was alive, in the mines in the North. Just as the queen and the Court said he was.

And yet a niggling doubt still managed to worm its way into my brain. Viggo's words had struck too close to home. On more than one occasion in the past, I, too, had wondered if Matrus could be lying about the boys' destination. The fear had plagued me on and off over the years, but I'd always tried to bury it. After all, how would any of us verify it? All we had to go on was the word of the Court because the only safe way to travel the depths of The Green in order to even have a hope of reaching the elusive North was by aircraft, and flying was illegal for all except the Court.

"What do you think Patrus would do if they had evidence of what you suspect is happening to some of Matrus' boys?" I managed.

Viggo shrugged, his eyes forward again as we turned down another road. "I don't know," he muttered. "Everyone is still trying to understand the mind of our new king… But if his father were still reigning, he probably wouldn't care—unless there was a particular political advantage to be gained by caring, if you understand what I'm saying."

"Not exactly."

"Then never mind," Viggo replied briskly, before pursing his lips.

Would Matrus really have attempted such a mass-scale lie, so confident that nobody would ever find out or let the truth slip? Because if the bubble ever burst, the queen and her courtiers would be decried as hypocrites of the worst kind. What difference would there be between our country and Patrus? We would be considered no better than them, just as prone to corruption, lies and bloody-minded leadership. What role would Matrus' national motto, "Freedom in Peace", play in all this?

Stop thinking.

Matrus wouldn't murder those boys. It's Viggo's biased speculation.

My brother is ALIVE. And I'm going to see him again, if I can just keep my act together.

Being so consumed by our conversation, I had lost track of our surroundings, and noticed we were heading to a large store at the end of the road. Dashner's Arms. The parking lot in front of it was empty. Arriving outside its reinforced entrance, Viggo knocked.

A short, balding man wearing a smart tweed suit opened after a minute and, eyeing me in confusion, he beckoned us inside.

Viggo didn't bother to explain my presence. He simply moved forward with me, following the bald man through a giant warehouse stacked with guns and ammunition, toward a pair of double doors. He opened them up and pointed out a dent against the metal, near the locking mechanism.

Viggo stepped outside into a messy backyard, piled with empty crates and boxes. He inspected the area, walking around the circumference of the yard, looking for what exactly, I wasn't sure. Then he returned to us, his arms crossed over his chest while gazing up the high back wall of the building. "The culprit has left no obvious tracks, but I'll send some colleagues round with dogs later today... I take it you don't have any canines guarding this place, Mr. Crighton?" Viggo asked the bald man.

"No," he replied.

"Then I suggest you get some."

Mr. Crighton nodded.

"I'm also surprised," Viggo went on, "that you don't have a better surveillance system in place. You need more cameras out here." He ran a hand over the dented doors. "And these doors are outdated. You're asking for a burglary without the latest technology."

"Okay, sir," Mr. Crighton replied. He pulled out a pad of paper and began jotting down notes.

Once Viggo finished giving him his analysis on the doors and the yard, we headed back into the building. We ended up spending a while in here—Viggo examined every other exterior door and window. Before we left he also had to commission some new weapons for his division. By the time Viggo was done, it was well into lunchtime.

He returned to where I'd been waiting—in a chair outside Mr. Crighton's office—and reached down a hand for me to take. I couldn't help but notice an odd tingle running down my arm as we touched. It remained for several seconds after he'd pulled me to my feet and let go of me.

Mr. Crighton thanked us and then we left the building, crossed the parking lot, and returned to the road.

"Let's get some lunch," Viggo said.

He stopped with me at the first eatery we passed, a small bakery. When we moved inside, it was empty except for two couples sitting together around a table by the window.

The man behind the glass counter grinned as he looked from me to Viggo.

"Good to see you again, Viggo. It's been a while!" he said. "And who's this? New girl?"

"Mrs. Bertrand," Viggo said tersely, before ordering two large sandwiches. "What do you want?" he asked me beneath his breath.

I opted for a slice of savory pie.

After paying, Viggo carried the tray to a table for two at the back of the bakery. We sat opposite each other— him with his back to the room—and dug into our food.

About halfway through Viggo's sandwiches, the couples by the window rose from their table and made their way over to us.

"Looks like we've got visitors," I whispered as they approached.

Viggo turned.

"Hey, Mr. Croft. I'm sorry to disturb you," one of the men said, eyeing the two of us tentatively, "but I wondered if we could have your autograph?" He held out two white napkins. "We were there at your fight two nights ago. Spectacular performance."

Viggo looked like the last thing he wanted to do was entertain the request, but he acquiesced, if only just to get rid of them quickly. Taking a pen and the tissues from the man, he scribbled his initials on each of the tissues and handed them back.

The men stowed them away appreciatively and Viggo returned to his food. I guessed they were going to leave us alone now, but then the second man said, "I wanted to ask one thing…"

Viggo was once again pulled from his meal.

"Do you ever plan to fight in the big league? You'd smash your way to the top!"

It would probably be physically impossible for Viggo to pull a more unenthusiastic expression. He merely shook his head.

At this, the man backed away, and the group took the cue to leave.

Viggo and I continued eating. Though I couldn't help but ask, "Why?"

Viggo groaned. "Why what?" he snapped.

"Why do you keep yourself at a level you're clearly above?"

He stopped chewing, eyeing me. "What makes you think I'm 'a level above'?"

"Well, it's the way people talk about you. These strangers who just came up to you, and Lee has also mentioned your abilities."

Viggo continued chewing. He waited until he had swallowed a mouthful before answering, "My current level serves its purpose. It pays me the money I need without the lack of privacy… Believe it or not," he added, "there are some things in life that aren't worth giving up for money."

"People already seem to know your name though," I said.

"Exactly," he countered. "And it would be ten times worse if I rose up in the game."

I paused, dragging my knife across the plate, before daring to go on. "I guess to me… it seems a waste. If I had the opportunity, I would go all the way."

His gaze leveled with mine briefly before averting to the table surface. Since he offered no leeway to continue the conversation, I dropped the subject. But I didn't drop thinking about it—my lack of opportunity versus Viggo's lack of desire. I wished in some fantastical twist of events, Patrus would establish a league for female fighters. That would probably be enough to tempt me to stay here permanently or at least try to visit frequently if I could be involved. But Patrus allowing female fighters seemed about as likely as Matrus suddenly halting their weeding out of "high risk" boys.

After Viggo finished his sandwiches, we left the bakery.

In the hours that followed, we didn't talk as much. We passed several other wardens as Viggo roamed the inner city, "making his presence felt," before he began leading me back to his office. He said he had some paperwork to attend to, but we never made it that far.

A sudden buzzing emanated from Viggo's right coat pocket, where he retrieved a phone.

"Okay," he said, his eyes glued to the device. "There's been an incident. An unusual one for this time of day."

Without further explanation, he grabbed my arm and began racing with me toward where he'd left his motorbike. He seated me first before leaping on himself and kicking off down the road.

"What happened?" I gasped as the lurch knocked the breath out of me.

"A kidnapping," Viggo replied.

"Who got kidnapped? By whom?"

"You'll see."

As we careered through the city, a blaring noise erupted from the back of Viggo's motorcycle—a siren. It caused all large obstructing vehicles to quickly clear the roads and let us pass.

As we arrived at the outskirts of the city, I caught sight of six wardens standing around in a huddle on the edge of the road. Viggo stopped next to them and leapt off the bike.

"We recovered her," one of them informed Viggo.

I slid off the bike and followed Viggo, trying to make out exactly what they were all huddled around. Then I heard a low groaning, and a whimpering. It sounded like someone was curled up on the ground. Viggo, who'd pushed his way to the front of the group, was staring downward. I reached for his arm and pulled myself to him, gaining as good a view as him.

Lying on the street was a thin woman wrapped in a lambswool shawl. Her right eye was swollen and bruised, her upper lip cut. The sight made me wince.

"Did you detain him already?" Viggo demanded.

"No," one of the men replied. "He's being pursued as we speak."

"*Where?*" Viggo pressed, his tone bordering on aggressive.

"Southwark Street, moving toward Lumber Avenue. A red car. Keep your phone on loudspeaker."

Viggo stepped away, pulling me back to his motorbike. He touched the screen of his phone before stowing it into his pocket. We both leapt on the motorbike. He pushed away so quickly this time that I didn't have time to find the handles beneath my seat; both nervousness and excitement filled me as I grabbed hold of his firm shoulders and we whizzed off.

Sirens from other warden vehicles blared around us. Reaching a junction, we took a sharp right turn, passed a line of stalled vehicles, and did a U-turn onto a parallel street.

"Brody Street." A voice crackled in Viggo's pocket. "Heading south."

Viggo hit the brakes so hard I almost went flying off the bike. He reversed into a road to our left and roared down it. He showed no signs of stopping at the next junction, but then, in a blur of red and shattering glass, a car came smashing through a shop front and skidded out onto the road directly in front of us. If Viggo hadn't had reflexes fast enough to make another emergency brake, we would have gone crashing right into it.

"Hey!" Viggo shouted. "Stop!"

There were apparently only two men in the vehicle, one in the passenger's seat and one in the driver's. They paid no heed to Viggo's warning and frantically revved the engine to pick up speed and continue driving in the opposite direction.

"Hand me a gun," Viggo called to me over his shoulder. "In my belt."

Reaching my hands through the folds of his trench coat, I felt his belt for a gun and yanked it out. I raised it to him and he took it with one hand. I was tempted to offer to help him, but I was still so new to handling guns, let alone shooting one at a speeding vehicle.

Clutching the motorbike's handle with his left hand, he unleashed bullets at the tires with his right. His aim was sharp. The tires punctured, causing the vehicle to slow.

As we had almost caught up with it, the doors opened and two men leapt out, revealing their full appearance for the first time. They looked unkempt and were dressed in similar rough fashion to the men I'd had a run-in with the night I ended up in the alley in my effort to avoid Cad. And they also had matching tattoos, only they weren't squares on the neck. They were small black triangles etched beneath the right eye. The square and the triangle must have been symbols of two different gangs.

Viggo stopped, leapt off the motorbike and raced after the men. "Stop where you are!"

He shot a bullet into the ankle of the shorter one, causing him to yelp and stumble. Before I could witness the fate of the other, a click sounded just in front of me. The trunk of the car pushed open and out climbed... two more men.

They took one panicked look at me before slipping round the side of the vehicle and darting off in the opposite direction.

I wasn't sure what possessed me, but the next thing I knew, I was darting down the street after them. "Hey!" I yelled.

They shot glances over their shoulders, eyes widening as they realized a woman was on their tail.

"Violet!" Viggo yelled behind me, but I was already turning a corner and chasing the criminals down another road. A dead end, the three of us realized. They stopped short and did a one-eighty, running back in my direction. They obviously thought they could just push past me.

After quickly verifying that their hands were devoid of weapons, I went charging at the nearest one to me. Diving for his knees, I floored him. He thrashed as he landed on his back, attempting to grip my throat. I grappled with him, twisting myself until my legs were in the perfect position to stretch out his arm and trap him in an arm bar. I tugged hard, tightening my hold and straining his ligaments. He grunted in pain.

Footsteps bounded down the street toward us. I glanced up to see Viggo's stunned face.

"There was another one!" I shouted. I hadn't managed to witness where exactly he'd run.

Viggo raised his phone to his ear while he continued to stare at me. "Need backup on Sullivan Street. Three detained criminals by the junction, and another one escaped on foot."

He slid the phone into his pocket before lowering and grabbing the man beneath me. I untwined my legs from the criminal and released him so Viggo could stand him upright, at which point he'd stopped attempting to struggle.

A sense of euphoria filled me, not so different than what I'd felt during my secret gym fight. I'd taken down a criminal—a male criminal, in Patrus. I'd looked him in the eye and shown him that I could match him. I could barely even bring myself to wonder what the consequences of this act might be. I was sure none by the law, since I was under Viggo's watch and guardianship.

Even as we escorted the criminal back to where Viggo must have cuffed and left the others, Viggo remained gazing at me.

"I feel like there's something you're not telling me, Violet," he muttered as we turned the corner.

I feel like there is, too.

CHAPTER 20

As backup arrived, both of us fell quiet. We returned to his motorcycle and headed to the lab, where we found Lee waiting in the parking lot.

Lee's face brightened. "How did everything go?" he asked. He must've been wondering why we were late.

"No doubt your wife will tell you," Viggo said. He nodded his head, his eyes flitting from Lee to me, where they lingered for a few seconds more before he revved his engine and sped away.

After Viggo was out of sight, we mounted Lee's motorcycle. "Why are your clothes torn?" Lee asked.

It was my knees—my pants had gotten frayed. "We, uh, got into an altercation on our way back here. There was an attempted kidnapping. Viggo went chasing after the guys involved and, well, I ended up helping a bit."

"Are you serious?"

"Yes," I said, a tad hesitant in spite of being proud of what I'd done. I wasn't sure how Lee was going to react.

"How did you help?" he asked.

"I tripped up one of the guys. Just held him down until Viggo arrived."

"And how did Viggo react to it?"

"He didn't really say much. I already mentioned to him that I took a few defense lessons in Matrus when I was younger, just like a hobby thing."

"Hm," Lee murmured, looking worried. "Then I guess it worked out okay… But getting involved the way you did was risky. Unnecessarily risky."

"I don't plan to do it again," I assured him, although I would like to, if the opportunity arose. "It was a spur of the moment thing; Viggo had brought me along on his motorcycle anyway, right into the heat of the scene, so helping him hardly seemed like a big extra step."

"Hm," Lee said again.

He went quiet and focused on the road for the rest of the journey. When we arrived back home, we cooked and ate dinner together, and then I retired to bed.

The next day, I awoke to the sound of drilling for the second time since my arrival here. I groaned, sitting up in bed and rubbing my face. *Lee's darn mechanic.*

After brushing my teeth and showering, I headed downstairs to the kitchen to find Lee awake and eating breakfast at the table.

"Viggo called," he said, as I took a seat beside him.

"What did he say?"

"He can't take you today until the afternoon," Lee replied. "He said that he'll pick you up during his lunch hour."

"Oh. Okay." I felt disappointed. This meant that I was going to have to find something to do with myself for the entire morning.

"Also," Lee added, "he's got a later shift tonight, so you can stay with him for that if you want. He said he'll drop you back afterward, say, around half past midnight."

"Okay." *Late night with Viggo.* I couldn't deny that this prospect excited me.

"Mr. Bertrand?" a man's voice called from outside the kitchen.

"Yes, Chris. In here."

A gray-haired man in scruffy blue dungarees arrived in the doorway. He met my eyes briefly with a polite nod, before turning his focus to Lee.

"So looks like I'm done for now," he said. "I trust you'll call me if you detect any problems."

Lee was already standing up and heading to the door.

"Excellent," Lee said, planting a hand on Chris's shoulder and leading him toward the front door. It clicked open and footsteps moved outside.

I fetched myself a bowl of oatmeal before wandering to the window. The two men were talking in the drive. Lee handed Chris a small black pouch, which I assumed contained his payment. They shook hands, and then Chris left through the gate.

I continued gazing out the window as Lee returned to the kitchen. It was a beautiful morning.

"So, what are your plans for today?" I asked Lee.

"I've got to go out again," he said. "I need to leave in five minutes."

He swallowed down the rest of his food before dumping his plate in the sink and heading to the entrance hall. "I'll see you later this evening," he called, before shutting the door behind him.

Okay...

And thus began my wait.

I ended up actively seeking out Samuel—who had been lazing around in the sun outside in the back garden—and recruited him for a game. I couldn't help but be entertained by the enthusiasm he showed for his ball.

But I was getting tired of playing with him in this confined backyard. He'd probably appreciate a change of scenery, too.

I gazed around at the trees enclosing the garden. Beyond the back fence was a road—you could hear the occasional car driving by. That was the same road we'd taken when we'd traveled to Viggo's cabin.

Most men were at work during the day, according to Lee. And women weren't allowed out. I couldn't imagine that there would be many people roaming these mountain roads. And if I wore my disguise...

Although I knew it would make Lee uncomfortable, I decided to head out anyway. I wouldn't go far. I would stay within ten minutes of the house in case I had to run back for some reason. But it would give my head some space and help make the time pass more quickly.

I changed into the male costume before returning downstairs to Samuel. I put on his leash and, grabbing a set of spare keys, headed out. Samuel didn't seem to notice that I was a different person to the one I had been just a few minutes ago. His tail wagged excitedly as we crossed the drive and slipped out of the gate.

We took a right and began strolling up the pretty mountain road, past the crystal-clear stream that ran nearby. I peered into each driveway as we passed, glimpsing the triangular-shaped buildings identical to Lee's.

Turning a corner, I felt the stretch in my calf muscles as we began to ascend a steeper slope.

What I would have really liked, in that moment, was to get away from everyone. Escape into nowhere, like Viggo wanted to do. I wished there was a footpath leading off into nature, away from all man-made constructions and other signs of civilization. But the only path was this road.

Samuel jerked forward, almost making me lose balance. He had spotted a squirrel scurrying across the road.

Gripping his leash more tightly, I reined him in.

We had walked more than ten minutes away from the front of Lee's drive by now. Probably more like fifteen or twenty minutes. My shirt had started to cling to my lower back. The morning sun, pleasantly mild against my skin when we had stepped out, was beginning to feel uncomfortable.

I sighed. We should probably head back now.

"Come on, boy," I said, tugging on Samuel and herding him back down the mountain.

But as we reached the corner and were about to wind our way back around it, the sound of a woman screaming made me stop still.

It had come from somewhere behind me... the house behind me. Number thirty-two.

Then it came again. Another scream. It drifted through one of the open downstairs windows.

"Stop it!" the shaking female voice cried. "Stop!" It grew more ragged, more desperate. "Don't pick that up!"

I heard the sound of smashing porcelain. There was a cry of pain, followed by a door slamming. Then all went quiet.

Barely breathing, I felt my consciousness return to the sunny world around me. To Samuel, tugging at me impatiently. But I remained staring at the house. The silence was more disconcerting than the screaming.

Viggo couldn't arrive soon enough.

Feeling shaken, I returned to the house with Samuel and waited indoors for the rest of the morning and early afternoon. Viggo ended up arriving just before three p.m., later than I had been expecting him.

I had been waiting near the window overlooking the front of the house and as soon as he pulled up on his motorbike, I hurried outside to meet him.

The first thing I did was inform him of what I had witnessed earlier at number thirty-two.

"You need to go and investigate," I concluded.

Inhaling, he ran a hand over his face before saying, "I can't."

"What? Why not?"

"That's not how things work here. Wardens can't just go barging into citizens' private homes like that. The first thing I would have to do is file a report at head office, prompting one of our people to summon the man for an interview. He would be asked questions about what was going on that afternoon, and if it is different from your report—i.e., if he denied anything happened—then they would move on to the woman for questioning to get to the bottom of it. However, because you are a woman, none of this can happen. Women can't be witnesses... especially not women who were out roaming illegally by themselves at the time."

His gaze sharpened.

I pursed my lips.

Lee was at work, so of course, Viggo knew that I would've gone by myself. Perhaps I had allowed myself to get a little too comfortable around Viggo already in assuming that he wouldn't report me.

"What would be required in order to launch an investigation," he went on, "would be for a man to witness the noises. Then something could possibly be done about it."

I sighed heavily. "Okay."

I felt his eyes on me as I looked down at my feet. Then he said, "Hop on," apparently choosing to turn a blind eye to my disobedient wandering after all.

I climbed on to the bike behind him and this time didn't bother gripping the handle beneath my seat for support. Instead I held Viggo as I'd done for the first time the day before, since it was more comfortable.

"Could we just drive past there now?" I ventured. "Number thirty-two. Maybe the cries will have started again."

"Okay." We pulled out of the driveway and took a right, further up the mountain.

We stopped outside the house and waited beneath the shade of a willow tree… But nothing happened. After five minutes of waiting in silence, Viggo started the engine again and we rode back down the mountain.

"So what if a woman witnessed a murder?" I posed, mulling over this particularly absurd rule. Men had a lot of disadvantages in Matrus, some arguably worse than the women in Patrus. But this particular law grated on my nerves. "If she actually witnessed, for example, one man attacking another man. Hacking his head off. Are you telling me she wouldn't be able to testify in court? That nobody would take her seriously?"

"She would need to have gained solid evidence somehow," Viggo said. "Like a videotape or an audio recording. But you are correct, her word alone would not be enough."

I exhaled in frustration. "*Why?*"

"You could ask that question about a lot of things," Viggo muttered.

He was right. I was asking the question more out of frustration than anything else. Not only would a male have to witness the noises, but he'd also have to be willing to testify. The idea that whatever was happening behind that door could continue happening indefinitely disturbed me to no end. I had been half-tempted to barge in there myself while in my costume—or rather, knock on the door—if only to disrupt whatever suffering that woman was going through.

But I guessed that this was just another thing that was best not to think about. Trying to make sense of rules that didn't make sense was rather a losing proposition.

That didn't stop me wondering whether things might change someday. Whether some queen and king might eventually ascend to the two nations' thrones and put an end to rules like this. Though I knew it was a dream. We had lived like this for centuries and it seemed that, as the years passed, both governments were only coming up with more enforcements to keep us ingrained in our ways. I didn't see why anything would change.

At least not in my lifetime.

Viggo parked outside Head Office. I followed him as he swept up the granite stairs, through the steel-gray reception room, and headed directly for an elevator. He punched the button for the sixth—and highest—floor. The doors shuddered and pulled closed. The cables creaked as we ascended and we listened to the sound of each other's breathing until the doors dinged open.

Viggo stepped out into an empty corridor and led me down to a room at the very end of it, a large room with windows that spanned the length of an entire wall. Drawn to the windows, I stared out at the view of Crescent River, the city on one side and the palace on the other. We still weren't high enough for me to be able to see beyond the walls of the palace, though it was the closest I'd ever gotten to the building. I gazed at the windows, and spotted the occasional shadow moving behind them.

I remained standing while Viggo took a seat behind his table and began sifting through a pile of papers. I gazed outside a while longer before joining him. Pulling up a chair opposite him, I took a seat.

I picked up a shiny black pen from a holder and tapped it against the table surface while my feet fidgeted.

"Anything I can help with?" I wondered.

"Nope," he said, not looking up.

I leaned back in my chair, stretching out my arms. Then I took another turn about the room.

"What sort of money do you get paid as a warden… assuming you were getting paid?"

He glanced up at me, raising a brow.

"What?" I asked.

He shook his head and returned his eyes to the papers. "That's not a question you should make a habit of asking around here," he said. "It's not considered appropriate for a woman to ask a man about his earnings."

I narrowed my eyes on him. "So you're not going to tell me?"

The shadow of a smile crossed his lips. Viggo's rebel smile. "If you really want to know, it works out to about four ounces of gold per month."

"And that's considered, like, good pay?" I asked.

"It's, uh, about the highest pay you can expect to receive as a warden."

"I see…" Admittedly, his answer didn't mean a lot to me. I'd never really had a chance to earn income. I'd been locked away too early in my youth. I just remembered getting the occasional silver piece thrown my way by Ms. Connolly when I'd done chores around the orphanage. I'd stored it in a tin box I hid beneath my bed. I wasn't even sure where that was now.

"So you earn double that as a fighter," I went on, leaning against the desk and gazing down at his papers.

"Yeah."

"Hm." I sank back into my chair. Removing my shoes, I lifted my legs and laid my feet to rest on the table.

Viggo looked up again.

"What?" I asked, feigning innocence. "Is this not considered ladylike either?"

At this he chuckled, shaking his head in mild disdain.

Well, I was comfortable like this, and Viggo didn't *actually* mind, so I kept my feet where they were.

In spite of the warden's hardened and usually brooding demeanor, I picked up on a leeway with him that I doubted existed in many other men here. The only way I could think to explain it was the fact that he had been married to a Matrian girl. Marrying her must say quite a lot about him. That he liked a woman who could think for herself. A woman who could challenge him. One whose nature wasn't to be a doormat.

"Do you have any friends?" I found myself asking, interrupting his work again.

"Depends on what you define as a 'friend,'" he replied.

"Well, someone you can trust, I guess. Someone you feel comfortable around. Someone you know has your back."

There was a beat before he answered, "Does that really matter to you?"

I shrugged. "Nope."

He clenched his jaw. "Then I'll ask you to keep quiet while I finish this paperwork."

I stopped annoying Viggo at his request. I moved to the window and sat down cross-legged on the floor. I gazed out at the city and what I could see of the palace for the next half hour. When I got bored with that, I took the liberty of helping myself to a few spare sheets of paper and a pen. Resuming my position by the window, I sketched the city out of boredom until Viggo announced that he was done.

As we headed out of the building and returned to Viggo's motorbike, the sun was on the verge of setting. He stuffed a couple of papers he had carried with him from the office into the compartment beneath the seat before retrieving two guns and stowing them into his belt. He covered them with his trench coat and then set his sights on the parking lot exit.

"We'll walk from here," he said. "There's a major fight on tonight. A 'big league' fight," he added, using air quotes. "So there may be some accompanying rowdiness."

"Where does the fight take place?" I asked, thinking back to Lee's scientist friends' conversation outside the restaurant. I didn't recall them mentioning the venue.

"Starkrum Stadium. We'll head there now."

We headed to the river bank and walked along the promenade before turning into a street and winding our way toward a giant dome-shaped building. Its walls were white, and at its base was a long set of glass doors, outside of which was a square where a crowd of people had already gathered to wait in line.

"*Rosen versus Cruz*" was the headline fight, according to the poster that hung above the entrances.

"How often are there big events like this?" I asked Viggo, my eyes running over the long line of people.

"Sometimes as many as five in a month," he said.

Approaching the building, Viggo led me around its wall, away from the crowd. We stopped outside a back entrance, a single, solid metal door. Viggo pressed a button on the intercom board and a voice crackled through it a few seconds later.

"Your name, please?"

"Croft."

"Okay. Come on in, sir."

The door clicked open and we moved inside. A staircase stood directly in front of us, which took us up to the first floor of the stadium. Surrounding us on either side were row upon row of red seats. I wasn't even sure how to start guessing how many were in here. The stadium held seven such levels altogether.

We moved to the barrier and gazed down toward the center of the building, where a huge cage was fixed. Employees in blue shirts ran about the floors like mice, scurrying to make final preparations before the doors opened. There were food vendors set up strategically, causing a scent of frying oil and fresh bread to pervade the arena.

According to the poster I'd spied outside, the fight was due to start in about fifty minutes. So I guessed that meant people should start being allowed in right about now...

Sure enough, the sound of heavy doors drawing open drifted up from downstairs, followed by thundering foot-steps and chattering. There were large groups of men, but also a fair number of couples and families.

I remembered I had to be careful not to make myself too visible, in case Cad was here. I reached into my jacket pocket, where I found the cap I'd been wearing earlier while in my manly disguise. I pulled my hair into a bun before placing the hat on my head and tucking my hair beneath it. Then I lowered the cap so that it shaded my eyes.

Viggo noticed, and gave me an inquisitive look. I didn't need to explain my every action. I let him go on wondering...

He soon repositioned us so that we stood directly opposite the main entrance. I imagined he looked quite intimidating from the ground, in such clear view of everybody entering… this big, towering figure, face stern, eyes sharp, like some kind of presiding deity of the cage.

After about half an hour, Viggo moved us again. He led me down to the ground floor, where he moved with purpose, his eyes fixed in one corner of the room, near the men's restrooms. The next thing I knew, he was running forward toward a bearded man in a faded brown coat, who also suddenly sped up.

The man yelped as Viggo's hand closed around the back of his neck and shoved him up against the wall. Viggo's hand dove into the man's right coat pocket where he pulled out a black wallet.

"I don't think this belongs to you, does it?" Viggo asked, his voice dangerously low. He opened up the wallet, revealing cash and an identity card which, indeed, pictured an entirely different man.

The thief's eyes bulged.

Retaining his grip on the man, Viggo pulled him away from the bathrooms and back toward the exit. Two other wardens were waiting outside the doors. Viggo shoved the thief toward one of the wardens and said, "Thief." He held up the wallet. "Take him downtown."

The warden nodded grimly before taking charge of the man.

Viggo returned with me to the building and headed straight to the front row, where he stopped in front of the man who matched the photo in the wallet. Viggo cleared his throat to get his attention.

"Oh!" the man said, leaping to his feet and patting down his coat disbelievingly. He took the wallet. "I didn't even realize it was missing. Thank you, sir!"

Viggo nodded curtly before turning away and heading back down the aisle to stand at the end of it, where he continued his perusal of the room. Dozens of people eyed Viggo and whispered among themselves, obviously having recognized him. This made me feel even more so that Viggo's excuse for not fulfilling his full potential as a fighter was a load of bull. He was already recognized practically everywhere he went. I couldn't imagine that moving up a league would make that much of a difference in his life when he was already used to being spotted and stared at. There was a deeper reason for Viggo's reluctance to fight, but I knew better than to bring up the subject again.

I turned my thoughts back to the thief. I hated to imagine what lay in store for him. One thing was certain, he wouldn't be going pickpocketing again in a hurry.

Finally, the main doors closed. The lights dimmed, and the spotlights shone down on the cage in the center, as well as two aisles on either side of the stadium where, presumably, the fighters were soon to emerge. Large magnifying screens that I hadn't even noticed before lit up around the arena.

Stirring music blasted from speakers and the screens mirrored the two brightly lit, yet still empty corners of the stadium. Not empty for long though. The first fighter, Rosen, stepped out to a round of cheers. He was dark-haired, six feet tall, and wearing bright red shorts. He beat his fists together, protected by stiff fingerless gloves. He stalked down the aisle, climbed into the cage, and bounced around, flexing his jaw and baring his tooth guard as he waited for his opponent.

Next was Cruz's entrance, to a much lesser welcome than Rosen. Half the crowd booed as he made his way down to the cage. His skin was tanned, and he was also about six feet tall. As the two fighters leveled with each other in the cage and the fight began, I looked discreetly in Viggo's direction. His jaw was set firmly, his expression stoic as he watched the fight begin. Though his eyes still roamed the audience, he was obviously interested in watching the fight.

I wondered what he was thinking. Not even the slightest bit of longing? Of reconsideration?

Who knew? His expression wasn't letting on, so I resumed my focus on the fight.

Cruz, the underdog, was already proving himself to be a very worthy opponent. As the first round progressed, he dominated at every turn, sending Rosen spiraling into defense mode. I found myself clenching my fists as I yelled out instructions to the losing fighter (in my mind). *Come on, get out of the corner! Watch his leg! No! He's going to—*

At the beginning of the second round, Cruz took Rosen down, where they began grappling.

I became so wrapped up in the fight, I only realized Viggo had been closely watching me at the end of the second round. As our eyes met, I felt an odd flurry in my chest. It was the idea of him taking interest in me enough to study me, when until now, his general instinct had been to look anywhere but at me.

His expression was curious, with a hint of amusement, his olive eyes reflecting the bright lights. "You really like all this, don't you?"

I nodded, grinning in spite of myself.

He went quiet as the third round began—Cruz still dominating—though I couldn't help but keep glancing at Viggo to see if he was still watching me. He stopped, or at least, didn't get caught by me again.

By the end of the fourth round, Cruz scored a knock-out. The stadium erupted in cheers, claps and whistles. Cruz had won himself some new fans.

"Do you want a drink?" Viggo asked me, flexing his shoulders.

"Yeah," I said. The atmosphere was hot and tense.

We moved over to one of the food stalls, where the vendor handed Viggo two bottles of water, free of charge. A perk of being a warden here tonight, apparently.

The water was deliciously cool as it glided down my throat. I breathed out in satisfaction as I downed the whole bottle in less than a minute. I scrunched it up in my hand and aimed it at a trash can. Viggo was slower in finishing his bottle. Now that everyone had a break before the next contenders entered the cage, he was alert again to monitor the crowd.

I joined him in examining the audience… and that was when I noticed a child. A girl wandering down one of the aisles by herself. She looked no older than five. Her blonde hair in bunches, she was clutching a stuffed bear to her chest and looking quite frightened as she gazed around.

I nudged Viggo with my elbow, drawing his attention to the girl as I began to move toward her.

Approaching, I bent down to her level before Viggo could, as I figured she'd take my advance better than his. "You okay?" I asked. "Where are your parents?"

The corners of her lips turned downward at my question, tears filling her eyes. She shook her head, clueless.

"Okay," I said, picking her up. "Come with us."

"We'll have an announcement made," Viggo said, leading me down the aisle. We circled the outskirts of the ground level until we arrived at a wide desk, behind which sat two men in smart black suits.

One of them picked up a microphone and made an announcement for the child, his voice filling the entire stadium. About three minutes later, a young couple came racing toward us, their faces glowing with relief.

The mother, a pretty blue-eyed blonde, looked at me with gratitude as I handed her the child.

"Thank you!" she breathed, before the three of them headed back to the seats.

I could guess what she must have been feeling because I knew what it was like to lose a child.

Five minutes later, another announcement was made for the commencement of the next fight. Everybody settled down and Viggo and I resumed our previous watching position, near the glass doors.

By the time the last fight was over, it was deep into the night. I wondered if Lee had intended for me to stay out this late. He had said that I could stay on with Viggo, though, so I guessed that he must have been aware of how long these events could last

I had a spare key in my pants pocket, anyway, so I wouldn't need to wake him in case he had fallen asleep.

Nothing else noteworthy had happened in Viggo's policing department since we'd spotted the lost child. The two of us waited by the doors until the crowd had piled out and we were alone in the arena except for a few employees tidying up. All the other wardens had left already.

Viggo sighed, his eyes raking over the seats on the ground floor one last time, before turning to face the main entrance. "We're done," he said.

His green eyes were glassy and he looked tired. I pitied him. He not only had to drive me back to Lee's, but then he had his own journey to make to his cabin in the mountains.

I wondered if on nights like this he ever regretted insisting on living so far away from everyone.

We left the stadium and emerged in the square. It was still busy out here. The crowds were dallying, standing, and talking excitedly about the fight, while others were piling into eateries that lined the adjoining street.

As we crossed the open plaza, a trio of men caught my eye. They were sitting squarely in front of the stadium's entrance, on one of the benches. They wore boots and their general scruffy demeanor reminded me of the men we'd chased yesterday. On examining them closer, I realized that they even had the same triangular tattoos beneath their right eye.

And they were staring right at me.

As they rose to their feet, I tugged on Viggo's coat sleeve. I tried to point them out to him discreetly, which was difficult, considering their focus was zoomed in on me.

"Those guys," I whispered, raising myself on my tiptoes to get closer to Viggo's ear while turning my back on them. "You see their tattoos? They're from the same gang who was involved in the kidnapping yesterday."

"Yes," Viggo said and stopped still to meet their gaze. His fists clenched and then he began walking toward them, with me trailing along after him.

He cleared his throat as we approached. "Evening, *gentlemen*," he said tersely. "What might you be staring at?"

It was unsettling that their attention remained on me, even as Viggo addressed them. *Why me? What's so interesting about me?*

Their focus ought to be solely on Viggo, and getting the hell out of here before getting themselves into trouble with him.

"Something wrong?" Viggo pressed.

The man in the middle with scraggly black hair looked steadily back at Viggo, not appearing the slightest bit intimidated.

"Is there a problem?" he asked coolly. "Is it a crime to sit here?"

"No," Viggo replied. His eyes raked over their tattoos. "But considering that you belong to the same gang as your friends who were arrested yesterday, I suggest you not get too cocky around here…" Viggo's glare intensified. "Know what I'm saying?"

"Not sure what you mean by 'gang,' sir," he replied. "You have no evidence that we belong to anything."

Viggo didn't bother arguing with him. These guys were gutsy. Used to living on the edge of the law, pushing its borders as hard as they could.

All three men's focus returned to me once more, their eyes dark and threatening, before they stalked off.

Viggo drew in a shallow breath as they turned down an alleyway. Then he glanced down at me, a slight look of concern in his eyes… Concern which, in turn, unsettled me.

"Why didn't you, like, arrest them or something?" I asked. "Isn't the tattoo evidence enough that they belong to the same gang?"

"It's not solid enough evidence. I can't simply arrest someone for having a tattoo. Or sitting and staring."

"So you're just letting them go," I murmured. "Letting them wander off into the city…"

"You seem to forget that I don't make the rules around here," Viggo reminded me pointedly.

"And why were they looking at me?"

"We can only speculate, can't we?" he said, before closing his hand around my wrist and leading me away from the square. We headed to the street that led back to the promenade. "We didn't manage to catch that guy who ran away," Viggo explained. "The escapee likely told his friends about the wardens who got involved in the kidnapping—and no doubt also mentioned you. It's not every day that a woman takes down a man in an arrest. In fact, I bet it's never happened in all of this nation's history—at least, certainly not the way you did it."

His grip tightened on me as we entered the crowded street, as if afraid I might slip away somehow. He remained holding me just as firmly until we had left the bustling promenade and returned to the parking lot where he had left his motorbike.

He opened up his seat and lowered his guns into the compartment.

"So…" I blew out, leaning against one of the bike's handles. "What's happening tomorrow then? Will I see you in the morning?"

He shook his head. He refastened the seat lid before meeting my eyes. "No. I have a day off tomorrow."

"A day off, huh? I guess that means you'll be fighting then?" I recalled a fight noted in the schedule I'd peeked at in his gym, but since he had already told me he spent his spare time in fights, this was hardly an amazing guess on my part.

"Yes, actually," he said. "I'll be at training throughout the day and then in the evening, I have a fight."

"Where?"

"Brunswick Arena."

Same small place as last time.

"I see." I wet my lower lip. An awkward span of silence descended between us. Suddenly neither of us were sure what to say—or, apparently, do—next. We stood, just looking at each other. Then, with equal awkwardness, we started speaking at once.

"I would—"

"You could—"

We both stalled, sharing a smirk.

"Ladies first," Viggo said, his eyes warming with his expression.

"I was just going to say that I, um, wouldn't mind tagging along with you tomorrow, if *you* don't mind."

He glanced down at his hands. "Yeah, I, uh… Seeing that you like fights so much, I was gonna say you could come to see my fight in the evening. If you wanted to. I could pick you up at about seven."

My smile broadened. *It's a date.*

CHAPTER 21

Viggo sped me back to Lee's home and stayed on his bike watching as I approached the house and made sure that I got inside okay.

Lee was still awake. He opened the door, emerging in his pajamas and carrying a mug of tea. I turned back toward Viggo to wave that he could go, but he was already riding off.

"How did the day go?" Lee asked. We headed to the kitchen. "You hungry?"

"No, thanks. And it went fine. Not much happened. Viggo had work to do in his office, then we headed to the Rosen-Cruz fight. We stayed until the end of the event and then he brought me straight back." I poured myself a glass of water before sinking into a chair opposite Lee. "Oh, and he's off work tomorrow," I added. "But he's invited me to attend his fight in the evening. Said he'd come to pick me up around seven. He's going to get there a bit early."

"Brunswick?" Lee asked.

"Yeah."

"Hm." He sipped from his mug.

"What?" I'd been expecting him to say something encouraging, like it was a good idea that I had accepted the invitation. I was supposed to be getting close to Viggo.

"Nothing," he said. He gave me a furtive glance. "I just, um… I don't want you to get carried away with this task."

"Carried away? What are you talking about?"

He sighed. "I just mean, keep sight of the goal… why you're seeing him in the first place."

My throat tightened. The "goal" in regards to Viggo was something I had to forget. Lee didn't understand. For my, my brother's, Lee's and Matrus' sake, I had to bury our plan for Viggo deep. Otherwise I couldn't do what was required of me.

"As long as you keep that goal in mind," Lee went on, "you'll automatically do and say the right things, and everything will run smoothly."

I nodded, though I knew I couldn't do what he was asking of me. I would pull this off in my own way. I knew myself and how I worked better than him.

I needed to change the subject.

"So what have you been up to?" I asked him.

"Preparing the site," Lee replied, rubbing his forehead. He looked exhausted. "It's not a simple process. A bunch of hoops to jump through, and each step has to be carried out gradually, slowly, and steadily, so that I don't cause

suspicion in anyone. The attendees have been almost confirmed, also... even King Maxen might make an appearance this year... There will be a lot of moving pieces when
the night finally arrives. A lot of moving pieces indeed."

I nodded briefly again before getting to my feet. "Yeah.
Well, I'm going to bed."

"Good night, Violet," Lee said, looking up and offering
me a small smile as I moved past him. A smile I couldn't
quite bring myself to return right now.

I just wanted to shut myself in my room, throw myself
into bed, and lose myself in sleep...

I slept in late. By the time I came downstairs, Lee had left
already for the city. I had another empty day ahead of me
before this evening.

I didn't want to risk taking Samuel out again. I had
already pushed the law enough since arriving here. So, I
found myself heading up to Lee's room. I sat in front of
his computer, which had been left unlocked, then nav-
igated to the map of Patrus and stared at the five red
moving dots. I could guess which one Viggo was—he was
already at his gym. I wondered what he was practicing
now. Whether he even had a trainer, or if he always prepared for fights on his own. Then I found myself watching the other four dots and wondering who those people
were. One of them was roaming the outskirts of the city,

while the other three were near the city center, the latter, like Viggo, pretty stationary.

I lost track of how much time I spent sitting in Lee's bedroom. But as afternoon bled into early evening, I returned to the garden, a pile of psychology books tucked beneath one arm. My attempts to focus on reading were shattered, however, when... I heard it again—a woman's cry, coming from the other side of Lee's back yard fence. Number thirty-two.

Dropping my book, I hurried to the fence and listened, trying to catch the words that the upset woman was speaking. I was too far away to hear them. Her speech was muffled.

I ran back inside the house to the kitchen and looked up at the clock. Ten minutes to seven. Viggo should be arriving anytime now and then we could dash around the corner and he could witness the noise for himself. But, fearing it would stop again before Viggo got here, I began looking for some kind of recording device or a camera. I rummaged through all of Lee's cupboards but failed to find anything I could use. *Dammit. I should have asked Lee if he had a camera.* But then I heard a roaring engine entering the front drive of the house.

Viggo had arrived.

I thundered down the stairs and, grabbing a set of spare keys, raced out to him. He smiled faintly on seeing me, but his expression soon turned to surprise as I dashed toward him like I was being chased.

"Number thirty-two!" I hissed. "It's started again…" I went quiet, straining to hear. Yes, I could make it out from the front yard, although it was very faint.

"Let's get closer," Viggo said. "Get on the bike."

I climbed onto the seat behind him. Wrapping my arms around his waist, he tore up the road and stopped on the sidewalk opposite the house.

We got off the motorbike and moved by foot to the other side of the road, where we ducked down beneath a line of bushes. We held our breath, listening as the noise continued. More smashing had started. More pleas. Our faces inches apart, our eyes locked as we concentrated.

"Okay," Viggo said after a minute. "I've heard enough. First thing tomorrow morning, I'll lodge a complaint and have a colleague take the man in for questioning."

"Good," I said, breathing out in relief. Hopefully whatever was going on in there would be stopped sooner rather than later.

"You know, Violet," Viggo said as we began rolling back down the mountain, "you *should* have become a warden."

Arriving at the Brunswick Arena, we descended to the basement and headed through one of the doors at the back of the auditorium. We passed down a narrow corridor and turned through another door into a small rectangular changing room equipped with a punching bag, a bench, a locker, towels, and other items of clothing. I also spotted a second door which led into an adjoined bathroom.

Viggo dumped his bag on the bench before sliding off his coat. Turning his back on me, he removed his black t-shirt. My eyes roamed his chiseled back, watching his muscles ripple as he rummaged in his bag for a pair of black shorts—the same pair he'd worn to his previous fight. He scooped up a towel and moved to the bathroom. "Taking a shower," he grunted. "Helps clear my head before a fight."

Viggo spent twenty minutes in the bathroom before emerging. His hair went straight and almost black when it was wet. The darkness of it somehow accentuated the sharpness of his eyes. His standing there damp and bare-chested made him look like some kind of wild, rugged warrior... and more attractive than I'd ever seen him.

He reached into a pocket at the side of his bag and pulled out a hair tie, fastening his long hair back. Then he pulled out a roll of bandage from his bag and began wrapping it around his knuckles. He used tape to tighten it before standing up and approaching the punching bag. He began to hit it, his punches gradually building in power, until the bag was swinging all over the place, hardly able to catch a break.

"Why don't you wear those thicker, tougher fingerless gloves I've seen the other fighters wear?" I asked him. "Why only bandages? Aren't you more likely to get injured?"

"Yes," he replied. "But it's standard at my level of fighting."

That made no sense to me. "What do you mean?"

"It's what the crowd is used to watching at sub-level. A portion of them prefer sub-level fights for this reason; it's less regulated. More danger involved without hard gloves. More pain."

"Sounds grim," I muttered.

He chose not to comment.

My eyes wandered again around the room. I noticed a pair of flat, cushioned gloves hanging from a hook near the locker. They were apparently designed for a trainer to catch punches. I reached for them and slid them on absentmindedly, as I flexed my wrists.

"Hey," I said, standing and raising my gloved hands. "Want to have a go at punching me instead?"

He paused and turned to me, his expression quickly turning incredulous.

"Why not?" I asked. "Nobody's watching."

He merely shook his head before resuming his focus on the punching bag.

I quirked a brow. "You don't think I can handle it?"

He didn't stop punching to face me this time as he replied through sharp breaths, "I can't throw a punch at a woman."

Hm.

I'd wanted to attempt to recreate the feeling I'd experienced in my gym sparring match with Viggo. But it seemed that wasn't going to happen.

Not wanting to be pushy, I sat down again, glaring at my gloves. Still, I couldn't help but inform him, "I've fought girls as strong as men before." My mind turned back to Dina. Not as strong as Viggo, of course, but he didn't need to know that.

"It doesn't matter how strong you are," Viggo breathed. "I saw how you took down that guy in the street. I know you're skilled. But if you asked me to punch you, it wouldn't be a punch. It would be a nudge, a light jab at the most."

He worked himself up into another flurry of punches until he appeared to be satisfied that he'd warmed up enough. He backed away from the punching bag, tightening his bandages.

"Okay. How about I punch you? " It wouldn't be the same as in the gym, but it would be better than nothing.

Viggo smirked. "That I could allow..."

I rose to my feet, removing the training gloves from my hands and handing them to him. But, on taking them from me, he discarded them on the floor. Apparently, he was going to use his bare palms as my target. *Suit yourself.*

He dipped into his bag and retrieved the roll of bandage. He moved to me, reaching for my hands, but I shook my head. "Come on," I said, rolling my eyes. "We're only going to be at it for a few minutes. You're gonna have to leave for the fight soon."

Still, he looked reluctant. "And what will I tell your husband if you go home to him with bruised knuckles? I already returned you once with grazed knees."

"My knuckles aren't made of flower petals," I replied.

He hesitated a moment more before resuming his position in front of me. "All right," he said, the corners of his mouth twitching in a half smile. He raised a daring brow. "We've got ten minutes. Have at me."

A rush ran through my body as I clenched my fists. Although he wouldn't see me eye to eye, Viggo was still a dream sparring partner. I had been one of the toughest girls in my defense classes; a lot of the other girls couldn't take blows as hard as I could throw them and I'd often ended up partnered with Ms. Dale for that reason. But with Viggo… I didn't have to hold back. He could take anything I threw at him. Plus, I didn't have any facial hair to worry about keeping in place.

I approached him, aiming my first swipe at his right palm, which was rock hard. But the contact felt good. Like scratching an itch. I threw a punch at his left palm, then right again, before moving on to a kicking combination. As my right foot rose to his stomach, he blocked it—firmly enough that I didn't reach him, but not hard enough to cause a bruise.

When I moved to punch him again, he surprised me by catching my wrist. He spun me around, my back against his chest, where he held me in a firm lock. I hadn't expected him to elevate the game. I supposed this was as close as he was going to get in treating me equally in terms of fighting.

Having been trained to get out of this kind of hold before, my next move was wired in my brain. It came as mere instinct for my right leg to slip backward and jerk forward. I caught him at the back of his right knee. He hadn't been expecting that, either. He lost balance, causing the two of us to tumble to the floor. I quickly scrambled to gain an advantage while he lay on his back. Gripping his arms and pressing them hard against the floor, I straddled his hips. I leaned over, my face leveling with his. As our eyes met, we both broke out in a tense laugh.

"Surrender?" I asked him.

I felt his stomach muscles tauten against my thighs. He narrowed his eyes. "Is that what you think this is?"

I didn't get a chance to respond, or see what he'd do next, as a sharp rapping at the door brought reality spiraling back.

Viggo cursed. I leapt off him and he stood up just in time before the door swung open.

Being in Patrus, there wouldn't have been an awful lot of ways a married woman and an unmarried man could have explained that position.

Catching my breath, I smoothed down my top and tried to pretend I'd just risen from the bench when a white-haired man poked his head through the doorway. Surprise registered in his eyes on seeing me here, but he quickly focused on Viggo.

"You're on in twenty-five minutes," he said.

"Yes, I know," Viggo said tightly. I could see he was trying to steady his breathing too. And was there a slight flush to his cheeks? It felt like there might be to mine.

"Good, good." With one last glance toward me, the man backed out of the room.

My cheeks definitely heated as Viggo and I were left alone again. That had been close. I coughed my throat clear and sat back down on the bench. Viggo didn't start punching the bag again. Avoiding eye contact, he moved into the bathroom, where he splashed his face with water and stood in front of the mirror for a while. Then he returned to the room and paced up and down.

I watched him while his focus was on the floor and wondered whether nerves ever bothered a man like Viggo Croft after all the fights he had experienced.

"Have you ever lost a fight?" I asked him. That might not have been the most sensitive question to ask a fighter minutes before he was due to step inside the cage, but Viggo didn't strike me as the superstitious type.

He shook his head.

A grin returned to my face. "Then let's not make tonight a first."

Finally, he looked at me again. His expression was dark, though I sensed a smile hiding somewhere behind it. "I don't intend to."

The next few minutes slipped through our fingers like sand. A round of boos echoed down the corridor. Viggo's opponent must have entered the arena. And then the elderly man was at the door again.

"Time to roll!" he announced excitedly.

I stood up and followed Viggo and the man out of the room. Viggo was my guardian, and even though he'd be in the cage, I was supposed to follow him as closely as possible. When we headed down the corridor, however, and reached the wide-open door to the arena, I had to hang back with the elderly man while Viggo stepped into the spotlight. The audience exploded. I caught Viggo drawing in a light breath before stalking down the aisle. The spotlight followed him, and I was able to move closer to the darkened doorway without worrying about being spotted. Viggo climbed into the cage opposite his opponent—a guy with ebony skin and cropped black hair. Going by appearance alone, they looked a very even match, Viggo perhaps slightly at a disadvantage—his opponent was a little taller.

"May I ask who you are, ma'am?" the white-haired man, who was still standing opposite me by the doorway, asked.

"Mrs. Bertrand," I replied quickly, my eyes reverting to the fight. I didn't want to miss any of it.

"Oh, I see. And how do you know Viggo?"

"My husband appointed him as my second guardian."

The man stopped talking to me after that. My spine tingled as the Deepvox man announced the start of the fight. His voice was almost drowned out by the cheering crowd.

I wished that I could get closer as the two men began to circle each other. I was still worrying about Cad or his parents spotting me. The chances that they'd be at the fight were probably slim, but I couldn't take any risks. I had brought my cap with me, however. If that had been enough to get by at the event the night before, it should be enough here, too.

"Excuse me," I said, taking my leave from the elderly man. I moved down the aisle, approaching the cage.

A security guard stopped me as I reached within a few feet. "Mr. Croft is my guardian," I told him before he could say anything. He let me pass and stand right next to the cage, where the water was kept and the attendants waited.

Up close was more exhilarating than I could have imagined. I could see every detail, every flicker of emotion in their eyes, every bead of sweat.

Viggo's opponent—Rod "Ruin" Ryland, according to the trim on his blue shorts—took aim at Viggo first. Viggo dodged before countering with a right hook which caught the side of Rod's face with a painful smack. Rod skipped back. The crowd yelled. Somehow, I felt that this was going to be another short fight.

Rod approached again, more cautiously, only to quickly swerve backward as Viggo launched a side kick. Viggo took the offensive, Rod backing away further. I could tell that Rod was trying to stay on his feet, jerking away whenever Viggo stooped or stepped closer. Rod clearly didn't want Viggo taking him to the ground. But that appeared to be exactly what Viggo's game plan was.

Viggo advanced, closing in like a panther, until Rod was up against the wall of the cage. Then he hurled himself at the guy's knees, going straight for the takedown. Rod desperately tried to keep his balance, but he only lasted a few seconds before his back went slamming down against the floor, Viggo on top of him. The audience howled and I found myself shouting along with them as Viggo proceeded to smother Rod's defensive punches and catch hold of his arms. "Yes! Come on!" I bellowed. I wondered if Viggo could hear me among the sea of other screams.

Rod proved to be more of a veteran on the ground than I had given him credit for. He squirmed and twisted beneath Viggo like an anaconda, and after about two minutes of intense grappling, to my dismay, he managed to free himself. The two men shot to their feet and resumed circling one another, though Rod was visibly tired by the grappling. His chest heaved and he bought himself some time by distancing himself a few steps. Viggo sensed his weakness. He swept forward and broke through Rod's defense, catching his nose with a hard punch. Rod staggered, then swung back with a flurry of quick, but rather sloppy punches. It did the job of fighting Viggo back a few feet. Then, as I sensed Viggo was about to go in for another flooring, the bell rang, announcing the end of the round.

A smile lit up my face as Viggo stalked toward my end of the cage. He noticed me as one of the attendants handed him a water flask through the bars. Viggo took a swig and I felt a twinge in my chest as his Adam's apple bobbed, the water gushing down his throat.

But I pushed the guilt down. *Down, down, down.* Deep, until it stopped existing.

After handing his flask back to the attendant, Viggo caught my eye again. He gave me the slightest wink before returning to the center of the cage for the second round. Cool as ice, Viggo was.

I hoped that Viggo would finish his opponent in this round. Rod didn't start out nearly as confident as he had in the previous one. Viggo, on the other hand, went in far more aggressively. He forced Rod to the edges of the cage with a slew of well-timed punches before finally opening up another opportunity to sweep Rod to the ground. This time, they fell in a peculiar way, twisting in mid-fall so that Viggo ended up landing on his back, Rod's back against his chest. Rod struggled to twist around to gain the advantage of being face forward and on top, but Viggo was too swift. His arm wrapped around the man's neck, pressing down hard against his throat and strangling him. Rod writhed and attempted to punch Viggo in the head, but Viggo held on tight. Rod even managed to roll over, but Viggo wrapped his legs around his waist, refusing to release his grip on Rod's neck. Rod managed to stand briefly before staggering and falling face forward. Viggo now on top, he served punches with his left hand while choking harder with his right arm, all the while maintaining control over the rest of Rod's body with his expert legwork. And then it was all over. Rod, draining of oxygen, tapped out.

The audience's celebration was deafening. It seemed even louder than at Viggo's previous fight. Viggo stood up, his eyes sweeping fleetingly around the room—over his adoring fans—before he stood by the referee.

Rod's team was hovering over the fighter, along with a physician, checking that he was all right, and then he rose—albeit on shaky feet—to stand on the other side of the referee. The booming voice announced Viggo to be the undisputed winner. The referee held Viggo's arm aloft. The second he let go, Viggo was heading back to his cage exit. He climbed out, his feet hitting the floor in front of me. His skin shining with sweat, he swept past me, catching my hand at the last moment and pulling me down the aisle alongside him toward the exit. This sent the females in the crowd into a frenzy. Wolf whistles abounded, every one of them obviously thinking that I was Viggo's new girl. Thank God Lee and I weren't actually in a relationship. If he'd been watching this, he probably would have been pissed.

I was just glad that I had my back to the crowd and they couldn't see my face. We entered the corridor, the noise of the audience fading a little as Viggo led me straight back to his room.

He shut the door behind us before he approached the bench. He picked up his towel and wiped down his face, chest and torso.

"Good one," I said.

"Yeah," he muttered, not attempting even a smidgen of enthusiasm. He gathered his clothes and shut himself in the bathroom.

After he turned on the shower, there came another knock at the door.

I doubted Viggo had been able to hear it over the running water. I wasn't sure what to do. Answer it, or ignore it? I decided to answer it.

Opening the door, I was expecting perhaps to see the elderly man come to congratulate Viggo. But instead, standing in the doorway was a middle-aged man with sleek brown hair and wearing a smart gray suit. He was holding a black briefcase, attached to which was a badge with black bold letters: *"PFL"*.

"And who are you, Madam?" he asked me. No doubt he'd witnessed my exit with Viggo.

"Mrs. Bertrand. Viggo is my second guardian."

"Ah..." He stole a peek inside the room. "And is Mr. Croft available?"

"He's in the bathroom, but I doubt he'll be long... What do you want to speak to him about?"

The man's brows lowered. Apparently, as a woman, I had just asked one too many questions.

"I'll just... wait inside here, if that's okay?" he said.

"I guess," I muttered grudgingly.

I let him inside before closing the door behind him. He took a seat on the bench, while I found myself standing outside the bathroom door. After five minutes of awkward silence, Viggo emerged, wearing his day clothes. As I was right near the bathroom door, his eyes were on me first. He frowned, and looked like he was about to ask why I was standing in this odd place, when his eyes fell on the… intruder.

I was surprised when the first thing Viggo did was groan. "Mr. Sands," he said, "I told you no."

Mr. Sands stood up, offering a hand to Viggo—which Viggo promptly ignored.

"And I do greatly apologize for the intrusion," Mr. Sands said smoothly, looking apologetic for nothing. "But we last spoke over a month ago. That was quite a few fights ago. I thought there might be a possibility that you changed your mind about joining the Power Fight League since then."

"I haven't," Viggo snapped, throwing his towel against the bench.

"I know you've said you don't want the fame," Mr. Sands bulldozed on, "but surely by now, you have already gained a very large following? After a certain number of fans, it hardly even makes much difference."

My jaw dropped. Mr. Sands was voicing my thoughts exactly!

Viggo shook his head, stubborn as an ox. "No. I'm not interested."

"Would you just take a look at the contract the PFL is proposing, Mr. Croft? I took the liberty of preparing this before coming to your fight this evening. I tried to address a number of the concerns you brought up in our previous talk, and have come up with some creative solutions that might make your rise to celebrity less steep. For example, we could agree not to broadcast the events on television or radio, make your fights only a live event… similar to what you're already used to."

Wow. These people are desperate to have him.

Still, Viggo shook his head.

Although this was really none of my business, I couldn't help but blurt out, "Really, Mr. Croft? They're bending over backward to have you!"

Viggo's scowl deepened as his eyes shot to me.

"You could earn, like, a *ton* more," I went on, disregarding his glare. "And they say they won't even broadcast it so widely." *Plus you'll start wearing proper gloves and not have your hands constantly beat up.*

Now Mr. Sands looked interested in what I had to say.

"Mrs. Bertrand," he said, his face shining with self-serving gratitude, "you truly have a point. Mr. Croft, I implore you to at least read through the contract before rejecting the move to PFL again so swiftly." Mr. Sands held out three sheets of paper.

Viggo dragged a hand down his face. He threw me another hard stare before slipping the contract from Mr. Sands's hands and dumping himself down on the bench to read it.

I approached him tentatively, peering over his shoulder.

After scanning through the three pages, I was nervous about what Viggo was going to do. Reject again?

"The contract's only for one fight," I said.

"Yes," Viggo muttered. "I can read."

"So you could back out of the whole thing easily if you truly hated it," Mr. Sands interjected.

Viggo swallowed.

"I think you should take it," I said quietly.

He perused the contract five minutes longer before he slapped it down on the bench and rose to his feet.

He inhaled, running a hand through his hair. Then he shook his head in resignation. "Okay. One fight… I'll do it."

Yes.

"Fantastic!" Mr. Sands said, positively bouncing on his feet. He was quick to draw out a pen from his briefcase and hand it to Viggo, who moved back over to the bench to sign it.

Mr. Sands didn't stay a lot longer after that. "I won't detain you further now," he said. "You must want to rest after the fight. But I have your number, Mr. Croft. I'll be in touch tomorrow morning."

Viggo nodded, the shadow of a grimace still lingering on his face. As Mr. Sands left the room, he clenched his jaw as if he had just tasted something bad. I let him stew in his own thoughts as he packed up his possessions and donned his trench coat.

"You ready?" he asked gruffly, casting me a fleeting look.

"Yes."

"Then let's get out of here."

I followed him to the door. Instead of taking a left turn which would lead back to the arena, he took a right which brought us to a rusty stairwell. It took us up to a single door, which led out to a quiet street around the back of the building.

He pulled up his hood so that it shadowed his face, while I kept my hat low on my forehead as we made our way to his motorbike. As he stowed his bag beneath the seat, I dared break the silence.

"I have a new name for you, by the way," I said.

He groaned, slamming the seat shut. He climbed on to the motorbike and I slid on behind him, wrapping my arms around his waist.

"Do you want to know what it is?"

"I'm sure you're going to tell me anyway," he grunted.

"Viggo 'The Victor' Croft."

He kicked off and joined the road. Beneath the roar of the engine, I caught him mutter, "You have a nerve, Violet Bertrand."

CHAPTER 22

There was bad traffic on the way back to Lee's. Apparently, there had been a major crash on one of the highways, which caused a ripple effect of solid jams throughout the city. Viggo ended up completely retracing our route, even back past the Brunswick, to take a longer route home. He rode through the city closer to his side of the mountains, northwest of the palace. It was a relief to leave the noise and smoke behind as we climbed the mountains; the fresh air, tinged with the scent of pine, was bliss.

It was a mild night. Viggo got hot beneath his coat at one point; I helped peel it off his shoulders and kept it on my lap so he wouldn't have to stop to remove it, leaving me to feel the muscles beneath his t-shirt as I resumed my hold on him.

Viggo smelled like the pines. Rugged, virile. Maybe it was because he lived out here. The ends of his loosened hair touched my forehead as I rested my cheek against his back. I felt sheltered, safe. Truth be told, I was feeling sleepy now, too, and I closed my eyes for the rest of the journey.

By the time we thundered into Lee's drive, it was later than Lee had been expecting. The kitchen lights were on, the blinds half closed.

I got off the motorbike.

"Good night," I whispered.

"Night," he murmured.

His eyes glinted in the moonlight as I held his gaze a few seconds longer before turning and heading to the house. As Viggo had done the night before, he waited until Lee had opened up before riding off.

Unlike the night before, Lee was still dressed in his work clothes. A navy blue suit.

"What took you so long?" he asked as he closed the door after me. His face was tense.

"A ton of traffic," I said. "We had to go a roundabout way to get here."

We moved into the kitchen. When he offered me dinner, I accepted it. As he went about heating something up, he asked, "So how was Viggo? What did you talk about?"

"He won in the second round," I said. "It was great. I waited right by the cage and watched up close—I wore my cap, of course. And after the fight some agent from the PFL came to see him in his changing room. I've been trying to encourage Viggo to move up to his level, and when the agent offered him a new contract tonight, he finally accepted it."

The spoon Lee had been using to stir a saucepan dropped to the stove with a clatter. He spun around to face me, his expression shocked.

"You *encouraged* him to do that? What were you thinking?"

I stared at him in confusion, my lips parting. "I-I don't understand."

"Why would you encourage him to move up to the PFL? It didn't occur to you that this could mess up his entire schedule? His training, his fights! For heaven's sake, Violet. I warned you not to lose focus!"

I found myself stumbling for words, unsure of what to say. Lee was right. I hadn't given the slightest thought what consequences might ensue if he joined the PFL. His entire schedule that I'd gone to the trouble of noting down could be turned on its head. For all we knew, Viggo might be offered a PFL fight on the night of the banquet.

"As it stood," Lee went on, "that night was completely blank for him. He even had a night off his duties as a warden—I checked. He was to be replaced by someone else that evening. We had this all battened down, dammit!"

Lee sank down in a chair, running his fingers nervously through his hair.

My breathing quickened. What had I just done? Of course, Viggo might've accepted the contract anyway. Mr. Sands and the contract might've been enough to convince him… though I couldn't help but feel that my encourage-ment had played a part in it. Viggo was a stubborn man. He might not have even heard Mr. Sands out if I hadn't been there encouraging him to listen.

"Oh, this is a mess," Lee breathed. "A complete mess… Did they discuss the next fight in the changing room? Any kind of schedule at all?"

I shook my head. "No. The agent just said that he would be in touch tomorrow morning."

"He might even shift gyms for this. How are we going to figure out his updated schedule?"

"I-I could just ask him when the fight is."

Lee let out a breath, still looking irritated.

The smell of burning filled the room. Whatever Lee was heating up was getting ruined. But he could hardly bring himself to care. I had lost all my appetite now, anyway.

Crap. What have I done?

I sat in my chair, frozen, watching Lee tentatively as he buried his head in his hands. Then, with a deep sigh, he raised his head and looked me. "I'm just… trying to understand how you could have possibly thought that encouraging him was a good idea."

I was thinking of Viggo, of him being paid more and treated better.

"I'm sorry," I said. "I've been trying to make friends with him and I… I slipped up."

"We can't afford slip-ups. And do I need to remind you that my life is on the line just as much as yours is in this?"

"I know," I said through clenched teeth. *Even though I seem to be the one taking on the major risks all the time.* I felt like snapping something back at him, but I held my tongue. I knew I had messed up.

Lee stood up and turned off the heat beneath the sizzling pan before proceeding to throw the food in the trash.

Even though I no longer wanted to eat, I remained in my seat while Lee prepared a second dinner for me. When he placed a plate in front of me, I picked at the food, hardly able to swallow.

I felt like I was losing myself on this mission.

I pushed the food away after I'd eaten all that I could and drank from the glass of water he'd set down for me.

Lee's mood had quieted. "Okay," he said, sighing. "Look, Violet. I know this is hard. Trust me, I do. And we all make mistakes… But you've *got* to stay focused. Everyone is counting on you."

I managed a nod. "A reunion with my brother is on the line, too." I wasn't sure whether he knew that.

Biting his lower lip, he stood up. "Okay. I'm heading to bed." He began moving toward the door, but as he passed my seat, he stopped. He glanced down at me still in my chair, a furtive look in his eyes. Unexpectedly, he stooped. A second later, his moist lips were pressing against the side of my neck, beneath my right ear, in a firm, chaste kiss. And then, just as suddenly, he drew away.

"Good night," he managed, before sweeping out of the kitchen.

I stared at the empty doorway in a daze, my fingers raising to the side of my neck. I felt the skin where his lips had been.

What was that about?

Why would he do it?

I struggled for the next ten minutes to make sense of Lee's kiss. It had come so abruptly. So unexpectedly. From nowhere.

In the end, there was only one thing I could conclude:

Maybe I'm not the only one losing focus.

CHAPTER 23

My sleep was fitful that night. A recurring nightmare plagued me, a nightmare about a young boy sitting in a row boat in the middle of a river, being swept away by a current. The harrowing feeling of being able to do nothing but stand and stare remained with me after I woke up drenched in sweat. I glanced out of the window, whose blinds I'd forgotten to draw last night. The horizon glowed orange with the first signs of dawn. I checked the clock by my bedside. Five-thirty a.m.

I breathed in deeply through my nose. I wished that I could take a pill and forget about everything. Become a robot. I grimaced to myself. King Maxen's Benuxupane pills didn't seem like such a bad idea right now.

I took a hot shower, which helped to calm me. Like with Viggo, running water had a way of clearing my head.

I was no stranger to adversity. I'd been through harder times than this before and pulled through. I'd pull through again now. We didn't have long to go anyway, and then this would all be over.

After finishing in the shower and dressing—I didn't bother to dry my hair—I went downstairs. The kitchen was empty, but I could hear Lee upstairs. His shower was running.

I fixed myself some honey and ginger tea and settled down at the table. Samuel came in to greet me with a groggy woof before allowing me to stroke his head. It was raining outside, the first rain since I'd arrived.

By the time I'd finished my tea, Lee creaked down the staircase and emerged in the kitchen.

The first few seconds of his arrival were the worst. My stomach somersaulted as last night replayed in my mind. He also seemed awkward. He murmured a quick good morning before busying himself by the sink.

It appeared that he was going to act like the kiss hadn't happened.

"So, uh, what's on the agenda today?" I asked him. I was wondering what time Viggo would come for me, though he wouldn't have called yet. It was still too early.

"You're not going to see Viggo today." Lee's answer came.

I stared at the back of his head as he hunched over the sink.

What? Why? I wanted to blurt. But I held back. Why was I so bothered anyway whether I saw Viggo or not?

It was the abrupt reminder of Lee's power over me that threw me off.

"I've already left a message on his phone," he said.

"All right," I replied, trying to sound unruffled. I needed to cooperate with Lee, not fight him, for everyone's sake.

"Instead," Lee went on, "you're going to help me with something down at the lab." He turned away from the sink and sat opposite me at the table with a glass of water, still not meeting my eyes directly. He reached into his right pocket and pulled out a phone. "Alastair is due to make a call in about… one minute."

Barely a few seconds after Lee had spoken, the phone rang. The number flashed up as "Mariana"—apparently a disguise, presumably in case Lee's phone ever got stolen. Lee picked it up and pressed it to his ear. "Yes."

He uttered a few more "yes's" and "fine's", before handing the phone to me.

"Yeah?" I said.

"Good to hear from you, Violet," Alastair's pitchy voice replied.

"Things are going fine," I told him flatly, before he could ask the question. "There's really not a lot to talk about. The banquet is drawing closer and we're preparing for it as best we can."

"Good. Good. We're very glad to hear that." A pause. "You'll be seeing your brother soon, and you're making your nation proud, Violet… Never forget that."

I answered with silence. Alastair requested to be handed back to Lee and I handed back the phone wordlessly for Lee to wrap up the conversation.

"So, about today," Lee went on. "We need to leave for the lab in half an hour. I'll explain more on the journey."

I stayed in my seat while Lee left the kitchen. I heard him open the front door, then came his crunching footsteps in the driveway. The garage door creaked, and then an engine sounded: not a motorcycle. It sounded more like a car.

I headed to the window to see a brown five-seater roll into the center of the drive. Lee killed the engine, got out and hurried back to the house.

I met him in the hallway. "I didn't know you had a car," I commented.

"I rented it yesterday," he said. "Forecast predicted it would be rainy, and we can't afford to get wet today." He eyed me. "If you're ready we might as well leave now… Though we'll need to fix you up with your disguise first."

My curiosity, or rather, apprehension, was growing regarding what exactly Lee had in store for us. I followed him up to my bedroom where my costume was kept. Things felt awkward again as he got up close to put on my wig and help me with my facial hair and contact lenses. But his expression remained businesslike.

I changed into the body suit before pulling on a deep brown suit. Then, after popping some Deepvox pills and checking my appearance with Lee, we left the house.

"You sure this costume is a good idea?" I asked as we got in the car. I felt uneasy about going to the lab dressed like this. People had seen me before as a woman. They might recognize me even in this disguise. Plus, how would Lee explain who I was if we bumped into someone?

"Don't worry," Lee replied. "I've thought about it."

Watching the road slip away beneath us, my eyes glazed over as we rolled down the mountain. I tried not to worry, but failed. I didn't like feeling dependent on anyone—man or woman. In fact, I abhorred it. I hated not being clear on the plan in my own head. But it wasn't worth causing more tension between Lee and me. I had to keep biting my tongue. *This will be over soon.*

"Since it's early on a public holiday—the late King Patrick's coronation," Lee said, "the city won't be crowded. And the lab should be mostly empty. You're going to install one of the explosives we'll need for the lab... The one we require to blast open the egg's glass casing."

My heart skipped a beat. "Are you serious?"

"Quite serious."

"I have no idea how to handle explosives."

"Again, don't worry. I'll advise you what to do."

"What about the other explosives?" I asked him. "Have you installed those already?"

"No, but the others I've figured out how to handle without you. It's just this one you need to take charge of."

Lee proceeded to tell me in detail about where and how to correctly install the explosive device.

Arriving at the lab, Lee punched in the code to get us into the parking lot and parked as close to the entrance as he could. He reached an arm around the back of my seat and removed an unassuming brown bag, which he placed between my legs. Then he handed me a pager, which I stuffed into my pocket.

Now all that remained was action. He gave me a firm nod before stepping out of the car.

I watched Lee hurry to the building through the rain. He let himself inside, and his shadow disappeared behind the glass.

I stared down at the pager. In about fifteen minutes, he should be buzzing me.

I kept watch of the digital clock above the dashboard, my fingers clenching around the handle of the bag. Soon only one minute was left. Thirty seconds. Ten seconds… The pager buzzed five seconds late.

I took my cue to leave.

I pulled on a raincoat that had been stuffed inside the back pouch of Lee's seat, positioning the hood low over my face. I slipped the bag beneath my arm, making sure the overcoat covered it, then exited the car and hurried to the entrance.

Lee was waiting behind the glass doors and after he let me inside, we immediately parted ways—I headed toward the staircase that was located near the elevators, while Lee headed to the room behind the reception desk.

I scaled the stairs as fast as I could, breathing hard by the time I arrived on the top floor. Stepping out into the corridor, I recognized it from my previous visit. I no longer had to keep the hood over my head here. Lee's job during the minutes I'd waited in the car had been to stall the cameras recording in the entrance area, the staircase and up here… Just for fifteen minutes. I had to be fast.

As I reached the door of the lab, I buzzed Lee. A few seconds later, the door clicked open, Lee manipulating it from the downstairs control panel.

Stepping inside, I held my breath and gazed around. The lab was empty, eerily quiet. I let the door close behind me before working my way toward the glass cabinet at the back of the room. Toward the silver egg.

This damn egg. There had really better be something valuable in it.

By using the word "installing", Lee had made this job sound far more complicated than it actually was, at least for today. All I had to do was drop off a package of small explosives and hide them here so that they would be ready for the night of the party. He had advised me where I should put them.

My eyes panned to the light above me. It was wide, flat, and circular and fixed into the ceiling. Sliding a hand into the front pocket of the bag, I drew out a few screwdrivers before standing on a table. I raised my arms and began trying to find the right fit. I found one that slotted into the screws perfectly, though they were tightly fit. It wasn't a quick process to unscrew all the screws, especially since my nerves kept causing the screwdriver to slip in my hands. I feared I wouldn't make the fifteen minutes in time.

I exhaled in relief as the light finally came off. I glanced down at the clock by the door—seven minutes left. I placed the light carefully on the table—the last thing I needed was for it to shatter. Then I dug another hand into my bag and pulled out a foil package. I felt four heavy cylindrical objects inside as I stuffed the package through the gaping hole in the ceiling. I positioned them just by the edge, easy for me to reach in a hurry. Then I stooped down for the light fitting and worked as quickly as I could to reposition the screws. It was depressing to think I'd have to go through this all again on the night of the banquet.

The buzzer vibrated in my pocket just as I had one screw left.

Ugh. Screw you, Lee. I'm almost done...

I had the screw at just the right angle. If I let go, I'd have to start this one again, and I was running dangerously low on time. I spent the next minute refining the angle before leaping down to the floor and tucking the chair beneath the table where I'd found it.

The pager had vibrated twice more since then. When I pulled out the device from my pocket and checked it, my blood ran cold.

"GET OUT OF THE LAB!!!"

My heart in my throat, I grabbed the bag and bolted for the door.

Out of the lab? What does that even mean? Out of this particular lab, or out of the building?

But as I reached within ten feet of the exit, I froze. Footsteps sounded outside. I should have checked the pager the second Lee sent the first message. It was too late now. I was trapped.

I looked frantically around the room for a hiding place. I had no time to even consider whether diving beneath the table closest to me would be the best option. A few seconds after I'd slid beneath the furniture, the door glided open. Footsteps entered.

I clasped a palm over my mouth, trying to stifle my breathing. A man in corduroy pants walked past my table, continuing down the aisle. He was dragging behind him a suction cleaner. Why hadn't Lee known about it? I was trusting him blindly. He was supposed to have thought through all this. *I'm putting my life in that man's hands!*

The intruder walked to the end of the aisle and started up the machine. The room filled with white noise.

My fingers unsteady, I reached for my pager and punched in a message. *"STUCK INSIDE. WHAT NOW?"*

I stared down tensely at the device after sending it. *Come on, man!*

Lee's reply arrived forty seconds later:

"STAY WHERE YOU ARE."

What? For how long?

The cleaner was moving slowly but steadily toward my end of the room. He was cleaning thoroughly, too, making sure that he got every last bit of dirt out from underneath the tables.

He was going to find me.

Just as I was contemplating darting beneath a different table—one further away that would hopefully buy me some more time—the door opened again, and in stepped a second cleaner... also with a suction machine. He started cleaning much closer to me. At the rate he was sweeping across the floor, he was going to reach me in less than a minute.

"*TRAPPED,*" I paged.

I clutched the device, waiting with bated breath for Lee's response. It wasn't coming.

The second cleaner arrived within five feet. Then four. Then three. Then...

The suction broom took its first swipe beneath my table, missing my left foot by a fraction. Clutching the bag, I spread myself as flat against the wall as I could, leaving as little of me touching the ground as possible. But it wasn't going to be enough. The machine moved forward again, this time aimed directly at my feet. Like a rabbit caught in the headlights, I closed my eyes, steeling myself for the impact while hoping against hope that he might mistake me for a table leg.

The broom hit me. But as it did, an alarm rang out, so loud it felt like my eardrums would split.

Although the broom had touched me, the guy became too distracted to check what he'd hit. He dropped the machine, and so did his colleague. The two of them rushed out of the room.

I took a moment to steady my breathing, drawing in a long, quiet breath.

Then I moved forward and peered out from under the table. Now I needed to get out while I could.

Making sure that my mustache, beard and hair were still on straight—just in case I got spotted outside—I left my spot beneath the table and headed for the door. But for the second time, it opened before I could reach it. There hadn't even been footsteps to warn me. I didn't even have time to throw myself under a table.

It was Lee and I had never been happier to see that man. He scanned the lab wide-eyed before taking my arm and pulling me out of the room.

The corridor was empty, but he did not head back to the same stairwell that I had come up. Instead we moved in the opposite direction down another hallway, before reaching a red door. As Lee opened it, a damp breeze swiped at my face. It led outside, to a narrow metal stair-case scaling the back wall of the building. Lee pulled me outside into the rain and we clambered down the steps as fast as we dared.

Then, as we kept close to the wall and pulled on our raincoats, Lee led me back to the parking lot. Reaching the car, he opened up the front passenger door. I collapsed inside, stowing the bag beneath my knees. I expected Lee to take a seat next to me and immediately drive off, but instead he whispered, "I'll be back in a minute. I have to go back in and restart the cameras."

He swept back to the building and through the glass doors. He didn't take long. Three minutes later he was back in the car and we drove toward the parking lot exit. We both were silent until we were firmly outside of the gate and speeding back toward home.

"What happened?" the two of us demanded at once.

"I'm sorry," Lee replied first. "The cleaners were *not* due in today. They were supposed to come tomorrow. A change in the schedule was obviously made, and whoever was responsible for it forgot to mark it in the works calendar. It couldn't have been prevented." He looked at me sideways. "Did you pull it off?"

"Yes," I huffed. "It's done."

Lee nodded, relief washing over his face. "Good girl."

CHAPTER 24

After we returned to Lee's house, he didn't have anything for me to do for the rest of the day, but he preferred not to call Viggo. My voice was too deep to see him, anyway. He suggested that I see him again tomorrow, when my main priority would be to figure out whether his schedule would be changing on the night of the banquet.

Lee drove me to head office in the morning and took me upstairs to Viggo's floor.

"Come in," came a familiar grunt as Lee knocked.

Lee pushed open the door and the two of us stepped inside.

Viggo sat behind his wide desk wearing a dark green t-shirt, his coat hanging from the back of his chair. A small pile of papers lay in front of him.

"All right, Viggo?" Lee asked pleasantly.

Viggo nodded, his eyes moving to me.

"Violet mentioned the contract. Congratulations!"

"Thanks," Viggo replied, monotone.

"Okay, I'd better head off. See the two of you later." Lee turned to me and leaned down to peck me on the cheek before leaving the room. The second kiss he'd laid on me. The first he had laid in public.

Trying not to get too caught up in mulling over Lee's weirdness, I approached Viggo's desk. As our eyes met, a smile spread across both of our faces.

I took a seat opposite him. "How was your day yesterday?" I asked him.

He shrugged. "Uneventful. Yours?"

I couldn't quite bring myself to say 'uneventful', so instead I replied, "Fine. Lee had the whole day free and wanted us to spend it together."

Viggo nodded stiffly, averting his eyes to the table.

"Mr. Sands must've called you, right?" I said.

"He did."

"Well?"

"They want the fight to be sooner than I had expected. Next week."

"Next week? Which day?"

"Saturday."

The banquet was to be held the Wednesday after. I supposed that meant Viggo's schedule would remain the same, if the fight was to be over days before. Any changes to his training routine would in theory take place prior.

"Are you able to get any extra time off from your warden duties to train? It's so soon."

"No extra time off above my yearly allowance," he replied. "I'll figure it out."

"Who are you up against?" I asked.

"They've decided they want to escalate me straight to Cruz."

"Seriously?"

"Yup," he said, rubbing his jaw.

"Are you nervous?"

He shrugged again.

I guessed that meant no.

"So, what's your plan for today? Warden duties until evening?"

"No, I've got the second half of today free. I plan to train a little, but I'll be heading back home. I think your husband is expecting that I take you with me, and then drop you at your house at the end of his work day."

"Okay," I said. This would be the first time I'd be alone with Viggo in his house, so far away from other people. I wondered if it might feel awkward.

Viggo returned his focus to his papers, but said, "By the way, you might be interested to know that the man we reported—or rather, you reported—at number thirty-two will be questioned today."

"Good," I muttered. I'd done my part, now I had to hope justice got served.

Viggo finished leafing through the papers in front of him before tucking them into a drawer.

We spent the rest of the morning outside. The rains of yesterday had given way to a bright blue sky. Viggo had to make another visit to the arms store for a meeting with the manager, which took up a good part of the morning, before returning to head office. He led me to a large conference room on the ground floor, where he met with about fifty other wardens—all of them working under him, apparently.

I sat in the chair by a corner, a little separated from the men. I didn't want to cause waves by taking a seat right among them. Viggo had three things on his agenda: first he informed them of new weapons that the force was bringing in, as well as giving them a demonstration. Next he spoke about new security protocols to be instigated near "Thickets Bridge"—apparently a bridge located somewhere in the mountains that connected a route to Porteque. And finally, he asked for an update on what was happening regarding the man who had escaped from the recent kidnapping incident, the man I hadn't managed to catch. There were no updates in that regard. Apparently he had escaped, well and truly.

After the meeting, everybody piled out of the conference room and headed to the canteen for lunch. Viggo and I accompanied them. As we collected trays and served ourselves a hot meal, I felt eyes watching me. Nobody looked directly at me for more than a few seconds, but I could tell the men were wondering who I was exactly, and why I was hanging around with their chief.

After we'd eaten, we left the building and headed to Viggo's motorcycle. Soon, we were speeding toward his side of the mountains.

We hit an unexpected spell of traffic along the way. I thought that maybe another accident had taken place and was clogging up all the roads again, just like the other night. But that didn't appear to be the case here. I strained my neck to see through the line of honking vehicles.

"Damn," Viggo murmured.

"What?"

"I forgot it was today."

"Forgot what was today?" I squeezed his waist, pressing him for an answer.

"King Maxen is making an appearance just up the road. You see that gold sedan?"

"Uh, yeah. Just about." A shiny golden vehicle was parked up near the sidewalk to our left.

"That's the king's. It's the inauguration of a new hospital... I'm off-duty now, otherwise I'd be there making sure things ran smoothly."

"A new hospital?"

"They say it's going to be the most technologically advanced we've ever had in Patrus," Viggo said.

"Lots of new, uh, technological stuff going on around here," I commented.

"Yeah," Viggo said. "And there will be a lot more to follow in the coming months. Don't ask me for details. I don't make a habit of reading the papers."

Or watching the news or listening to the radio, if his cabin was anything to go by.

I guessed life was a lot quieter that way. More peaceful without the constant bombardment of headlines.

I had lived that way for a lot of my life too—not that I'd had much of a choice in recent years, being stuck in detention centers. It wasn't exactly a priority there to keep the girls informed of current events.

I inhaled deeply as we approached the foothills, once again relishing the crisp, pure air.

"Do you always train by yourself?" I asked.

"Of course not. There are guys I spar with in the gym. But sometimes it's good to be out in the open."

I agreed.

Ascending higher and higher, I finally caught sight of Viggo's cabin as we traveled the last stretch of road. This was the first time I had seen it in daylight.

It really was small for a guy like Viggo. I wondered if he ever felt claustrophobic. Then again, if he did, he could sit out in the open, which I guessed was what the chair on his porch was for…

After disembarking and parking his motorcycle, he led me up the steps to the wooden platform that ran around the cabin, and opened the door.

"Come in if you want," he told me, already heading toward his bedroom. "I need to change."

Closing the door politely behind me, I headed to the sitting room. It looked the same as the night I'd last visited. Even the ointment and bandages were in the same place, although the hearth was not ablaze.

I was left to look out of the window—down at the bustling city—for a couple of minutes before Viggo returned barefoot, sporting a loose pair of pants and a looser black shirt that revealed a flash of his chest.

"Want something to drink?" he asked me. "I only have water."

"I'm okay for now."

We returned outside and I followed him around to the back of the cabin, where he had a sprawling backyard. Most of it was overgrown, but there was a stretch in the center where the grass had been kept trimmed. A make-shift log shelter stood by its border. Beneath it was various exercise equipment. Weights, benches, and other strength training gear I couldn't put a name to.

The view from this side of the house took me by surprise. Viggo's home being on a high plateau, it afforded a view of the *other* side of this mountain. The cliffs and peaks dipped down into a lush valley, through which ran a glittering river. And on the other side, more regal mountain ranges sprawled out for as far as I could see. Some peaks were so high, I couldn't even see their tips. Low clouds hung over them in an otherwise spotless sky.

Viggo's view was unique. Cityscape on the one side. Wilderness on the other.

He caught me staring in awe.

"So, deeper into these mountains is where you plan to buy land, once you quit being a warden?" I asked him.

"Not too deep, but deeper."

I squinted, trying to gauge how far my vision would stretch into the distance. "What's too deep?"

"Certainly no further than Thickets Bridge."

Wherever that was…

Viggo moved over to the log shelter and picked up some weights. I knelt on the grass as he began to warm up, my attention half on him, half on the view that was still taking my breath away. So far, things didn't feel awkward, and I suspected that wouldn't change. He was the same man as he was down in the city… just with a bit more breathing space.

Viggo worked out for the next hour and then retreated into the cabin for water. He brought out a steel jug and two glasses.

"Hope I'm not distracting you by being here," I told him, accepting a glass.

"No," he said, dropping down on the grass next to me. "I planned to give myself a bit of a break today anyway.

Still some days to go before the fight… and I know Cruz's style. Seen it many times before."

He removed his shirt, wiping the sweat from his face, chest and neck.

I stood up and wandered over to his equipment, testing the weight of his dumbbells. They were heavy. Very heavy. I played with a few other items before turning to face him. He was watching me.

I slipped my hands into my pockets, kicking at the ground casually as I asked, "Would you teach me a thing or two about what you know?"

"Teach you what, exactly?"

"I don't know. Some punching and blocking tips. Some grappling techniques. You're like a snake when you get a hold of someone."

He glanced toward the front of his cabin, as if to check no one was watching. "Okay." Putting down his glass, he strode over to me. "Let's start with some blocks… Say I go to punch you like this"—he moved his fist toward me in slow motion—"how would you block it?"

I swiped it aside with a swift chop of my right forearm. Not the most elegant move, but it usually did the trick.

"Okay," Viggo said. "And what about like this?" He came in with a slow round hook. Since there was enough space between us, I ducked down and went for his knees.

"Now I would floor you," I said, hooking the back of my ankles against the back of his.

"Try it," he said.

I jerked my ankles forward, causing him to lose balance. He caught his fall expertly with his arms rigid and palms spread out.

"And now," he said, sitting up and twisting me around so that my back was against his chest, "if I held you in this choke…" He locked one arm around my neck, the other fastening my arms behind my back. "How would you get out?"

Hm. Good question.

This was difficult because neither of us were standing. I couldn't knock him to the ground like I had done back in his changing room when he'd held me from behind.

I tried to maneuver my legs to distance myself and loosen his grip on me, but I failed. I realized that I actually did not know—or remember—how to get out of this.

"What's the answer?" I asked.

"What if I told you the answer is, there's no way out of this one?"

"I'd call bull."

He chuckled. "Then get out of it."

His challenge got my creative juices flowing.

I realized what I would do. My knees were touching the ground, which meant that I had leverage. Due to the nature of his hold, his face wasn't far from the back of my head. I would jerk my body upward suddenly, catching him with a head-butt strong enough to weaken his grip on me for a few seconds. Then I'd slither out.

Obviously, I wasn't going to actually do that now. I didn't want to give Viggo a bloody nose before his fight, so I just explained it to him.

"Hm. That might've worked," he said. "But I guess we'll never know. Now that you've told me your idea, I'll be sure to watch the back of your head."

Still his grip remained on me. "Hey, come on!" I said, grinning.

"There is another way out of this, though," he said. "At least one other way that wouldn't require you to smash my face in. Figure it out."

Viggo was a hard taskmaster, but I liked it.

Another idea came to me, and this time I acted instantly. Using my knees, I shoved all my weight to the right as I leaned backward. The mix of movement and direction was enough to rock Viggo's balance. We both toppled to our sides on the grass. As we made contact with the ground, there was a second where Viggo's hold loosened on my arms. I managed to slide them out in front of me and then break his hold on my neck enough for me to squirm and twist until I was facing him, our noses inches apart. I froze, realizing just how close we'd come to each other. Closer than we'd ever been. I paused for a few seconds to take in the details of his eyes, his dark lashes, every hue of green in his irises and the way they seemed to gleam as he looked back at me. Then, experiencing a flush of bashfulness, I switched back into fighting mode. Curving my right arm around him, I shoved myself further upward until my right shoulder dug into his neck, while I flattened his left arm beneath me. His right arm was still free, but I kept my head pressed close to his, which made it tougher for him to gain control of me.

Of course, if he was actually fighting with me, he would've made things a lot more difficult. But as I released him and we both sat up, there was still a shine to his eyes. He seemed pleased.

We spent the next few hours discussing techniques and putting them into play—mostly grappling, which was what I enjoyed the most, but also some punching and kicking. Before we knew it, dusk was upon us. That was just as well, I supposed. Viggo had worn me out. I was fit from manual labor, but I hadn't done resistance training for years. Of course I didn't have anywhere close to Viggo's lasting power. He could have continued all night.

Although evening had fallen, we still had some time left before Lee arrived back home. Viggo strolled over to the wooden shelter, gripped its roof, and, with one fluid motion that caused every muscle in his back and arms to flex, he lifted himself onto it. He glanced down at me. "Wanna come up here? The view's pretty good."

Heck, yes.

I wasn't tall enough to reach the top of the roof, so Viggo offered a hand and helped me up. We sat down facing the wilderness, our legs dangling over the edge. The mountains glowed orange in the evening light, enhancing their raw beauty to something of fantasy.

I had gained a new appreciation for why Viggo wanted to live up here. The view alone was worth the absence of electricity.

"Thanks for that," I said to him, leaning back, my eyes ahead.

"Welcome."

A span of silence fell between us, but it was not uncomfortable.

I glanced over my shoulder, toward Viggo's second view. The city. My eyes traced the shape of the river, and that of the buildings extending around it; they melded together, forming one giant crescent around the palace. Then I asked a question that had been nagging me for a long time.

"What is the actual meaning of your crescent symbol?"

Viggo followed my gaze and joined me in eyeing the city. "It symbolizes strength and potential. Growth, like the waxing moon."

"Ah," I said softly. "That makes sense."

It was ironic that it was Patrus' crescent mark that Matrus authorities stamped on boys who failed the test, when Patrus was the last place they'd ever be allowed to go.

I turned my thoughts to the symbol on the Matrus flag—a curved grain of wheat. It was fairly self-explanatory. It signified growth and fertility, but it was intended more to be an ode to a society rooted in pragmatism, diligence, and most importantly, peace.

I sensed Viggo watching me as I gazed upon the city, but I didn't let on. I felt that strange flurry in my chest again.

He seemed to hesitate, then asked, "How did… you and Lee meet, Violet?"

I realized that this was the first time I'd heard Viggo use Lee's first name.

"I thought he told you," I said, my jaw tightening.

"Yeah," he said. "He did mention it in passing, I guess… Never mind."

I let him fade into quiet. The less we discussed Lee and me, the better.

But since he'd posed a question about my relationship, it seemed only natural that I should turn a question on him that ran along the same lines. "Have you always been single?"

"No. I haven't. I… I was married. But things didn't work out."

I sensed the discomfort in his voice and immediately regretted asking the question. I didn't want to dredge all those painful memories up for him. Not on such a beautiful evening as this, when his mood appeared to be lighter than it had been since I'd met him.

"I'm sorry," I said and glanced away, hoping to make it clear that I didn't expect him to offer anything more on the subject.

My eyes traveled further over the city of Patrus to its vast surrounding suburbs. Then northward, where The Green began on Patrus' side of the river, extending like an infinite ocean of trees. Then to the river itself, whose hanging mist was tinged with the evening sun… And then beyond that, blurred by the fog, the faint outline of Matrus.

Sitting here with Viggo, it felt somewhat painful to stare in my homeland's direction for long. I'd had enough of the cityscape, anyway. I twisted back around and faced the wilderness. Viggo did the same.

Only a quarter of the sun was visible now above the peaks. Soon we would have to leave. I didn't want Lee getting tense with me again, under more suspicion that I was getting "carried away".

But we still had a few minutes left.

Enveloped by the peaceful atmosphere, on the cusp of light and darkness, a question bubbled up in me.

"You ever wonder if things will always be like this?"

"What do you mean?" Viggo asked, his voice husky.

"Just… how we find ourselves living."

Viggo's gaze lowered to his hands. There was a pause before he replied, "More often than I should probably admit."

Having both been victims of the law in our countries, I supposed we were more vulnerable to wondering. Grief did that to you. It made you wish for a life that wasn't yours. It made you dream.

But dreaming wasn't encouraged in my world. Just like expressing views opposing that of our Queen wasn't. Doing the latter publicly was an offense that led to serious consequences—jail time, or occasionally even banishment.

Criticism of the Court was something that had to be done behind closed doors, with people whom you trusted wouldn't rat you out. I suspected Patrus was similar in that respect, given Viggo's caginess to clarify certain comments he'd made about Patrus' leadership.

My eyes fixed on a family of eagles swooping down upon a rocky cliffside, settling in for the night.

"Do you feel like you belong in Patrus?" I asked him in almost a whisper.

Viggo furrowed his brows. "I s'pose I don't really understand the question. I was born and raised here. I am a man."

I didn't really understand the question either. I'd been born and raised in Matrus. I was a woman. Matrus was where I belonged. Matrus was my home…

"I guess I just wonder what happens to someone who doesn't feel they belong on either side of the river."

Viggo didn't have an answer to that one.

CHAPTER 25

We didn't stay much longer on the roof. Viggo pushed himself off, landing on the grass, and I was about to jump off after him when he reached up to help me. I hesitated, unsure of how this was going to work. Holding his hands at this angle would be silly.

"Hold my shoulders," he said.

His hands positioned on the roof on either side of my hips, he beckoned me closer with a gentle nod. I leaned down to grip his shoulders. As I slid into his arms, his hands engulfed my waist. Warmth flooded through me. My feet touching the ground, I was suddenly acutely aware of my erratic heartbeat. I withdrew my hands from Viggo's shoulders and he let go of my waist, but we shared the same two feet of soil for a few seconds, his eyes reflecting the fading evening light.

Then I staggered backward. I looked toward the cabin, feeling lightheaded. *What's gotten into me? It's this mountain air or... something.*

"Let's go," Viggo said. His voice came as a croak. He left me and strode toward the front of his home; I found my balance and followed him.

Mounting the motorcycle, neither of us spoke as we traveled back to Lee's house.

We arrived well on time. Lee had only just gotten in and he smiled on opening the door to me, before the two of us waved Viggo goodnight.

"Any change of schedule for him? No press release has been made yet involving a date." Lee asked as soon as we were inside.

"It'll be kind of a last-minute fight," I said, my throat feeling parched. "It's been fixed for Saturday."

"Hm. Okay," Lee said, stroking his chin. "That gives us four days before the banquet. I don't see why his schedule would change much immediately after the fight... Everything should still run as planned."

The next few days passed quickly. Almost too quickly. Except for Lee reporting a scare in the lab, where he'd witnessed a group of men huddled around the egg, evidently trying to coax it open, nothing very eventful happened.

Lee assured me that they'd failed to open it, though for all we knew, they might be getting closer to figuring it out. It was a good thing the banquet would soon be upon us.

Lee continued to drop me off with Viggo in the mornings, and when he and I weren't in his office, roaming the city, or in some meeting, Viggo would be in the gym. I watched from the bench while Viggo worked out, sometimes by himself and sometimes with others. The two of us didn't go up to his cabin again.

I had no more 'special' jobs to accomplish for the mission. My next and final task would be on the night of the banquet. The night I was due to leave Patrus. Lee's own prep work was almost done, according to him. It was no wonder that he had been so busy. He not only had to keep up with the demands of his job in the lab, but, on top of that, fulfill his end of the deal for Matrus. He had a lot of weight on his shoulders. We both did. I regretted resenting him for not taking on as much danger as me— although my tasks might be more out in the open and carry more immediate risks, he was still working hard in the background.

I didn't ask Lee for details about his own work, though. I didn't want to know his business, and I was glad that he didn't offer the information.

I was also glad that he didn't make any more advances toward me, though I still felt an undercurrent of awkwardness around him.

I was relieved when Saturday came around. The day of Viggo's fight. It marked a milestone—only four days left to go.

Although Lee was at home, and in Viggo's eyes there was no reason for me to hang around with him, Lee suggested that going to his fight would be helpful. I'd seen Viggo regularly up until now, and I needed to keep the momentum going for the last few days.

The fight was due to take place at night, and since Viggo had a number of other things to do before then—PFL formalities, like final weigh-ins and such—he didn't come to pick me up until the evening. The fight was to be held in the same stadium as the Rosen-Cruz fight. I could only imagine how crowded it would be.

As I hopped on Viggo's motorbike and we headed down the mountains, Viggo confirmed that we should expect a lot of people; the tickets had sold out in record time, spurring the PFL to set up screens around the outer walls of the arena so that people could watch from the square and bordering streets. Although the PFL had agreed not to broadcast the fight on television or radio, broadcasting it to extra people outside the stadium was apparently something that they could get away with in the contract.

Something told me that I was feeling more nervous than Viggo for the fight as we rode around the building to a back entrance. He looked calm and collected as ever as we entered the building. His confidence was something that I admired—he wasn't cocky or arrogant, but pragmatic. He simply knew what he was capable of.

A man in a suit was there to greet us at the end of the entrance hallway. He introduced himself as Mr. Doherty, cofounder of the PFL. He shook hands with Viggo before leading us to a changing room—certainly a step up from Viggo's previous room. It was more than twice the size, everything more luxurious, from the front of the door engraved with his name in gold letters, to the soft, fluffy towels, to the air-conditioning, to the tray of refreshments waiting on a table. My eyes lingered on the padded, fingerless gloves hanging from a hook by the door.

Viggo nodded briefly in appreciation before Mr. Doherty left us alone.

I wandered about the room and approached the frosted window. I opened it just a little to gaze outside at the crowds already forming.

Viggo dumped his bag down and fished out his fighting shorts, also a step up from his previous fights. These were black with gold trim, sporting the bold letters "PFL".

Viggo headed to the ensuite bathroom to shower and change. When he emerged wearing the shorts, he removed the gloves from the hook and sat down next to me on the bench. I watched as he strapped them on. Finally some decent protection for his knuckles.

"Those look good," I commented.

He flexed his fingers in the gloves. "Yeah."

He stood up and began swinging air punches.

"PFL makes a huge fuss about everything," Viggo muttered as he continued to warm himself up. "There must have been over fifty journalists at the weigh-ins. My picture will be everywhere tomorrow." He scowled. "Then there's all the trash you're expected to talk about the opponent… Can't stand hype."

"Well, you don't have to play along," I said to him. "You can do whatever you want. You're Viggo Croft, remember?"

He scoffed.

"What happens after you win this fight?" I asked. I was confident that he would win. It seemed silly to use the word *if*.

"Then I suppose I will wait a week or so to see what the aftermath is like. If the buzz is somewhat bearable, I guess I'll sign up for a second fight. If it's intolerable, I won't."

Someone knocked on the door. Some guy in black PFL uniform, one of the event organizers.

"A gentleman from *The Sportster* would like to have a few words with you in the final lead up to the fight," he said. "Would you be willing to talk to him?"

Viggo's expression darkened. "Is that the same guy who brought Miriam up earlier?" he asked.

"Uh… yes."

"Then you can show him the exit."

The organizer looked disappointed, but didn't press. He backed out of the room.

Miriam.

"Who's Miriam?" I asked, hoping he wouldn't mind the question.

Viggo turned his back on me, busying himself in his locker. "My late wife."

I regretted asking. We both went quiet.

Another interruption came barely five minutes later. As Viggo opened the door, it was another man in black PFL uniform, blond with a scratchy beard and holding a clipboard.

"Sir," he said, his eyes passing me as they swept around the room, "you need to come to meet Cruz now. The referee needs to have his final word with the two of you together."

"Okay." Viggo sighed. He glanced back at me, indicating that I follow, but as I headed with him to the door, the employee objected.

"I'm very sorry, Mr. Croft," he said, "but if your female friend could wait here in your changing room…"

Viggo's jaw twitched in annoyance. Then he exhaled. "Okay. Violet, wait here. Don't go anywhere."

"I won't," I assured him.

He left the room with the man, shutting the door none too gently behind him.

I roamed around the room a second time, stooping to pick up a bottle of chilled water from the refreshment basket. Then I approached the window again and peered through the crack. We were on the ground floor, so I couldn't see the full extent of the crowd, but it had bal-looned since the last time I'd looked out just a few minutes ago.

After finishing my water, I needed the bathroom. I locked myself inside, and realized I'd been sweating in spite of the air conditioning. It was the buzzing stadium, being surrounded by crowds of people, the atmosphere wrought with tension and excitement.

But the second I stepped out of the bathroom, a heavy fist flew at me from nowhere and caught me square in the face. I reeled, pain searing through my nose. Stars circled before my eyes. Before I could attempt to defend myself, a heavy weight was flung at me, knocking me from my feet and pinning me facedown against the floor. As I tried to yell, a hand clamped around my mouth, and then a second hand, lined with some kind of pungent-smelling tissue, folded around my nose.

My brain became foggy. I could no longer struggle. And then all went black.

CHAPTER 26

I woke up to a splitting headache and a coppery taste in my mouth. Blood. My own blood. I was lying flat on my back, the floor hard and rough beneath me. And cold. Terribly cold. Prying my eyelids open, I sat upright. Metal clanked and I realized that my wrists and ankles were fastened with chains—chains that were fixed to the wall behind me, immovable, no matter how hard I strained against them. And my clothes were ripped, my hair a matted mess.

I sat in a small, windowless room, whose walls and floor were stone. The only light emanated from a dim gas lantern on the floor.

Where am I?

My heart pounding, I fixed my eyes on the opposite wall, where jagged words had been scrawled in red paint.

"WELCOME TO PORTEQUE."

I stopped breathing.

Attached to the wall, beneath the words were… photographs? I squinted in the gloom. Each depicted a woman, curled up in a fetal position on a floor that looked very much like the one I was currently sitting on. Behind, and looming over her was a man. His body was cut off at the waist, so all I could see were his legs and heavy boots. Just as every woman was different, so appeared to be every man; different leg heights and shoe sizes. Then, as my eyes fell to the lowest photograph on the wall… I recognized the clothes the girl was wearing.

That girl was me.

What is this?

Before I could consider yelling, I heard footsteps.

The heavy wooden door opened and in stepped a man whom I had seen before. He wore different clothes—unkempt, Porteque-style clothing—but I recognized that scratchy beard. It was the PFL attendant who had taken Viggo away and insisted that I stay behind in the changing room.

A second man entered behind him. He had a tattoo beneath his right eye. I recognized him too. He was the man who had seen me take down his friend in the road—the man who'd gotten away.

They moved toward me, their leering eyes raking me over.

Arriving in front of me, the tattooed man lowered and grabbed my throat. I attempted to fight him off, but there was only so much I could do while my hands and feet were bound. I'd never felt more vulnerable and powerless in my life.

He tilted my head upward and gestured to a shadowy corner in the room that I had not paid much attention to until now. Fixed to the wall was a camera, pointed directly at me. They had been watching me.

"What do you want?" I breathed. The men seemed to be deliberately keeping their backs to the camera.

"First," the tattooed man replied, his voice as scratchy as his companion's beard, "to teach you your place."

His right hand balled into a fist. Gripping my hair with his left hand, he dealt me a crushing blow in the gut. Once, twice, thrice. Winded, I coughed and spluttered, clutching at my sides. I collapsed as he kicked me in the kidney, curling myself up into as tight a ball as I could.

"Ada!" the second man shouted, his voice resounding in the chamber.

I dared glance up as more footsteps echoed.

A short woman entered the room; she was bone-thin, with lanky mousy-brown hair. I didn't think that she was any older than twenty-five, yet she had deep lines around her mouth and forehead. Beneath her right eye, she, too, sported a triangular tattoo.

The moment she laid her dark eyes on me, she lurched forward. Her fingers dug against my scalp and ripped at my hair, forcing me into an upright position.

She bent down to my level and spat in my face.

"You know that it was my husband you took down?" she hissed.

I tried to protect myself as she dealt me a stinging slap across the face. Her thinness was deceiving—she had muscles in those arms.

She struck me again and again, her bony fingers like whips against my skin. Then, reaching for a belt around her waist, she clasped at a handle and drew out a knife. Holding the back of my head, she pulled me closer to her.

"Stop," I wheezed.

She ran the tip of the blade against my upper cheek, beneath my right eye socket, in one sweeping crescent motion.

I cried out again, tears leaking from my eyes.

"Stop," I rasped. "Stop it!"

She came at me again with the knife, but before she could make a second contact with the blade, one of the men gripped her by the arm and snatched the weapon from her hand.

"Enough," he said gruffly. "We don't want her so cut up just yet."

Ada, eyes still glimmering with rage, grabbed my neck and forced my head downward, toward the feet of the tattooed man. She squashed my face against his boots, their grime soiling my skin.

"Know your place before a man!" she hissed.

She held me there for five seconds before releasing me and stepping backward.

I pressed my back against the wall in a feeble attempt to distance myself from the men I was left with.

"The second reason you are here," the tattooed man went on, as if there had been no interruption, "is to assist us in sending a message to any other bitches like you who have managed to leech their way into Patrus."

He moved to me and, holding my hair, panned my head to the camera again. "Say hello," he whispered, his mouth inches from my ear. He snickered, reaching into his pocket and drawing out a strip of brown fabric with two holes gouged into it. His male companion produced the same and so did Ada. They tied them around their heads so that the upper halves of their faces were obscured but for their eyes.

Another man entered the room, both of them sporting similar masks... and one of them carrying a hot iron bar.

The man carrying the bar handed it to Ada. She waved it around before my face, taunting me with it, bringing it closer until its heat caused my skin to break out in a heavy sweat.

She gathered a strand of my hair and trailed it over the hot iron, singeing it and producing a sickening burning smell. She waved the frayed ends of my hair before my face, pressing them to my nostrils.

"Imagine what your skin will smell like."

She grabbed my arm and extended it before glancing at the camera. An oily smile glided across her face as she addressed the lens. "This is for every woman out there who thinks it's okay to shout back at her man."

She lowered the iron bar against my sensitive inner wrist.

My skin exploded in agony. A screech erupted from my throat. I was sure that I would pass out.

Still eyeing the camera, the woman went on, "For every woman who thinks she can cheat, or talk behind his back."

Another strike of the iron bar, a few inches further up my arm. Somehow, it was even worse this time, knowing what was coming. Tears spilled from my eyes as I struggled to break away from her grasp.

Still, she went on addressing the camera, "For every woman who thinks she knows better."

Another burn, climbing up my shoulder. My entire body, drenched in sweat, had begun to shake uncontrollably.

"And this," she said, in a lower voice, a terrifying sense of finality to her tone, "is for every bitch who thinks she's equal."

I was sure that the madwoman was going to strike me in the chest, maybe even drive the sharp end of the rod through my heart… So it came as a surprise when she stalled, and instead placed the rod down on the floor.

The runaway criminal standing behind Ada gave me a knowing smile, relishing my fear.

Bastard. I saw your cowardly ass run away from me back on that street.

He bent down to my level and I flinched as his hand gripped the side of my face, his calloused thumb touching my cheek.

"It's a shame," he said. "Look at you—young, blessed with good looks, a nice body… We don't treat all female visitors to Porteque like this, you know. Some of them we even make wives out of, like Ada. We found her at sixteen."

"Why are you telling me this?" I croaked.

He sighed. "I'm not telling you as much as I'm telling the women who will watch this."

He let go of my face and rose to his feet. He addressed his companions surrounding us. "Bring in the table."

One of the men exited and returned a few seconds later, pushing along a rickety steel table on wheels. It had wrist and ankle holds attached to either end of it. Ada manifested a key and freed me from my current chains one at a time. I immediately leapt for the door, but it was a hopeless endeavor. My captors crowded around me, wrestling me into submission. They dragged me to the table where they strapped me down. These restraints were tighter and it felt like they stopped the blood flowing to my feet and hands. Maybe that was the idea.

As they gathered around me, the runaway man spoke: "Cut her."

I writhed as they reached into their belts and withdrew knives. They used the steel edges of the table to sharpen the blades, Ada on my right even gouging me in the thigh as she did so, deliberately careless.

These people are insane.

"Stop!" I begged. "Please, I'll do anything! Just stop!"

That I had resorted to begging these animals cut me to the core, deeper than any knife could. It felt like renouncing any semblance of dignity I had left.

These people needed to be lined up and shot. If only I had a gun. Ms. Dale's last-minute training would've actually been useful.

"How do you want to do this?" Ada asked the runaway. They appeared to have finished sharpening their knives.

The runaway, standing closest to my head, replied, "Same as the last."

His answer brought a dozen nightmarish visions to my mind. As their knives descended on me, all I could do was close my eyes and pray. I thought of Viggo, about the chance I'd never have to see him again, and about the mission and my lost opportunity to reunite with Tim.

As the blades began to press into me, piercing skin, a man yelled outside.

"EVACUATE!"

The door burst open and in stepped another man, face shining with sweat, eyes alight with alarm. "Wardens!" he panted.

The word sent relief rolling through my body.

"WHAT?" the runaway man yelled back. "Impossible! They can't have reached us so quickly!"

"They're here!" he insisted.

Ada and the men surrounding me swore. Shoving their knives back in their belts, they loosened me from the table before grabbing hold of me. The tallest man—the runaway—hauled me over his shoulder, dangling me upside down, while a second man grabbed my wrists and held them tightly together. That didn't stop me from thrashing my legs. As they carried me out of the dank room and up a flight of grimy stairs, the man holding my wrists connected his knee with my face, sending my head into another tailspin.

I could no longer keep track of where we were going or who was around me. All I knew was that their route was dark and bumpy, and then the air suddenly became a lot colder. A chill wind caused my skin to break out in goosebumps. We were outside.

I caught the glare of headlights to our right, and a loud roaring noise in the distance. Then came gunshots. We reached some kind of vehicle and I was shoved into a spacious trunk and locked inside.

I had no idea how much time had passed since I had been kidnapped. But the man had said that the wardens' arrival was quick. I had no idea how the "wardens" had managed to locate me so quickly, given that Porteque was supposed to be tucked away in the depths of the mountains—somewhere even Viggo seemed hesitant to enter.

I was rolled from side to side as the vehicle picked up speed, in spite of the hard bumps in whatever road—or track—we were following. I tried to grab hold of something to avoid more injury, but soon we were traveling so fast, the bumps so wild, it was impossible to avoid getting banged about.

What's going on?

Where are they taking me?

The ground tilted in a slope. I rolled to the other side of the trunk. My stomach dropped. We were going downhill. Fast.

The gunshots grew louder behind us.

The base of the vehicle vibrated, then we shuddered to a stop that sent the back of my head smashing against the trunk's side wall.

The truck bobbed as people climbed out, unloading it of weight, and then the trunk opened. Two hands shot inside and grabbed me, yanking me out, and my feet sank into shallow water. We were in the dip of a wooded area and, as I gazed around wildly, I noticed we were surrounded by a crowd of men—and one woman—and five trucks. I gazed up at the slope we had just descended. Its steepness made me feel nauseated. The gunshots echoing down came from somewhere near the top.

The man, whom I realized was the same coward who had run away, tugged on me, pulling me through the water as everyone else began to cross the stream.

I wouldn't let them drag me further.

The man must've thought that I was too weak to put up much of a fight now. My nose had started bleeding again, and my brain was clouded, but desperation had a way of making you find strength you thought you'd lost.

I dropped all of my weight downward, my backside hitting the rocky bed of the stream. My wrist slipped from the man's grasp and I lurched for his knees, toppling him backward into the water. As he landed, his right hand instantly moved to his knife. But I had already predicted that.

I slid the blade out of its sheath and without a second's hesitation slashed his throat in a fit of fury. His blood drenched my hands and arms and flowed around me as I fought to stand up… only to be instantly struck by a vicious blow to the back of my head. The jolt caused my grip around the knife to slacken and it flew from my hands as I tripped. The upper half of me fell on land, but my legs and feet still trailed in the water.

I cried out as a foot stamped down on my back. Then hands gripped my neck, fingers gouging into my throat. With whatever renewed energy I'd managed to summon rapidly ebbing away, I fumbled around on the ground, searching for a sharp rock. Discovering a stone that felt jagged enough to cut skin, I raised my arms and pressed down hard against the man's hands with one palm, while using the other hand to rip sharply with the pointed tip of the stone where I estimated his wrist was.

Wherever I'd managed to strike, it worked. His hold on me loosened enough for me to gasp for air. I twisted myself around, only to see my latest attacker joined by five other men. They weren't going to mess around this time. They knew it. I knew it. The deprivation of oxygen had made me too weak to stand up anymore. I couldn't even attempt to continue defending myself.

As the closest man leapt for me, all I could think to do was curl myself up in a ball, as if that would somehow soften the pain of the impact.

His full weight crashed down on me, knocking my head back.

But I did not feel the tip of the knife or slash of the blade.

No. All I felt was his crushing weight.

I managed to slither out from beneath him and glanced up to see the other men had stopped in their tracks. Not just stopped, but they were beginning to scatter, racing across the stream and into the woods on the other side.

That was when I realized why the man on top of me had become so… motionless. As I slid out from under him completely, his face thunked against the ground. At the back of his head was a round, bloody bullet hole.

I scrambled backward and tried to stand up, but I felt too dizzy. When I looked toward the slope where the bullet must have come from, my eyes found a tall figure running toward me through the trees. With the silhouette of a long gun in his right hand, his outline was familiar, even in the darkness. Wavy hair. The straight shape of a trench coat.

I almost cried out in relief as Viggo's face emerged, illuminated by soft shafts of moonlight. His eyes gleamed with anxiety as he took in my bloodied state.

"Whose blood is that?" he uttered in a strained whisper.

I looked toward the stream and pointed to the corpse of the man whose throat I'd torn open. Then I spotted the knife, still coated with blood. It had fallen on the ground, not far away.

Shouts of wardens drifted down from the slope. Viggo cursed. Throwing a sharp glance in their direction, he hurried into the stream and dragged the corpse out. Then he scooped up the knife. Wrapping his hands around its handle, to my shock, he drove it back into the dead man's throat.

Leaving the blade erect, he leapt toward me, slipping one strong arm beneath my knees, the other wrapping around my waist. Then he picked me up and began to run with me.

But not in the direction I'd expected him to; not back up the slope he'd come from. Instead, confusingly, he dashed across the stream and reached the opposite side. Shooting another look over his shoulder toward his rapidly approaching colleagues, he hurtled into the woods with me. The same woods the Porteque men were escaping into. The same woods the wardens were firing bullets toward. One hissed past us now, frighteningly close.

"Viggo," I panted. "What—?"

"Don't talk," he breathed, his eyes trained ahead of us.

I clung to him more tightly as the slope on this side steepened. I pulled myself closer against him, my bloodied hands slipping against the skin behind his neck.

My heart hammered as I caught sight of silhouettes of the Porteque gang up ahead.

What is Viggo thinking? Is he going after them? While carrying me? *Has he gone mad?*

As I had become almost fully convinced that he was chasing after the criminals, Viggo's direction diverged from them. He swerved diagonally to our left, while they were moving decidedly right.

The trees became denser as he continued to run, and the bullets no longer reached us. The gunshots grew fainter, and the loudest noises became Viggo's heavy boots crunching in the brushwood and his harried breathing so close to my ear. I could practically feel his heart pounding against me.

I had never witnessed Viggo so tense. For the first time since I'd met him, he showed fear.

I needed first aid. I needed to visit a hospital.

The gushing of water came within earshot. Then a clearing came into view, through which ran a river. Its surface glistened in the moonlight as we approached. Finally, Viggo came to a stop.

He looked down at me. "Can you stand?"

"I-I'm not sure."

He exhaled. "Okay."

Lowering me gently, he seated me at the edge of the bank. He proceeded to remove his coat, belt and gun and hang it on a branch. Then he returned to me, wearing the same shirt and pants he'd worn earlier in the day before the fight. He sat down next to me and swung his legs into the water and the next thing I knew, he'd dropped into it, submerging his upper chest, still fully clothed. Apparently, he was tall—and steady—enough to touch the bottom, even with the current.

He winced. "It's cold. But we have to get you cleaned up. There was no time back in that stream."

I examined myself more closely. It wasn't just my hands, arms and face that had gotten splattered with the blood. There were stains on my neck, upper chest, lower torso and clothes. I removed the torn garments, balled them up, and discarded them in the river. Now I wore only my underwear, which was also stained.

"Come," he coaxed softly.

My body tensed up as I slipped off the bank's edge, into his open arms. My chest constricted, my skin breaking out in goosebumps. I wound my arms around Viggo's neck and pulled my body flush against his, for support amidst the current, and for warmth.

"You're worried I could be punished for killing that man?" I panted against his hair.

I felt him swallow against my shoulder. A pause ensued.

"Do you want to know what happened to Miriam? My wife?" His voice was hoarse.

"What?" I whispered, as my stomach clenched with guilt at the thought that I already knew.

"She was hanged for defending herself in a situation not all that different from this. She killed an attacker without a neutral witness." Viggo's chest heaved beneath me. I sensed an undercurrent of guilt to his tone. *Does he blame himself for her death?* "I… I'm not saying the same insane rule would apply to you. Even the court doesn't care much about what happens to these Porteque dregs. But it's not worth the risk."

He created a few inches' gap between us. His eyes studied my arms before he began to run a palm along them, down to my hands, rinsing me of the blood. The current was doing a good job of cleaning my torso and chest on its own.

"I'll say I killed him if anyone questions it," he continued. "I planted my handprint on the knife."

"There'll be no consequences for you?"

"None to speak of."

"How will you explain both of us being sopping wet when we return?" I asked, shivering as one of his hands ascended to tenderly brush against the side of my face.

"I'll tell them one of the guys split from the group with you, and I found the two of you crossing a river, where I headed him off. He got away, but I managed to get a hold of you."

"You're a good liar."

He gritted his teeth and held my gaze. "Sometimes that's what's required to do what is right in Patrus."

I looked down, experiencing a spike of discomfort.

"Okay. I think you're done." He gathered me to him and moved us back to the bank. Climbing out, he settled me on the ground before heading to the branch where he'd hung his possessions. He retrieved the coat and brought it to me, hanging its heavy weight around my shoulders. The smell of him immediately made me feel safe and protected. "Better remove your underwear, too. Just throw it in the river and keep my coat."

I breathed in. "Okay. "

Viggo turned his back on me while I maneuvered my way out of my bra and panties. I hurled them into the river before pulling on his long coat. I fastened up the zipper to my neck. "You can turn around," I murmured.

He turned and bent down and scooped me up. As he rose and I tightened my grip around his shoulders, I realized my hands were trembling. Aside from the cold, I was still recovering from shock.

When Viggo began to run again—gripping me as though he feared I might loosen my hold—my cheek fell against his shoulder. His fear was not unfounded. I fought to maintain consciousness, but exhaustion finally claimed me. I faded out.

CHAPTER 27

I woke to the noise of whirring rotors. I was lying on something soft. Narrow, but comfortable. Someone's palm was pressed on my forehead. I opened my eyes.

Viggo's handsome face hung over me. His hair was wet, and tied back. His dark brows had been deeply furrowed, but became less so as our eyes locked. He removed his hand from my head. I tried to sit up, but he pushed me back down.

We were in the belly of some kind of aircraft. The walls were rounded and lined with metal panels. This was the first time I'd ever been in an aircraft, let alone flown in one. The sensation was unsettling. My ears felt blocked.

I was lying on a cushioned stretcher, Viggo sitting beside me on a stool. Memories of the night washed over me and I relived every terrifying moment. Waking up in the dark and the cold. The lack of control. The fear. The pain. The humiliation. The anger. The relief.

I was still wrapped in Viggo's coat. I felt its inner lining brush against my bare skin; it took the edge off my still-damp hair and body. I reached up to my face. I had a bandage over my nose.

I stared up at Viggo. "How did you find me?"

"Thanks to your husband," Viggo replied. His voice was low, like he hadn't spoken in a while.

"Lee?" I breathed. "Where is he?"

"He's back in the city," Viggo explained. "But he was able to communicate to me your location. The moment I realized you were gone, I called him and he was able to guide me and my team."

"But how would Lee know?"

Now it was Viggo's turn to look confused. "You didn't know that he has you tracked?"

My breath hitched. *No. I didn't know that.*

Since when had Lee been tracking me?

I had looked at his computer only recently to watch Viggo's red dot on the map, and I hadn't shown up there. As I turned my mind back to the last few days, I realized he must have done it the night he got annoyed with me. The night I'd told him I had encouraged Viggo to enter the PFL, and potentially mess up our whole schedule. The night Lee had first kissed me.

Whatever Lee's motives—be they borne out of some kind of possessiveness or not—I could only be grateful now that he had done it. Otherwise, I would have likely died in that dark basement.

"I did know," I lied, rubbing my head. "I just—with everything, I didn't put two and two together."

"As soon as we touch down in the city, I'll take you to the hospital. Your husband said that he will be waiting there for you."

"Okay," I said, swallowing. My mind turned back to earlier. "Hey, what happened with the fight?"

"Forget the fight!" he growled. "I left the arena as soon as I found you gone. It was that damn attendant, wasn't it? The one who told you to stay in the room."

I nodded. "And the runaway criminal, from the other day…" *The man I killed.* I explained to Viggo who else I'd seen, including Ada.

Viggo scowled. "That arena needs better screening as to who gets in and out. As for the others, I still have men back there making arrests… You remember we saw members from that gang, sitting in the square after the Rosen-Cruz fight. They were watching you, probably trying to find a way to get at you then, too. The gangs of Porteque don't take kindly to women rising above their role, God forbid when it's against one of their own. They took your felling one of them as an insult to their entire clan."

"They're insane," I breathed.

"They'd call themselves law-upholding," Viggo said darkly.

We lapsed into a span of silence. Trying to turn my mind away from the horrors of the night, I thought once again of Viggo's missed fight. He had just… walked out.

Abandoning Cruz, the organizers and thousands of fans. Guilt gripped me.

"Thank you, Viggo," I whispered, my throat thick.

He didn't acknowledge my words. He averted his gaze over his shoulder. "How much longer?" he called to an unseen colleague.

"Five minutes," a man called back.

We sat wordlessly for the rest of the journey. On descending, Viggo slipped his arms beneath me, picking me up again. He carried me out of the aircraft and we emerged on a landing strip on top of a towering building. Surrounding us was Patrus City.

"How far is the hospital?" I asked him as he carried me through a door which led to a stairwell.

"This is the hospital."

His answer came as a disappointment, which confused me. I'd been beaten up; I needed to see a doctor and be treated. But somehow I'd been expecting a little more delay until meeting Lee again... until leaving Viggo.

Viggo wound down the stairwell and pushed us through a set of double doors, which led us to a bustling hallway. Doctors—all male, of course—were moving in and out of rooms, pushing carts, speaking with patients. And then we spotted Lee, sitting tensely on a bench at the end of the corridor. He sprang up as soon as he spotted us and hurried to close the distance.

His face was deathly pale. His chest heaved in relief as Viggo transferred me to his arms, Lee's citrusy scent overtaking Viggo's.

"Good man, Viggo," Lee said hoarsely. "Good man."

Viggo merely nodded, his green eyes locking with mine for a second longer, before he turned and disappeared down the crowded corridor.

CHAPTER 28

Lee and I didn't get the opportunity to talk much about what had happened before I was called in for my appointment with Dr. Milman, which turned out to be a lot more intrusive than I had anticipated. In Matrus, all doctors were females (with the exception of just one male who was the son of one of Queen Rina's courtiers). I guessed now I knew what it felt like for Matrus males every time they needed an examination.

Dr. Milman focused on doing everything he could for my injuries—stitched up the cuts, applied a thick white cream to my burns before bandaging them—and after Lee returned to the room, he informed me that I could leave. He equipped us with several bottles of medication and cream along with extra bandages, and said that the best thing I could do for recovery was rest.

The doctor arranged for a wheelchair for Lee to borrow so he didn't have to carry me everywhere. I was still feeling dizzy whenever I stood, but the doctor said that should resolve itself in a day or two.

Lee wheeled me downstairs and outside to the road where he hailed a taxi. Once inside, I found myself rehashing everything that had happened, with Lee asking for every harrowing detail.

I was relieved when we arrived back at Lee's house and once inside he carried me up the stairs, to my room. He laid me down on the bed and tucked me beneath the covers.

"How are you feeling now?" he asked, looking me over with concern as he stood by my bedside.

My eyelids felt heavy as lead. I needed to sleep.

Lee took the hint. "I'll leave you alone," he said. "You have to recover as quickly as possible. We have only four days left… Whatever happens, we can't let this interfere with the banquet."

CHAPTER 29

*T*he banquet.

As much as I tried to put off thinking about it, the time was drawing too close now. As much as I struggled to continue brushing it aside, I couldn't. I could no longer keep it thrust down to the depths of my subconscious.

Only four days left.

Four days, and I will be calling Viggo to the scene of the crime.

Four days, and I will be framing him for an atrocity he didn't commit.

Four days, and I will have ruined his life… Maybe given the Court reason to take it from him.

None of my previous techniques for numbing myself worked anymore. Maybe it was the stillness I was forced to inhabit, the quiet of my room as even Lee left me alone for hours on end.

It was as if every emotion I'd kept pent up since the beginning of this mission came flooding out at once. Overwhelming me. Drowning me.

How could I have ever agreed to do this?

Viggo had rescued me from death and here I was contemplating in only a few sleeps' time, pulling the rug out from under his feet. Stabbing him in the back in the worst possible way. I had made him trust me enough to show his vulnerability: the loss of his wife, his struggle with Patrian society, and his readiness even now to defy the rules. I had become his *friend*. Why else would he have left the fight to save me if he didn't value our friendship? If he didn't like me? He could have informed Lee of my disappearance and then left the rest of his team to look for me. He'd been off-duty at that time, anyway. He hadn't needed to leave the fight for me, nor had he needed to cover up the murder I'd committed. And yet he'd done all this. He'd foregone the mass of money he could have made from that fight, angered thousands of people, and maybe even put his sparkling future career on the line... all for me.

I shook my head as I lay in bed with my eyes closed.

No. No. I can't do this. I can't do this.

The hours slipped away at terrifying speed. Soon night had come around again. Then morning.

Lee's brief appearances to check in on me came as simply blips in time, brief interruptions to my agonizing over Viggo. He informed me that he'd washed Viggo's coat and taken it to the wardens' head office for him to collect.

Alastair called the evening of the third day before the banquet to speak to both of us. Lee told me that it was best not to tell him about the kidnapping—that it would only freak him out.

So I told Alastair that everything was going smoothly, even as I was screaming inside.

I told him that Lee and I would be ready for the banquet, even as I ached.

I didn't know what to do, or what to say—if anything—to Lee. I felt trapped in a web of my own making. Tangled up in knots with no hand to free me.

Although I should be focusing on nothing but my recovery, I was barely even aware of my physical state anymore. I used the cream and medication as the doctor prescribed, mechanically, by rote, barely even bothering to check the progress of my healing in the mirror.

I was too far gone, my mind lost on a different stratum.

Do I tell Lee what I'm feeling?

I feared his reaction, and I didn't want to lay any more stress on him than he was under already, but I finally reached a precipice where I felt I would lose my mind if I kept my emotions bottled up even an hour longer.

So, when I heard him return to the house, I called for him. He came climbing up the stairs and entered my room, sitting on the edge of my bed.

"Are you okay?" he asked, tensing.

I propped myself upright against the headboard and drew in a breath. "Lee..." My voice came out uneven.

"I-I don't know that I can do this." *I can't do this.* I could hardly believe what I was thinking. *I have a reunion with my brother on the line!*

Lee heaved a sigh. He reached out a hand and cupped my knee, squeezing gently. "Violet, I understand your nerves. In spite of my preparation, I still find myself doubting. Can we really pull this off? Will we get out alive? Etcetera, etcetera. You need to stop thinking. We have only two days left, and then there will only be *doing*. Two days, and you should be out of here... back home. Safe. Two days left, that's all. So just... keep it together. Okay?"

"But Viggo," I croaked. "He saved my life. He sacrificed—"

"Violet," Lee said, sterner this time at the mention of Viggo. "Remember what I said. Don't lose sight of the bigger picture. In fact, you should *only* be thinking of the bigger picture. Nothing else. That's all you're here for. Once you keep your mind focused on the goal, all the details become insignificant... just moving pieces on the board. Pawns in the game. You understand?"

I didn't. I neither understood nor agreed with what Lee was saying. I could no longer accept that implicating Viggo was the *only* way. And yet even I could see that there was no point continuing this discussion. As much as I wished I could speak honestly with Lee to release some of the pressure escalating within me, he was a closed book. It was far too late in the game to be bringing up feelings and sentiments. None of it mattered. In Lee's mind, the plan was already chalked out for us, set in stone. After his preparation in the lab, the explosives he'd set up, the destruction they would cause, and the lives they would claim, there was no moving backward.

We were on a freight train with broken brakes.

We had to execute, or die trying.

But as Lee left me to rest again and get an early night, I knew that I had become a different kind of passenger. The kind of passenger to leap from a runaway train. The kind who would not wait until the end.

CHAPTER 30

Once midnight fell, I swung my legs off the bed.

I stood up and didn't feel dizzy.

I walked around the room, my back straight, head up high. Still no dizziness. Then I moved to the bathroom and stared at myself in the mirror. My face was still bruised, of course, and the stitching beneath my eye still fresh. I searched my drawers to check my mustache and facial hair hadn't been removed and found them still there along with the adhesive and my wig.

I padded to the door and opened it a crack. The corridor outside was dark. I poked my head out fully, then stepped out. I couldn't hear any sounds indicating that Lee was downstairs, so I headed to his room and pressed my ear against the door. Deep, heavy breathing. He was asleep.

I hurried back to my room and applied the facial hair and wig in record time, then pulled on a jacket. I didn't need to bother with the bulky body suit. It was nighttime, so hopefully nobody would see me anyway.

Finishing in the bathroom, I approached my bed and stuffed three spare cushions beneath the blanket to make it look like my form was lying there—in case Lee came in for a brief glance during the night. I needed to buy myself as much time as possible.

Samuel was asleep in his basket outside the kitchen, and I hardly dared to breathe as I made my way to the front door. I picked up Lee's chain of keys hanging from the coat rack, pulled on a pair of shoes, and then slowly, carefully, went about opening the door. The metal was well-oiled and the mechanism opened with a soft click. I closed it and locked it behind me before heading round the building to Lee's motorcycle that was leaning against the wall.

Even though I was able to drive whatever vehicle I wanted in Matrus—I had never actually learned. I had spent too much time in detention to have come across the chance. Now, as I rolled the motorcycle out of the driveway, out of view from the house, I felt terrified. I barely knew how to start it—everything I was about to do was based on witnessing Lee and Viggo drive their motorcycles.

But this was the only way I could make it to Viggo's house.

This was the only way.

After strapping one of the helmets to my head and pushing the motorcycle a comfortable distance away from

Lee's house, I dared attempt to start it up at the side of the road. It took a minute before I managed it. It came alive more easily than I expected. Now I had to hope that riding it would come just as smoothly... It didn't.

As I hopped on, I immediately lost balance and my right leg almost got crushed beneath the falling machine. It took a good five minutes for me to feel comfortable raising my feet from the ground again. I revved the engine, causing the motorcycle to jerk forward. I almost lost balance a second time. I feared I might swerve off the road before I ever reached Viggo's.

But there was no time for second thoughts. I couldn't afford to entertain doubts.

I spurred the vehicle ahead, as slowly as I could without having the engine conk out due to the slope we were ascending, before gradually building confidence and rolling faster. I had two advantages at least: first, the roads up here weren't busy, and second, I knew the way to Viggo's cabin fairly well.

So, I found myself hurtling through the night, the road slipping away beneath me.

Framing Viggo wasn't the only way. I knew it wasn't. There had to be other scapegoats we could use. We could pin the whole operation on the men of Porteque. Leave a message behind on a building in big red letters or something, declaring it to be an act of rebellion. They were already anarchists, so this could follow on naturally from their recent kidnapping of me.

Whatever the case, once I'd seen Viggo, Lee and I would have no choice but to scramble around for another solution to prevent the blame falling on Matrus. Lee would be mad at me, but I didn't care. We'd figure out a last-minute alternative, because we'd have to. We both had too much at stake to fail in this mission.

Drops of rain began to fall. Drops which soon multiplied and came down harder and heavier, until I was drenched to my underwear.

Still, it didn't matter.

Almost there now. Almost there.

I was shivering by the time I recognized the turn down Viggo's lane. The rain had become torrential and it was a wonder that I hadn't skidded off the road entirely. I trundled down the dirt track—fast turning to thick mud—and skidded to a stop ten feet before Viggo's cabin.

No gas lamps shone through the gaps in the shutters. Perhaps he wasn't even home.

I had to pray that he was only asleep.

Discarding the motorcycle, I stood, my knees feeling shaky from the journey. The first thing I did was reach for my fake hair and tear it off, shoving it into my pockets. I might not even need it again after tonight.

My blood pounding in my ears, I hurried to Viggo's porch and scaled the steps to his front door. I hesitated to catch a breath, then knocked four times.

No answer.

I knocked again, five times, more loudly.

Still nothing.

Oh, no. Don't say he's out after all.

I left the porch, striding back out into the rain, and circled the building. Shutters covered every window. I couldn't see through a single one of them. Moving back toward the front of the building, I stopped dead in my tracks.

A light had been lit. As I turned a corner, at the bottom of the porch stairs was Viggo, wearing nothing but boxer shorts. His hair was mussed, his eyelids hooded. I had obviously woken him up.

But his expression came to life on realizing his intruder was me.

"Violet!" He gaped. "What are you doing here?" His eyes shot to the motorcycle, his face falling. "Where is your husband?"

I stood rooted to my spot as though paralyzed. "He's not here," I rasped.

Viggo launched forward and grabbed me by the hand, pulling me toward his porch, up the stairs and through to his cabin. He slammed the door behind us, towering over me in the hallway. He turned on me, backing me against the wall, his expression a mixture of alarm and utter confusion.

"You… You *drove* here?" he demanded.

My hands balled up. I nodded, holding his intense gaze.

"What the *hell* has gotten into you? Do you know the punishment you could receive for that infraction? And that's leaving aside the fact that you've roamed across a mountain at night completely on your own—have you forgotten what just happened to you?" He gripped my shoulders in frustration as I merely stared back at him. "Say something, dammit!"

I'd gone over what I was going to say to him in my mind already, but now that I was here, standing in this stupidly narrow corridor, Viggo so close to me we were practically touching, I felt breathless. Claustrophobic.

"I, uh, I need to tell you something," I managed, my voice deeper than it should have been.

His brows rose, eyes widening. "Clearly!"

I couldn't go so far as to tell him the truth, obviously. He couldn't know that I was a spy, that I'd been trying to frame him all along, or anything about our mission. After telling him all that, he'd likely not trust another word I said. Why should he? I had no idea how he'd react or what he'd do, and I couldn't run the risk of losing the chance to see my brother again. A chance I *still* was convinced that I had.

I just needed to make sure that Viggo didn't come anywhere near the lab tomorrow—even if I failed to convince Lee that the Porteque men would be better scapegoats.

Gathering confidence, I looked Viggo seriously in the eye, parting my lips to speak… but before I could utter a word, my jacket pocket vibrated. When I slipped a hand inside my pocket, it closed around my pager. I'd forgotten it was still in there. My throat drying out, I lifted the pager and glanced at the screen.

"SAY ANYTHING, AND HE WILL BE ASSASSINATED."
My blood ran cold.

Lee had woken up and tracked me down. I'd known all along this was a possibility, but I had been hoping against hope that I would make it back in time.

But what is Lee talking about?

Have Viggo assassinated?

Why?

How?

"Violet?" Viggo drew my attention back to him. "What's going on? Did your husband send a message?"

I hurriedly stuffed the pager back into my pocket. My first instinct was to assume that Lee had panicked on seeing me at Viggo's and was now bluffing out of desperation. *Lee doesn't even have those sorts of contacts here, does he?* I thought back to the moving red dots on Lee's computer screen. Lee had told me that they were people whose "help" he'd used. I wasn't sure to what extent that "help" could stretch, or how much he trusted them. Obviously not enough to work with him in directly stealing the egg; otherwise, why did he need me? Or maybe Lee would find a way to pull off the assassination himself.

I supposed it was possible that Lee wasn't bluffing.

But why? Why was assassination necessary? It was as though Lee was assuming that I'd lost myself to guilt and was about to spill everything to Viggo.

"Violet!" Viggo urged.

I parted my lips, on the verge of going through with my original plan. But Lee's message had burned itself into my brain.

Assassinated.

Maybe there were other reasons he (or his mysterious "helpers") would be forced to end Viggo. Reasons I wasn't aware of. Lee had said from the very beginning that Viggo was one of our biggest obstacles... and that was why Lee had sent me in to neutralize him.

Only in the process, I've become neutralized myself. I'd gotten "carried away". Exactly what Lee had repeatedly warned me against.

I tried to forecast Viggo's life in a few days' time, assuming that I went ahead with Lee's plan. Viggo would be facing death on that path, too. The state would offer him no less punishment for the crime. But maybe down that route, there was a chance that he would find a way out. A chance that he would find some evidence to prove himself innocent. Maybe Viggo could convince the authorities to conduct an in-depth investigation into the matter... Viggo would suspect me, having received my call to the crime scene. Maybe he wouldn't even link me to Matrus; maybe he'd think that I'd been traumatized and threatened so severely by the men of Porteque during my time captive there that I was doing their bidding in causing disruption. As I recalled the brainwashed Ada, that could be a plausible assumption.

And perhaps people would assume that I'd burned in the blast, so there would be no wondering where I'd gone.

And I'd be back in Matrus. Maybe even already reunited with my brother by the time investigations came to any conclusion.

As strange as it sounded, letting Viggo face Patrus' judicial system seemed like a better chance of survival for him.

"Violet!" Viggo clutched my shoulders and shook me again, forcing me to look him in the eye. "What did you come to tell me about? What could have *possibly* been so important that you felt the need to travel to me in the middle of the night without your husband?"

In his exasperation, Viggo had moved closer to me still. I could no longer take the pressure of his imposing form in such proximity. Pushing past him, I strode into the living room, clutching my head, my back turned to him.

Now I couldn't think of a single good reason I could offer as to why I had come here. Why I had gone behind my husband's back...

I might have already done irreparable damage by coming here tonight. Piqued his interest in Lee's and my relationship to a point where it should never have been piqued.

Viggo entered the living room after me. His tone had become calmer, quieter—more hesitant—as he said, "Has Lee... done something to you? Did you have an argument or..."

"No," I said, shaking my head firmly. "Nothing like that. We-We're okay." My pitch rose as I repeated, "We're okay."

The floorboards creaked. Viggo stood just a foot behind me now. I could hear his breathing. Breathe in his scent. My heartbeat quickened as his hand closed gently around my shoulder, endearing me to turn around.

"Then... what?" he asked.

I faced him. Blood rushed to my cheeks as I took in his tired face, his forehead lined with confusion. The stubble around his jaw had grown noticeably since the last time I'd seen him a few days ago, adding to his jaded appearance.

His confusion stabbed me with guilt. But more than confused... he looked concerned. Concerned, just as he had been after finding me wandering the streets alone, the second night of my arrival in Patrus. As he had been when he'd held my arm tightly after our encounter with the gang members outside the Rosen-Cruz fight. As he had been when saving me from Porteque and covering up my murder. After I'd woken up to him in the helicopter. And just now, as I'd arrived outside his house with a motorcycle in the pouring rain.

Viggo Croft was a good man.

Better than my Matrian upbringing had ever allowed me to imagine existed on this side of the river, or on my side.

He was the best I'd known on either side.

As he sighed, apparently giving up hope of ever receiving an answer from me, I no longer needed to wonder how to respond.

When I gazed at his face, adrenaline surged in me. My pulse raced. For the first time, I knew exactly what to do. It didn't require any thinking. Any weighing of the pros and cons. Just instinct. Pure, inescapable instinct.

"If you're not going to talk, then I need to take you—"

Viggo's voice trailed off as I closed the small distance between us. My arms acted of their own accord as they wound around his neck and shoulders. Then they were pulling me upward, closer, until I was standing on my tiptoes. My brows furrowed, my eyelids shut… and then my lips were on his. Heat rolled through my body.

His lips were firm. Voluminous. Lips that cushioned mine in a way that made me want to take them in my mouth one at a time, experience their fullness slowly, thoroughly. Lips that could engulf mine if he responded. But I didn't expect him to respond. He had frozen, arms stiff at his sides, every muscle beneath his bare shoulders and chest tensed against me.

Any second, I expected him to grab my arms and push me away. Insist that I leave.

But he didn't pry me off. Although he remained static… he was allowing me to kiss him. My chest fluttering, I dared raise my eyelids half open. His eyes were closed tight. A deep frown marring his features, he looked stricken with conflict.

Still, he didn't push me away.

He must have sensed I'd opened my eyes, for his opened a few seconds later—only halfway, like mine. We gazed at each other like two people drowning, neither of us having the strength to surface, even in the face of sinking deeper.

Then, at some point during those few dazed seconds, something sparked in Viggo's green irises. Fervor. Hunger... Need. And suddenly, my lips were no longer maintaining control. His lips moved, prying from my grasp, before returning a second later to establish dominance. His mouth claimed mine, unhurriedly at first, the way he might scope out a new opponent in the cage. Then it escalated to a strength that left me struggling to breathe. His kiss forced every muscle in my mouth to awaken as the rest of his body loosened, coming alive. His hands dove into my hair, his powerful fingers threading through its length before trailing down my back. His lips refusing to unlock from mine for even a second, he lowered himself, dragging his hands down to my thighs before hoisting me up against his hips. He moved to the nearest wall and pressed me against it. His palms ran the length from my knees to my thighs. Then they slid beneath my shirt. The coarseness of his hands against my bare skin lit me up. He stopped above my navel, his fingers curving round my waist as he held me firmly in place.

He'd pinned me, and now he had me.

His tongue parted my lips, allowing me to feel it for the first time. It brushed against the tip of mine before moving deeper. Exploring. Then devouring.

My senses were lost in him. His scent, his taste, his hard breathing. He had overpowered me completely, and I was losing this fight. Willingly losing it.

When I'd moved in, I'd had no game plan, no clear idea of what I was even doing, let alone how long I'd let it last. I'd just felt the overwhelming need to release my tension around him. To finally provide him with a response he'd been hounding me for. *Perhaps even to say goodbye.*

But I didn't think it would last long.

Time had lost its meaning, however. My mind had become comfortably numb. Viggo's mouth, taut skin and forceful grip became all that existed in my world.

I was afraid now to pull apart. Having figured out a pattern to regulate my breathing against the rhythm of his passion, I found myself slipping out of defense mode. Anchoring myself higher up against him, I wrapped my legs tightly around his waist, pulling my chest flush against his. I clutched the sides of his face, relishing the prickle of his stubble beneath my fingers. Like the mountains he insisted on living among, everything about Viggo was raw. Wild. *Real.* He was unadulterated masculinity. From his thick waves of hair to his rough, cut-up fists. I hadn't thought it possible for one person to crave another as I did in this moment… least of all a woman for a man.

I feared we might drown even deeper that night, the two of us alone in this cabin. Especially as his hands moved higher beneath my shirt, his thumbs tracing the top of my breasts, his palms grazing my bra cups.

But we never got the chance to test our self-restraint.

As a sharp rapping sounded at the door, Viggo and I were torn apart.

We stood, frozen, lips and cheeks flushed red, our hearts thumping. Reality slammed into us, and our delicate illusion shattered. We stared at each other as strangers would, stunned by what had happened. By what we had *allowed* to happen.

There was no time for words. Viggo, trailing a quick hand through his hair, snatched up a shirt hanging over the back of his armchair and jerked it over his head. While I—with no mirror to assist me—attempted to pat down my hair, straighten my clothes and look as though Viggo's hands hadn't just been up my shirt.

Searching my face, Viggo's eyes were still glassy, shining with desire, as I suspected mine were.

His expression was questioning. I nodded, even as I tried to tame my erratic breathing, still my trembling hands.

I was as ready to face Lee now as I ever would be.

CHAPTER 31

Viggo opened the front door to reveal Lee standing on the porch in a long black anorak with an umbrella tucked beneath one arm, dark circles beneath his eyes. "Viggo," he said. I could hardly hold Lee's gaze as he glanced my way. "I'm so sorry for this." Lee held out a hand to me and I had no choice but to brush past Viggo and take it, like an obedient child, allowing Lee to pull me next to him on the porch. His arm found my waist and he held me against him. "Violet has been unstable since Porteque. The doctor said it could be a long time before she recovers from the trauma. She's been sleep-walking, going blank when I ask her questions… I didn't think she'd ever do something as crazy as this."

Viggo didn't say a word. He stood, his face stoic, his eyes remaining determinedly on Lee. I averted my own gaze to the floor. It was torture to look Viggo in the eye now. Every fiber of my being still burned for him. My lips still tingled from his kiss. The scent and feel of his bare skin still tantalized me. Standing there in his doorway, his hair loose and mussed, eyes alight with a gleam that told me his consciousness, too, was still trapped living in the moments before Lee's arrival… he was temptation personified to me. I guessed I was the same for Viggo, given his refusal to look at me.

"I understand that you are bound to report my wife for this transgression," Lee said, giving my waist a tense squeeze. "But given everything she's been through… Would you be able to wait at least a few days? I fear what being taken to court will do for her mental health."

There was a pause before Viggo's baritone voice replied, "I cannot promise anything, Mr. Bertrand."

"Of course not," Lee said quickly. I was sure that even requesting Viggo to engage in "obstruction of justice" would put Lee on the line for punishment too, if Viggo decided to report us.

"Once again," Lee went on. "I'm deeply sorry for the inconvenience. I will deposit all the money I owe you to date. Just let me know the number of hours—you've been keeping track, I assume? As for the motorcycle she came with, can I figure out a way to pick it up tomorrow? If you wouldn't mind my leaving it here…"

"You can leave the bike here," was all Viggo said. His response made me wonder if he was even planning to accept Lee's money in the end.

Lee thanked Viggo again before pulling me away from the porch, down the stairs and into the rain—much lighter than when I had arrived—toward his second motorcycle, a dark red one.

I resisted the urge to look back at Viggo as he watched us move away. Move away, when all I wanted was to race back and throw myself into his arms. Wrap my legs around his waist and lose myself in him all over again.

But this wasn't a fairytale.

Viggo's and my story was everything but.

I couldn't be sure how long Viggo remained watching us leave, but the light from the gas lamp on his porch still cast shadows as we arrived at the end of the dirt track.

Only once we had joined the road and picked up speed did Lee break the silence.

"I think you owe me an explanation."

I felt his tenseness beneath my hands as I was forced to hold on to him for support.

I wasn't sure what to say. I had betrayed his trust and been caught red-handed. I figured there was nothing to say other than the truth.

"I couldn't help it."

"Couldn't help *what*?"

"I had to see him. I wanted to stop him from showing up tomorrow. I didn't…" My voice faltered. "I *don't* want to do this to him."

I expected a barrage from Lee, but instead he remained silent.

And he stayed silent until we reached his home. Entering the hallway, he removed his anorak and hung it over the coat holder before slowly turning around. His face was ashen. His eyes flickered to meet mine.

"Do you…" He hesitated, drawing in a breath. "Do you have feelings for him?"

I swallowed. "You could say that."

"What happened when you were alone in the cabin? Before I arrived? I need you to tell me."

"I didn't say anything, and I never planned to tell him anything about the mission. As I said, my only intention was to keep him away from the lab. But then… I shut up completely because of that damn message you sent me."

From pain and frustration rose anger.

"What did you mean by that message?" I asked him, my gaze turning into a glare. "Why would you assassinate him?"

"You know the seriousness of this mission. I don't need to remind you all that hangs in the balance. For Matrus. For you. For me. We can't afford any leaky holes." Lee's tone had become quite flat, past anger, and drenched in disappointment.

"Why do we need to use Viggo at all?" I demanded. "Why can't we pin this on Porteque?"

"It's too late to change the plan now. The banquet is tomorrow! There's no way we could pull that off in a believable manner with such short notice."

"I'll do it!" I stormed. "I'll find a way!"

"No, you won't," Lee said. "There is no time! And besides, it would be against our queen's orders. Before you even arrived, she and Alastair agreed that Viggo would be the best person. Porteque is too easy and obvious a scapegoat. If you defy them, I doubt they'll fulfill their end of your deal when you return."

My hands balled into fists. "It doesn't make sense! Porteque might be easier to set up, but there would be fewer potential holes with them than with Viggo. Hell, those sick bastards might even be happy to step up and claim credit for the deed."

Lee's nostrils flared. I could tell that it was taking a lot of effort to keep his voice calm as he replied, "Violet. I repeat: it is too late to be having this conversation. Alastair has relayed the queen's wishes. We cannot change everything at such a late hour. If you want her to keep her promise to you, you're going to have to go through with this."

Exhaling in aggravation, I drove my fists against the wall. The sound made Samuel bark and scamper into the hallway.

"Now I need you to answer a question," Lee went on. "How can I trust that you didn't tell Viggo anything? How do you expect me to believe you now?"

It took more than a minute before I could bring myself to reply.

"Well"—I breathed heavily—"if we're going through with this, you'll see tomorrow, won't you? You can listen to the conversation. You'll hear his response to my request and you'll know that I told him nothing."

Still, his gaze remained on me, searching me.

I dropped down to rip off my shoes, brushing Samuel away as he moved in to sniff me.

"So what actually happened?" Lee asked. "How did you explain your appearance?"

The way he was eyeing me, it was as if he sensed something deeper had gone on. Almost like he suspected me of kissing Viggo. Was that jealousy that twitched his jaw?

But I was tired of this conversation now. Tired of anger. Tired of everything. I wanted to lose myself in sleep. After the workout Viggo had given me, I probably could even coax myself into slumber.

"Nothing happened that would be of any interest to you," I said. "I made up a stupid excuse for why I was there and we waited until you arrived."

Avoiding his gaze, I moved to push past him. But he gripped my arm and pulled me back, forcing me to face him.

"Did he touch you?" Lee's expression was serious, his blue eyes glimmering in the soft hallway light.

"No," I replied through gritted teeth.

But Lee wasn't buying it.

"Are you sure?"

"*I* kissed him!" I exploded. "What does it matter to you?"

His lips parted at my admission. "It matters to me more than you think."

"Well, it shouldn't," I shot back, brushing him aside and running to the stairwell. I felt hot tears brimming in my eyes. I did not want Lee to see them. I rarely cried, and much more rarely showed it.

"Violet, wait," Lee called to me, but I ignored him. I thundered up the stairs to my room and slammed the door behind me.

I threw myself against the mattress and buried my head in the pillows, letting them absorb my tears. My body shook in silent sobs. I squeezed my eyes tight. I felt ashamed to cry, even on my own.

I wished that I was a robot. That I could simply do, and not think or feel. That was what Lee required on this mission. A robot. Not a girl.

I staggered to the bathroom and splashed my face with cold water in an attempt to calm myself, then crawled back into bed and willed myself to sleep.

But my door slid open before I could manage it.

I groaned internally, wishing Lee would leave me alone, at least until the morning.

To my surprise, he had brought in a tray and he set it down on my bedside table. Upon it sat a jug of water, a glass, and a small white sachet.

He knelt by my bedside. I met his eyes through the gloom.

"Have some water," he said.

I was actually grateful for it. I felt dehydrated and I finished the glass and replaced it on the tray. He refilled it, then picked up the sachet.

"I've brought you something that will help you push through tomorrow," he said, his voice somber.

I sat up in bed, staring at the sachet cradled in his fingers. "What?" I asked.

"A diluted dose of the drug we talked about. The emotion-suppressing drug - Benuxupane. This is enough to make an impact for the next twenty-four hours."

My eyes widened. This drug wasn't supposed to be publicly available yet. Lee must have gotten it from the lab. As wary as I was about this mysterious new drug, there was only one logical way to respond to Lee's offer.

I nodded. Indirectly, it was exactly what I had been wishing for only minutes before his arrival. I would usually be the last person to want to give up control over my feelings and emotions. But now, I needed to. If I was to survive tomorrow without breaking down, I had to swallow this thing.

Lee nodded back curtly before tearing open the sachet and handing it to me. I squeezed it over my mouth and out popped a small powdery pill, landing on the center of my tongue. Lee handed me a glass of water and I quickly downed it.

I sank back against the pillows. Lee stood up and gazed over me. "You see," he said quietly, "I had a reason for asking what went on with Viggo." He cleared his throat. "Now, there are some known side effects like a mild head-ache, heartburn, and, occasionally, anxiety. But they won't last. You should be fine."

I closed my eyes. *I'll be fine...*

Lee's palm brushed over my forehead briefly before he collected the tray and left the room.

Benuxupane... What a good idea of King Maxen's after all.

CHAPTER 32

An additional side effect of the drug seemed to be sleepiness. I must've drifted off within ten minutes of swallowing the pill, and by the time I woke up, it was almost midday.

I sat up slowly in bed, rubbing my head and trying to make sense of what, if anything, was different about me. My head throbbed mildly. I also felt a slight churning in my stomach, though that was not necessarily a result of the pill.

I thought of last night. Of my visit to Viggo's cabin. Of our kiss. And I experienced the strangest feeling, if it could even be described as a feeling. I remembered everything, of course—every detail and every emotion that I had experienced then—yet recalling them did not bring the same pain they had last night.

Where longing and guilt had thrived was now a sense of hollowness. Of numbness. A dull, monotonous ache.

That pill was like a painkiller for the brain. My emotions were still there, somewhere beneath the surface, but I was not close enough to them for them to hamper my objectiveness. The pill didn't eradicate emotions, but smothered them. At least, at the dosage Lee had fed me.

My brain felt sharp. Clear. Alarmingly clear.

I thought of the day ahead of me. Of tonight. And I saw the goal with clarity. For the first time, I was able to separate feelings from duty. Something Lee had urged me to do all along.

I slipped out of bed and took a shower, then headed out of my room. I found Lee, sitting in front of the computer in his bedroom, fully dressed.

Our eyes locked.

He raised a brow, expectant. "Well? How are you feeling?"

I shrugged. "Not a lot."

"That's good," he said. "Very good."

He offered me a chair next to him at his desk. He had been staring at the map of Patrus City and he pointed to one of the red dots. "That's Viggo. He's at Head Office. Let's hope he's not reporting you for last night."

I knew that Viggo wouldn't.

"So," Lee went on briskly, "Let's go over the plan." He reached into his pocket and drew out his phone, placing it on the table. "During Viggo's lunch break, you need to call him and set the appointment for this evening. You're going to say that you want to talk to him about last night.

Don't give him too many details—the point is to pique his interest. You will say that you are going to be accompanying me to the lab's banquet tonight, and that you want to meet him outside the camera room. He knows where that is. There's a quiet, private space outside the camera room, so he won't find it strange that you are asking him to head there."

I nodded.

"You need to tell him that you will try to slip away from me and be there at seven-fifteen p.m. But request him to wait for up to thirty minutes in case you can't leave me that quickly. Promise him that you will meet him."

Again, I nodded.

"The cameras will catch him heading to the security room. Soon after that, the cameras on the ground floor will stall. And fifteen minutes later, the first round of bombs will detonate at the back of the banquet hall."

"*First* round of bombs?" I asked, frowning.

"Yes," Lee said. "Plans changed in the last week—we will be blowing not just the ground floor, but also upstairs. Not only will this create an additional distraction, but it will choke the sky more thickly with smoke which, as you'll see, will be important."

"And where will we be?"

"Up until the bombs go off, we will be attending the banquet, of course. We will arrive at the lab at about six-thirty. Everyone will be chatting and relaxing in the lounge until about seven-ten, when we'll head to the dining hall. The banquet will be served at seven-thirty—which is when the first bombs are due to explode. I'll be watching the clock, and four minutes before, at seven twenty-six, I will receive a blank call. We'll be in the main hall, which is large. The bombs have been installed within the walls of the furthest end of the room from the door. We'll use the blank call as an excuse to stand by the exit, on the opposite corner of the explosives. I'll tell them that your aunt, who is sick, has called and you need to take a few minutes to talk to her. I'll accompany you to the door, where we'll hold an imaginary conversation in view of everyone.

"Then, as soon as the bombs go off, you'll rush to the egg's lab using the staircase, while I'll head off in a different direction to arrange transport for us…" I listened carefully as he began to explain how to set up the bombs around the glass casing of the egg and have them implode without blowing myself up.

He made me repeat the process three times until he was satisfied that every detail had sunk in, though I would've appreciated a practice run.

"Then," he went on, "all you'll have to do is retrieve the egg, hurry to the stairs, and head up to the roof. You will find the door leading out to the rooftop open, and I'll be waiting for you there. From the time you leave me downstairs, you'll have exactly fifteen minutes. You mustn't be any later than that."

Fifteen minutes was tight for all that. The light fitting hiding the package was fiddly. At least I'd opened it once already. I had to hope the second time wouldn't take me as long.

"So," Lee said, clasping his hands together, "that's all you'll have to do. Alastair is due to call to check in on us in about fifteen minutes. And we'll make the call to Viggo in an hour."

I sat in the kitchen opposite Lee, clutching his phone in my hands and staring down at Viggo's number. I pressed dial. My palms grew sweaty as it rang.

"Mr. Bertrand?" Viggo's deep voice spoke in my ear after five rings.

"Mrs. Bertrand," I replied.

Viggo went quiet. So did I.

Lee widened his eyes at me.

"I'm sorry to disturb you," I said, wetting my lower lip, "but I need to talk to you about last night."

There was a beat before he replied, "I'm not sure that's a good idea."

"It probably isn't," I said. "But I need to speak to you. I'll be at the lab's banquet with Lee tonight. I need to… get something off my chest."

"Where is your husband now?"

"Taking the dog for a walk. He's off work today."

"Then why can't you tell me now?" Viggo posed.

"It's something best said in person."

Another span of silence. Then I heard him drawing a breath. "All right," he muttered. "I'll meet you, but after that, I think it's best that we don't see each other again. I doubt your husband will ask me to have a lot more to do with you."

"Okay," I said, my voice going a tad scratchy.

"Where do you want to meet?"

"In the lab building. Outside the camera room."

"Hm. Okay."

"At seven-fifteen. I'll do my best to arrive at that time, but if I have some trouble getting away from Lee, could you wait for up to thirty minutes? If I don't arrive by seven forty-five, feel free to leave."

Asking anybody to hang around for thirty minutes was disrespectful. I could hear his reluctance, but he agreed. He was probably regretting ever having gotten involved with me in the first place.

"Okay, I'll see you later," I concluded. "Goodbye, Viggo."

"Goodbye, Mrs. Bertrand."

CHAPTER 33

Lee was pleased by my performance.

"Now you can relax for the next few hours," he said. "We will be leaving here at five-thirty to allow us some leeway with the traffic, but I suggest you get ready in good time. And wear something nice."

I wished that we didn't have hours to wait. I wished that we could leave now and get it all over with.

But the time passed quickly. Before I knew it, I was in my room getting ready. I chose the same blue dress that I had worn for Lee's and my wedding. When I ran, I would have to hike it up, but the only thing suitable for an occasion such as a banquet would be a long dress, according to Lee. I would wear my heels too. Those would definitely have to come off.

After I finished dressing and trying to make my hair look presentable, I left my room and found Lee sitting at his computer again. He was already dressed in a black tuxedo. His hair was gelled back, his face clean-shaven. He looked bland, nondescript. The polar opposite of Viggo's rugged style.

He looked me over as I eyed him, then reached into a drawer and handed me the same pack of tools that I'd used the last time I'd ventured into the egg's lab. Screwdrivers for the light fitting. He also retrieved a small lady's handbag and gave it to me.

"Got this for you in anticipation."

I couldn't quite bring myself to say thanks. I took the bag from him and stuffed the tools into it.

Lee returned his focus to the screen. "We still have about fifteen minutes before we're due to leave," he said. "Viggo is there." He pointed to a red dot near Crescent River. I couldn't find the other four dots, though I spotted my own. I hadn't questioned Lee about the tracker he'd given me and he hadn't mentioned it either. There wasn't much to say, given that I'd be dead by now if he hadn't thought to do it.

Lee shut down the map. "We won't need this after tonight," he said. "I'm going to be uninstalling it from my system and wiping all traces of it."

After he'd finished getting rid of the map, we headed downstairs.

"I've called a car service," he explained as he led me out of the house.

It was a warm evening, the clear sky streaked with hues of orange. A shiny black vehicle rolled up on the gravel five minutes later. The chauffeur got out to let us into the back of the car.

As we drove off, I glanced back at Lee's pyramid house. It was strange to think that this would be the last time I ever laid eyes on it. My sanctuary since I'd arrived. I felt a dull tug of guilt that I hadn't bidden farewell to Samuel.

Even though it was rush hour, the journey went quickly. Time seemed to have sped up, and I was grateful for it.

Soon, the car was drawing into the parking lot of the laboratory, and Lee was helping me out. I checked my watch. Six twenty-eight.

Entering the building's reception, I could hear the sound of male chatter. Lee led me past the lobby, along a corridor, and into the same lounge I had visited during my first trip to the lab. Extra seating had been placed in here, along with two extra billiards tables. The room was packed. I spotted a couple of familiar faces from my first visit: Simon, and then Richard, Lee's boss. It was as my eyes fell on the latter that I realized I wasn't the only woman here. There were two other wives, both apparently belonging to Richard—a blonde and a brunette. Wearing tightly fitted gowns, teetering heels, and long earrings that tangled with their curled hair, they didn't look much older than me. They stood on either side of him, clutching his arms. I looked away as they caught my eye.

Lee began to mingle with the crowd, introducing me to people as we passed. My mind was too distant to retain names. I merely smiled and nodded my head politely, which was all they expected from me anyway.

I kept glancing at my watch as Lee engaged in conversation. At six forty-five, Lee made his way with me over to an empty snack table as an excuse to get a bit of breathing—or rather, talking—space. "You heard what Simon said?" he asked me beneath his breath as he popped a salt-encrusted nut into his mouth.

"No." I wasn't able to concentrate on the conversations.

"He said King Maxen confirmed his plan to come. He's expected at seven-ten, about the time we're due to head into the banquet hall."

Five minutes before Viggo.

"So does that change anything?" I murmured.

"We just have to hope he's not late."

We returned to the sofas. The next twenty-five minutes slipped away in a blur of dark-colored suits and jovial chatter. As seven-ten drew in, the room became noticeably quieter, everyone anticipating the king's arrival. Then a man poked his head through the door to announce that the king would be delayed by five minutes.

Lee's face noticeably tightened at the information. That would give everyone ten minutes to settle into the banquet hall before the bombs imploded at half past. Assuming King Maxen didn't arrive even later—the banquet wouldn't start without him. If the bombs went off before we made it to the hall, they would still cause a distraction, of course, but Lee and I wouldn't be able to slip away so easily and discreetly to do what we needed to do.

But none of this worry was necessary. At seven-sixteen, the same man who'd come to announce King Maxen's lateness returned to announce his arrival. About a minute later, a tall, broad-shouldered man wearing a light gray—almost silvery—suit appeared in the doorway. He had thick sandy brown hair that extended to his jawline, which sported an immaculately groomed goatee. Clutched in his right hand was some kind of walking stick, though to call it that would be an injustice. It looked more like a scepter, forged of what appeared to be solid silver, its rounded clutch engraved with gold. Behind him stood two burly-looking men who hardly fit into their straight tuxedos. Bodyguards, no doubt.

A smile peeled across King Maxen's face, flashing a set of pearly white teeth. I had seen his picture before, but it was quite a different experience meeting him in the flesh. I could understand why people called him charismatic. There was an energy he brought to a room. "Gentlemen," he said, his voice smooth and deep. "I do apologize for keeping you waiting. Apparently, even the king is susceptible to rush hour in Patrus City."

Chuckles swept around the room.

"Shall we proceed to the hall?" he posed.

Everybody who had been seated rose immediately and bowed. The king turned and headed down the hallway with his bodyguards, while the rest of us filed after him.

The banquet hall was several doors along and the aroma of food filled my nostrils as we entered. The hall contained a huge table spanning the entire length of the room. Shiny steel warmers and platters were already laid out down the middle of the table, along with plates and cutlery. I pitied the man who ended up at the opposite end of the table. It was so close to the furthest wall. That person ended up being Richard, his two wives seating themselves on either side of him, while King Maxen sat at the head on the opposite end, his bodyguards occupying the chairs immediately next to him. The rest of us chose our seats. Everybody was obviously hungry. We were all seated and settled by seven-twenty... Leaving us ten minutes.

The king rose to his feet. He didn't need to tap a glass to call for silence. Everyone's eyes were already fixed on him.

He beamed around the table. "I am delighted to be here for this momentous occasion. More than anything, tonight is a celebration of you fine gentlemen. With your intelligence and determination, we have made progress this year many predicted impossible. It is you who are the building blocks of our society. You are the future. The lives of our future generations are in your hands. This year, you have all demonstrated that you are fully capable of bearing such a responsibility, and I anticipate you will do your nation proud for years to come. Thank you for your service to mankind."

Everybody clapped. The king, raising his glass, sat down. "Now, let us feast!"

His speech hadn't lasted long. It was seven twenty-four now. Dinner was to be served early. Servers piled into the room and began to assist the guests in laying appetizers on their plates... and then Lee's phone went off.

Now seven twenty-six.

Lee pulled the phone from his pocket, making a show of embarrassment. "Violet, it's your aunt. She couldn't have called at a worse time." He turned to Simon—who sat on the other side of him—apologetically, as well as the other men looking our way. "Excuse us for a minute."

Lee betrayed his nerves as he gripped my hand far more firmly than necessary to lead me toward the exit. We stopped at the door, still in clear view of everyone, where he "accepted" the call and handed me the phone.

"Are you out of the hospital yet?" I asked of my imaginary aunt. "Oh. Since when? Did you ask the doctor about that?"

My heart was in my throat as I spent the next minute conversing with myself. Then two minutes. Then three minutes...

And then came the blast.

I felt the heat as Lee jerked me through the doors and out of the room. Shouts and screams erupted amidst the explosion, chilling me to the bone. Lee raced faster down the hallway than I'd thought him capable of. I yanked off my heels and strapped them to an arm in order to keep up. We reached the reception area. Now it was time to part ways. Lee pointed to the stairwell and I darted for it, not even checking to see which direction Lee headed in. I didn't have a split second to waste. I had only fifteen minutes to blow open the casing around the egg and then reach the roof.

I raced up the staircase as fast as my legs could carry me. By the time I'd reached the top, I had burned through almost two minutes.

Panting, I raced along the corridor to the egg room. I stopped outside it, staring at the closed door.

Crap.

Before I'd had to page Lee for it to open, but now… I stopped panicking as I pushed at the door. It was already open. Of course, Lee had thought of this.

Emerging in the familiar lab, I hurtled across the room toward the egg. I stood on the nearest table beneath the light fitting and, reaching into the small handbag that had remained hanging from my arm since I left the taxi, I drew out the tools. My hands were shaking as I began to work on the screws. Even though I was several floors up, I could hear the noise from below. *Block it out. Focus.*

I loosened the first bolt, then the second and third, until I arrived at the last one. I quickly realized that I had made a grave mistake when replacing this fitting last time. The teeth of the screw were damaged, chipped. Which meant that none of my tools could gain a grip on it, and I had no leverage to open it.

But I had already opened the others successfully. Inserting my fingers at the edge of the fitting, I pulled downward and managed to create a gap large enough to fit a hand through. I felt for the package and found it where I'd left it. Gripping it, I coaxed it out, pressing downward against the fitting to make the gap wider. As I slipped it through, the edge of the fitting must have been too sharp and it caused a tear in the foil package—two small red cylinders fell to the floor.

I leapt off the table and scooped them up, praying that they hadn't been damaged. I planted them on the table where I emptied the rest of the bag's contents. There were five red cylinders altogether, a wire that split into five at one end, with a black button-like object at the other end, and a small black device with a round red button in the center of it: the activator.

I checked my watch.

Eight minutes.

I can do this.

Recalling Lee's detailed instructions, I began to set up the bomb. Each cylinder contained a sticky pad which allowed it to attach to the glass around the egg. Then I clipped the split wire into the ends of each of the cylinders before switching on a button at the base. It began to flash.

I took the activator in my hands, and pressed a switch on this one too. It also began to flash.

Six minutes.

I hurried backward to the other end of the room, as far as I could, and ducked beneath a table. Then, closing my eyes, I pressed the activator.

Nothing happened.

I waited for ten seconds—even though Lee said that it was supposed to go off within three. The ten seconds turned into twenty, and then I could wait no longer.

Dammit.

Whether the cylinders were faulty to begin with, or the fault had something to do with the two cylinders that I'd dropped, I didn't know.

I hurried back to the explosives and examined the wires, thinking that perhaps I hadn't inserted some properly. I thought I'd been so careful to check them, but now that I scrutinized them, one looked slightly out of place. On one of the cylinders that I'd dropped, the fitting had become loose. I needed to push the wire further inward, but that could cause the explosives to detonate too soon.

I had no choice now. I gazed around the lab, looking for some—any—kind of utensil that could assist me. I found a pair of longish tongs and grabbed them. Gripping the wire, I pushed inward.

A beep sounded.

It had worked.

"3" flashed up on my activator's tiny screen.

Adrenaline surging through my veins, I threw myself against the floor and tried to get beneath a table as the bombs erupted. Although I'd managed to duck beneath a steel table which bore the brunt of the blast and shattering glass, the billowing heat scorched my face and inflamed my Porteque injuries. An alarm blared.

Three minutes.

Coughing, I gripped the hem of my dress and pulled it up to cover my mouth and nose. I stood up and gazed at the explosion's aftermath. Setting off something like this in a lab was extremely dangerous—Lee had warned me of that. Any number of flammable substances could ignite at any moment now. That was why I had to grab the egg and get the hell out.

I picked up a chair and planted it a few feet in front of me, using it as an island to draw closer to the unprotected egg, still perched in its stand, until I could lean over and close my hands around it, touching it for the first time. It was cool and sleek and heavier than I had expected it to be. My palms being sweaty didn't exactly help my grip around it, but I held on to it for dear life as I raced to the lab's exit.

I dashed along the corridor, back to the stairwell. I scaled the first flight of stairs, and as I reached the second I heard the second round of explosions, higher up in the building. Lee hadn't been joking when he'd said I needed to get out in time.

The door at the top of the stairwell was like a gateway to heaven as I reached it. I pulled down hard on the handle, pushing it open, and staggered out into the cool night breeze.

I'd done it. I'd made it out alive. *And now… where was Lee?*

I gazed around the rooftop, whose atmosphere was quickly clogging with smoke. Lee wasn't up here.

Did something go wrong?

Rotors whirred above me. My immediate fear was that it was one of Patrus' helicopters called to the incident.

I was sure that they would arrive soon, but this… this was not one of them. This was something… I wasn't even sure how to describe. It was a bizarre hybrid aircraft. Its body was a large motorcycle, long enough to fit four people. Above it, fixed to a thick pole that ran down the center of the motorcycle, were spinning rotors. And on either end of it—where the wheels should have been— were two square wooden boxes, big enough to fit two men: I guessed some kind of balancing mechanism. Sitting on the seat and clutching the handles was Lee. He was twisting the latter to navigate the aircraft.

This must have been what he had been working on all along in his garage. "Fixing" his third spare motorcycle. I had assumed that by "arranging transport" for us, Lee had meant that Matrus would have provided something. But no. All this time he had been building an illegal aircraft in his basement. His engineer Chris had also broken the law. Lee must've bribed him well… and hidden the aircraft somewhere nearby in anticipation of tonight.

Lee looked relieved to see me, to say the least. He lowered the aircraft within two feet of the ground. Clutching the egg with one arm, I hauled myself up onto the seat and sat behind him.

"Hand me the egg," Lee said.

I placed it on his lap. He carefully slid it into a basket at the base of his seat, keeping it protected with both feet.

I wrapped my arms firmly around his waist as we took off. As we moved past the rooftop of the lab, my stomach flipped. As we flew over a sheer drop, I couldn't even see the ground because of the smoke, and certainly nobody could see us.

Lee sped up—we had to get out of here before Patrian aid arrived.

We headed firmly eastward, leaving the smoke-infested area. The river came into view, and Matrus' border loomed in the distance. Screams and shouts still echoed in my head as I glanced back over my shoulder at the destruction we had left behind. Then my eyes dragged over the rest of the city, and the looming mountains beyond.

So long, Patrus… So long.

CHAPTER 34

Lee and I had been quiet the whole journey. As we reached Matrus' border, he hovered a little lower, closer to the tops of the building. When I realized we were headed straight for Queen Rina's palace, I asked, "Are you going to finally tell me what's in the egg or not?"

"Not," Lee replied, clipped. "I don't have permission. That doesn't change because we've crossed borders. You'll have to ask the queen or Alastair and see if they'll reveal it to you. Alastair will have the key, and no doubt he'll want to verify the egg's contents are intact."

I ground my teeth. After everything I'd been through, I felt I was owed an explanation. I would ask Alastair when I next saw him. When I'd spoken to him before we left for the banquet earlier this evening, he'd said that he and the queen would be waiting to receive us on the highest floor of the palace—which was where the queen's private residential quarters were.

Passing over the wall of the palace compound, we flew to a circular landing pad on its roof and, with a shudder, touched down. My knees felt weak as I slipped off the seat, my bare soles touching the concrete. I still had my heels strung around my right arm. I shook them off, letting them fall to the floor.

"You don't have any spare shoes with you, do you?" I asked Lee. My shoulder bag was too small to hold much other than the tools.

Lee got off the motorbike and opened up the seat, pulling out a black backpack with a pair of shoes inside. "I did bring these, actually. In case anything went wrong and we had to do some extra running." They were my old shoes, the ones I'd arrived in Patrus with. I gave my handbag—which I had no further use for—to Lee, who dropped it into the underseat compartment before I slipped the shoes on and tied up the laces.

After snapping the seat shut, Lee turned his focus to a door fifteen feet away. I was about to start walking toward it, but he caught my hand and held me back.

"Wait here with the egg," he said. "I need a private word with them first."

I stayed put as Lee disappeared through the door. I breathed in deep, gazing around at the sparkling lights of Matrus City. It felt so strange to be back. I suspected it would take a few days to erase Patrus from my brain. To remember that I didn't legally require a man for anything anymore. That men were the ones who submitted to us.

But I didn't feel as liberated as I should have.

I was still feeling numb. I had several hours to wait until the Benuxupane wore off. I would see what emotions flooded back to me then.

Lee was longer than I had expected him to be. I wondered what he was talking about. *Something about me?*

Finally I heard footsteps returning up the stairwell. He emerged from the doorway, his bunched tuxedo jacket and bag over one shoulder, while stuffing black gloves into one pocket.

His expression was serious as he said, "Okay, you can go down now. First door on your right after leaving the staircase. I'll fetch the egg."

I ventured down the stairwell, which consisted of two flights of steps, through an open reinforced door, and into a long quiet hallway. It was lined with embroidered silk carpets, and the high walls were bedecked with portraits of Queen Rina's family and lineage. I paused to gaze at her seven daughters. They shared her features prominently: slanted brows and sharp cheeks. Their ages ranged from seven to twenty-six. All conceived via insemination—all female. Matrus' doctors had methods of maximizing the chances of conceiving a female, but they weren't always accurate. Abortion wasn't permitted in Matrus, however— not even of male children—so I supposed the queen must have gotten lucky. (To my knowledge, abortion wasn't allowed in Patrus either.)

I continued and stopped outside the first door on my right. It was half open. I knocked briefly before stepping inside a warmly-lit library, bordered by towering cherry-wood bookcases. My eyes fell on the round table in the center of the room, surrounded by high-backed chairs. I could make out the queen and Alastair sitting next to each other, backs toward me.

I approached the table and circled it to greet them... only to lay eyes on two corpses.

Their heads lolled over their chests, their backs slumped, their fronts drenched in blood. Etched across their throats were wide, still-oozing gashes.

I stood, paralyzed. I blinked hard and fast, wondering if it was a hallucination brought on by the drug. I touched Queen Rina's stiff shoulder.

It wasn't a hallucination.

It was real.

A bloodstained knife lay in front of the bodies, a few centimeters away from a message that had been scratched into the wooden table surface:

"FOR THE BOYS OF MATRUS."

My veins turned to ice.

"Lee," I choked. "Lee!" I staggered out of the room and rushed to the staircase as I continued to call for him. My voice gained volume as I ascended the steps... and caught the sound of whirring rotors.

"LEE!" I screamed, leaping the final steps and bursting out onto the roof.

Lee and his aircraft were already four feet in the air, and soaring toward the edge of the building.

"LEE! NO!"

His head tilted toward me, an almost apologetic expression on his face as he called down in a steady, steely voice, "I'm sorry, Violet. If we want truth in our world, some things must be done, and sacrifices must be made."

His words barely registered in my brain. My mind couldn't make sense of what was happening.

I had just walked in on the queen and Alastair murdered. And now Lee was flying away. With the egg.

In a haze of panic, my throat clamped up. I could no longer even scream.

Adrenaline then took over. His aircraft still being within reach, I lunged forward and, with a jump I'd hardly thought I was capable of, I grabbed hold of one of the bars that lined the aircraft's undercarriage just three seconds before it crossed the roof's perimeter. Thrust over a sheer drop of over thirteen floors, I fought to maintain my grip on the bars as the aircraft dipped with my weight.

Pulling my legs upward, I hooked them over another bar on the other side of the carriage, gaining a better hold while the aircraft continued to speed away from the palace.

As I was on the verge of attempting to pull myself higher, Lee's heavy boot crashed down against my right hand. Bone cracked. Pain erupted from my middle finger and seared up my wrist. My right hand slipped.

Hanging now by only one hand and my legs, I thrust my right arm toward a bar near the center of the under-carriage and forced my throbbing hand to wrap around it.

As Lee moved to drive his boot down against my left hand, I could afford to relinquish my grip. I let go a second prior to his boot hitting the metal. Before he could with-draw it again, I clamped my fingers around his ankle and jerked downward with all the strength I possessed.

I heard the scraping of his second boot against the motorcycle's uneven metal floor. He was sliding. Then he was shrieking. He was falling. Past me. Way past me. Down, down, down. And then, within the blink of an eye, he was lying spread-eagled on the pretty brick path that ran through the queen's back garden. Rigid and still.

CHAPTER 35

The dose of Benuxupane Lee had given me wasn't strong enough to suppress the fear ripping through my chest. Clinging to the base of the aircraft, the blood rushing to my head as I gaped down at Lee's dead body, I felt paralyzed. I was barely even aware that the aircraft was continuing to soar ahead unmanned. I was lost in the past, reliving every second of the last ten minutes.

What just happened?

Why?

Why did he do it?

My sweating right hand sliding on the bar snapped me back to the present. I felt numb all over from shock, but I had to climb up onto the motorcycle unless I wanted to join Lee in the queen's ornamental grounds.

Gradually, I managed to maneuver my way upward, making use of my left hand over my right as much as I could, until I was perched on the motorcycle's seat, my feet planted firmly on either side of me. I gripped the base of my seat and gazed back at the increasingly distant palace. Lee's form fell out of my vision, the high wall bordering the palace concealing him. The aircraft no longer seemed to be ascending much, but it was hurtling forward with unnerving speed. I looked ahead of me, over the sprawling city, and the suburbs beyond. Terror clawed at me. I had not the first clue how to navigate this thing. It was a wonder to me that it was even still flying, that it hadn't crashed to the ground the moment Lee fell out.

Where am I going?

What. Just. Happened?

I didn't know how to start making sense of it. But what I did know was that I had to put as much distance between myself and that palace as possible, as fast as possible. I didn't know how long it would take for the queen and Alastair's bodies to be discovered. I cursed myself for making so much noise when shouting for Lee. After discovering their corpses, I'd fallen into a stupor of disbelief and been so stupid as to place a hand upon the queen's shoulder. A bare hand. I'd left behind my trace. And whoever discovered them would notice that the door that led up to the rooftop had been left open. They'd search the roof, notice Lee's body, if that hadn't been discovered beforehand. And realize I would be missing.

I didn't know whether anyone else in that palace was aware of the mission Lee and I were supposed to be carrying out in Patrus. Whether they knew that we were due to return in Lee's makeshift aircraft. But if anyone did know, surely the first thing they would assume was that I had gone flying off with it. They'd send a horde of helicopters after me.

This could be happening at any moment.

My heart quivering, I fixed my eyes ahead and dared place my hands on the handlebars for support.

How does this thing work?

I'd caught a glimpse of Lee twisting the throttle while riding it, the way you would twist the throttle of a regular motorcycle. Was that action spurring the aircraft forward? Were any of the bike's other parts used for similar functions? The brakes for slowing?

God. This is insane.

Sweat dripped from my forehead as I mustered the courage to twist the throttle. The engine chugged. The rotors spun faster. The aircraft's speed increased. I blew out unsteadily. I'd figured out how to accelerate. Stopping—and eventually landing—would be another terrifying experience entirely. But I had no idea when I could stop or land. I couldn't anywhere in the city, or in the suburbs. With the queen's death, this entire area would soon be swarming with wardens. I had to go further. Beyond the suburbs.... The Green. That was where I would reach if I kept moving. And then? Once I reached The Green? Then what?

What had Lee been thinking? Where had he been planning to head? Back to Patrus? Was that where his loyalties really lay?

Then why the hell would he agree to blow up the lab and attempt to kill the king in the process?

He couldn't have been loyal to Patrus. And I couldn't believe that he would head back there. He had been navigating northward. In the same direction I was going now. The Green.

Where was Lee's backpack? I couldn't see it hanging anywhere. And, for that matter, where was the egg? *That blasted egg.* They must be in the compartment beneath my seat.

Before I could even begin trying to formulate my next step, I had to attempt to figure Lee out. How could he have been playing both sides all along? And why? For the egg? Why did he want it? It struck me that he must have taken the key from Alastair before he murdered him. Hopefully it hadn't still been on Lee's person when he'd fallen.

I threw another anxious glance over my shoulder. I could barely even make out the palace anymore.

The city was slipping away beneath me, and soon, so were the suburbs. I twisted the throttle, increasing the aircraft's speed further.

Daring to stand, I unlatched the seat to reveal a much larger compartment than I'd expected to find. Shafts of moonlight escaping through the clouds revealed Lee's backpack, dozens of tins of food, bottles of water, three guns, four knives, five aerosol sprays (the same variety that Ms. Dale had brought with us to The Green), spare clothing, a flashlight, a breathing mask, thick gloves… and the egg, safely stowed in one corner. He had come prepared for The Green.

I grabbed the flashlight and the backpack before closing the seat and resuming my sitting position. Switching on the light, I unzipped the main compartment and began to rummage in search of the key. Within it was another knife, a box of matches, a loop of rope, an unlabeled white tube of pills that looked suspiciously like Benuxupane, a compass, a camera… and then two photographs. I removed the compass and placed it in a small holder that was fixed beneath the gears. Then I picked up the photographs and shone my light down on them. My breath hitched. One of them displayed an all-too-familiar sight: the table in the queen's library, etched with the words "*FOR THE BOYS OF MATRUS*". The second displayed a different message. "*FOR THE MEN YOU WILL DECEIVE*" was scratched into the tinted windshield of a shiny gold sedan. It looked like King Maxen's vehicle. Perhaps Lee had scratched that message while it was pulled up in the lab's parking lot, after the blast. We had parted ways on the ground floor.

What does all this mean?

What about the boys of Matrus?

Fear surged through me as I recalled Viggo's speculation. *No. They can't be killing the marked ones. They can't be.*

As I dove deeper into the backpack, my fingers closed around a crumpled piece of paper. I pulled it out and flattened it. It was covered with smudged black handwriting. My mouth fell open as I began to read.

"Desmond,

I regret what I will have to do. To Violet Bates the criminal. Chris Patton the engineer. Duncan Friedman the arms specialist. Seb Morrissey the camera technician. Jacob Venn the immigration officer. But when we have the egg and its key, I will remember that each served their purpose.

Sacrifices must be made.

I imagine the furor I will have created in both nations tonight. I can't be sure that King Maxen will be killed, but Patrus' prize lab will be shaken, and on Matrus' side, the queen and Alastair will be wiped out.

And neither nation will have the egg.

It's possible Patrus will piece together the puzzle and discover that the terrorist was not Viggo Croft. Even if they consider my and Violet's sudden absence a casualty of the explosion, we will have hardly left a hole-free trail. It doesn't matter. I don't give a damn whether a war sparks between the two nations on the back of my actions.

Every step I've taken to "conceal" Violet's and my tracks and place the blame on Viggo has been mostly a front for Violet so that she continues to trust that I'm in line with Matrus' wishes, as well as to satisfy Alastair, who continues to hound me for updates.

Alastair intends for me to assassinate Viggo after he shows up at the lab. Make it look like he committed the crime and then claimed his own life as some kind of statement. That would ensure Matrus' involvement being ruled out of the picture. But I won't bother with that.

Because, again, I don't care.

As I've sensed Violet beginning to get more out of control, however, it's been important that I rein her in. She is still of use to me, and I need her obedience. I've tried to command it with affection (albeit half-heartedly). That's had no effect on her. I've had to control her by other means, like monitoring her with the tracker. And I'll feed her a pill. I think that will be needed in order for the night to run smoothly.

God knows, I've had enough obstacles already. But it will all come through in the end. I know it will.

Patrus believes me to be Patrian. Matrus believes me to be Matrian. They don't know that I belong to neither.

I am a man of no nation.

Many people see that as a curse. But for me, it's a gift. It's allowed me to perceive the world in a way that others can't. Others who are too embedded in the two systems to even consider a life beyond that which has been chalked out for them.

I'm not sure how far back my discontent has dated with the two societies. Perhaps as early as eight. But I remember the day I finally decided I needed to escape.

It was only recently, soon after King Maxen's ascent to the throne. By some twist of providence, two incidents I haven't been able to ignore occurred within the space of a few days. I discovered the real reason King Maxen commissioned Benuxupane, and the truth about the marked boys of Matrus.

Since the two incidents, it's simply been a matter of waiting for the right opportunity. If I am going to escape, I want to leave with a bang, so to speak. I want to leave a mark on both nations—one neither will forget in a hurry.

When the egg went missing from Matrus, I saw my opportunity and seized it.

The truth is, even I don't know what's within that sleek metal egg. All I know is that anything both governments want can't be a good thing for anyone, no matter how many self-serving lies they spout.

And so, with this mission, I will be able to accomplish both objectives in one strike. Mark, and flee.

Just as I will leave a note for Matrus, I will also leave one for Patrus.

I don't know where I will head, or if I will survive. If there is anything at all beyond that mass of forest.

But even if The Green is indeed as endless as people believe, if my aircraft gives way before I manage to cross it and I never live to discover what lies beyond the trees… I don't care.

I will have lived a fuller life in the past twenty-four hours than in all of my twenty-five years of living.

I will die a free man.

Not a pawn in someone's game.

Lee."

As I finished reading, my hands were trembling so hard I could no longer hold the paper straight. This strange letter exploded a dozen questions in my mind, but I could focus on only one.

The boys. What had Lee discovered about the boys?

Folding up the paper, I slipped it back into the bag. My heart palpitating, I continued to search through its contents. I discovered a small silver key in one of the side pockets. Retrieving it, I stood up again and opened the seat. I planted the backpack inside before reaching down to scoop up the egg. I placed it on my lap as I resettled.

The keyhole was near the base. Attempting to still my hands, I managed to insert the key into the hole and twisted it clockwise. It moved two hundred and seventy degrees before stopping. There was a click, and then a smooth crack appeared around the center of the egg. Drying my hands of perspiration against my ripped dress, I eased open the egg's lid… and stared.

Only the top half of the silver casing would unlatch and it lifted to expose a second, smaller egg that fit snugly inside it. Its walls appeared to be made of some kind of extremely thick glass, and within it swirled… a sack of liquid. The sack's wall was thick, spongy and transparent. It stuck flush to the glass like it had been glued there. The liquid's texture was gooey and semi-transparent, its color brownish-amber. I touched the exterior with my finger. It was warm. Shockingly warm. The very bottom of the egg was taken up by a black plate whose base was concave, to fit the shape of the egg. I guessed that was some sort of temperature-controlling device. Shining my flashlight directly through the murky liquid, I spotted something else. It was small, smaller than the center of my palm.

It looked like an embryo.

What type of embryo, exactly, I wasn't knowledgeable enough about biology to tell. It was still in early stages of development. I could make out the bulge of a head, the curve of a back, several bumps which I guessed would be limbs. A translucent cord was attached to its midriff. The cord connected the fetus to the center of the egg's base, that strange plate thing.

What is this?

Why do Matrus and Patrus want it so badly?

What did Lee want with it?

It could be an animal… It could be a human.

A sudden gust of wind shook me out of my stupor. It was strong enough to wobble the aircraft. Given that I hadn't been holding on to anything for support—and I still couldn't with the egg in my hands—my feet shot outward over the floor to steady myself. In the process, my heel shifted a lever at the base of my seat that I hadn't even noticed.

Two alarmingly loud creaks emanated from the wooden boxes fixed to either end of the motorcycle. I tensed up, petrified I'd done something fatal.

What I was not expecting was for the bases of the wooden boxes to suddenly flap open, and for four bodies to tumble out.

Four male bodies.

I almost choked on my tongue as I realized I recognized one of them: his faded dungarees, his gray-speckled hair. His frozen, stubbled face. It was Chris the mechanic.

Hurtling down with the other three men to a quiet suburban street, they made contact with the concrete with a sickening splat.

The other three men. They had to be the other three red dots on Lee's monitor. Duncan, Seb, and Jacob.

Lee was a madman. What was he doing carrying them in his aircraft? He must have murdered them shortly before the banquet, and stored them in the boxes out of convenience. Maybe he'd been planning to dump them in The Green. Clearly, I'd never known the real Lee. The flat, Matrian-male persona he'd put forward throughout my stay with him had been an act.

Unable to focus on the egg any longer, I closed and locked it up before replacing it in the seat compartment with more care than I'd previously handled it. There was a life in that thing.

After zipping up the key in the backpack, I sat down and faced forward. I gripped the handles for support. I felt like throwing up.

Lee's letter replayed in my mind.

Desmond.

Why was it addressed to Desmond? That was one of the strangest things about the letter.

Desmond was Lee's middle name. Perhaps the letter was some kind of journal entry, an upheaval of guilt before the night. But still, it didn't make any sense to me that he would use his middle name. Why not address it to Lee? He'd called himself only Lee around me, and I hadn't heard a single person address him as Desmond either.

As I recalled the explanation Lee had given me for the name, the very first night I had arrived in Patrus, a thought struck me.

"My full name is Lee Desmond Bertrand. Named Lee by my father, Desmond by my mother... I'm native to neither Matrus nor Patrus. In fact, I was born in the middle."

It drew my mind back to a question I had mulled over and posed to Viggo the evening we'd sat atop the roof in his backyard.

What happens to someone who doesn't feel they belong in either nation?

Lee's father was a Patrian. His mother a Matrian.

Lee of Patrus.

Desmond of Matrus.

A chill ran down my spine as I wondered if Lee truly was insane.

Maybe he had some kind of split-personality disorder. Maybe his childhood had messed him up.

Maybe I finally had an answer to my question and Lee was an extreme case of what could happen to a person who felt they belonged in neither nation. They rebelled against both.

Suddenly, the night seemed to grow much colder. I shivered.

I was beginning to near The Green.

Ms. Dale had been right. She'd told me, not far away from where I soared now, that once I reached the other side of the river I should trust no one. I just hadn't considered Lee to be a member of the other side.

Now, whether I liked it or not, I didn't belong to either side, either. I was a fugitive from both nations.

And I was sitting exactly where Lee would be sitting right now. On an illegal aircraft, accompanied by the egg, some meager supplies, and a few pieces of survival equipment.

My eyes fell to the compass I'd placed in the holder.

Lee had intended to head north. But my heart felt torn in two directions. North and west. My brother and Viggo. They were the only two people who mattered to me anymore. It felt like the world could implode (which it might do anyway after tonight's events), but if I could find those two alive, I would be content.

But now I feared that both of them were already dead. Although Lee had decided not to kill Viggo earlier, for all I knew, he could have gotten caught up in the blast. Maybe

Lee had set off more bombs on the ground floor than I was aware of. He'd seemed keen to destroy the building as much as possible.

And my brother. After Viggo's suspicion and now Lee's words, I feared that Queen Rina had lied to me all along about a reunion. I had only a sliver of hope left in my heart that Tim was still alive.

But, somehow, I had to find out. My soul would not rest until I had.

However many days or hours I had left to live after tonight's disaster, I had to make them count. I had nothing left to lose.

I didn't know how I would pull any of this off, or in what order. I still barely knew how to navigate this darn aircraft. I didn't know how to change its direction, and I sure didn't know how to land.

But whatever I ended up doing, and however I ended up doing it, there was one thing I knew for certain:

From this moment on, like Lee Desmond Bertrand, I had to be a player of my own rules.

No longer a pawn in someone's game.

READY FOR THE NEXT PART OF VIOLET'S STORY?

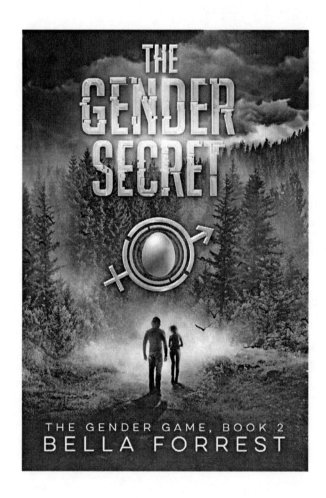

Dear Reader,

Thank you so much for reading. I hope you enjoyed The Gender Game.

Book 2, The Gender Secret releases November 21st 2016!

If you visit WWW.MOREBELLAFORREST.COM and join my email list, I will send you an email as soon as The Gender Secret is available.

You can also visit my website for the most updated information about my books: www.bellaforrest.net

Until we meet again between the pages,

—Bella Forrest *x*

ALSO BY BELLA FORREST:

A SHADE OF
VAMPIRE SERIES:

SERIES 1:
Derek & Sofia's story:

A Shade of Vampire (Book 1)
A Shade of Blood (Book 2)
A Castle of Sand (Book 3)
A Shadow of Light (Book 4)
A Blaze of Sun (Book 5)
A Gate of Night (Book 6)
A Break of Day (Book 7)

SERIES 2:
Rose & Caleb's story:

A Shade of Novak (Book 8)
A Bond of Blood (Book 9)
A Spell of Time (Book 10)
A Chase of Prey (Book 11)
A Shade of Doubt (Book 12)
A Turn of Tides (Book 13)
A Dawn of Strength (Book 14)
A Fall of Secrets (Book 15)
An End of Night (Book 16)

BEAUTIFUL MONSTER DUOLOGY:
Beautiful Monster 1
Beautiful Monster 2

FOR AN UPDATED LIST OF BELLA'S BOOKS,

please visit www.bellaforrest.net

Join Bella's VIP email list and she'll personally send you an email reminder as soon as her next book is out.

Visit to sign up: www.morebellaforrest.com

CPSIA information can be obtained
at www.ICGtesting.com
Printed in the USA
FSOW02n1755020917
38088FS